MICHELLE MAJOR
DANI WADE
BARBARA WALLACE

MILLS &
BOON

First Published in Great Britain 2017
By Mills & Boon, an imprint of HarperCollins*Publishers*
1 London Bridge Street, London, SE1 9GF

I DO. . . © 2017 Harlequin Books S. A.

Her Accidental Engagement, *A Bride's Tangled Vows* and *The Unexpected Honeymoon* were first published in Great Britain by Harlequin (UK) Limited.

Her Accidental Engagement © 2014 Michelle Major
A Bride's Tangled Vows © 2014 Katherine Worsham
The Unexpected Honeymoon © 2014 Barbara Wallace

ISBN: 978-0-263-92957-7

05-0317

Our policy is to use papers that are natural, renewable and recyclable products and made from wood grown in sustainable forests.The logging and manufacturing processes conform to the legal environmental regulations of the country of origin.

Printed and bound in Spain
by CPI, Barcelona

HER ACCIDENTAL ENGAGEMENT

BY
MICHELLE MAJOR

Michelle Major grew up in Ohio, but dreamed of living in the mountains. Soon after graduating with a degree in journalism, she pointed her car west and settled in Colorado. Her life and house are filled with one great husband, two beautiful kids, a few furry pets and several well-behaved reptiles. She's grateful to have found her passion writing stories with happy endings. Michelle loves to hear from her readers at www.michellemajor.com.

To Mom and Dad: for your love,
support and the years of off-key harmonies

Chapter One

Julia Morgan lit the final match, determined to destroy the letter clenched in her fingers. She was well aware of the mistakes she'd made in her life, but seeing them typed on fancy letterhead was more than she could take at the moment. She drew the flickering flame toward the paper but another gust of damp wind blew it out.

The mountains surrounding her hometown of Brevia, North Carolina, were notoriously wet in late winter. Even though it hadn't rained for several days, moisture clung to the frigid March air this afternoon, producing a cold she felt right to her bones.

With a frustrated groan, she crumpled the letter into a tiny ball. Add the inability to burn a single piece of paper to her colossal list of failures. Sinking to her knees on the soggy ground, she dropped the used matchstick into a trash bag with all the others.

She ignored the wail of a siren from the highway above

her. She'd pulled off the road minutes earlier and climbed down the steep embankment, needing a moment to stop the panic welling inside her.

For a few seconds she focused her attention on the canopy of pine trees below the ridge where she stood, her heartbeat settling to a normal rhythm.

Since she'd returned to her hometown almost two years ago, this love of the forest had surprised her. She'd never been a nature girl, her gypsy existence taking her from one big city to another. Thanks to her beautiful son, Julia was now rooted in Brevia, and the dense woods that enveloped the town gave her the sense of peace she hadn't known she'd missed for years.

The makeshift fire hadn't been much of a plan, but flying by the seat of her pants was nothing new for Julia. With a deep breath, she smoothed the wrinkled letter against the grass. She'd read it compulsively over the past week until the urge to destroy it had overtaken her. She knew the words by heart but needed the satisfaction of watching them go up in flames.

Unfit mother. Seeking custody. Better options.

Tears pricked the backs of her eyes. Burning the letter wouldn't change the potential it had to ruin her life. She'd tried to dismiss the contents as lies and conjecture. In a corner of her heart, she worried they were true and she wouldn't be able to defend herself against them.

Suddenly she was hauled to her feet. "Are you hurt? What happened?" A pair of large hands ran along her bare arms, then down her waist toward…

Whoa, there. "Back off, Andy Griffith," Julia sputtered as parts of her body she thought were in permanent hibernation sprang to life.

As if realizing how tightly he held her, Sam Callahan, Brevia's police chief, pushed away. He stalked several yards up the hill toward the road, then turned and came at her again. Muscles bunched under the shoulders of his police uniform.

She had to work hard to ignore the quick pull of awareness that pulsed through her. Darn good thing Julia had sworn off men. Even better that big, strong alpha men were *so* not her type.

Julia gave herself a mental headshake. "What do you want, Sam? I'm sort of busy here."

She could have sworn his eye twitched under his aviator sunglasses. He jabbed one arm toward the top of the hill. "What I *want* is to know what the hell you're doing off the side of the road. *Again.*"

Right. She'd forgotten that the last time Sam had found her, she'd been eight months pregnant and had wrapped her ancient Honda around a tree trunk. He'd taken her to the hospital where her son, Charlie, had been born.

That day a year and a half ago had been the start of a new life for her. One she'd protect at any cost.

Sam had been new to Brevia and the role of police chief then. He'd also been a whole lot nicer. At least, to Julia. He'd made the rounds of the single ladies in town, but ever since Charlie's birth Sam had avoided her as though he thought he might be the first man in history to catch a pregnancy. Which was fine, especially given some of the details she'd heard about his history with women.

"Julia."

At the sound of her name, she focused on his words.

"There are skid marks where your car pulled off."

"I was in a hurry," she said and swiped at her still-moist cheeks.

His hands bunched at his sides as he eyed her bag. "Do I smell smoke?"

"I lit a match. Lots of them." Her chin hitched. "Wanna call Smokey Bear for backup?"

He muttered something under his breath at the same time a semi roared by on the road above.

"I didn't quite catch that."

Sam removed his sunglasses and tucked them into the front pocket of his shirt. He was almost *too* good-looking, his blond hair short but a little messy, as if he needed a trim. The effect softened his classically handsome features and a square jaw that fell just short of comic-book chiseled. His gaze slammed into hers, and Julia knew if ice could turn molten, it would be the exact color of Sam's blue eyes.

"You were on your knees," he said slowly.

Julia swallowed. "I lost a contact."

"You don't wear contacts."

"How do you…? Never mind." She bent to retrieve the bag of worthless matches.

His finger brushed the back of her arm. "What are you doing out here, Jules?"

Something about the sound of her name soft as a whisper broke through her defenses. She straightened and waved the letter at him. "I have a meeting in town and needed some fresh air to collect my thoughts."

"At the salon?"

She shook her head. "No. Hair dye doesn't require much mental fortitude. I have a real meeting, with an attorney."

He didn't ask for details but continued to watch her.

"It's about Charlie," she offered after a minute. "About my custody." To add to her humiliation, she choked on the last word.

"You're his mother. Of course you have custody."

"I know." She lifted the letter. "But Jeff and his parents think—"

"Who's Jeff?"

"My ex-boyfriend." She sighed. "Charlie's father."

Sam's eyes narrowed. "The one who's never set eyes on him?"

"He's a college professor and travels the world doing research. His dad runs an investment firm in Columbus, Ohio, and his mom is a retired cardiologist. They're rich, powerful and very intellectual. The whole family is off-the-charts smart. I guess they have…concerns. For Charlie's future and my ability to provide the right environment. Jeff wants a new custody arrangement."

"Have Jeff's parents met Charlie?"

"No. They called a couple of times after he was born. They didn't approve of me when I was with Jeff, and since he didn't want anything to do with the baby…" She paused then added, "I let my mom deal with them."

That made him smile. "In my opinion, Vera is also off-the-charts smart."

Julia ignored the shiver in her legs at his slow grin. Her mother, Vera Morgan, was a pit bull. But also keenly intelligent. Everyone in her family was smart. Everyone but her.

"Jeff's mother is here with their family attorney to meet me. To make sure everything's okay—that Charlie is in good hands."

"Of course he's in good hands." Sam's voice gentled as he repeated, "You're his mother."

"I've done a lot of stupid things in my life, made a lot of mistakes. Jeff knows the sordid details and I'm sure his parents do, too." Emotion clogged her throat.

Sam was not the man she wanted to have see her like this. She made a show of checking her watch. "What I could use is some damage control for my reputation. White picket fence, doting husband, pillar of the community stuff. It's a little late for me to join the Junior League." She shook her head. "Anyway, thanks for your concern today, but as you can see, I'm peachy keen."

"You shouldn't talk to anyone until you get an attorney of your own."

"Frank Davis said he would help me, but I hope it won't come to that. I'm sure the Johnsons want what's best for Charlie. I should at least hear them out. That boy deserves everything this world has to offer." She gave a humorless laugh and started back toward the road. "What he's got is me."

As she moved past Sam, his hand reached out, but she jerked away. If he touched her right now she'd be a goner, and she needed to keep it together. For Charlie.

"You're more than enough," he called after her.

"From your lips to God's ears, Chief," she whispered and climbed up to her car.

"Who are you and what have you done with my father?"

Sam shifted in his chair at Carl's, Brevia's most popular restaurant, still reeling from his unbelievable afternoon. From the bizarre encounter with Julia he'd been called to a domestic disturbance that ended up being a chicken loose in Bobby Royall's kitchen. It had made him almost thirty minutes late to dinner with his dad. Now he wished the bird hadn't been so easy to catch.

Joe Callahan adjusted his Patriots baseball cap and chuckled. "It's me, son. Only better."

Said who?

His father had been a police officer in Boston for almost forty years, most of which had been spent working homicide. Joe Callahan had dedicated his life to his career, and his family had suffered from the on-the-job stress and risks he took daily. Although it wasn't intentional, Sam had modeled his own life after his father's. Sam had put his job before everything and everyone in his life—just like Joe.

Recently, though, Joe had begun conducting programs for police departments on emotional awareness. Sam had resisted his father's repeated attempts to help him "get in touch" with his feelings. But now Joe was here and impossible to ignore.

"The boys down at the precinct loved my seminar. At least four of 'em were in tears by the end. I got thank-you notes from a half-dozen wives."

"That's great, Dad." Sam took a long drink of iced tea, wishing he wasn't on duty. A cold one would be mighty helpful tonight. "I don't see what that has to do with me or your unexpected visit to Brevia."

His father pulled a flyer out of the briefcase at his feet and pushed it across the table. "While I'm down here, I thought we could organize a workshop."

Sam glanced at the pamphlet. His stomach gave a hearty gurgle. *Law with Love, Presented by Retired Police Captain Joseph Callahan.* A picture of Joe hugging a group of uniformed officers filled the front page. Sam couldn't remember ever being hugged by his craggy, hard-nosed father. Holy mother of…

"I don't know. It's only me and one deputy on the force."

Joe tapped the sheet of paper. "It's for firefighters and paramedics, too. We could bring in neighboring towns— make it a regional event. Plus civil servants, city council. You're looking at a long-term reappointment, right? This could make quite an impression as far as your potential."

At the mention of his possible future in Brevia, Sam lost the battle with his temper. "My potential as what? I'm the chief of police, not the hug-it-out type."

His father's sharp intake of breath made Sam regret

his outburst. "Sorry. You know what a small town this is and—"

Joe held up a hand. "Don't apologize." He removed his bifocals and dabbed at his eyes with a napkin.

"You aren't going to cry," Sam muttered, disbelieving. "You don't cry."

"Yes. I *am* going to cry. To take a moment and *feel* my pain."

Great. This was the second time today he'd brought someone to tears.

After a loud nose blow, Joe's watery gaze met his. "I feel my pain, and I feel yours."

"I'm not in pain." Sam let his eyes drift shut. "Other than a raging headache."

Joe ignored him and continued, "I did this to you, Sammy."

Sammy? His father hadn't called him Sammy since—

"When your mother died my whole world collapsed. I didn't think I could live without her. I didn't want to. It broke me a little more every day to see you and your brother that sad. I did the only thing I could to survive. I shut off my heart, and I made you do the same. I was wrong. I'm here to make it right again."

Sam saw customers from the surrounding tables begin to stare. "It's okay. Let's go outside for a minute."

Joe followed Sam's gaze and shook his head. "I'm not embarrassed to show my feelings. Not anymore." He took another breath, this one steadier. "Ever since the incident with my ole ticker." He thumped his sweatshirt. "They say facing death can make you reevaluate your whole life."

"It was indigestion, Dad. Not a real heart attack. Remember?"

"Doesn't matter. The change to my heart was real. The

effect on my life was real." He readjusted his glasses. "I want the same change for you. I want you to be happy."

"I'm fine." Sam gulped a mouthful of ice and crunched. "Happy as a clam."

"Are you seeing anyone?"

Alarm bells went off in Sam's head. "I…sure…am actually. She's great." He looked away from his father's expectant face, unable to lie to him directly. He glanced around the crowded restaurant and his gaze landed on Julia at a booth in the back. He hadn't noticed her when he'd first walked in, but now he couldn't pull his eyes away.

This must be the meeting with her ex-boyfriend's family she'd told him about. The faces of the two women seated across from her were blocked, but Julia's cheeks flamed pink. Her palm smacked the table as if she was about to lose control.

Easy there, sweetheart, he counseled silently.

As if she'd heard him, her eyes met his and held for several moments. His pulse hammered against his throat. Then she squared her shoulders and folded her hands in her lap.

He turned back to his father. "You'd like her. She's a real spitfire."

Joe smiled. "Like your mother."

Sam forced himself not to look at Julia again. "I was ten when she died. I don't remember that much."

"This one's different than your other girls?"

Sam caught the waitress's attention and signaled for the check.

"Because I think you need a new perspective. After what happened with…"

"I don't want to rehash my relationship history."

Joe reached across the table and clasped Sam's hand in his. "I know you want to find love and settle down."

Sam heard a loud cough behind him and found the young waitress staring. Her look could only be described as predatory. *Fantastic.* Sam had dated some when he'd first come to town but had kept to himself recently, finding it easier and less complicated to be alone. The way gossip went viral in Brevia, he'd have a fresh line of eligible women in front of his office by morning.

"I told you," Sam said, loud enough for the waitress to hear. "I've got a girlfriend. We're very happy."

The waitress dropped the check on the table with a *humph* and stalked away.

"It's serious?" Joe asked.

Sam's gaze wandered to Julia again. "Very," he muttered as she jabbed a finger across the table. This time his mental warning to not lose control didn't reach her. Her voice grew so loud that people at surrounding tables turned.

"I want to meet her," his dad said, rubbing his palms together, oblivious to the commotion behind him. "Why don't you give her a call and see if she can meet us for dessert? If she's so wonderful, I can help make sure you don't blow it."

At the moment, Sam wasn't worried about screwing up anything himself or producing a nonexistent girlfriend for his dad to fawn over. Instead he felt the need to avert someone else's disaster. "I'll be right back."

Joe grabbed his arm as he started past. "Don't be sore, Sammy. I was joking. You're a great catch."

Sam shrugged out of his father's grasp. "I need a minute. Stay here."

He darted around a passing waiter as he made his way to Julia, who now stood in front of the booth.

"You have no idea what I'm capable of," she shouted. All eyes on this side of the restaurant were glued to her.

Just as he reached her, Julia picked up a glass of water from the table. Sam leaned in and wrapped his fingers around hers before she could hurl it at anyone.

"Hey there, sugar," he said as he pulled her tense body tight to his side. "I didn't realize your meeting was at Carl's tonight. You doing okay?"

"Let go of me," she said on a hiss of breath. "This is none of your concern."

"Well, I *am* concerned," he whispered then plastered on a wide smile. "I haven't met your new friends yet."

She squirmed against him. "They aren't my— "

"Howdy, folks," Sam interrupted, turning his attention to the two strangers staring at him. "I'm Sam Callahan. A…uh…friend of Julia's."

The woman in the corner practically screamed "old money," from her sophisticated haircut to her tailored suit. A thick strand of pearls hung around her neck and a massive diamond sparkled on her left hand. The way her gaze narrowed, she must be Charlie's paternal grandmother. Next to her was a younger woman, tiny and bookish. Her big owl eyes blinked from behind retro glasses. Faint streaks of color stole up her neck from the collar of her starched oxford shirt as she watched the two of them.

"Friend?" The older woman scoffed. "Latest conquest, no doubt." She nudged the woman beside her. "Are you taking notes on this? She's now flaunting her boy toy in front of us."

Boy toy? Sam's smile vanished and he worked to keep his voice pleasant. "Excuse me, ma'am, you have the wrong idea—"

She continued as if he hadn't spoken. "Can you imagine what my grandson's been subjected to when his mother is obviously a tramp? When the judge hears—"

Sam held up a hand. "Wait just one minute, lady. If you think you can waltz in here—"

Julia's fingernails dug into his arm. "I *don't* need your help. Walk away."

He glanced down at her and saw embarrassment shimmering along with anger in her expression. And fear. At the mention of the word *judge,* he'd felt some of the fight go out of her. He wished he hadn't interrupted, that he'd let her handle her own problems, the way she'd wanted to in the first place. But a part of Sam needed to be the hero just so he could feel something. It was what he was used to, one of the few things he could count on. That part of him couldn't walk away.

He released Julia and leveled his best law-enforcement stare at the grandmother. As he expected, she shrank back and darted a nervous glance at her companion. "I'm Sam Callahan, Brevia's police chief." Hands on hips, he held her gaze. "To be clear, I am *no one's* boy toy and would appreciate if you'd conduct yourself in a more civilized manner in my town. We don't take kindly to strangers spreading malicious rumors about our own. Do I make myself clear?"

Several beats passed before the studious-looking woman cleared her throat. "Mr. Callahan—"

Sam squared his shoulders. "You can call me Chief."

The attorney swallowed. "Chief Callahan, I'm Lexi Preston. I represent the interests of Charlie Morgan's father, Jeff Johnson, and grandparents, Dennis and Maria Johnson. My father is the Johnsons' family attorney and he asked me—"

"Get to the point."

"Yes, well…" Lexi mumbled as she shuffled papers around the table. "I was simply explaining to Ms. Morgan the facts of her case, or lack thereof, when she became hostile and confrontational. My client is not to blame for this unfortunate disturbance. We have statements from a number of Ms. Morgan's former acquaintances as to her character, so Dr. Johnson's assertion, while ill-advised, is not without foundation."

He heard Julia suck in a breath but kept his attention on the two women. "I don't care what your so-called statements allege. You're not going to drag Julia's name through the mud."

Preston collected the rest of the papers. "Why is Ms. Morgan's reputation your business? Is she under investigation by local law enforcement?"

"This can't get any worse," Julia whispered so low only he could here. "Go away, Sam. Now."

From the corner of his eye, Sam saw his father standing a few feet away, watching him intently. Sam was a good cop and he played things by the book, having learned the hard way not to bite off more than he could chew.

But some lessons didn't stick.

He peeled Julia's hand from its death grip around his upper arm and laced her fingers with his. "It's my business, Counselor, because I'm not going to let you or anyone hurt the woman I intend to marry."

Chapter Two

Julia thought things couldn't get worse.

Until they did.

She glanced around the restaurant, as dumbfounded as the people who stared at her from the surrounding tables. She recognized a lot of them; Carl's was a popular spot for Brevia locals.

Yanking Sam away from the table a few steps, she smiled up into his face, well aware of their audience. It took all her willpower to resist the urge to slap him silly. "Have you lost your mind?" she said, keeping her voice low.

The corners of his mouth were tight as he returned her smile. "Apparently."

"Fix this. You have to fix this."

"That's what I'm trying to do." He smoothed a stray hair from her cheek. "Trust me."

No way. Julia didn't trust men. She had a long line of

heartbreak in her past. Mountains of collateral damage that made her sure she was the only person she could trust to take care of her and Charlie. "Don't touch me," she whispered through gritted teeth.

His hand dropped from her face. "I'm going to help you. But you can't fight me. Not here."

She glanced over his shoulder at the attorney and Charlie's grandmother. For a fraction of a second, worry marred Maria Johnson's perfect features. Julia didn't understand the break in the ice queen's armor, but it must have had something to do with Sam.

"Fine." She reached forward and clasped both of his rock-solid arms, as if she could make him understand the gravity of her situation through a simple squeeze. "You better make it count. Charlie's future is on the line."

He searched her gaze for a long moment, then bent onto one knee. He took her fingers in his, tugging softly when she would have pulled away.

"I didn't mean…"

"Julia Morgan," he said, and his deep, clear voice rang out in the restaurant. "We've kept this quiet—no easy task in Brevia—but it's long past time to make things official." He cleared his throat, adjusting the collar of his starched uniform shirt. "Would you do me the honor of becoming my wife?"

Julia blinked back sudden tears. A marriage proposal was what she'd wanted, once upon a time. She'd wanted Jeff to see they could build a real life together. Foolishly sure he was the one, she'd been reckless and selfish. Then the universe had blessed her with a beautiful son. She was working day and night to make a good life for Charlie. Now that she wanted to do the right thing, she risked losing him.

Not for the first time, she wondered if he'd be better off

with the Johnsons and the privileged life filled with opportunities they could provide.

She squeezed her eyes shut to clear her thoughts. She was Charlie's mother, no matter what, and wouldn't ever stop fighting for him.

Sam ran his finger along the inside of her wrist. "Are you going to answer the question? My leg is cramping."

"Oh, no. Sorry."

"No?" he asked over the collective gasp.

"I mean yes. Get up, you big oaf." Heat flooded her face and her stomach churned. What was she doing? She'd learned not to rely on a man for anything and now she was putting her entire future in Sam's hands. Impulsive as ever, she repeated, "Yes. My answer is yes."

He stood, rubbing one knee. "Cool it on the name-calling. We're in love, remember."

"You betcha, honey-bunny."

That produced a genuine grin from him, and she was again caught off guard by her body's reaction as tiny butterflies did a fast samba across her belly. Oblivious to his effect on her, Sam turned to the booth.

Before he could speak, an older man wrapped them both in a tight hug. "This is amazing."

Amazing? Not quite.

Sam caught her gaze, his eyes dark and unreadable. "I forgot to tell you earlier. My dad came to town today. Meet Joe Callahan, your future father-in-law."

Uh-oh.

Joe cupped her face between his large hands. "You're just what he needed. I can already tell." Tears shimmered in eyes the same color as Sam's, only sweeter and looking at her with such kindness a lump formed in Julia's throat. "You remind me of my Lorraine, rest her soul."

"Okay, Dad." Sam tugged her out of Joe's embrace. She took a step back but Sam pulled her against his side.

Joe turned to the booth. "I'll buy a round to celebrate. Any friends of…"

"Julia," Sam supplied with a sigh.

"Any friends of my future daughter-in-law are friends of mine."

"We're *not* friends," Lexi Preston ground out. "As I said earlier, I represent her son's biological father and his parents. They're interested in exploring a more viable custody arrangement. The Johnsons want what's best for the child. They can give him opportunities—"

"They want to take my baby," Julia mumbled. Sam's arm tightened around her waist.

If Joe was surprised to hear she had a child, he didn't let on. His posture went rigid. "That's ridiculous. She's the boy's mother."

"Dad, this isn't the time or place—" Sam began.

Joe wagged a finger at Lexi Preston and Maria Johnson. "Now listen here. I don't know what all this nonsense is about, but I can tell you my son will take care of that child and Julia. He's the law around here, for heaven's sake." He leaned closer and Lexi's nervous swallow mimicked Julia's. Joe Callahan might look like a teddy bear but he had a backbone of steel. "You'll have to come through both of us if you try to hurt her. We protect our own."

"I've had quite enough of this town for tonight." Maria pushed at the attorney, who stood quickly. "I don't care who you've got in your backwater little corner of the world, we're going to—"

Lexi put a hand on Maria's shoulder to silence her. "The less said tonight, the better. We have a court date next week." She gave Julia a curt nod. "Ms. Morgan, we'll see you then."

"Take care of the check, Lexi." Maria Johnson barked the order at her attorney before stalking out of the restaurant.

"Does that mean she's leaving Brevia?" Julia asked.

"For now. I'll stay for the duration of the process. The Johnsons will fly back and forth." Lexi leaned toward Julia. "I don't want to get your hopes up, but a stable home environment could change the situation." She clapped a hand over her mouth as if she'd said too much, then nodded to the group and scurried away.

Julia reached forward to hug Joe. "Thank you, Mr. Callahan. For what you said."

"I meant it. Sam isn't going to let anything happen to you."

Sam.

Julia turned, but focused her attention on the badge pinned to Sam's beige shirt, unable to make eye contact with him. Instead she looked out at the tables surrounding them. "Sorry for the commotion. Go back to dinner, and we'll get out of your way."

"Wait a minute." Sam's voice cut through the quiet.

Julia held her breath.

"As most of you heard tonight, Julia and I have something to celebrate." He grabbed her hand and drew her back to him. Her fingers spread across his broad chest of their own accord. "We need to make this believable for the gossip mill," he whispered against her ear.

A round of applause rang out in the restaurant followed by several clinks on glasses. "Kiss. Kiss. Kiss," came the call from the bar.

Julia froze as Sam gazed down at her, his expression heated. "Better give them what they want."

"It's totally unbelievable and I had garlic for dinner," she muttered, squirming in his arms.

"I'll take my chances," he answered with a laugh.

"Have it your way." Cheeks burning, she raised her head and pressed her mouth to his, a chaste peck fit for the balcony at Buckingham Palace. When she would have ended the kiss, Sam caught hold of her neck and dipped her low. She let out a startled gasp and he slid his tongue against the seam of her lips. Ever so gently he molded his mouth to hers.

A fire sparked low in her belly as she breathed in the scent of him, warm and woodsy and completely male. Lost in her reaction, her arms wound around his neck and her fingers played in the short hair along his collar. She heard his sharp intake of breath and suddenly he righted them both to a chorus of catcalls and stomping feet.

"That's what I'm talking about," someone yelled.

"Okay, folks." Sam's gaze swept across the restaurant and he smiled broadly. "Show's over. I'm going to see my lovely bride-to-be home."

Julia pressed her fingers to her lips and looked at Sam. The smile didn't reach his eyes.

When she turned, Joe watched her. "You're a breath of fresh air if I ever saw one," he said and gave her trembling hand a squeeze.

She led the group into the night but not before she noticed several members of the ladies' auxiliary huddled in the corner. They'd have a field day with this one. The salon would be buzzing with the news by morning. Her chest tightened as she felt Sam behind her, frustration pouring off him like a late-winter rainstorm. Maybe he'd already come to regret his stupid proposal.

This entire situation was his fault. She'd told him she didn't need a hero, and that was the truth.

Still, his announcement had rattled Maria Johnson and

her attorney. She couldn't figure out how a fake engagement would benefit Sam, but he wasn't her problem.

Charlie was Julia's only priority. She'd do anything for her son.

Right now she needed time to think, to figure out how to make this bizarre predicament work in her favor. "It's been a long day, boys," she said quickly. "Joe, it was nice to meet you. How long will you be—"

"We need to talk," Sam interrupted, gripping her arm when she tried to break away.

"I thought I'd be around for a while. Give my boy some lessons in tapping into his feelings, finding his passion and all that." Joe gave Sam a hearty thump on the back. "After that little display, I think he may have wised up on his own. You're good for him, Julia. Real good."

Sam's hold on her loosened. He studied his father. "You mean one kiss convinced you I can do without a dose of your emotional mumbo jumbo?"

Julia swatted his arm. "That's your father. Show some respect."

Sam shot her a withering look. "I'll remember that the next time your mom's around."

Joe laughed and wrapped them in another hug. "Not just any kiss. It's different when you kiss *the one.* Trust me, I know. I bet they could see the sparks flying between the two of you clear down to the coast."

Looking into Joe's trusting face, she couldn't let Sam's father pin his hopes on her. She had to tell him the truth.

"Mr. Callahan, I don't—"

"You're right, Dad," Sam agreed. "It's different with Julia. I'm different, and I don't want you to worry about me anymore." He pinched the tip of Julia's nose, a little harder than necessary if you asked her.

"Ouch."

"Such a delicate flower." He laughed and dropped a quick kiss on her forehead. "What would I do without you?"

"Troll for women over in Charlotte?" she offered.

"See why I need her by my side?"

Joe nodded. "I do."

Sam turned to Julia and rubbed his warm hands down her arms. "Where are you parked?"

Julia pointed to the blue Jetta a few spaces down from where they stood, her mind still reeling.

"Perfect. I'm going to walk Dad back to the hotel and we'll talk tomorrow."

She didn't like the look in his eye. "I'm kind of busy at the salon tomorrow."

"Never too busy for your one true love."

Julia stifled the urge to gag. "I guess not."

"Get going, then, sugar." He pinched her bottom, making her yelp. She rounded on him but, at the calculating gleam in his eye, turned back toward her car. Sam and his dad watched until she'd pulled out.

Despite this peculiar evening, his announcement had served its purpose. Lexi Preston had said having Sam in the picture might change things. That could be the understatement of the year, but if it kept Charlie safe, Julia would make it work.

No matter what.

Sam took a fortifying drink of coffee and watched as another woman walked through the door of The Best Little Hairhouse. He knew Julia had worked at the salon since her return to Brevia two years ago, but that wasn't why he avoided this place like the plague. It was too girlie for him. The bottles of hair product and little rows of nail polish on the shelves gave him the heebie-jeebies.

The one time he'd ventured into the Hairhouse, after the owner had reported a man lurking in the back alley, he'd felt like a prize steer come up for auction.

He adjusted the brim of his hat, buttoned his jacket against the late-morning rain and started across the street. He'd put the visit off until almost lunchtime, irritated with himself at how much he wanted to see Julia again. Part of him wanted to blame her for making him crazy, but another piece, the part he tried to ignore, wanted to get close enough to her to smell the scent of sunshine on her hair.

He scrubbed a hand across his face. Sunshine on her hair? What the hell was that about? Women didn't smell like sunshine. She worked at a salon and probably had a ton of gunk in her hair at any given moment. Although the way the strands had felt soft on his fingers when he'd bent to kiss her last night told another story.

One he wasn't interested in reading. Or so he told himself.

Sam opened the front door and heard a blood-curdling scream from behind the wall at the reception desk. He jerked to attention. He might not spend a lot of time in beauty salons but could guarantee that sound wasn't typical.

"I'm going to choke the life out of her," a woman yelled, "as soon as my nails dry."

Nope. Something wasn't right.

He glanced at the empty reception desk then stepped through the oversized doorway that led to the main room.

A pack of women huddled around one of the chairs, Julia in the center of the mix.

"Is there a problem here, ladies?"

Seven pairs of eyes, ranging from angry to horrified, turned to him.

"Sam, thank the Lord you're here."

"You would not believe what happened."

"Congrats on your engagement, Chief."

The last comment produced silence from the group. He met Julia's exasperated gaze. "Not a good time," she mouthed and turned back to the center of the cluster, only to be pushed aside by a woman with a black smock draped around her considerable girth. Sam tried not to gape at her head, where the neat curls framing her face glowed an iridescent pink.

"There will be time for celebrating later. I want that woman arrested," Ida Garvey announced. Sam was used to Ida issuing dictatorial commands. She was the wealthiest woman in town, thanks to a generous inheritance from her late husband. Other than the clown hair, she looked like a picture-perfect grandma, albeit one with a sharp tongue and a belief that she ruled the world.

For an instant, he thought she was pointing at Julia. Then he noticed the young woman hunched in the corner, furiously wiping tears from her cheeks.

"Ida, don't be a drama queen." Julia shook her head. "No one is being arrested. Accidents happen. We'll fix it, but—"

"She turned my hair pink!" With a screech, Ida vaulted from the chair and grabbed a curling iron from a stand. "I'm going to kill her!" Ida lunged toward the cowering woman, but Julia stepped into her path. The curling iron dropped, the barrel landing on Julia's arm before clattering to the floor.

Julia bit out an oath and Ida screamed again. "Look what you made me do," she bellowed at the now-sobbing stylist. "I burned her."

Sam strode forward with a new appreciation for the simplicity of breaking up a drunken bar brawl. Ida looked into his face then staggered back, one hand fluttering to her chest. "Are you gonna arrest me, Chief?"

"Sit down, Mrs. Garvey." He waved at the group of women. "All of you, back off. Now."

Ida plopped back into the chair as the group fell silent again.

Julia winced as he took her arm in his hands. A crimson mark slashed across her wrist, the skin already raised and angry. "Where's a faucet?"

"I'm fine," she said through gritted teeth. "Happens all the time."

"I sure as hell hope not."

"Not exactly like this. I can use the sink in back." She tugged her arm but he didn't let go.

"Don't anyone move," he ordered the women. "That means you, Ida."

"I don't need your help," Julia ground out as he followed her to the back of the salon.

"You aren't leaving me alone with that crowd."

"Not so brave now." Julia fumbled with the tap.

He nudged her out of the way. "I'll do it. Nice ring. I have good taste."

"I had it from… Well, it doesn't matter." Her cheeks flamed as she glanced at the diamond sparkling on her left hand. "I thought I should wear something until we had a chance to figure things out. Fewer questions that way. You know how nosy people are, especially in the salon."

They needed to talk, but Sam couldn't get beyond Julia being hurt, even by a curling iron. "Tell me what happened."

"Crystal, the one in the corner, is our newest stylist. Ida came in without an appointment and she was the only one available. When she went to mix the color, Ida started barking orders. Crystal got so nervous, she mixed it wrong.

Instead of a fluffy white cotton ball, Mrs. Garvey's head is now glowing neon pink."

Sam hid a smile as he drew her arm under the faucet and adjusted the temperature. She closed her eyes and sighed as cold water washed over the burn. He drew small circles on her palm, amazed at the softness of her skin under the pad of his thumb.

After a moment he asked, "Do you want to press charges?"

Her eyes flew open, and then she smiled at his expression. "Assault with a deadly styling tool? No, thanks."

Her smile softened the angles of her face, made her beauty less ethereal and more earthy. God help him, he loved earthy.

She must have read something in his eyes because she yanked her hand away and flipped off the water. "I need to get out there before Ida goes after Crystal again."

"Did you hire Crystal?"

"About three weeks ago. She came over from Memphis right out of school to stay with her aunt and needs a break..." She paused, her eyes narrowing. "You think I'm an idiot for hiring a girl with so little experience."

"I didn't say that."

"Everyone thinks Val's a fool to leave me in charge. They're waiting for me to mess up." She wrapped her arms around her waist then flinched when the burn touched her sweater. "And here I am."

Sam knew Val Dupree, the Hairhouse's longtime owner, was planning to retire, and Julia was working to secure a loan to buy the business. She was acting as the salon's manager while Val spent the winter in Florida. "No one expects you to mess up."

"You've been in town long enough to know what people think of me."

The words held no malice, but she said them with a

quiet conviction. Sam wanted to take her in his arms to soothe her worry and at the same time shake some sense into her. "Was it a mistake to hire Crystal?"

"No." She looked at him as though she expected an argument. When he offered none she continued, "She's good. Or she will be. I know it."

"Then we'd better make sure Ida Garvey doesn't attack your future star again."

"Right." She led him back into the main salon, where Ida still pinned Crystal to the wall with her angry stare. Everyone else's attention was fixed on Julia and Sam.

Julia glanced over her shoulder. "It's been twenty questions about our relationship all morning."

He nodded. "Let's take on one disaster at a time."

She squared her shoulders and approached Mrs. Garvey, no trace of self-doubt evident. "Ida, I'm sorry." She bent in front of the chair and took the older woman's hands in hers. "I'm going to clear my schedule for the afternoon and make your hair better than before. You'll get three months' worth of free services for your trouble."

Mrs. Garvey patted her pink hair. "That would help."

"Lizzy?" Julia called. A young woman peeked around the doorway from the front of the salon. "Would you reschedule the rest of my clients? Everyone else, back to work."

"I'm sorry," Crystal said from the corner, taking a step toward Julia.

Ida shifted in the chair. "Don't you come near me."

Sam moved forward but Julia simply patted Ida's fleshy arm. "Take the rest of the day off, Crystal. I'll see you back here in the morning."

"Day off?" Ida screeched. "You're going to fire her, aren't you? Val would have fired her on the spot!"

Color rose in Julia's cheeks but she held her ground. "No, Mrs. Garvey. Crystal made a mistake."

"She's a menace. I knew she was doing it wrong from the start."

"She made a mistake," Julia repeated. "In part because you didn't let her do her job." She looked at Crystal. "Go on, hon. We'll talk in the morning."

"I have half a mind to call Val Dupree this minute and tell her how you're going to run her business into the ground."

"I'd watch what you say right now, Mrs. Garvey." Sam pointed to her hair. "Julia may leave you pink if you're not careful."

"She wouldn't dare." But Ida shut her mouth, chewing furiously on her bottom lip.

"Get comfortable," Julia told her. "We'll be here for a while."

She turned to Sam. "I think your work here is done, Chief."

He leveled a steely look at her. "We're not finished."

"Unless you want to pull up a chair next to Ida we are. The longer that color sits on her hair, the harder time I'll have getting it out."

"You don't play fair."

Her eyes glinted. "I never have."

Chapter Three

Julia rubbed her nose against Charlie's dimpled neck and was rewarded by a soft belly laugh. "Who's my best boy?" she asked and kissed the top of his head.

"Charlie," he answered in his sweet toddler voice.

"Thanks for keeping him today, Lainey." Julia's younger sister and their mother, Vera, took turns watching Charlie on the days when his normal babysitter was unavailable. "Things were crazy today at work."

She couldn't imagine balancing everything without her family's help. Two years ago, Julia's relationship with Lainey had been almost nonexistent. Thanks in large part to Charlie, she now felt a sisterly bond she hadn't realized was missing from her life.

"Crazy, how?" Lainey asked from where she stirred a pot of soup at the stove.

"Ida Garvey ended up with hair so pink it looked like cotton candy."

Lainey's mouth dropped open.

"She freaked out, as you can imagine." Charlie scrambled off her lap to play with a toy fire truck on the kitchen floor. "It took the whole afternoon to make it better."

"I thought you meant crazy like telling people about your secret boyfriend and his public proposal." Lainey turned and pointed a wooden spoon at Julia as if it were a weapon. "I can't believe I didn't even know you two were dating."

Julia groaned at the accusation in her sister's tone and the hurt that shadowed her green eyes. When she'd gone along with Sam's fake proposal last night, Julia hadn't thought about the repercussions of people believing them. Thinking things through wasn't her strong suit.

She didn't talk about her years away from Brevia with Lainey or their mother. They had some inkling of her penchant for dating losers and changing cities at the end of each bad relationship. When the going got tough, it had always seemed easier to move on than stick it out.

From the outside, Julia knew she appeared to have it together. She was quick with a sarcastic retort that made people believe life's little setbacks didn't affect her. She'd painted herself as the free spirit who wouldn't be tied to anyone or any place.

But her devil-may-care mask hid a deeply rooted insecurity that, if someone really got to know her, she wouldn't measure up. Because of her learning disabilities and in so many other ways.

Her struggles to read and process numbers at the most basic level had defined who she was for years. The shame she felt, as a result, was part of the very fiber of her being. She'd been labeled stupid and lazy, and despite what anyone told her to the contrary, she couldn't shake the belief that it was true.

Maybe that was why she picked men who were obviously bad bets. Maybe that was why she'd been a mean girl in high school—to keep people at arm's length so she wouldn't have a chance of being rejected.

She wondered for a moment how it would feel to confide the entire complicated situation to Lainey. For one person to truly understand her problem. She ached to lean in for support as fear weighed on her heart. But as much as they'd worked to repair their fractured relationship, Julia still couldn't tell her sister how scared she was of failing at what meant the most to her in life: being a mother to Charlie.

"I'm sorry. I didn't mean for half the town to find out at Carl's." No one in her family even knew about Jeff's interest in a new custody arrangement.

She stood, trying to come up with a plausible reason she wouldn't have shared big boyfriend news. "My track record with guys is common knowledge, and I didn't want Sam to have people beating down his door to warn him away from me."

Lainey's gaze turned sympathetic. "Oh, Jules. When Ethan and I first got back together I didn't want anyone to know, either. I felt like the town would hold my past mistakes against me and you were back and… Never mind now. I'm going to forgive you because it's so wonderful." She threw her arms around Julia. "Everyone loves Sam, so…" Lainey's voice trailed off.

Julia's stomach turned with frustration. "So, what? By default people are suddenly going to open their arms to me?"

Lainey shrugged. "It can't hurt. Do you have a date?"

"For what?"

Lainey pushed away. "The wedding, silly. You'll get married in Brevia, right?"

Julia blinked. "I suppose so. We're taking the planning slowly. I want a long engagement. It'll be better for Charlie."

"Sure." Lainey frowned but went back to the stove.

"Just enjoying each other and all that," Julia added quickly, guilt building with every lie she told. "So in love. You know."

"I want to be involved in the planning."

"Of course. We can have a girls' day out to look for dresses and stuff." With each detail, the difficulty of deceiving her family became more apparent.

She reminded herself that it was only for a short time, and she was protecting everyone from the stress of the custody fight. "I should go. Thanks to the commotion today, I'm late on the product order I should have sent. If Charlie goes down early enough, I'll be able to get it in tomorrow morning. A night full of numbers, lucky me."

"Do you want some help?"

Julia tensed. "I can handle it. I'm not a total idiot, despite rumors to the contrary." She saw hurt flash again in her sister's gaze and regretted her defensive tone.

She did most of the paperwork for the salon when Charlie went to bed to minimize her hours away from him. She spent many late nights pouring over the accounts and payroll information, terrified she'd make a mistake or miss an important detail. She was determined no one would ever see how unqualified she was to run her own business.

"No one thinks you're an idiot," Lainey said quietly. "You're doing an amazing job with the salon, but I know how things get when you're tired. I'm offering another set of eyes if you need them."

"I'm sorry I snapped." Julia rubbed two fingers against each temple, trying to ward off an impending headache.

"I'll take it slow. It's routine paperwork, not splitting the atom."

"Could you delegate some of this to the receptionist or one of the part-time girls? Why does it all have to fall on you? If you'd only tell them—"

"They can't know. No one can. What if Val found out? The deal isn't final. She could change her mind about selling to me."

"She wouldn't do that," Lainey argued.

"Someone could take advantage, mix things up without me understanding until it's too late." Julia gathered Charlie's sippy cup and extra snacks into the diaper bag.

Lainey shook her head, frustration evident as she fisted her hands at her sides. "Learning disabilities don't make you stupid, Julia. When are you going to realize that? Your brain processes information differently. It has nothing to do with your IQ, and you have the best intuition of anyone I know. No one could take advantage of you—"

"Have you seen my list of ex-boyfriends?"

"—without you letting them," Lainey finished.

"Point taken." Even as much as Julia had wanted her relationship with Jeff to work out, she should have known it was doomed. He'd been the opposite of most guys she'd dated, and she should have known someone so academic and cultured wouldn't truly want her. They'd gone to museums and gallery openings, his interest in her giving her hope that someone would finally see her for more than a pretty face.

She'd craved his approval and made the mistake of sharing her secret with him. None of the men before him had known about the severe learning disabilities that had plagued her since grade school. She'd managed for years to keep her LD hidden from almost everyone.

Only her family and certain trusted teachers had known

the struggles she'd faced in learning to read and process both words and numbers. She wasn't sure any of them understood how deep her problems were. The embarrassment and frustrations she'd felt as a kid had prevented her from letting teachers, interventionists or even her parents truly help her.

It had been easier to play the part of being too cool for school or, as she got older, not wanting to be tied down to a real job or responsibilities. Only for Charlie was she finally willing to put her best effort forward, constantly worried it wouldn't be enough.

"Are you still working with the literacy specialist?"

"Every week. It's a slow process, though. Between my visual and auditory learning deficiencies, I feel like a lost cause. Sometimes I wonder if it's even worth it."

"It's worth it," Lainey said as she lifted Charlie from the floor and gave him a hug before depositing him into Julia's arms. "LD is complex and I'm proud of you for everything you've accomplished despite it. I'm here if you need me. Ethan and Mom can take Charlie, so—"

"Mom's back?" Julia swallowed. She'd assumed her sister hadn't heard about the engagement. But their mother had her finger on the pulse of every snippet of gossip from Brevia to the state line. "She wasn't scheduled back until next week." Long enough for Julia to get a handle on her mess of a life.

"She flew in this morning. I can help contain her, you know. You'll need reinforcements for damage control on that front."

Julia stopped in her tracks. Even though she'd worried about her mother finding out, hearing Lainey say it made her knees quiver the tiniest bit. "Mom knows? I thought she just got back."

"She knows," Lainey answered with an eye roll. "I think she's waiting for you to call and explain yourself."

Another layer of dread curled in the pit of Julia's stomach. Her mother would support her. Vera was a big part of Charlie's life and would fight tooth and nail to protect him. But she understood Julia's limitations better than anyone. Julia didn't want to know if her mom had any doubts about her ability to give Charlie a good life on her own.

Now was the time to come clean, but with Charlie in her arms, she couldn't bring herself to voice her fears. It might make them too real.

"I'll call her. She'll understand. I'll make her understand."

Lainey only smiled. "Good luck."

Julia needed a lot more than luck.

She tried to ignore the persistent knocking at her apartment door later that night. She hadn't called her mother and silently debated whether Vera would make the twenty-minute drive to Julia's apartment to rake her over the coals in person.

But Charlie had just fallen asleep after six verses of "The Wheels on the Bus," and Julia wasn't going to risk the noise waking him, so she opened the door, prepared for the mother–daughter smackdown of the century.

Sam stood in the hallway watching her.

Even better.

"Long day, Chief. I'll call you tomorrow." She tried to close the door but he shoved his foot into the opening. Blast those steel-toed boots.

He held up a white cardboard box and a six-pack of beer. "It's been a long day for both of us. We eat first and then dig ourselves out of this mess."

She sniffed the air. "Pepperoni?"

"With extra cheese."

She took a step back and he eased around her into the tiny apartment. It actually didn't feel so small with just her and Charlie in it. Somehow, Sam not only filled the room but used more than his fair share of the oxygen in it. Julia drew a shaky breath and led the way to the small dining area.

"Sorry," she apologized automatically as she picked macaroni noodles from the maple tabletop. "Charlie's been practicing his QB skills at mealtime."

"Nothing wrong with starting early. Where's the little guy?"

"Asleep. Finally."

Sam put the box on the table and handed her a beer as he cocked his head. "Is that classical music?"

"Beethoven."

"Sounds different than I remember. More animated."

She picked up a remote and pointed it at the television on the other side of the room. "It's a Junior Genius DVD."

"Come again?"

"A program designed to increase a young child's brain activity." She clicked off the television. "They have research to show that it works."

His brows rose. "I still hear music."

She felt color creep into her cheeks. "I play a Mozart disc as he falls asleep." She walked past him to the kitchen and pulled two plates from a cabinet.

"Are you a classical-music fan?"

She spun around and stalked back to the table. "Why? Do you think classical is too highbrow for someone like me? Would it make more sense if I was a Toby Keith groupie?"

He took a step back and studied her. "First off, don't hate on Toby Keith. Secondly, it was a question." He waved one hand in the direction of the bookcases that flanked the television. "You have more classical CDs on your shelves than I've seen in my entire life. It's a logical assumption."

"Sorry." She sighed. "I like some composers but it's mainly for Charlie. I figure he needs all the help he can get, living with me. You may have heard I'm not the sharpest knife in the drawer."

"Is that so?"

"It's a well-known fact in town. My mom will tell you I have 'street smarts.'" She met his gaze with a wry smile. "I'm sure any number of my former friends would be happy to tell you how I skated through school by charming teachers or bullying other students into helping me." She broke off as Sam watched her, worrying that she'd somehow given him a clue into her defective inner self. She plastered on a saucy smile and stretched up her arms in an exaggerated pose. "At that point my life's ambition was to be a supermodel."

"Personally, I wanted to be Eddie Van Halen." He shrugged. "Were you really a bully?"

"I like to remember it as a benevolent dictatorship. I had my reasons, but have discovered that the kids I ordered around back in the day have become adults who are more than happy to see the golden girl taken down a few pegs." She opened the pizza box and pulled out a slice, embarrassed at her silly adolescent dream. "I was the ring leader and the 'pretty one' in Brevia, but couldn't cut it in the big leagues."

"You started over. There's nothing wrong with that. People do it all the time."

"Right. I went to beauty school, dated a string of losers, partied too much and tried to live below my potential." She tipped her beer in a mock toast. "And that's pretty low."

"Somebody did a number on you, sweetheart. Because

the way you handled that mess at the salon today took some clever negotiation skills. Not the work of a fool."

"We'll see what Val thinks once Ida spins it." She slid a piece of pizza onto his plate. "Sit down and eat. Unless the pizza was a ruse to get in the door so you could rip my head off without the neighbors hearing. Might be easier than going through with your *grand proposal*."

His knee brushed against her bare leg as he folded himself into the chair across from her. It occurred to Julia that she was wearing only boxer shorts and a faded Red Hot Chili Peppers T-shirt with no bra. Bad choice for tonight.

"Such violent thoughts," he said, sprinkling a packet of cheese flakes on his pizza.

She sat back and crossed her arms over her chest. As soon as she'd realized she was braless, her nipples had sprung to attention as if to yell "over here, look at us." Not something she wanted Sam to notice in a million years.

"Why did you do it? This crazy situation is your fault."

He frowned. "You weren't exactly convincing as the levelheaded, responsible parent. You were about to dive across the table and take out the grandma."

"She deserved it." Julia popped out of her chair and grabbed a fleece sweatshirt from a hook near the hallway, trying not to let her belly show as she pulled it over her head. "But I didn't need to be rescued. Especially not by Three Strikes Sam." She sat back in her chair and picked up the pizza. "We're quite a pair. Do you really think anyone is going to believe you're engaged, given your reputation?"

"What reputation, and who is Three Strikes Sam?"

She finished her bite. "You don't know? Brevia is a small town. But we've got more than our share of single ladies. Apparently the long line of women you've dated since you arrived has banded together. The story is that you don't go on more than three dates with one woman. You've got your own fan club here in town. The ladies blog, tweet and keep track of you on Facebook. They call you Three Strikes Sam."

Sam felt as though he'd been kneed in the family jewels. Never mind the social-media insanity, what shocked him more was that Julia acted as if she knew the details of his dating history. That possibility was fright-night scary.

"You're making it up."

"I'm not that creative. You can log on to my computer and see for yourself. I only found out a couple of weeks ago, when Jean Hawkins was in the salon."

Sam swallowed hard. Jean was the dispatcher for the county sheriff's office. They'd had a couple of casual dinners last month but had agreed not to take it further. Or so he'd thought.

"She got a blowout and a bang trim. A 'wash that man right out of her hair' afternoon." Julia wrinkled her pert nose. "You know how it is—stylists are like therapists for some people. Get a woman in the chair and she has to spill her secrets."

"And *she* told you about this fan club?"

Julia nodded and took a drink of beer. "Three seems to be the magic number for you. You're a serial get-to-know-you dater."

Sam pushed away from the table and paced to the end of the narrow living room. "That's ridiculous." He ran a hand through his hair. "There's no arbitrary limit on the number of dates I'll go on with one woman."

"A dozen ladies claim there is," she countered. "They say you've more than made the rounds."

"I haven't dated a *dozen* ladies in Brevia. Besides, why would anyone gossip about dating me?"

"You've been in Brevia long enough to know how it

works." She laughed, but he found no humor in the situation. Sure, he'd been on dates with a few different women. When he'd first come to town, it had sort of happened that way. He'd always been a gentleman. If things led to the bedroom he didn't complain, but he also didn't push it. No one had grumbled at the time.

He wasn't a serial dater. The way she said it made him sound like a scumbag. So what if he was a little gun-shy? Walking in on your fiancée with her legs wrapped around another guy would do that to a man. It had been almost three years now since he'd had his heart crushed, and he wasn't itching to repeat that particular form of hell. "You're telling me I'm a joke with these women because I'm not in a relationship?" His voice started to rise. "In case they haven't noticed, I have a serious job. One that's more important to me than my damned social life."

"It's not like that," she said quickly, reaching out to place her cool fingers on his arm. A light touch that was oddly comforting. "No one is laughing at you. It's more like a challenge. Scary as it may sound, you have a town full of women who are determined to see you settle down. According to my sources, you're quite the catch."

He dropped back into the chair. "I came to Brevia because I wanted a fresh start."

"As Mick Jagger would say, 'you can't always get what you want.'"

"You think this fake engagement is what I need?"

"It was your idea to start. Plus, it's quieted the gossips, and your dad seemed to approve."

He nodded and took a long drink of beer. "My father loved you."

"Who can blame him?" she asked with a hair toss.

Sam smiled despite himself. "He wants to help me tap into my emotions."

She studied him as she took another bite. "Is that so bad?"

"I don't need to be more emotional."

"Your fans beg to differ."

"Don't remind me," he muttered.

A tiny cry came from the corner of the table and Julia adjusted a baby monitor. "I'm going to check on him." She padded down the hall, leaving Sam alone with his thoughts. Something he didn't need right now.

He preferred his emotions tightly bottled. It wasn't as if he didn't have feelings. Hell, he'd felt awful after calling off his engagement. He would have made a decent husband: loyal, faithful...

Maybe those were better attributes in a family pet, but he managed okay.

In Sam's opinion, there was no use wearing his heart on his sleeve. The scraps of memory he had from the months after his mother died were awful, his dad too often passed out drunk on the couch. Neighbors shuttling Sam and his brother to school and a steady diet of peanut butter and jelly sandwiches. When Joe finally got a handle on his emotions, it had saved their family.

Sam would never risk caring for someone like that. Feeling too much, connecting to the feelings he'd locked up tight, might spiral him back into that uncontrolled chaos.

He looked around the apartment, taking in more details with Julia out of the room. The dining area opened directly onto the living room, which was filled with comfortable, oversized furniture covered in a creamy fabric. Several fuzzy blankets fell over the arm of one chair. A wicker box overflowed with various toys, most of which looked far more complex than he remembered from childhood.

In addition to the classical CDs, framed pictures of Charlie with Julia, Vera, Lainey and Ethan sat on the bookshelves. Sam had also noticed an impressive collection of books—several classics by Hemingway, Dickens, even Ayn Rand. For someone who clearly didn't see her own intelligence, Julia had sophisticated taste in reading material.

The baby monitor crackled, drawing his attention. He heard Julia's voice through the static. "Did you have a dream, Charlie-boy?" she cooed. "Can Mommy sing you back to sleep?"

Charlie gave another sleepy cry as an answer and a moment later Sam heard a familiar James Taylor song in a soft soprano.

He smiled as he listened to Julia sing. Classical for Charlie, Sweet Baby James for his mother.

Sam felt a thread of unfamiliar connection fill his heart. At the same time there was a release of pressure he hadn't realized he'd held. In the quiet of the moment, listening to her sweet and slightly off-key voice, the day's stress slipped away. He took a deep breath as his shoulders relaxed.

"I love you, sweetie," he heard her whisper, her tone so full of tenderness it made his heart ache all the more.

He understood in an instant how much it meant for Julia to keep her son. Knew that she'd do anything to keep Charlie safe.

Suddenly Sam wanted that for her more than he cared about his own future. But he was a man who'd made it through life taking care of himself, protecting number one at all costs. No matter how he felt about one spirited single mother, he couldn't afford to change that now.

Hearing footsteps, he quickly stood to clear the dishes from the table.

"I think he's back down," she said as she came into the kitchen.

Sam rounded on her, needing to get to the crux of the matter before he completely lost control. "You're right," he told her. "This deal was my idea and I'll play the part of doting fiancé because it helps us both."

"Doting may be pushing it," she said, fumbling with the pizza box, clearly wary of his change in mood. "We don't need to go overboard."

He propped one hip on the counter. "We need to make it believable." He kept his tone all business. "Whatever it takes."

"Fine. We'll make people believe we're totally in love. I'm in. Whatever it takes to convince Jeff to drop the custody suit."

"Will he?"

"He still hasn't even seen Charlie. I get the impression his parents are pushing for the new custody deal. The attorney is really here to figure out if they have a viable case or not before they go public. Jeff didn't want kids in the first place. He'd even talked about getting the big snip. They probably think Charlie is their only shot at a grandchild, someone to mold and shape in their likeness."

"I don't think that's how kids work."

She shook her head. "I don't think they care. If we can convince Lexi that Charlie has a happy, stable home and that he's better off here than with Jeff and his family, that's the report she'll give to them. It will be enough. It has to. Once I get the custody agreement—"

"You'll dump my sorry butt," Sam supplied.

"Or you can break it off with me." She rinsed a plate and put it into the dishwasher. "People will expect it. You're up for reappointment soon. It should earn extra points with some of the council members. Everyone around here knows I'm a bad bet."

"I thought you and Ethan had been the town's golden couple back in the day."

"He was the golden boy," she corrected. "I was the eye

candy on his arm. But I messed that up. My first in a series of epic fails in the relationship department."

"Does it bother you that he's with Lainey?" Sam asked, not willing to admit how much her answer meant to him.

She smiled. "They're perfect together in a way he and I never were. She completes him and all that."

"Do you think there's someone out there who'd complete you?"

"Absolutely." She nodded. "At this moment, he's drooling in the crib at the end of the hall."

He took a step closer to her and tucked a lock of hair behind her ear. "We're going to make sure he stays there."

Her lips parted as she looked up at him. Instinctively he eased toward her.

She blinked and raised her hands to his chest, almost pushing him away but not quite. "We have to establish some ground rules," she said, sounding as breathless as he felt.

"I'm the law around these parts, ma'am," he said in his best Southern drawl. "I make the rules."

"Nice try." She laughed and a thrill ran through him. "First off, no touching or kissing of any kind."

It was his turn to throw back his head and laugh. "We're supposed to be in love. You think people will believe you could keep your hands off me?"

She smacked his chest lightly. "I'm surprised your ego made it through the front door. Okay, if the situation calls for it you can kiss me. A little." Her eyes narrowed. "But no tongue."

He tried to keep a straight face. "Where's the fun in that?"

"My best offer," she whispered.

He traced her lips with the tip of one finger and felt

himself grow heavy when they parted again. "I think we'd better practice to see if I'll be able to manage it."

He leaned in, but instead of claiming her mouth he tilted his head to reach the smooth column of her neck. He trailed delicate kisses up to her ear and was rewarded with a soft moan. Pushing her hair back, he cradled her face between his palms.

Her breath tingled against his skin and she looked at him, desire and self-control warring in the depths of her eyes. He wanted to keep this arrangement business but couldn't stop his overwhelming need. As out of control as a runaway train, he captured her lips with his.

Chapter Four

It should be illegal for a kiss to feel so good. The thought registered in Julia's dizzy brain. Followed quickly by her body's silent demand for more…more…more. Her arms wound around Sam's neck and she pressed into him, the heat from his body stoking a fire deep within her. His mouth melded to hers as he drew his hands up underneath her shirt.

A man hadn't kissed her like this in so long. As though he meant it, his mouth a promise of so much more.

A familiar voice cut through her lust-filled haze. "So, the rumors are true. Doesn't seem right your mother should be the last to know."

Sam's eyes flew open as he stepped away from her. Julia let out a soft groan.

"Ever think of knocking?" she asked, pressing her hands over her eyes.

"No" was her mother's succinct answer.

"Nice to see you, Mrs. Morgan." Although Sam's voice sounded a little shaky, Julia had to admire his courage in holding her mother's gaze.

Almost unwillingly, Julia turned and met her mom's steely glare. "I'm sorry, Mom. We wanted to keep things quiet a bit longer."

Vera Morgan was a tiny blonde dynamo of a woman. Her hair pulled back into a neat bun, she retained the beauty of her youth mixed with the maturity of decades spent overseeing her life and everyone in it. She crossed her arms over her chest. "Until you could announce your engagement in the middle of a crowded restaurant?"

Julia cringed. "Not the exact plan."

"I don't understand what this is about. It sounds like one of your typical impetuous decisions. Your father and I raised you to be more careful with how you act. I thought you'd have learned to be more responsible about the choices you make. Have you thought of Charlie? What's best for him?"

"He's all I think about and of course I want what's best for him. You have no idea…" Julia wanted to lay it all on the line for her mother—Jeff's family, the attorney, her fear of losing Charlie. She paused and glanced at Sam. He nodded slightly as if to encourage her.

How could she admit her years of bad choices could jeopardize Charlie's future? She knew her mother thought she was irresponsible, fickle and flighty. For most of her life, Julia had been all of those things and worse.

Her mother waited for an answer while the toe of one shoe tapped out a disapproving rhythm. Julia could measure the milestone moments of her life by her mother's slow toe tap. She swore sometimes she could hear it in her sleep.

"I don't expect you to understand, but this is good for Charlie. For both of us."

Vera's gaze slanted between Julia and Sam. "Having the hots for a guy isn't the same as love. From what I just witnessed, you two have chemistry, but marriage is a lot more than physical attraction."

Julia felt a blush rise to her cheeks. "I'm not a teenager anymore," she mumbled. "I get that."

"I worry about you rushing into something." Vera paused and pinned Sam with a look before continuing. "Especially with a man who has a reputation around town. I don't want you to be hurt."

"I know what I'm doing. Trust me. For once trust that I'm making the right decision." She hated that her voice cracked. She'd made some stupid choices in her life. So what? Lots of people did and they lived through it. Did she have to be raked over the coals for every indiscretion?

Sam's hand pressed into the small of her back, surprisingly comforting. "Mrs. Morgan," he began, his voice strong and confident. Julia wished she felt either right now. "Your daughter is the most amazing woman I've ever met."

Julia glanced over her shoulder, for a moment wondering if he was talking about her sister.

The corner of his mouth turned up as he looked at her. "*You* are amazing. You're honest and brave and willing to fight for what you want."

Charlie's sweet face flashed in Julia's mind, and she gave a slight nod.

"You're a lot stronger and smarter than you give yourself credit for." His gaze switched to Vera. "Than most people give her credit for. But that's going to change. I want people to see the woman I do. Maybe we shouldn't have hidden our relationship, but it wasn't anyone's business. To hell with my reputation and Julia's, too."

"I hear a couple town-council members are making a big deal about your single status as they're starting to review your contract. They think only a family man can impart the kind of values and leadership Brevia needs."

"Another reason we were quiet. I don't want to use Julia and Charlie to get reappointed. The job I've done as police chief should be enough."

He sounded so convincing, Julia almost believed him. At the very least, his conviction gave her the courage to stand up for herself a little more. "Sam's right. We're not looking for anyone's approval. This is about us."

"Have you set a date yet?" Vera asked, her tone hard again.

"We're working on that."

Sam cleared his throat. "I'm going to head home." He dropped a quick kiss on Julia's cheek. "I'll talk to you tomorrow."

"Coward," she whispered.

"Sticks and stones," he said softly before turning to Vera.

"Mrs. Morgan, I'm sorry you found out this way. I hope you know I have Julia and Charlie's best interests at heart."

Her mother's eyes narrowed.

"That's my cue." Sam scooted around Vera and let himself out the front door.

"I only want what's best for you." Vera stepped forward. "Your father and I didn't do enough to help you when you were younger. I won't make that mistake again." She wrapped one arm around Julia's waist. "I don't understand how this happened and I don't trust Sam Callahan. But I know Charlie is your number one priority. That's what counts."

Julia didn't want her mother to feel guilty. As a child, she'd tried to hide the extent of her problems from her parents, as well as everyone else. They weren't to blame. She let out a slow breath. "I'm doing this for Charlie."

"You love him?"

"He's my entire life."

"I meant, do you love Sam? Enough to marry him."

"Sam is a wonderful man," Julia answered quickly. "I'd be a fool not to want to marry him." Not exactly a declaration of deep and abiding love but it was as much as she could offer tonight. "I'm sorry you had to come over."

Her mother watched her for several moments before releasing her hold. "You're my daughter. I'll do anything to protect you. You know that, right?"

Julia nodded. Once again, she had the urge to share the whole sordid mess with her mother. She swallowed back her emotions. "It's late. I'll bring Charlie by in the morning before I drop him at the sitter's."

Vera patted her cheek. "Get some sleep. You look like you could use it. You can't keep up this pace. You're no spring chicken."

"Thanks for the reminder." That was the reason Julia wanted to handle this on her own. Vera couldn't help but judge her. It was in her mother's nature to point out all the ways Julia needed improvement. She'd have a field day with the custody situation. Julia had enough trouble without adding her mother's opinion into the mix.

She closed and locked the door behind her mother then sagged against it. She'd done a lot of reckless things in her life but wondered if this time she'd gone off the deep end.

The baby monitor made a noise. Charlie gave a short cry before silence descended once more. Her gaze caught on a framed photo on one end table, taken minutes after his birth. She'd known as soon as the nurse had placed him in her arms that Charlie was the best part of her. She'd vowed that day to make something of her life, to become worthy of the gift she'd been given. While she had a difficult time tamping down her self-doubt, she never questioned how far she would go to protect her son. She'd do whatever it took to keep him safe, even this ridiculous charade with Sam. If it helped her custody case in the least, Julia would become the most devoted fiancée Brevia had ever seen.

That commitment was put to the test the next morning when a posse of angry women descended on the salon. Two to be exact, but it felt like a mob.

She'd swung by her mother's after breakfast then dropped Charlie with Mavis Donnelly, the older woman who watched him and one other toddler in her home. She'd gotten into town by eight-thirty, thanks to Charlie's propensity to wake with the sun. She wanted time to look over the monthly billing spreadsheets before anyone else arrived.

No one outside her immediate family knew about her condition, and she intended to keep it that way, afraid of being taken advantage of or thought too stupid to handle her own business. She put in the extra time she needed to get each financial piece right. Sometimes she studied the numbers until she felt almost physically ill.

When the knocking started, she straightened from her desk in the back, assuming it was one of the stylists who'd forgotten her key. Instead the front door swung open to reveal two pairs of angry eyes glaring at her.

"How'd you do it?" Annabeth Sullivan asked, pushing past her into the salon without an invitation. Annabeth had been in the same high-school class as Julia, a girl Julia would have referred to as a "band geek" back in the day. She hadn't been kind, and Annabeth, who now managed the bank reviewing Julia's loan application, hadn't let her forget it. Annabeth's younger sister, Diane, followed her inside.

"Morning to you, ladies."

"He never goes on more than three dates." Annabeth held up three plump fingers. "Never."

"Can I see the ring?" Diane asked, her tone gentler.

Reluctantly, Julia held out her hand. "It's perfect," Diane gushed.

"Kind of small," Annabeth said, peering at it from the corner of one eye. "I figured you'd go for the gaudy flash."

Julia felt her temper flare. "You don't know me, then."

Annabeth took a step closer. "I know you, Julia Morgan. I know you had your minions stuff my locker with Twinkies the first day of freshman year. And made my life hell every day after that. I spent four years trying to stay off your radar and still you'd hunt me down."

The truth of the accusation made Julia cringe. "I'm sorry. I tried to make amends when I came back. I was awful and I'm truly sorry. I offered you free services for a year to try to repay a tiny portion of my debt."

"A year?" Diane turned to her sister. "You never told me that."

"Be quiet, Diane. That doesn't matter now. What I want to know is how you cast your evil spell over Sam Callahan."

"I'm not a witch. No spells, no magic." She paused then added, "We fell in love. Simple enough. Is there something else you need?" She took a step toward the front door but Annabeth held up a hand.

"Nothing is simple with you. Sam is a good man. He went on three dates with Diane."

"Almost four," Diane added. "I thought I'd made it past the cutoff. But he got called to a fire and had to cancel our last dinner. After that, he told me he wanted to be just friends."

"So, how come you two are all of a sudden engaged when no one even knew you were dating?"

"Even Abby was surprised and she knows *everything* about Sam." Diane clamped a hand over her mouth as Annabeth leveled a scowl at her.

As Julia understood it, Abby Brighton had moved to Brevia to take care of her elderly grandfather. She was the police chief's secretary and dispatcher. She didn't know about Abby's relationship with Sam, but the way Annabeth was looking at her sister, there was more to the story.

"Plus, you're a little long in the tooth for Sam," Annabeth stated, getting back to the business at hand.

Her mom had just said she was no spring chicken and now this. Lucky thing she'd chucked her ego to the curb years ago. "I'm thirty-two, the same age as you, Annabeth. We're not quite over the hill."

Annabeth pulled a small notebook out of her purse. "That's old for Sam. He usually dates women at least four years younger than him."

"And how old is that?"

"Don't you know how old he is?" Diane asked.

Julia met Annabeth's shrewd gaze. Calculated error on her part. "Of course. What I don't understand is why you carry a notebook with Sam's dating stats in it."

Annabeth snapped the notebook shut. "I don't have his dating stats, just a few pertinent facts. He and Diane seemed closer than any of the other women he dated. I want my sister to be happy. She had a chance before you came into the picture."

Julia studied Diane and couldn't begin to picture the dainty woman and Sam as a couple. "Did Sam break your heart?"

Diane scrunched up her nose. "No," she admitted after a moment. "Don't get me wrong, he's supercute and such a gentleman. But he's a little um…big…for me."

Julia's mouth dropped open. "Big?"

"Not like that," Diane amended. "He's just…with the uniform, all those muscles and he's so tall. It's kind of intimidating."

"I know what you mean," Julia agreed, although Sam's size appealed to her. She was five-nine, so it took a lot of guy to make Julia feel petite, but Sam did it in a way that also made her feel safe.

"You have real feelings for him." Annabeth interrupted her musings.

"I… We're engaged. I'd better have real feelings."

"Frankly, I thought this was another one of your stunts to show up the other single women in town. Prove that you're still the leader of the pack and all that." She glanced at Diane. "I didn't want my sister to fall prey to you the way I did."

"I'm *not* the same person I was. I can apologize but you'll need to choose whether to forgive me. I don't blame you if the answer is no, but it's your decision. My priority is Charlie. I want to live a life that will make him proud. I don't intend to re-create the past. You're married now, right?"

The other woman nodded. "Five years to my college sweetheart. He's my best friend."

"Why is it so strange to believe that I might want that for myself? My parents had a great marriage and you probably remember my sister recently married the love of her life, who just happened to be *my* high-school sweetheart. They're happy and I want to be happy. Last time I checked, that wasn't a crime in this town."

Julia pointed a finger at Diane. "If your sister wants to find a man, she will without you hunting down potential suitors for her or tallying lists of how far ahead of other women she is in the dating pool. Sam is a real person, too. I don't think he intended to become such a hot topic of gos-

sip. He's living his life the best way he can. We both are."
She stopped for breath and noticed Annabeth and Diane
staring at her, eyebrows raised.

She realized how much she'd revealed with her little
tirade and tried to calm her panic. Maybe she didn't want
to be known as the town's head mean girl anymore, but
she had a reputation to protect. She made people think
she didn't take things seriously so that they'd never notice when she got hurt. She plastered a smile on her face.
"What? Was that a little too mama grizzly for you?"

Annabeth shook her head, looking dazed. "I didn't realize that's how you felt about things. Sam is lucky to
have you."

"I'm not sure—"

"I'm sure."

The three women turned to see Sam standing in the
doorway. Julia's face burned. "How much did you hear?"

"Enough to know that I agree with Annabeth. I'm
damned lucky to have you."

Annabeth and Diane scooted toward the front door. "If
you'll excuse us. We'll leave you two alone."

He didn't move. "Is this going to hit the gossip train or
however it works?"

Diane shook her head. "We weren't the ones who started
analyzing you. It was—"

Annabeth gave her sister a hard pinch on the arm. "It
doesn't matter anymore. It's clear you're not the person
everyone thought."

Sam eased to the side of the doorway. "I think that could
be said for more than just me."

Annabeth threw a glance at Julia and nodded.

"Maybe you should spread that news around."

"I'll get on it, Chief." The two women hurried out of the
salon, and Sam pulled the door shut behind them.

"I'm a real man?" he said, repeating Julia's earlier comment. "I'm glad you think so, Ms. Morgan."

Julia slumped into a chair, breathing as if she'd just finished a marathon run. Her eyes were bleak as they met his. "It's pointless, Sam. This is never going to work."

Chapter Five

Sam stared at Julia. Her blond hair curled around her shoulders and fell forward, covering one high cheekbone. His fingers itched to smooth it back from her face, to touch her skin and wipe the pain from those large gray eyes. She looked so alone sitting in the oversized stylist's chair.

Sam knew what it felt like to be alone. Hell, he'd courted solitude for most of his life. He'd learned early on only to depend on himself, because when he relied on other people for his happiness he got hurt. First when his mother died and his dad had almost lost it. Then, later, in the relationship that had ended with his fiancée cheating on him.

He'd come to believe that happiness was overrated. He wanted to work hard and make a difference—the only way he knew to chase the demons away for a little peace.

When he'd heard Julia defending his character, something tight in his gut unwound. He was used to making things happen and having people depend on him. He prided himself on not needing anyone. It bothered him to know that women were spreading rumors about him, but he would have soldiered through with his head held high. Hearing Julia take on those ladies had made him realize he liked not feeling totally alone.

Her declaration that they couldn't make it work made no sense. "Why the change of heart?" He moved closer to her. "You convinced Annabeth and Diane."

"How old are you?"

"Thirty-three."

"Why do you only date younger women?"

He stopped short. "I don't."

"Are you sure? I've heard you average women at least four years younger. I'm thirty-two. My birthday's in two months."

"I don't ask a woman about her age before we go out. If there's a connection, that's what I go on."

"You never asked me out."

"I asked you to marry me," he said, blowing out a frustrated breath. "Doesn't that count?"

She shook her head. "I mean when you first came to town. When you were making the rounds."

"I didn't make the rounds. Besides, you were pregnant."

"I haven't been pregnant for a while."

"Did you want me to ask you out?" The attraction he'd denied since the first time he saw her roared to life again.

She shook her head again. "I'm just curious, like most of the town is now. We've barely spoken to each other in the last two years."

"I thought the idea was that we were keeping the relationship under wraps."

"What's your favorite color?"

"Green," he answered automatically then held up a hand. "What's going on? I don't understand why you think this won't work. You made a believer of Annabeth Sullivan, the town's main gossip funnel."

Julia stood and glanced at her watch. "The girls will start coming in any minute. I don't know, Sam. This is complicated."

"Only if you make it complicated."

"What's my favorite food?"

"How the heck am I supposed to know?"

"If we were in love, you'd know."

Sam thought about his ex-fiancée and tried to conjure a memory of what she'd like to eat. "Salad?" he guessed.

Julia rolled her eyes. "Nobody's favorite food is salad. Mine is lobster bisque."

Sam tapped one finger on the side of his head. "Got it."

"There's more to it than that."

"Come to dinner tonight," he countered.

"Where?"

"My place. Five-thirty. I talked to my dad this morning. He didn't mention delving into my emotions once. Huge progress as far as I'm concerned. He can't wait to spend more time with you."

"That's a bad idea, and I have Charlie."

"The invitation is for both of you." He took her shoulders between his hands. "We're going to make this work, Julia. Bring your list of questions tonight—favorite color, food, movie, whatever."

"There's more to it than—"

"I know but it's going to work." As if by their own accord, his fingers strayed to her hair and he sifted the golden strands between them. "For both of us."

At the sound of voices in the salon, Julia's back stiffened and her eyes widened a fraction. "You need to go."

"We're engaged," he reminded her. "We want people to see us together."

"Not here."

He wanted to question her but she looked so panicked, he decided to give her a break. "Dinner tonight," he repeated, and as three women emerged from the hallway behind the salon's main room, he bent forward and pressed his lips against hers.

Her sharp intake of breath made him smile. "Lasagna," he whispered against her mouth.

"What?" she said, her voice as dazed as he felt.

"My favorite food is lasagna."

She nodded and he kissed her again. "See you later, sweetheart," he said and pulled back, leaving Julia and the three stylists staring at him.

"Abby, how old are you?" Sam stepped out of his office into the lobby of the police station.

Abby Brighton, who'd started as the receptionist shortly after he'd been hired, looked up from her computer. "I'll be twenty-eight in the fall."

"That's young."

"Not really," she answered. "Maggie Betric is twenty-six and Suzanne over at the courthouse in Jefferson just turned twenty-five."

"Twenty-five?" Sam swallowed. He'd gone out to dinner with both women and had no idea they'd been that much younger than him. When did he become a small-town cradle robber? Jeez. He needed to watch himself.

"Julia's in her thirties, right?" Abby asked.

"Thirty-two."

"When's her birthday?"

"Uh…" Wait, he knew this. "It's in May."

Abby turned her chair around to face him. "I still can't believe I didn't know you two were dating."

"No one knew."

"But I know everything about you." She looked away. "Not everything, of course. But a lot. Because I make the schedule and we work so closely together."

He studied Abby another minute. She was cute, in a girl-next-door sort of way. Her short pixie cut framed a small face, her dark eyes as big as saucers. They'd worked together for almost two years now, and he supposed she did know him better than most people. But what did he know about her? What did he know about anyone, outside his dad and brother?

Sure, Sam had friends, a Friday-night poker game, fishing with the boys. He knew who was married and which guys were confirmed bachelors. Did knowing the kind of beer his buddies drank count as being close?

"Do you have a boyfriend, Abby?"

Her eyes widened farther. "Not at the moment."

"And your only family in town is your granddad?"

She nodded.

Okay, that was good. He knew something about the woman he saw every day at work. He looked around her brightly colored workspace. "I'm guessing your favorite color is yellow."

She smiled. "Yours is hunter green."

How did she know that?

"Does Julia make you happy?" she asked after a moment.

"Yes," he answered automatically. "Why?"

"I just wouldn't have pictured her as your type." Abby fidgeted with a paper clip. "She's beautiful and everything, but I always saw you with someone more…"

"More?"

"Someone nicer, I suppose."

"You don't think Julia's nice? Has she been unkind to you?"

Abby shook her head. "No, but I hear stories from when she was in high school. I'm in a book club with some ladies who knew her then."

"People change."

"You deserve someone who will take care of you."

"I'm a grown man, Abby. I can take care of myself."

"I know but you need—" She stopped midsentence when the phone rang. She answered and, after a moment, cupped her hand over the receiver. "Someone ran into a telephone pole out at the county line. No injuries but a live wire might be down."

Sam nodded and headed for the front door. "Call it in to the utility company. I'm on my way."

He drove toward the edge of town, grateful to get out and clear his head. He'd done more talking about himself and what he needed and felt in the past twenty-four hours than he had in the previous five years. His dad's fault, for sure.

This engagement was supposed to help Sam dodge his father's attempts to make him more in touch with his feelings. Hopefully, this dinner would smooth things over enough so life could return to normal. Other than the pretend engagement.

It wouldn't be as difficult as Julia thought to fool people. They'd hold hands, be seen around town together for a few PDAs and everyone would believe them. Kissing Julia was one of the perks of this arrangement. He loved her moment of surprise each time he leaned in. Sam hadn't been with a woman for a long time, which must explain why her touch affected him so much.

He understood the importance of making this work. Tonight, they'd come to an understanding of how to get what they both wanted.

* * *

Julia lifted Charlie out of his car seat and turned to face the quaint house tucked onto one of the tree-lined streets near downtown Brevia.

"He even has a picket fence," she said to her son, who answered her with a hearty laugh and a slew of indecipherable words.

"My sentiments exactly." She kissed the top of Charlie's head.

"Do you need a hand?"

Joe Callahan stepped off the porch and headed toward her.

"I've got it, Mr. Callahan. Thank you."

He met her halfway up the walk. "Call me Joe. And you—" he held out his hands for Charlie "—can call me Papa."

"Pap-y," Charlie repeated in his singsong voice and leaned forward for Joe to scoop him up. Her son, the extrovert.

"You don't have to do that."

Joe was already swinging Charlie above his head, much to the boy's delight. "What a handsome fellow," he said. He smiled at Julia. "He favors his beautiful mother."

Julia couldn't help but return his grin. "Are you always this charming?"

Joe gave an easy laugh. "For decades I was a real hard—" He lifted Charlie again. "I was hard-nosed. A walking grim reaper. Sam and his brother got the brunt of that. I've learned a lot since then."

"Wisdom you want to impart to your son?"

"If he'll let me." Joe tucked Charlie into the crook of his arm and the boy shoved his fist into his mouth, sucking contently. "You've already helped him start."

It was Julia's turn to laugh. "I don't have much wisdom to share with anyone."

Joe started toward the house. "Mothers have inherent wisdom. My late wife was the smartest, most insightful woman I've ever met."

"How old was Sam when she died?"

"Ten and Scott was seven. It was a dark period for our family."

"Was it a long illness?"

Joe turned and immediately Julia realized her mistake. "Sam hasn't told you about his mother?"

She shook her head, unable to hide her lack of knowledge. "It's difficult for him to speak about."

Joe sighed as if he understood. "That's my fault. After Lorraine passed, I was so overcome with grief that I shut down and made the boys do the same. Looking back, it was selfish and cowardly. They were kids and they needed me."

Julia patted his arm. "How did she die?"

"A car accident," he said quietly. Charlie rested his small head on Joe's shoulder as if sensing the older man needed comfort.

"How tragic. I'm so sorry for all of you."

"The tragic part was that it was my fault. I'd been on the force over ten years. I became obsessed with being the most dedicated cop Boston had ever seen. Like a bone-head, I took on the most dangerous assignments they'd give me—whatever I could do to prove that I was the baddest dude on the block. Lorraine couldn't handle the stress. She begged me to slow down. I wouldn't listen, brushed aside her worries and only focused on what I wanted."

He ran his hands through his hair, so much like Sam, then continued, "She'd started drinking at night—not so much that she was falling-down drunk, but enough to numb her. I was tuned out and didn't realize how bad it had gotten. I got home late one night and we fought. She went for a drive after the boys were in bed—to cool off. She wasn't even a half mile from the house when she ran the red light. She swerved to avoid another car. Wrapped her car around a telephone pole. She was gone instantly."

Julia sucked in a breath. The first time she'd met Sam had been when he'd found her after she'd hydroplaned on a wet road and gone over an embankment, her car slamming into a tree. She'd been pregnant at the time, and thinking the accident might have hurt her baby had been the scariest moment of her life. Sam had gotten her to the hospital and stayed with her until Lainey had arrived. She wondered if he'd thought about his mother during that time, or if it had just been another day on the job.

"How devastating for all of you." She leaned forward and wrapped her arms around Joe. Charlie squealed with delight then wriggled to be let down.

"Okay." She lifted him from Joe's arms and deposited him on the porch.

Joe swiped at his eyes. "I would have followed her in a minute. I could barely function and had two boys at home who needed me more than ever. Instead, I threw myself into the job like I was tempting fate. If they gave awards for stupidity and selfishness, I would have been a top candidate."

"Nothing can prepare you for something like that. I'm sure you did the best you could. Sam and his brother must know that."

Joe held open the screen door and Charlie headed into the house. "It should have been a wake-up call but it took me another twenty years to get my priorities straight. I want to make it right by Sam."

She looked into Joe Callahan's kind eyes and her stomach twisted. Julia didn't have much luck making things right by anyone, and if Joe knew the details of their arrangement, it would break his heart.

"Mama, come." Charlie peered around the doorway to the kitchen. Charlie. He was the reason she'd entered into this deal in the first place.

"Where's Sam?" She held out her hand to her son, who ran toward her to take it.

Joe smiled. "Grilling out back."

She scooped Charlie into her arms and followed Joe down the hall. She'd guess Sam's house had been built in the early 1900s, and he'd obviously renovated, drawing inspiration from the Craftsman tradition with hardwood floors throughout. In the open kitchen, beautiful maple cabinets hung on each wall. The colors were neutral but not boring, a mix of classic and modern traditions.

Joe led her through one of the French doors that opened to the back patio. It hadn't rained for a couple of days, and while it was cool, the evening air held the unmistakable scent of spring, with the elms and oaks surrounding the green yard beginning to bud.

Sam stood in front of a stainless-steel grill, enveloped in smoke. He turned and smiled at her and her chest caught again. He wore a dark T-shirt, faded jeans and flip-flops. Julia hadn't often seen him out of uniform, and while the casual outfit should have made him less intimidating, certain parts of her body responded differently.

"Ball," Charlie shouted and squirmed in her arms. When Julia put him down, he ran toward an oversized bouncy ball and several plastic trucks stacked near the wrought-iron table.

Sam closed the grill's lid and met her questioning gaze. "I thought he'd like some toys to play with over here."

She nodded, a little dumbfounded at the impact the small gesture had on her.

"Sammy said you two are mainly at your place."

"It's easier that way."

"Have you given any thought to where you'll live once you're married?"

"Here," Sam answered at the same time Julia said, "Not really."

Joe's brows furrowed, so she added, "My apartment is a rental, so I assumed we'd move in with Sam."

Sam came to her side and placed a quick kiss on her forehead. "We're going to make the spare bedroom into Charlie's room."

Julia coughed wildly.

"Can I get you a glass of water?" Sam asked.

"I'll grab it," Joe said and disappeared into the house.

Sam clapped her on the back. "Are you okay?"

"Not at all." She drew in a breath. "Charlie's room?"

"We're engaged, remember. It's going to seem strange enough that the kid barely knows me. I didn't have any of his stuff or toys in the house and my dad started asking questions."

At that moment, the bouncy ball knocked against Julia's leg.

"Ball, Mama. Ball." Charlie squealed with delight.

Sam handed Julia a pair of tongs. "Will you pull the steaks off the grill?" He picked up the ball and tucked it under his arm. "I'm going in for some male bonding."

Julia watched, fascinated as Sam walked over to Charlie and held out a hand. Without hesitation, Charlie took it and Sam led him into the yard to roll the ball back and forth.

The only man in Charlie's life was Ethan. Julia tried not to depend too much on him. Lainey, Ethan and Julia had a long history between them, and Julia didn't want to push the limits of their relationship.

Charlie did his best to mimic Sam's motions as he rolled

and threw the ball, and Julia realized how important it was for her son to have a father figure.

"I knew he'd be great with kids," Joe said as he handed her a tall glass of water. "Scott is a wild one, but Sam…"

"Why do you think Sam never married?" Julia asked, tapping one finger against her lips. Annabeth's story about Sam's record as a three-dates-and-done serial dater came back to her.

"It's not for lack of trying," Joe answered candidly then amended. "But I can tell you're a better fit for him than Jenny."

Julia tried not to look startled. "Jenny?"

Joe studied her. "His ex-fiancée. He *did* tell you about her?"

"He was really hurt when it ended," she offered, not an outright lie but enough to cover her lack of knowledge. She and Sam had a lot they needed to get clear about each other if this charade was going to work.

Joe nodded. "Not that he would have told anyone. He bottled up his emotions just like I'd done when his mom passed. But Jenny's infidelity was a huge blow to him."

"I can understand why." Julia's mind reeled at this new information. Sam had been previously engaged and his fiancée had cheated on him. That might explain a little about his commitment issues.

"She wasn't a good match even before that. Sure, she was perfect on paper—a schoolteacher, sweet and popular with his friends, but she didn't get him. They were marrying what they thought they wanted without paying attention to what they needed."

Julia understood that line of thinking better than most. It was what had led her to believe her ex-boyfriend could make her happy. She'd thought she loved Jeff but realized what she loved was the image she'd had of him, not who he truly was. Was that what Sam had thought about his ex, as well, or had this Jenny been the love of his life? The thought gave Julia a sick feeling in the pit of her stomach.

Sam looked up from where he was currently chasing Charlie across the backyard. "How about those steaks, sweetie?"

"I'm on it," she called and headed for the grill.

Much to Joe's delight, Charlie insisted on sitting on Sam's lap during dinner. Sam looked vaguely uncomfortable as the toddler fed him bites of meat but dutifully ate each one.

In addition to the steak, Sam had roasted vegetables and made a salad. She'd brought a loaf of bread from the bakery next to the salon, along with a bottle of red wine. The dinner was surprisingly fun and Julia found herself relaxing. Joe did most of the talking, regaling her with stories, of his years with the force and more recently of the workshops he facilitated around the region.

"Someone needs a diaper change," she said as they finished the meal. At the look of horror on Sam's face, she laughed. "I'll take it from here."

"Good idea," he agreed.

"You'd better get used to stinky bottoms," his father chided.

Sam's eyes widened and Julia laughed again. "All in good time, Joe. For now, I'll take the poop duty."

Sam stood quickly and handed Charlie to her. "I'll clear the dishes." To her surprise, he placed a soft kiss on her mouth. Charlie giggled and Julia felt her world tilt the tiniest bit.

"Right," she said around a gulp of air. She met Joe's gaze as she turned for the house and he winked at her. Right. Sam was her fake fiancé. Of course he was going to kiss her sometimes. They'd discussed that it was all part of the act. It didn't mean anything.

At least, not to her.

Right.

She changed Charlie's diaper on the floor of Sam's living room. Unlike her cozy apartment filled with well-worn flea-market finds and hand-me-downs from her mother, the furnishings in this room appeared very new and hardly used.

A sleek leather couch faced an entertainment center with an enormous flat-screen television and several pieces of stereo equipment. He had a few books scattered on the shelves, mainly fly-fishing manuals and guidebooks for the North Carolina mountains. A couple of pieces of abstract art hung on the walls. Unlike her family room, there wasn't a single framed photo of any of Sam's family or friends.

Julia loved the reminders of each stage in Charlie's life on display around her house. It was as though Sam didn't have a personal life. Maybe it was just a guy thing, she thought, but then remembered how Jeff had documented each of his research trips with photos spread around their condo in Columbus.

Maybe not.

She pulled on Charlie's sweatpants and watched as he scrambled to his feet and headed back toward the kitchen.

"Hey, little man, where are you headed in such a rush?"

Joe picked him up as Charlie answered, "Ou-side," and he planted a raspberry on the boy's belly, making him laugh out loud.

"I'll see you later, gator." Joe put Charlie on the ground and he made a beeline for the back of the house.

"It was nice to spend time with you." Julia gave the older man a quick hug.

"I hope it's the first of many dinners. I'd love to meet

your family while I'm in town. Sammy said your mom is famous around here for the animal shelter she runs."

"It was a labor of love after my dad died." The thought of Joe Callahan and her mother getting together made her want to squirm. Keeping their respective families separate would make the summer much simpler. The complications of this arrangement were almost more than she could handle.

"I meant what I said at the restaurant," Joe told her. "Sam will protect you and Charlie. I don't know the details of your custody arrangement, but I believe that boy is better off with you than anyone else in the world."

Julia blinked back sudden tears. "Thank you. I better go track him down."

Joe nodded. "Good night, Julia. I'll see you soon."

The front door shut behind him, and Julia thought about Joe's last words. Charlie was better off with her. She had to believe that. He belonged to her and she to him. Nothing and no one was going to change that.

She turned for the kitchen just as Charlie's high-pitched scream came from the backyard.

Chapter Six

Julia raced onto the patio, following the sounds of her son's cries, her heart pounding in her chest.

Sam stood in the backyard, cradling Charlie against his chest with one arm. With his free hand he waved the tongs she'd used for the meat. A large gray dog hopped up and down in front of him.

"What happened?" Julia yelled as she sprinted down the back steps. "Is Charlie hurt?"

At the sound of his mother's voice, the boy lifted his tear-streaked face from Sam's shoulder. "Ball, Mama. No doggy." He pointed a slobbery finger at the Weimaraner running circles in the yard, the deflated bouncy ball clamped in his jaws.

His eyes never leaving the dog, Sam scooted closer to Julia. "Charlie's fine. Take him back to the house. I've never seen this animal before. He could be rabid."

Charlie shook his head. "No doggy," he repeated. "Charlie ball."

Julia looked from her son to Sam to the dog bounding and leaping, his stubby tail wagging, clearly relishing this impromptu game of keep-away. Rabid? Overenthusiastic and in need of some training. Not rabid.

Julia had grown up with a variety of animals underfoot. Her dad had been Brevia's vet for years, and the shelter her mother had built and run after his death attracted animals from all over the South. Her mom's ability to rehabilitate strays was legendary—Vera had even written a dog-behavior book that had become a bestseller a few years ago. Julia might not be the expert her mother was, but she had a fairly good sense for reading canine energy. And every inch of the Weimaraner was shouting "let's play."

"Sam, the dog isn't going to hurt you."

"It bared its teeth. It's a lunatic."

"You've never seen it before?" Julia moved slowly forward.

"No. I told you to get back on the porch. I don't want you or Charlie hurt."

She gave a quick whistle. The dog stopped and looked at her, its tail still wagging.

"Julia, you can't—"

"Drop it," she commanded, her finger pointed to the ground.

"Dop." Charlie mimicked her. "Charlie ball."

The dog waited a moment then lowered the lump of plastic to the ground.

"Sit."

The dog's bottom plopped to the ground.

She held out her palm. "Stay."

She took a step toward the dog. His bottom lifted but she gave a stern "No," and he sank back down.

"I'm sorry about your ball, sweetie," she told Charlie.

"Bad," he said with a whine.

"Not bad, but he needs someone to help him learn."

As she got nearer, the animal trembled with excitement.

"You shouldn't be that close."

"Do you have any rope?"

"I'm not leaving you out here. I'm serious. Back off from the dog."

"What is your problem? This dog isn't a threat."

"You don't know—"

As if sensing that her attention was divided, the dog stood and bounded the few feet toward her. The skin around its mouth drew back and wrinkled, exposing a row of shiny teeth.

"Get back, Julia. It's snarling." Sam lunged forward, but before he got the animal, the dog flopped at Julia's feet and flipped onto his back, writhing in apparent ecstasy as she bent to rub his belly.

Sam stopped in his tracks. "What the...?"

"He's a smiler."

"Dogs don't smile."

"Some do."

Charlie wriggled out of Sam's arms and, before either of them could stop him, headed for the dog. "Good doggy. No ball."

Julia put an arm around Charlie, holding him back, as Sam's breath hitched. "You shouldn't let him so near that thing."

She offered what she hoped was a reassuring smile. "My mom runs an animal shelter, remember? Charlie's been around dogs since he was born. I'm careful to supervise him and make sure he's safe." She tickled her fingers under the dog's ear and got a soft lick on her arm for the effort. "This boy is gorgeous."

"A good-looking animal can still be crazy."

Julia's shoulders stiffened. "What makes you think he's crazy?" Before he'd left for good, Jeff had said something similar to her. He'd told her she was beautiful but a nut job. He'd thrown in a dig about her intelligence as icing on the cake.

Her mother was the expert on stray animals, but Julia knew a thing or two about being damaged on the inside. Her gut told her this dog had a heart of gold.

"He snarled at me."

"He *smiled* at you," she insisted. "Pet him. He's a real sweetie."

"I don't like dogs," Sam said simply.

"I wouldn't have guessed it." She ran her hand along the length of the dog's side. "He's way underweight. No collar and he's dirty. I'd guess he's been on his own for a while now. You haven't seen him around?"

Sam shook his head. "A section of the fenced yard came loose in the storm a few nights ago. He must have smelled the grill and come in that way."

She straightened. "Would you take Charlie for a minute? I have a leash in the trunk of my car."

"You don't have a dog."

"Mom makes everyone keep an extra in case we come across a stray." The Weimaraner jumped to his feet and nudged at Julia's pants leg.

"Mama doggy," Charlie said as Julia shifted him into Sam's arms.

"No, honey, not mine. We'll take him to Grandma in the morning and she'll find a good home for him."

Charlie frowned. "Mama doggy."

Julia noticed Sam tense as the dog trotted over to sniff him. "Are you scared of dogs, Chief Callahan?"

"Wary, not scared." He held Charlie a little higher in his arms.

"If you say so." She headed up the steps toward the house and the dog followed.

"What if he runs away?"

"I have a feeling he'll stick close by. Weims are usually Velcro dogs."

"Are you going to keep him overnight?"

She nodded. "It won't be the first time. Mom says the strays have a knack for finding me. The scrappier they are, the harder I work to bring them in. I've rescued dogs from Dumpsters, highway ditches—"

"Stop!" Sam shook his head. "The thought of you luring in unknown dogs from who knows where makes my head pound."

"What can I tell you?" She laughed. "I have a soft spot for lost causes."

Sam met her gaze then, and for an instant she saw the kind of longing and vulnerability in his eyes she'd never imagined from a man as tough and strong as he seemed. "Lucky dogs," he whispered.

The hair on her arms stood on end and her mouth went dry. He blinked, closing off his feelings from her.

"Add this one to the lucky list," she said, her voice a little breathy. Quickly, she led the dog through the house, grabbing a piece of bread off the counter for good measure. But she didn't need it. The dog walked by her side, his early rambunctiousness tempered because he had her attention.

She pulled the leash out of her trunk and looped it over his head. He shook his head, as if he wasn't used to a collar. "Easy there, boy," Julia crooned and knelt to pet him. The dog nuzzled into her chest. "I bet you've had a rough time of it. If anyone can find you a good home, it's my mom."

She walked the dog back onto the porch, where she could hear the sound of the television coming through the open screen door.

"Is it okay if I bring him in the house?"

"As long as he doesn't lift his leg on the furniture," came the hushed reply.

She leveled a look at the dog, who cocked his head at her. "Keep it together," she told him, and his stubby tail wagged again.

"I should get Charlie home and to bed," she said as she walked into the family room then stopped short. Sam sat on the couch, Charlie nestled into the crook of his arm, their attention riveted to the television. An IndyCar race was on the big set, and Sam was quietly explaining the details of the scene to Charlie.

"Lubock thinks he's got this one in the bag. He's in the blue-and-yellow car out front."

"Blue," Charlie said, his fist popping out of his mouth to point to the screen.

"That's right, but watch out for Eckhard in the red and white. See where he's coming around the outside?"

Charlie nodded drowsily then snuggled in deeper.

"I thought you didn't like kids," Julia said quietly, as Charlie's eyes drifted shut.

Sam glanced at the boy then tucked a blanket from the back of the couch around him. "I like kids. Everyone likes kids."

Julia scoffed. "Hardly. Most people like dogs. You don't."

"That's different."

She watched the pair for several seconds then added, "Charlie's father doesn't like kids."

Sam met her gaze. "His loss."

"You've never even said hello to Charlie before this week."

"He and I don't run in the same circles," he countered.

"You know what I mean."

Sam picked up the remote and hit the mute button. He knew what she meant. Ever since he'd found Julia after her car crashed, he'd avoided both her and her son. That moment had terrified him more than it should someone in his position. He didn't know whether it was the memory of losing his mother, or the strange way his body reacted to the woman sitting across from him. Or a combination of both. But when he'd lifted her out of that car and carried her to his cruiser, his instinct for danger had been on high alert.

Sam was used to saving people from mishaps. It was part of the job. But she'd looked at him as if she'd put all her faith in him. That had made it feel different. More real, and scary as hell. Charlie had been born that same day, and Sam had decided it was better for both of them if he stayed away. He had nothing to offer a single mom and her child. His heart had shut down a long time ago.

Holding Charlie in his arms, he felt something fierce and protective roar to life inside him. If he wasn't careful, he could easily fall for this boy and his mother. He had to keep his distance but still play the part. His dad had spent most of the evening fawning over Julia and her son, leaving Sam blessedly alone.

He wanted to keep up the charade long enough for his father to leave town satisfied. When the eventual breakup came, Sam was sure he'd have a better chance of convincing Joe how heartbroken he was over the phone than in person.

"We should go over a few things before you leave," he

said, trying to make his tone all business but soft enough that he didn't wake Charlie.

Julia nodded. "I can take him from you first."

Sam shook his head and adjusted the blanket. "He's fine. Thanks for bringing him. You saw how happy it made my dad."

"He's going to be devastated when this doesn't work out."

Sam shrugged. "He'll get over it. You've given him hope that I'm not a total lost cause in the commitment department. That should hold him over for a while."

Julia adjusted in her chair as the dog settled at her feet with a contented sigh. Sam had heard a lot about Vera Morgan's exceptional skills with animals. It appeared the gift was genetic.

"He mentioned your ex-girlfriend."

Sam flinched. If he didn't have Charlie sleeping against him, he would have gotten up to pace the room. "Leave it to dear old dad to knock the skeleton from my closet."

"We're engaged. He assumed I already knew."

"And you thought knowing my favorite color was going to be a big deal."

"We need to understand the details about each other if this is going to work. Otherwise, no one is going to believe we're legitimate."

"Why not?" he countered. "People run off to Vegas all the time. Maybe you fell so head over heels for me that you didn't care about the details."

"Highly unlikely. You're not that irresistible."

Her comeback made him smile, which he realized was her intention. It was strange that this woman he knew so little could read him so well. "I was engaged for six months. She cheated on me a month before the wedding."

"That's awful."

"I caught her with my brother."

Julia's jaw dropped. "Wow."

"That's an understatement."

"What happened? Do you still speak to your brother? Are they together? What kind of awful people would do that to someone they both loved?"

"The way Scott explained it, before I kicked him out of my house, was that she was bad news and he was saving me from making a mistake. The way Jenny spun it before she followed him out the door was that he'd seduced her." He expected to feel the familiar pain of betrayal but only emptiness washed over him. "They aren't together and weren't again as far as I know. Turns out he was right. I found out later it wasn't the first time she'd cheated. She'd also been with one of the guys on the squad. Made me look like a fool."

"She's the fool." Julia came to stand before him. She lifted Charlie from his arms and sat down, laying her son beside her on the soft leather. "And your brother?"

"Scott was in the army for several years. Now he works out of D.C. for the U.S. Marshals."

She squeezed his arm and the warmth of her hand relaxed him a little. "I'm not interested in his job. What about your relationship?"

"My dad had a health scare almost two years ago. I passed my brother in the hall at the hospital. That's the extent of it."

"Oh, Sam."

"We were never close. My dad didn't encourage family bonding."

"Still—"

"This isn't helping our arrangement." Sam took her hand in his. "How long have we been dating?"

"Four months," Julia answered automatically.

"Favorite color?"

"Blue."

"Where we going on a honeymoon?"

"A Disney cruise."

"You can't be serious."

"Because of Charlie."

He laughed. "Fine." Some of the tension eased out of his shoulders and he asked, "Big or small wedding?"

"Small, close friends and immediate family."

"Who are your close friends?"

Her eyes darted away and she took several beats to answer. "The girls from the salon, I guess. A few of them, anyway. My sister."

"What about your friends from high school?"

"I didn't really have friends. Followers was more like it, and most of them have outgrown me."

"Their loss," he said, using his earlier phrase, and was rewarded with a smile. "What about your ex-boyfriend? Do you still have feelings for him? Should I be jealous?"

"Of Jeff? No. We were over long before he left me."

An interesting way to phrase it. Sam couldn't help but ask, "Could I kick his butt?"

She smiled. "Absolutely."

"Good. When is your next court date?"

"Friday."

"Do you want me to come?"

She shook her head and Sam felt a surprising rush of disappointment. "I might be able to help."

"You already are."

"You can't believe the judge will award custody to Jeff and his family. Is he even going to be here?"

"I don't know. But I can't take any chances. Even if he gets joint custody, they could take Charlie from me for extended periods of time. I won't risk it. Jeff made it clear he didn't want to be a father, so I don't understand why he's letting this happen. He was never close to his family."

"Have you talked to him directly?"

"I left a message on his cell phone right after the letter came. I might have sounded hysterical. He hasn't returned my call."

"You're going to have to tell your family what's going on before it goes too much further."

She nodded. "I realized that tonight. If my mom finds out your dad knew before her… It's all too much. I'm finally starting to get my life on track, with the salon and Charlie. For the first time in as long as I can remember, my mother isn't looking at me with disappointment in her eyes. When she finds out…"

"Vera will want to help. This isn't your fault."

"It sure feels like it is." She sank back against the couch and scrubbed her hands across her face. Sam saw pain and fear etched in her features. It gnawed away at him until he couldn't stand it. Why was she so afraid of her mother's judgment? Why did she think so little of herself, to believe her son was at risk of being taken away? Maybe she'd made some mistakes in her past but Sam didn't know anyone who hadn't. She couldn't be punished forever.

He might not be willing to give his heart again, but he needed to give her some comfort. He wasn't great with words and knew that if he got sentimental, she'd only use her dry wit to turn it into a joke. Instead, he placed a soft kiss on the inside of her palm.

She tugged on her hand but he didn't let go. "You don't need to do that now," she whispered, her voice no more than a breath in the quiet. "There's no one watching."

One side of his mouth quirked. "It's a good thing, too, because what I want to do to you is best kept in private."

Her mouth formed a round *oh* and he lifted a finger to trace the soft flesh of her lips.

"Charlie."

"I know." He leaned closer. "You're safe tonight. Almost."

"We shouldn't…"

"I know," he repeated. "But I can't think of anything I want more."

"Me, too." She sat up and brought both of her hands to the sides of his face, cupping his jaw. "This isn't going to get complicated, right?"

"Other than planning a pretend wedding, a custody battle, my meddling father and a town filled with nosy neighbors? I think we can keep it fairly simple."

She smoothed her thumbs along his cheeks and her scent filled his head again. "I mean you and me. We're on the same page. It's all part of the show, the time spent together, pretending like we're in love. It ends when we both get what we want."

He agreed in theory, but at the moment all Sam wanted was her. He knew telling her that would make her more skittish than she already was. He didn't want this night to end quite yet, even if her sleeping son was going to keep the evening G-rated. So he answered, "That's the plan."

She nodded then licked her lips, and he suppressed a groan. "Then it won't matter if I do this…" She brought her mouth to his and they melted together. When her tongue mixed with his, he did groan. Or maybe Julia did. Her fingers wound through his hair and down his neck, pressing him closer, right where he wanted to be.

He deepened the kiss as his hands found their way underneath her blouse, his palms spread across the smooth skin on her back.

"Stop." Julia's breathing sounded ragged.

His hands stilled and he drew back enough to look into her big gray eyes, now hazy with desire.

A small smile played on the corners of her mouth. "I want to make sure we both stay in control. No getting carried away."

Like to his bedroom, Sam thought. All the wonderful, devilish, naked things he could do to her there ran through his brain. He wanted to know this woman—every inch of her—with a passion he hadn't thought himself capable of feeling.

He didn't answer, not sure his brain could manage a coherent sentence at the moment. They stared at each other and he wondered if Julia's heart was pounding as hard as his.

He heard Charlie snore softly and let his eyes drift closed for a few seconds. He counted to ten in his head, thought about the pile of work waiting in his office and tried like hell to rein in his desire and emotions.

He withdrew his hands, smoothed her shirt back down and forced a casual smile.

"My middle name is control, sweetheart."

She cocked her head. "That's a good point," she said and didn't sound at all as affected as Sam felt. "What *is* your middle name?"

He shook his head slightly. "Matthew."

"Mine's Christine," she told him, as if she had no memory of a minute earlier when she'd been kissing him as if her life depended on it. "I'm going to get Charlie home." She stood and picked up the sleeping boy. The Weimaraner jumped to attention and stayed close by her side.

Sam felt off balance at her switch in mood but didn't want to admit it. "I'll walk you to your car," he said, keeping the frustration out of his voice. This *was* a business arrangement, after all, passionate kissing aside. Maybe Julia had the right of it.

She nodded and grabbed the diaper bag, pushing it at Sam. "If you could carry that," she said, as if she didn't trust him with his hands free.

The night had cooled at least ten degrees and she shivered as she hurried down the front walk. "Do you want a jacket?" he asked, taking large strides to keep up with her.

"I'm fine."

While it might be true that Sam hadn't had any long-term relationships since moving to Brevia, and had stayed out of the dating pool totally for the past few months, his evenings never ended like this.

Usually he was the one who put the brakes on, sexually. More than once, he'd been invited back to a woman's house—or she'd asked to see his place—on the first date and gotten a clear signal that she'd been eager to take things to the next level. Sam was cautious and tried to not let an evening go there if he thought someone wanted more than he could give.

Never, until tonight, could he remember a woman literally running out of his house when he so badly wanted her to stay.

Julia opened the back door and placed Charlie in his car seat then gave the dog a little tug. The Weim jumped up without a sound, as if he knew enough not to wake the sleeping boy.

Turning, Julia held out her hand for the diaper bag.

"Are we good?" Sam asked.

"Yep," she said, again not meeting his gaze. "I'll talk to you in a few days."

A few days? They were engaged. He told himself it wouldn't look good to the town, but the truth was he couldn't wait a few days. Before he could respond, she'd scurried to the driver's side, climbing in with one last wave and "Thanks" thrown over her shoulder.

Sam was left standing alone at the curb, wondering what had gone so wrong so quickly. He headed back to the house, hoping a cold shower would help him make some sense of things.

Chapter Seven

Julia swiped under her eyes and focused her attention on her mug of lukewarm coffee, unable to make eye contact with her mother or sister.

Lainey paced the length of Vera's office in the All Creatures Great and Small animal shelter. By contrast, their mother sat stock-still behind her desk.

"That's the whole story," Julia finished. "The judge ordered us into mediation and that meeting is tomorrow morning. I don't think it will do any good. I know what I want and Jeff's parents know what they want. If we can't come to an agreement with the mediator, there will be a final hearing where the judge makes a ruling."

"Is Jeff going to be there?" Vera asked, her tone both soft and razor-sharp.

"I guess so, but it will be better if he isn't, if it looks like it's his parents who want this." Her breath hitched. "The latest document I got from their attorney asks for an every-other-year joint-custody arrangement. There's an opportunity for it to be amended if Charlie's well-being is in jeopardy with one of the parties."

"Every other year?" Lainey stopped pacing. "How can they think of taking him away from you for that long? You should have told us this as soon as you knew, Jules. Maybe we could have done something—"

"What, Lainey?" Julia snapped then sighed. "I'm sorry. I don't mean to take it out on you. But what could have been done? I hoped if I made it difficult for them, they might give up. The first letter said they wanted full custody and offered a hefty payment for the expenses I've already incurred in raising Charlie."

"They thought you'd sell them your son?" Lainey's voice was incredulous.

"That's one way of looking at it. The last Jeff knew, I'd gotten pregnant as a way to keep him. He could have told his parents I didn't really want to be a mother or wouldn't be able to handle it on my own."

"You're not on your own." Vera tapped one finger on the desk. "You have us. And Sam."

Conflicting emotions welled in Julia's chest again as she thought of Sam. He'd told her to talk to her mom and sister. She knew it was inevitable, so she'd called them both on the way home last night and asked them to meet her at the shelter before work. At the time, it had been a good way to distract herself from Sam and the way he made her feel.

He must have been baffled by her behavior after they'd kissed. Most women he knew could probably handle a simple kiss. Not Julia. Maybe it had been too long since she'd been in a man's arms. It had taken every ounce of her willpower not to beg him to take her to bed. His touch had rocked her to her core and she'd had to beat a quick retreat so she wouldn't do or say something she'd later regret.

When he'd proposed the pretend engagement, she'd had no idea how much her emotions would get in the way. She'd had no idea how it would affect her to see Sam cuddling Charlie against his broad chest. How much her body and heart would react to his arms around her. How quickly she'd come to depend on the comfort he gave her and how he made her feel strong by believing in her.

"I'm the one they're going after," she told her mom. "And Charlie." A sob escaped her lips and she clamped her hand over her mouth.

Lainey rushed to her side and Julia let herself be cradled in her sister's warm embrace. Silence descended over the trio. This was the time Julia would normally make a joke or sarcastic remark about her propensity to ruin her own life. But, right now, she was just struggling to not break down completely.

This was the reason she hadn't told her family. Their sympathy and the disappointment she felt from them brought back too many memories of the past and the feelings that went with it. Her LD and the shame that went with it had made her put up walls against everyone around her. She'd gotten used to getting by, keeping secrets, not letting on how bad things really were. It was a difficult pattern to break.

From the time she'd been younger, Julia had made an unintentional habit of disappointing the people she loved. She'd let other people's judgments guide the way she lived her life. The belief that she was lazy and stupid had stopped her from getting help so many times. It was easier not to open up to her family about her emotions. She was too afraid of being exposed as weak and lacking in their eyes.

Even when she'd shown up on her mother's doorstep, pregnant, broke and alone, she hadn't cried or offered long explanations or excuses. She just kept moving. Now she felt stuck in quicksand, as though nothing could save her.

Vera's palm slammed onto the desk. "We won't let this happen. Have you consulted Frank?"

Julia nodded. Frank Davis had been practicing law in Brevia for as long as she could remember and was a friend of her mother's. After Sam's suggestion that she see an attorney, she'd hired him to represent her. "He's helping with the case."

Vera nodded. "That's a good start. You need to talk to Jeff. To understand why he's doing this now when he had no previous interest in being a dad. Surely you'll be awarded sole custody. You're Charlie's mother and you do a wonderful job with him."

"I don't know, Mom. Jeff's family is arguing that they can give Charlie opportunities he'll never have with me."

"A child doesn't need anything more than a loving family. Let them set up a college trust if they're so concerned with opportunities."

"What do you want to see happen?" Lainey asked.

That question had kept Julia up many nights. "I'll support them having a relationship with Charlie. I'm sure as he gets older he'll have questions about his father's family. I want him to be surrounded by all the people who love him." She paused and took a breath. "I'm afraid he'll eventually choose them."

"He won't," Lainey said softly.

"You can't know that. But he needs to live with me now. Full-time. Swapping him back and forth is ludicrous."

"I'm going to the mediation," Vera announced.

Julia's stomach lurched. As much as she appreciated and needed her family's support, she was afraid it would only make her more nervous to have her mother with her.

"That's not a good idea. I appreciate the offer but I need to handle this on my own."

Lainey squeezed her shoulder and asked, "Has Jeff contacted you directly or tried to see Charlie?"

Julia shook her head. "No. Neither have his parents, other than when I got messages about discussing the custody arrangement."

"When did that start?" Vera came around the side of the desk.

"About a month ago. I ignored them until the certified letter arrived last week."

"Ignoring your problems doesn't make them go away."

Funny, it had always worked for Julia in the past. She'd taken the easy way out of every difficult situation that came her way before Charlie. And thanks to the complexity of her difficulties processing both words and numbers, problems seemed to plague her. From bad rental agreements to unfair terms on a car loan, her inability to manage the details of her life took its toll in a variety of ways. Still, nothing had prepared her for this.

A knock at the door interrupted them.

"Come in," Vera said.

A member of the shelter staff entered, leading in a gray dog. Or more accurately, the gray dog led her. Upon seeing Julia, the animal pulled at the leash, his stubby tail wagging. His lips drew back to expose his teeth.

"That's quite a greeting," Lainey said with a laugh.

"Sam thought it was a snarl when the dog first came at him." Julia bent to pet him. The dog wiggled and tried to put his front paws on her chest. She body blocked him. "Down."

"What's the report?" Vera asked the young woman.

"We've done his blood work and tested him for heartworm and parasites. Surprisingly, he got a clean bill of health."

"That's great." Julia felt relief wash over her. "Have you had any calls about a lost Weim?"

The young woman shook her head. "Not yet."

"We'll do a three-day hold before he moves onto the available-dog list." Vera dropped to her knees next to Julia. The dog lunged for her, teeth gleaming, but Vera held up a hand and gave a firm "No." The dog's rear end hit the carpet, although one corner of his mouth still curled.

Julia met her mother's gaze. "The smile's not good for him, is it?"

Vera shrugged. "It depends on the potential adopter, but a lot of people might think the same thing Sam did. We'll find a place for him. We always do."

Julia stroked the dog's silky ear. She'd planned on leaving the Weimaraner at the shelter this morning. "Can I foster him? Until the waiting period is over or someone shows interest. I'll work on basic training commands to help offset the shock of the smile."

Vera hesitated. "You've got a lot going on right now, honey. Weims aren't easy dogs. They can have separation anxiety and get destructive."

Frustration crept across Julia's neck and shoulders. "You know being in a foster home is better for a dog's well-being." She couldn't believe her mother would insinuate the dog would be better in the shelter than with her.

"Of course," Vera agreed, as if she realized she'd crossed some imaginary line. "If you're willing to, it would help him immensely."

"Have they named him yet?" Julia knew the shelter staff named each animal that came in to make their care more personal.

The young woman shook her head.

"Call him Casper," Julia said.

"The friendly gray ghost?" Lainey asked, referring to the breed's well-known nickname.

Julia nodded. "It fits him and will give people a sense of his personality."

"Perfect," her mother said then asked the young woman, "They've done a temperament test?"

She nodded. "He's a big sweetie." The walkie-talkie clipped to her belt hissed. "I'll finish the paperwork with Julia as the foster." When Vera nodded, the woman smiled and walked out of the office.

"It's settled." Julia was going to make sure this dog found the perfect home. She straightened. "Charlie will be thrilled."

She turned to her mother. "I need to get Charlie from Ethan and drop him to the sitter before heading to the salon."

"I'll take him today," her mother said, in the same no-argument tone she'd used earlier.

"Really? I'm sure your schedule is packed after your trip."

"I'd love to."

Julia gave her mother a quick hug. "Thank you." She turned to Lainey. "Both of you. It helps to know I'm not alone."

"You never have been," Vera told her.

"And never will be," Lainey added.

As she gave Charlie a bath later that night, Julia had to admit Sam had been right. Talking about the situation with Lainey and her mother had made her feel more hopeful. She might have flitted from job to job and through a number of cities during her twenties, but now she'd settled in Brevia. She was close to the point where she could make an offer to buy the salon, assuming this custody battle didn't wipe out her meager savings.

She wrapped Charlie in a fluffy towel, put on a fresh diaper and his pajamas, Casper at her side the whole time. She didn't mind the company. She'd taken him for a walk with Charlie in the stroller earlier, after the dog had spent the day with her in the salon.

A few of the clients had been shocked at his wide grin, but his affectionate nature had quickly won them over. It also made Julia feel more confident about his chances for adoption.

When the doorbell rang, Casper ran for it and began a steady bark. Carrying Charlie with her, she put a leash on the dog. A part of her hoped Sam was making another unexpected evening call.

Instead, Jeff Johnson stood on the other side of the door. Casper lunged for him but Julia held tight to the leash. She stumbled forward when the shock of seeing her ex-boyfriend combined with the dog's strength threw her off balance.

"Watch it," Jeff snapped as he righted her.

Casper smiled.

"What the…? Is that thing dangerous?" Jeff stepped back. "He looks rabid. You shouldn't have it near the baby. Are you crazy?"

"Casper, sit." Julia gave the command as she straightened. The dog sat, the skin around his mouth quivering. "Be careful, or I may give the attack command." She made her voice flip despite the flood of emotions roaring through her.

For a satisfying moment, Jeff looked as if he might make a run for it. Then his own lip curled. "Very funny."

"Good doggy." Charlie pointed at the canine.

"He talks," Jeff said, surprise clear.

"He does a lot of things," Julia answered, her eyes narrowed. "Not that you'd know or care since you beat a fast escape as soon as you found out I was pregnant."

Jeff flashed his most disarming smile, a little sheepish with his big chocolate eyes warm behind his square glasses. That exact smile had initially charmed her when he'd come in for a haircut at the salon where she'd worked in Columbus, Ohio.

For several months dating Jeff had been magical for her. He'd taken her to the theater and ballet, using his family's tickets. They'd gone to poetry readings and talks by famous authors on campus. Some of what she heard was difficult to process, and in a moment of vulnerability, she'd told Jeff about the extent of her learning disabilities. He'd been sympathetic and supportive, taking time over long evenings to read articles and stories to her, discussing them as if her opinion mattered. It was the first time in her life Julia felt valued for her intelligence, and she became committed to making their relationship work at any cost.

Soon she realized what a fool she'd been to think a well-respected professor would be truly interested in someone like her. It was clear that Jeff liked how his friends reacted when he'd shown up at dinner parties with a leggy blonde on his arm. He'd also gotten a lot of use out of the way she'd bent over backward cooking and cleaning to his exacting standards when she'd moved in with him. If she couldn't be on his level intellectually, she'd fulfill the other roles of a doting girlfriend. She'd wanted to believe that a baby would make him see how good their life together could be. She'd been dead wrong. Once she wasn't useful to him, he'd thrown her off like yesterday's news.

"Come on, Julia," he said softly, his grin holding steady. "Don't act like you aren't glad to see me." She'd been fooled by that smile once and wasn't going to make the same mistake again.

She flashed a smile of her own. "I don't see anyone throwing a ticker-tape parade. You can turn right around. I've got no use for you here."

"I'm here to see my son," Jeff said, as any trace of charm vanished.

Charlie met his biological father's gaze then buried his face in Julia's shoulder, suddenly shy.

"Why now, Jeff?" She rubbed a hand against Charlie's back when he began to fidget. "Why all of this now?"

He sighed. "The custody request, you mean."

Jeff's IQ was in the genius range, but sometimes he could be purposefully obtuse. "Of course the custody request. Do you know the hell you and your parents have put me through? We've barely scratched the surface."

"Invite me in, Jules," he said, coaxing, "and we can talk about it. I have an offer that may make this whole mess go away."

It had felt different when Sam stood at her door waiting to be invited through. Her stomach had danced with awareness and her only doubt had been worrying about her heart's exhilarated reaction to him. Still, Julia relented. If she had a chance to make this better, she couldn't refuse it.

Jeff stepped into her apartment but froze when Casper greeted him by sticking his snout into Jeff's crotch. "Get away, you stupid mutt." Jeff kicked out his foot, hitting Casper in the ribs. The dog growled.

"Casper, no." She pulled him back to her side with the leash then leveled a look at Jeff. "Don't kick my dog."

"It was going for my balls. What do you expect?"

"I wouldn't worry too much. As I remember, your mother keeps them on her mantel."

Jeff gave a humorless laugh. "Always one for the quick retort. I miss that about you."

"Good doggy. Charlie doggy." The boy wiggled in her arms and Julia put him on the floor. His chubby finger pulled the leash from her hand and he led the dog toward the kitchen. "Doggy nice." Casper followed willingly.

"You trust that beast with him?"

"More than I trust you." Julia folded her arms across her chest. "For the record, there's nothing I miss about you."

Jeff's eyes narrowed. "He's still my son. Whether you like it or not, I deserve to be a part of his life. There's no judge in the world who will deny me access."

"I never wanted to deny you access. I called you after he was born, emailed pictures and never heard one word back. You haven't answered my question. Why now?"

His gaze shifted to the floor. "Change of heart."

"You need a heart for it to change. You made it clear you never wanted to be a dad. What's the real story?" Before he could answer, Charlie led the dog back into the family room. He pulled a blanket off the couch and spread it on the floor. "Mama, doggy bed." She smiled as her son took a board book from the coffee table and sat on the blanket with Casper, making up words to an imaginary story.

Her gaze caught on Jeff, who yawned and looked around her apartment, obvious distaste written on his face for the kid-friendly decorating style. He didn't pay a bit of attention to his son. Since she'd opened the door, he'd barely looked at Charlie. It was the first time he'd laid eyes on his own flesh and blood. She realized he couldn't care less.

Unable to resist testing her theory, she said, "He's about to go to sleep. Do you want to read him a story? He loves books."

Jeff held up his palms as if she'd offered him a venomous snake. "No, thanks."

"I've got paperwork that says you want joint custody of my son. You act like you'd rather be dipped in boiling oil than have any interaction with him."

"I told you. I've got a proposition for you."

"What?"

"Marry me."

Julia stared at him, disbelief coursing through her. He couldn't have shocked her more if he'd offered her a million bucks. "Is that a joke? It's sick and wrong, but it must be a joke."

"I'm serious, Jules. You're right—I have no interest in being a father in any sense of the word. Ever. In fact—" he paused and ran his fingers through his hair "—I got a vasectomy."

"Excuse me?"

"After you, I was determined no woman would try to trap me again."

"It takes two. I'm sorry, Jeff, that I ever believed we could be a family. I know how wrong I was. But I don't understand why you've changed your mind now?"

"Are you kidding? I love my life. I've been on two research expeditions in the past year. I make my own schedule and can teach whatever classes I want. Why would I want to be tied down to a woman or a baby?"

"Then why are you suddenly proposing? Why the custody suit?"

Jeff had the grace to look embarrassed. "My parents found out about my surgery. It made them interested in our kid. You know I'm an only child. They expected me to marry and 'carry on the family line.'" He rolled his eyes. "Whatever. But my dad's company is a big funder of my grants. If he wants a grandchild, I need to give him one."

Julia's gaze strayed to Charlie, who was snuggled against Casper's back, sucking on his thumb. His eyes drifted closed. She felt a wave of nausea roll through her. "You need to *give* him one? And you think you're going to give him mine?"

Jeff shrugged. "Technically, he's *ours*. When my parents want something, they don't stop until they get it."

"How is anything you're saying good news for me? Why don't you get the hell out of my house and out of my son's life?"

"Not going to happen."

"When the judge finds out your plan…"

"No one is going to find out. I'm the father. You can't keep him from me."

"I want to keep him safe and protected."

"That's why you should marry me. Oh, I heard all about your engagement to the cop. He's not for you. I know you. You want someone who's going to make you look smart."

Julia sucked in a breath. "You have no idea what you're talking about."

"Does he know about your problem?"

When she didn't answer, Jeff smiled. "I thought so. I'm guessing you don't want him to. It hasn't come up in the court proceedings, either, but that can change. Here's my proposal. Marry me, move to Ohio. My parents' property is huge. They have a guesthouse where you can live with the boy. All of your expenses will be covered."

"Why would I agree to that, and what does it have to do with us being married?"

"A marriage will seem more legit to my parents' precious social circle. They'll get off my back with someone to shape and mold into their own image."

"Like they did you?"

"My parents are proud of me."

"I thought your father wanted you to give up the university and take over his business."

"Not going to happen."

"Instead, Charlie and I should spend our lives at their beck and call?"

"They'll keep fighting until they take him away from you. We all will."

Her temper about to blow, Julia yanked open the front door. "Get out, Jeff."

"On second thought, maybe I should read the kid a story. Get to know him before he comes to live with us."

"Get out!"

Jeff must have read something in her eyes that told him she would die before she let him touch her son tonight. He hesitated then turned for the door.

She slammed it behind him. The noise startled the dog and woke Charlie, who began to cry. She rushed over and cradled him in her arms.

"It's okay, sweetie. Mama's here." Tears streamed down her face as she hugged Charlie close. "No one's going to take you away from me. No one." She made the promise as much to herself as to him, wanting to believe the words were true.

Chapter Eight

Julia stepped into the afternoon light and put on her sunglasses, more to hide the unshed tears welling in her eyes than for sun protection.

Frank Davis, her attorney, took her elbow to guide her down the steps of the county courthouse. They'd spent the past two hours in a heated session with Jeff, his parents and their lawyer. She couldn't believe how much information they'd dug up, from the details of her finances, including the business loan that had yet to be approved, to her credit history. Thanks to a loser boyfriend who'd stolen her bank-account information, her credit was spotty, at best.

They knew all of the dead-end jobs she'd had over the years, including those she'd been fired from or quit without notice, and had a detailed record of her habit of moving from city to city for short periods of time.

They'd brought in statements from one of her ex-boyfriends and a former employer stating she was flighty and irresponsible. Her old boss even said that she'd threatened to set fire to her hair salon. No one mentioned the woman had skimmed Julia's paycheck without her knowledge for over nine months after she'd discovered Julia's learning disabilities. Torching the place had been an idle threat, of course, but it hadn't sounded that way today.

"They made me seem crazy," she muttered.

Frank clucked softly. "It's all right, darlin'. A lot of mamas in the South are a bit touched. No one around here's gonna hold that against you." He checked his watch. "I got a tee time with some of the boys at one. Give me a call tomorrow and we'll plan our next move." He leaned in and planted a fatherly kiss on her cheek, then moved toward his vintage Cadillac parked at the curb.

Frank had known her since she'd been in diapers. He'd been one of her father's fraternity brothers in college. Not for the first time, she questioned the wisdom of hiring him to represent her. It was no secret Frank was close to retirement, and from what Julia could tell, he spent more time on the golf course and fishing with his friends than in his office or working on cases.

Lexi Preston might look like a pussycat, but she was an absolute shark. From her guilty expression every time they made eye contact, Julia knew Lexi was the one who'd researched her so thoroughly. Julia would have admired her skills if they hadn't been directed at her.

She glanced toward the courthouse entrance. Jeff and his parents could come out at any minute and she didn't want them to see her alone and on the verge of a breakdown. She wished now that she'd let her mother or Lainey come with her today.

She turned to make her way to her car and came face-to-face with Sam.

"Hey," he said softly and drew the sunglasses off her

nose, his eyes studying hers as if he could read what she was thinking. "How did things go today?"

"I told you not to come," she said on a shaky breath.

"I don't take direction well." He folded her glasses and pulled her into a tight embrace. "It's okay, honey. Whatever happened, we can make it better."

She tried to pull away but he didn't let her go. After a moment, she sagged against him, burying her face in the fabric of his uniform shirt.

As his palm drew circles on her back, her tears flowed freely. She gulped in ragged breaths. "So awful," she said around sobs. "They made me seem so awful."

"I don't believe that," he said against her ear. "Anyone who knows you knows you're a fantastic mother."

"What if they take him from me?"

"We're not going to let that happen. Not a snowball's chance."

Julia wiped her eyes. "They're going to come out any minute. Jeff can't see me like this."

"My truck's right here." Sam looped one arm around her shoulders, leading her away from the courthouse steps. He opened the passenger door of his truck then came around and climbed in himself. He started the engine but didn't make a move to drive off.

Julia kept her face covered with her hands and worked to control her breathing.

"Is that him?" Sam asked after a minute.

Julia peeked through her fingers as Jeff, his parents and the attorney walked out of the courthouse. Shading his eyes with one hand, Jeff scanned the area.

"He's looking for me so he can gloat." Julia sank down lower in the seat. "Jerk," she mumbled.

The group came down the steps.

"They're heading right for us."

"Sit up," Sam ordered, and she immediately straightened. "Smile and lean over to kiss me when they come by."

The urge to duck was huge, but Julia made her mouth turn up at the ends. "Here goes," she whispered as Jeff led the group closer, his father clapping him hard on the back. She waited until he noticed her through the windshield then leaned over and cupped Sam's jaw between her hands. She gave him a gentle kiss and pressed her forehead against his.

"That a girl," he told her. "Don't give him the satisfaction of seeing you upset."

"I can do this," she said, and Sam kissed her again.

"They've passed."

Julia stayed pressed against him for another moment before moving away. She leaned against the seat back in order to see out the side-view mirror. Jeff and his parents headed away, but Lexi trailed behind the group, looking over her shoulder every few steps.

"This isn't going to work."

"Yes, it is."

She shook her head. "I told you before, I made a lot of stupid decisions in my life. It's like they've uncovered every single one of them to use against me."

"Did you kill someone?"

Her head whipped toward him. "Of course not."

"Armed robbery?"

"No."

"Do you know how many people I meet in the course of my job who do bad things every day? Their kids are rarely taken away."

"Maybe they should be," she suggested, too unsettled to be comforted. "Maybe if they had people with buckets of money and tons of power going after them, they'd lose their babies."

He wrapped his fingers around hers. "You aren't going to lose Charlie. Stop thinking like that."

"You don't know, Sam. You weren't in that room."

"A mistake I don't intend to repeat. I should have been there with you. For you."

The tenderness in his voice touched a place deep within her: an intimate, open well of emotion she'd locked the lid to many years ago. She wanted to believe in him, to trust that he could protect her the way she'd never been willing to protect herself or even believed she deserved. The part of her who'd been hurt too many times in the past wanted to run.

She excelled at running away. She'd practically perfected it as an art.

That was what she'd been thinking in the courthouse. People disappeared all the time with no trace. She'd wanted to slip out of that room, gather up Charlie and whatever would fit in her trunk and drive away from the threat looming over her. She could cut hair anywhere. Why not start over in a place where no one knew her or her insecurities or all the ways she didn't measure up? She had friends around the country who'd help her if she asked.

The weight of trying to make a new life in a place that was as familiar to her as a worn blanket seemed too heavy. Of course trouble had followed her to Brevia. This was where it had started in the first place.

Sam's faith had made her feel as though things could work out, the same way Charlie's birth had renewed her hope in herself and her desire to really try.

What was the use? This morning was a cold, harsh dose of reality and she didn't like it.

"Stop it," he said quietly. "Whatever's going through your mind right now, put it out. It's not going to do you or Charlie any good for you to give up."

Because she couldn't help it, she met his gaze again. "I'm scared, Sam." A miserable groan escaped her lips. "I'm terrified they're going to take my baby and I won't be able to stop them."

"We're going to stop them." He took her hand. "What did Frank say?"

"That all Southern women were crazy, so it wouldn't be an issue, and he needed to make his tee time and we'd talk tomorrow."

"Tell me what happened in there."

"I can't." She bit her lip again and tasted blood on her tongue. "I put my mistakes behind me. Or I thought I did. Their attorney knew things about my past I hadn't even told Jeff. They went after my character and I had nothing to offer in my defense. Nothing as bad as me killing someone, although the urge to wipe the smug smile off of Maria Johnson's face was almost overwhelming. They made me seem unstable and irresponsible. Two things I can't afford if I'm going to keep sole custody of Charlie."

"Then we'll come up with something."

"This isn't your problem, Sam."

"Hell, yes, it's my problem. You're my fiancée."

The lunacy of that statement actually made her laugh. "Your fake fiancée. Not the same thing."

"For the purposes of your custody case it is. You're not alone, Julia. We both get something out of this arrangement. My dad has talked about heading back home before the wedding. That's huge for me. Dinner was a big success. It's my turn to repay you."

Sam knew there was more to his interest in her case than wanting to repay her. Yes, his dad had backed off, but it was more than that. Sam cared about Julia and Charlie, about keeping them safe. No one should be able to make her feel this bad about herself. He also knew it was dangerous territory for him. He'd let his heart lead him before, with disastrous results.

His father might be the king of emotional diarrhea these days, but Sam remembered clearly the months after his mother's death. He'd fixed lunches for his little brother, made sure they both had baths at night and taken money out of his dad's wallet to buy groceries on his way home from school. He'd walked a mile out of his way once a week so no one at the local grocery would recognize him and be concerned. When he wasn't at work, his father had sat in the darkened living room, paging through photo albums, a glass of amber-colored liquid in his hand.

That was what loving someone too much could do to a man. Sam had learned early on he wasn't going to make that mistake. When he'd caught his brother, Scott, with his ex-fiancée, he'd been angry and embarrassed, but mainly numb.

When he'd broken off the engagement, Jenny had told him the entire situation was his fault. He'd been too cold and distant. She wanted to be with a man who could feel passion. She'd thought seeing her with someone else would awaken Sam's passion. Talk about crazy, and she wasn't even Southern.

He'd known he didn't have any more to give her or any woman. Even though his pattern of dating hadn't been deliberate, the look a woman sometimes got in her eye after a couple of dates scared him. The look said "I want something more." She wanted to talk about her feelings. Sam felt sick thinking about it.

As far as he was concerned, a pretend engagement suited him fine. He cared about Julia and he wanted to help her, but their arrangement was clear. He didn't have to give more of himself than he was able to, and she wasn't going to expect anything else.

"Jeff asked me to marry him," she said, breaking his reverie.

"During the mediation?" he asked, sure he must have heard her wrong.

She shook her head. "Last night. He came to my apartment."

Sam felt his blood pressure skyrocket. "You let him in? What were you thinking?" Especially since Sam had practically had to hold himself back from making the short drive to her apartment. He'd had a long day at work, and as he was pulling into his driveway, he'd realized how much he didn't want to be alone in his quiet house. He'd resisted the urge, telling himself that he shouldn't get too attached to Julia or her son. They had boundaries and he was a stickler for the rules. Now to find out that her creep of an ex-boyfriend had been there?

"He came crawling back." Sam kept his tone casual. Inside, his emotions were in turmoil. This was the guy she'd wanted to marry so badly. What if she still carried a torch for him? He'd obviously been an idiot to let her go once. If he came back now, trying to rekindle a romance and wanting to be a real family, would Julia consider taking him back? That thought hit Sam straight in the gut. "What did you say?"

She studied him for a moment. "He didn't quite come crawling. More like trumpeting his own horn. He told me the reason they're coming after Charlie is because his parents want an heir to the family business."

"They've got a son. Let him take over."

"Not his deal, and Jeff isn't going to have other children. He's made sure of that. Although it's crazy to think they could start grooming a mere toddler. No wonder Jeff has so many issues. If only I'd been smart enough to see it when we were together. You know what the strange part of this is? No one in Jeff's family has tried to get to know Charlie. It's like they want him on paper but they don't care about having a grandson. I want him to know their family if they have a real interest in him. But I saw how Jeff suffered from being a pawn in his parents' power games. I can't let the same thing happen to Charlie."

He held her hand, his brilliant blue eyes warm with emotion. "Your son needs you. He needs you to fight for him."

She nodded and wiped at her nose.

"What you need is a plan of defense. You flaked on some jobs. It happens."

"There's a reason," she mumbled, almost reluctantly.

"A reason that will explain it away?"

She shrugged and shook free from his hand, adjusting the vents to the air-conditioning as a way to keep her fingers occupied. "I have severe learning disabilities."

When he didn't respond she continued, "I've been keeping it a secret since I was a kid. It's a neurobiological disorder, both visual and auditory. Only my family and a few teachers knew, and I kept it from them for as long as I could. Everyone else assumed I was lazy or didn't care."

"Why would you hide that?"

"You have no idea what it's like, how much shame and embarrassment is involved. To people who've never dealt with it, it seems cut-and-dried. It's not." Her hands clenched into fists as she struggled with her next words. "I'm a good mimic and my bad attitude served me well as a way to keep everyone from digging too much. I got by okay, but I can barely read. Numbers on a page are a puzzle."

"All those books on your shelf…"

"I'm nothing if not determined. I'll get through them someday. Right now, I'm working with a literacy specialist. They have a lot of methods that weren't available when

I was in school. But it never gets easier. For years, I tried so hard in school but people thought I was a total slacker. Ditzy blonde cheerleader with no brain. A lot of the time that's how it felt. Once I was out on my own, I hid it as best I could. People can take advantage of me pretty easily when it comes to contracts or finances. And that's what happened. A number of times. It always seemed easier to just move on rather than to fight them."

"Every time someone got wind of it, you left."

She nodded. "It was cowardly but I don't want to be treated like I'm stupid. Although, looking back, I acted pretty dumb most of the time. Especially when it came to boyfriends. I trusted Jeff. He never let me forget it."

"That you had a learning disability?"

"That I'm just a pretty face. The blond hair and long legs. When I told him I was pregnant, he told me that once my looks faded I wouldn't have anything left to offer."

"He's a real piece of work." Sam couldn't believe how angry he was. At her idiot ex-boyfriend and all the others who took advantage of her. But also with Julia. Watching her, Sam could tell she believed the garbage people had fed her over the years. He threw the truck into gear, not wanting to lose his temper. "Where's your car?"

"Around the corner." She pointed then shifted in her seat. "Thanks for coming today, Sam. I was a mess after the mediation. You helped."

"I could have helped more if you'd let me be in there with you." He pulled out from the curb and turned onto the next street. Her car was parked a few spaces down.

"Maybe next time," she said quietly. She reached for the door handle but he took her arm.

"You have a lot more to offer than looks. Any guy who can't see that is either blind or an enormous jackass." He kept his gaze out the front window, afraid of giving away too much if he looked at her.

"Thanks."

He heard the catch in her voice and released her. After she'd shut the door, he rolled down the window. "The Mardi Gras Carnival is tonight. I'll pick you and Charlie up at five."

"I'm beat. I wasn't planning on going."

"I'll pick you up at five. You need to take your mind off this, and it's a good place for us to be seen together."

Her chest rose and fell. "Fine. We'll be ready."

After she'd gotten into her car, Sam pulled away. Although the air was hot for mid-March, he shut the windows. Julia's scent hovered in the truck's cab. Sam wanted to keep it with him as long as he could.

He'd meant what he said about taking her mind off today. As police chief, he was obligated to make an appearance at town events, but he looked forward to tonight knowing he'd have Julia and Charlie with him.

Chapter Nine

Julia dabbed on a bit of lip gloss just as the doorbell rang. She picked up Charlie, who was petting Casper through the wire crate.

"Let's go."

"'Bye, doggy."

Casper whined softly.

"We'll be back soon," Julia told him. The doorbell rang again. "Coming," she called.

She grabbed the diaper bag off the table and opened the front door, adjusting her short, flowing minidress as she did.

"We're ready."

"Sammy," Charlie said, bouncing up and down in her arms.

"Hey, bud." Sam held out his hands and Charlie dived forward.

Julia worried for a moment about Charlie bonding so

quickly with Sam. In a way it worked to their advantage, at least as their pretend engagement went. But she had concerns about Charlie's clear affection for Sam. She didn't want her son to be hurt once their time together ended.

"You don't have to take him."

"My pleasure." Sam looked her over from head to toe then whistled softly. "You look amazing."

Julia felt a blush creep up her cheeks. "You, too."

It was true. Tonight he wore a light polo shirt and dark blue jeans. His hair was still longer and her fingers pulsed as she thought about running them through the ends. He hadn't shaved, and the dusting of short whiskers along his jaw made him look wilder than he normally did as police chief.

It excited her more than she cared to admit. She hadn't been on a real date in over two years. This wasn't real, she reminded herself. This was showing off for the town, convincing people their relationship was genuine.

Not that being in this relationship had helped her earlier. She'd barely said two words in her own defense as the Johnsons' attorney had put forward more and more information about her deficiencies as a person and how they might be detrimental to raising her son.

The mediator, an older woman who was all business, hadn't said much, nodding as she took in everything and occasionally looking over her glasses to stare at Julia.

Sam was right. She needed to get her mind off the custody case. So what if this night wasn't a real date and Sam wasn't her real boyfriend? It wouldn't stop her from enjoying herself.

Because of Charlie's car seat, she drove. Once they were close to the high school, she could see the line of cars. Half the town was at the carnival. She knew Lainey and Ethan would be there along with her mother.

"Is your dad coming tonight?" she asked, a thought suddenly blasting across her mind.

Sam nodded. "I told him we'll meet him."

"My mom is, too."

Sam made a choking sound. "Okay, good. They can get to know each other. It'll be great."

"That's one word for it."

"Does your mom believe the engagement? I haven't seen her since she walked in on us."

"I think so." Julia slowed to turn into the lower parking lot. "It's not the first time she's seen me be impulsive."

Sam shook his head as she turned off the ignition. "You never give yourself a break."

"Why do I deserve one?" She paused then said, "It's fine. I'm repairing my reputation with my family. It's a long progress, but I'm getting there. What makes you ask about my mom?"

"I saw Ethan downtown yesterday and he gave me the third degree about my intentions toward you."

"Ethan?"

"His big-brother routine was going strong. Told me how special you are and that if I hurt you or Charlie I'd have him to answer to."

"I don't know why he'd care. He went through hell because of me, although it's ancient history now."

"There you go again with the self-flagellation. We're going to need to work on that."

"Whatever you say." She got out of the car and picked up Charlie from his car seat. As she turned, she took in her old high school. It looked the same as it had almost fifteen years ago.

She filled her lungs with the cool night air. This was her favorite time of year in the North Carolina mountains. It smelled fresh and clean, the scent of spring reminding her of new beginnings. Coming off of the cold, wet winter, the change of seasons gave her hope.

Just like Sam.

Julia knew hope was dangerous. She was a sucker for believing in things that would never come to pass. She'd been like that in high school, too—wanting to believe she'd be able to keep up. Or, at least, admit how deeply her problem ran.

For some reason, that never seemed an option. Sam could say what he wanted about her learning disabilities being beyond her control. She knew it was true. But by high school, when elementary-age kids read more clearly than she could, it felt like stupidity.

None of her teachers had understood what was going on in her head. She'd never truly opened up to anyone about how bad it was. It had been easier to act as though she didn't care, to limp through school with a lot of blustering attitude and paying smarter kids to write her papers.

Charlie tapped her on the cheek. "Hi, Mama."

She shook off the memories. Sam stood next to her, watching with his too-knowing eyes.

"I'm guessing you haven't been back here for a while?"

"Not since graduation." She adjusted Charlie and headed for the gymnasium entrance. "Remind me again why we're here."

Sam put his hand on the small of her back, the gentle touch oddly comforting. "The annual Kiwanis carnival not only celebrates Fat Tuesday but raises a lot of money each year for local kids. It's a great event for the town."

"Spoken like a true pillar of the community." She gave an involuntary shiver. "Which I'm not and never will be."

"You never know. Either way, I promise you'll have fun. Greasy food, games, dancing."

Since she'd been back, she hadn't attended any town

events. It was one thing to reconnect with people she'd known within the relative safety of the salon. No one was going to rehash old resentments while she wielded scissors. Here she was out of her element and not confident about the reception she'd get from the girls she once knew. Especially since she'd taken Brevia's most eligible bachelor off the market.

A memory niggled at the back of her mind. "Didn't you do a kissing booth last year or something like that?"

Sam's confident stride faltered. "They auctioned off dates with a couple local guys."

She flashed him a smile. "How much did you go for, Chief?"

In the fading light, she saw a distinct trail of red creep up his neck. "I don't remember."

"Liar." She stood in one spot until he turned to look at her. "Tell me."

"A thousand," he mumbled.

"Dollars?" She gasped. "Who in the world paid that much money for you?" When he leveled a look at her, she added, "Not that I don't think you're worth it. But not a lot of people around here have that kind of cash."

"It was for a good cause" was his only answer.

Another thought struck. "Unless…it was Ida Garvey!"

He turned and she trotted to catch up with him, Charlie bouncing on her hip. "Let me take him." Sam slid his arms around Charlie and scooped him up.

"It was Ida, wasn't it? She's the only one around here rich enough to pay that amount."

He gave a reluctant nod. "I got the most money."

"What kind of date did you take her on?"

"Would you believe I escorted her to her fiftieth high-school reunion over in Asheville? She had me wait on her hand and foot. Kept calling me her 'boy toy' in front of her old friends." He shook his head. "I swear my butt had bruises from being pinched so often."

Julia laughed harder than she had in ages. "You really are a hero, you know?"

"It's not funny."

"Yes, it is." She looked at him and saw humor shining in his eyes, as well. Then she noticed they were at the gym entrance, light spilling out into the darkening night. She studied Sam for another moment, wondering if he'd told her that story to ease her nerves.

He really was a good guy, she thought. He should be with someone like him—a woman who was smart and sweet.

Someone nothing like her.

He smoothed the skin between her eyebrows. "Stop frowning," he said gently. "We're going to have fun."

He dropped his hand, intertwined his fingers with hers and led her into the gymnasium. He greeted the two women working the ticket counter, neither of whom Julia recognized. Sam made introductions, and both women gave her a genuine smile and shook her hand, offering congratulations on their engagement. She flashed her ring but noticed Sam stiffen when one of the ladies complimented him on it.

Charlie became suddenly shy and buried his face in the crook of Sam's neck, something Julia would have loved to do, as well.

"Come on, buddy," Sam coaxed. "Let's find some cotton candy."

"I don't think so," Julia said. "He hasn't had dinner yet."

Charlie gave Sam a wide grin. "Can-ee."

"We'll get a hot dog first," Sam promised her and moved into the crowd.

"Kids can always count on their dad for a good time," one of the women said with a laugh.

"While Mom cleans up the sick stomach," the other added.

"He's not…" Julia began, wanting to explain that Sam wasn't her son's father. Then she realized they already knew that, although Sam was certainly acting like the doting dad.

"He's quite a catch." The blonder of the two women winked at her.

Julia's stomach flipped because she knew how right the woman's statement was. "I'd better stick with them," she said and hurried after the two, emotions already at war in her mind and heart.

"Julia!" Lainey's voice carried over the crowd, and a moment later, she was surrounded by her sister, Ethan and their mother. Lainey gave her a long hug. "Sam said today was rough. Are you feeling any better?"

"I knew I should have come with you." Vera shook her head. "I'd like to get ahold of that family and talk some sense into them."

"When did you see Sam?" The thought of Sam giving information about her to her family made her more than a little uncomfortable.

"I ran into him downtown," Lainey said. "What's the big deal?"

"He shouldn't have said anything."

"He's going to be your husband," Vera corrected. "He has a right to worry."

"We all do," Lainey echoed. "Jules, you've got to let us help you. You're not alone."

"Where's the little man?" Ethan asked, his internal radar about conflict between the three Morgan women practically glowing bright red through his T-shirt.

"Right here," Sam answered, balancing a huge cotton

candy and a paper plate with hot-dog chunks and small pieces of watermelon on it.

Charlie reached for a piece of fruit and babbled a few nonsense words.

"You cut up the hot dog," Julia said, stunned.

Sam's forehead wrinkled. "I thought you were supposed to cut up round food when kids are little."

"You are." Julia felt ridiculous that something so minor had such an effect on her emotions. "I didn't realize you'd know it."

"Don't be silly." Vera reached for Charlie and snuggled him against her. "He's spent enough time around you and Charlie to realize that."

Julia saw Lainey studying her, a thoughtful expression on her face. "That's right. Isn't it, Jules?"

Julia nodded and stepped next to Sam, leaning up to kiss him on the cheek. "Of course. Thanks, hon."

Lainey's features relaxed and Julia blew out a quiet breath of relief.

"There's my favorite son and future daughter-in-law." So much for her short-lived relief. Julia heard Sam groan.

She turned and was enveloped in one of Joe Callahan's bear hugs. He moved from her to Sam. "Look at you, Sammy. Surrounded by friends with the woman you love at your side." His meaty hands clasped either side of Sam's jaw. "I'm so proud of you, son. You're not a loner anymore. I thought my mistakes had cost you a chance at a real life. But you're making it happen."

"Dad, enough." Sam pulled Joe's hands away. "Not the time or the place."

"There's always time to say 'I love you.'"

Sam met Julia's gaze over his father's shoulders. His eyes screamed "help me," and as fascinating as everyone seemed to find the father-son interaction, she intervened.

"Joe, I'd like you to meet my family."

He turned, his smile a mile wide.

"This is my sister, Lainey, and her husband, Ethan Daniels."

Joe pumped their hands enthusiastically. "Pleasure to meet you both. I'm Joe Callahan."

"Are you in town for long, Mr. Callahan?" Lainey asked.

"As long as it takes," Joe said with a wink at Sam.

A muscle in Sam's jaw ticked and his eyes drifted shut as he muttered to himself. They flew open a moment later when Ethan added, "You, Sammy and I should do some fishing once the weather warms up."

"Don't call me Sammy."

"I'd love to."

Vera cleared her throat.

"Sorry. This is my mother, Vera Morgan. And you've met Charlie."

Joe's eyes widened as he looked at Vera. "Well, I certainly see where you two girls get your beauty. Ms. Morgan, you are a sight to behold."

Vera held out her hand like the Southern belle she'd once been. Joe bent over her fingers and kissed them lightly. "Why, Mr. Callahan," she said, her accent getting thicker with every syllable. "You are a silver-tongued devil, I believe."

"Shoot me now," Sam muttered.

Julia's eyes rolled. She was used to this routine with her mother. Vera had been a devoted wife to her late husband, but since his death, she'd reinvented herself not only as an animal-rescue expert but as a woman with a long list of admirers. Unlike Julia, her mother always made sure the men with whom she was acquainted treated her like a lady, fawning around her until Vera moved on to the next one in line.

"Here she goes," Lainey whispered, as Vera tucked her chin and fluttered her eyelashes. Charlie watched the two for a moment then reached for Sam.

"Can-ee," the boy demanded, and Joe took the cotton candy from Sam.

"Come here, Charlie," Joe said and lifted him from Vera's arms. At this rate, Charlie would be held by more people than the Stanley Cup.

"Why don't I take him," Julia suggested.

"Joe and I will take him to the carnival games," Vera said.

"That's right," Joe told them with a wink. "You young folks can head to the dance floor or grab a drink."

Before she could argue, Joe and Vera disappeared into the sea of people, Charlie waving over Joe's shoulder.

"I'm up for a beer." Ethan looked at Sam. "How about you, Sammy boy?"

"Don't go there," Sam warned.

"Stop—you're going to make me cry." Ethan laughed until Lainey socked him in the gut. "Hey," he said on a cough.

"I thought Sam's dad was sweet." Lainey grinned at Sam. "He obviously loves you." Her gaze switched to Julia. "You and Charlie, too. Mom's going to eat him up with a spoon."

"A terrifying thought." Julia'd known this night was a bad idea.

"Come on," Lainey said to all three of them. "Let's get something to eat. They had a pasta booth in the corner."

Ethan wrapped one long arm around Lainey and kissed the top of her head. "Yeah, like a double date."

Julia couldn't help it—she burst out laughing. "This is going to be great. We'll be besties." Who would have thought that she'd be double-dating with her first boyfriend and her sister? It was too crazy to imagine.

She looked at Sam, expecting him to be laughing right along with her. Instead, his brows were drawn low over his vivid blue eyes.

"Fine by me." He took her hand to follow Lainey and Ethan toward the back of the gym.

"What's wrong?" she whispered, pulling him to slow down so they were out of hearing range. "Is it my mom and Joe? She's harmless, I promise. Her former admirers still adore her. Whatever happens, she won't hurt your dad."

Sam's arm was solid as a rock as his muscles tensed. "Does it seem strange to be so chummy with your ex-boyfriend?"

Julia thought about Jeff, then realized that was not who Sam meant. "Ethan's married to my sister. We've been over more than a decade. He's so much like my brother, I barely remember he's seen me naked."

Sam stopped on a dime, causing her to bump into the length of him. "Is that a joke?"

She wrinkled her nose. "I thought it was funny."

"It's not."

"Come on, Sam. You see how he looks at Lainey. He never once looked at me in that way. He's different with her, and I couldn't be happier. For both of them. It's old news, even around Brevia. That's an accomplishment, given how gossip takes on a life of its own in this town." She flashed him a sassy grin. "Chief Callahan, is it possible you're jealous?"

"I don't want to look like a fool. I've been down the road of public humiliation and the scenery sucks. Why would I be jealous? You said yourself Ethan's like your brother."

Julia studied him then placed a soft kiss on his mouth.

"I'd never do something to make you look like a fool. Scout's honor."

"I can't imagine you as a Girl Scout." Sam forced his lips to curve into a smile, wondering at his odd reaction. He wasn't the jealous type, and he knew how happy Ethan and Lainey were together. "Let's find them." He took Julia's hand again.

A number of people waved or stopped to say hello as they made their way through the crowd. At first, Julia tensed at every new greeting. Eventually he felt her relax, but she never loosened her death grip on his hand. He wanted to protect her, he realized, and also to show her she could belong to this community again. The people of Brevia had welcomed him, and if Julia gave them a chance, he was sure they'd accept her.

They caught up with Ethan and Lainey and grabbed a table near the makeshift dance floor. The sisters bantered back and forth, making Sam wish for a better relationship with his own brother.

Even before Scott had cheated with Sam's fiancée, they hadn't been close. Sam had been the responsible brother, stoic and toeing the line, while Scott had been wild, always getting into trouble and constantly resenting his older brother's interference in his life.

"How are things around town these days?" Ethan asked as he set a second beer on the table next to Sam.

"Quiet for a change." Sam took another bite of pasta then swallowed hard as Julia tilted back her head to laugh at something Lainey said. The column of her neck was smooth and long. He ached to trail a line of kisses across her skin.

He pushed away the beer, realizing he was going to need his wits about him to remain in control tonight.

"Were you involved in the drug bust over in Tellet County a few nights back?"

Julia stopped midsentence as her eyes snapped to his. "What drug bust? Sounds dangerous. Why didn't I hear about a drug bust?"

Sam threw Ethan what he hoped was a *shut your mouth* look.

"Sorry, man," Ethan said quickly. "Hey, Lainey, let's hit the dance floor."

Lainey popped out of her chair. "Love to."

"Cowards," Julia muttered as she watched them go. She turned her angry gaze back to Sam. "You were saying?"

"A meth lab outside the county lines," he told her. It had been a long time since anyone had cared about what he was doing and whether it was dangerous or not. "It's been kept quiet so far because the sheriff thinks it's part of a bigger tristate operation. We want to see if we can flush out a couple of the bigger fish."

She tapped one finger on the table. "I don't like you being involved in something like that."

"It's my job, Julia."

"I need to know about these things. I bet Abby Brighton knew where you were during the drug bust."

"She's my secretary. Of course she knew."

"We're engaged."

"Is that so?"

To his great amusement, she squirmed in her chair. "As far as everyone around here thinks. I need to be kept informed."

"Why?"

"To know whether I should worry."

"One more reason I wouldn't be a good bet in a real relationship. Ask my ex. I don't like to report in. I don't like anyone worried about me." He blew out a frustrated breath. "My job is dangerous almost every day. I deal with it, but I don't expect you or anyone else to."

"No one's allowed to care about you?" Her eyes flashed, temper lighting them.

"I don't need anyone to care."

"The Lone Ranger rides again." Julia pushed away from the table. He grabbed her wrist so she couldn't escape.

"Why are you mad? This doesn't have anything to do with you. We have a business arrangement. That's what we both wanted. It's not going to help either of us to be emotionally involved with the other one's life."

"Some of us care, whether we want to or not."

Her eyes shone and his heart leaped in his chest. He pulled her tight against him, aware they were gathering stares from people standing nearby. "Thank you for caring. I'm not used to it, but it means a lot." He pressed his forehead to hers. "I'm sorry I'm bad at this. Even for pretend."

"You're not *so* bad," she whispered.

"Do you want to dance?"

"Do you?"

He grinned at her. "Hell, no. But I can make it work."

"Give me a minute. I need to catch up with my mom and Joe, make sure Charlie's okay."

He studied her. "If I didn't know better, I'd say you're avoiding me right now."

She shook her head. "I want to find Charlie."

"They headed back toward the game booths. I'm going to say hi to the mayor and I'll meet you over there."

The gym was full, and without Sam at her side, Julia got a little panicked by the crowd.

She moved toward the far end of the gymnasium where the carnival booths were set up, then veered off quickly when she saw two women from her high-school class standing together near one of the attractions. One was

Annabeth Sullivan, whom Julia felt friendlier toward after their conversation at the salon. The other was Lucy Peterson, their graduating class's valedictorian. Julia had always been uncomfortable around her. She'd made it clear during high school that Lucy was persona non grata and knew the slightly chubby teen had suffered because of it.

Lucy had gotten her revenge, though. Because of her work in the school office and her access to the files, she'd found out about Julia's learning disabilities. She hadn't told anyone outright, but had spread the rumor that Julia had only graduated because she'd slept with one of her teachers and he'd fixed her grade.

She'd told Julia that if she denied it, Lucy would tell people the real reason she had so much trouble in school. Having a reputation as a slut hadn't been half as bad as the school knowing about her LD.

She ducked out a door and into the cool night air, walking toward the football field situated next to the main building. Two streetlights glowed in the darkness as her eyes scanned the shadowy length of the field.

She'd spent so much time here in high school. If she'd been queen of her class, this was her royal court. She'd felt confident on the field in her cheerleading uniform or on the sidelines cheering for Ethan. She'd hated falling back on her looks, but the insecure girl who had nothing else to offer had exploited her one gift as best she could.

Now she breathed in the cool night air and closed her eyes, remembering the familiar smells and sounds.

Her memories here were a long time gone. She was no longer a scared teenager. She had Charlie to protect. She'd made mistakes and was trying her damnedest to make amends for them. There was no way of moving forward without finally confronting her past, once and for all.

Chapter Ten

She took another breath and headed toward the school, determined to hold her head high. She had as much right to return to her high school as anyone.

Once inside, she stopped at the girls' bathroom to sprinkle cold water on her face. When a stall opened and Lucy Peterson stepped out, Julia wondered if she'd actually conjured her.

"Hi, Lucy." The other woman's eyes widened in surprise.

Lucy hadn't changed much since high school. She was still short and full figured, her chest heaving as she adjusted the wire-rimmed glasses on her face.

"Hello, Julia. I didn't expect to see you here. I'm in town for the weekend for my parents' anniversary. Normally I wouldn't be caught dead back in this high school. I live in Chicago. I'm a doctor." Lucy paused for a breath. "I'm babbling."

"What kind of doctor?" Julia asked.

"Molecular biologist."

Julia nodded. Figured. Julia knew better than to compare herself to a genius like Lucy. "That's great."

The two women stared at each other for several long moments. At the same time they blurted, "I'm sorry."

Relief mixed with a healthy dose of confusion made Julia's shoulders sag. "I'm the one who should apologize. I know I was horrible in high school. You were on the top of my list. Not that it matters, but you should know I was jealous of you."

Lucy looked doubtful. "Of me? You were the homecoming queen, prom queen, head cheerleader, and you dated the football captain. I was nobody."

"You were smart."

"I shouldn't have spread that rumor about you." Lucy fiddled with the ring on her left finger. "You weren't a slut."

"There are worse things you could have said about me."

"You weren't stupid, either."

Julia made her voice light. "The grade record would beg to differ."

"I read your file," Lucy said slowly. "It was wrong, but I know you had significant learning disabilities, which means…"

"It means there's something wrong with my brain," Julia finished. "*Stupid* is a much clearer description of my basic problem."

"You must have been pretty clever to have hid it all those years. I'm guessing you still are."

"I cut hair for a living. It's not nuclear science. Or molecular biology."

"That's right. My mom told me you'd taken over the Hairhouse."

"I'm working on it. The loan still needs to go through."

"Are you going to keep the name?"

Julia relaxed a little as she smiled. "I don't think so. 'The Best Little Hairhouse in Brevia' is quite a mouthful."

Lucy returned the smile then pulled at the ends of her hair. "I'm in town until Tuesday. Could you fit me in?"

"You don't hate me?"

Lucy shook her head. "In high school, I thought I was the only one who was miserable. Once I got away from Brevia, I realized lots of kids had problems. We were all just too narcissistic to see it in each other. Some people can't let go of the past. I've moved on, Julia. I'm happy in Chicago. I have a great career and a fantastic husband. I don't even mind visiting my mom a couple times a year, although I avoid the old crowd. I know in my heart they can't hurt me because their opinions don't matter. I don't hate you. You probably did me a favor. You made me determined to escape. Now I can come back on my own terms."

"I'm glad for you, Lucy." Julia checked her mental calendar. She'd trained herself to keep her schedule in her head so she didn't have to rely on a planner or smartphone. "How about eleven on Monday?"

Lucy nodded. "Maybe we could grab lunch after. I may not care too much about certain ladies' opinions but I wouldn't mind seeing their faces if we showed up at Carl's."

"I'd love that."

"I'll see you Monday." With a quick, awkward hug, Lucy hurried out the door.

Julia studied herself in the hazy mirror above the row of bathroom sinks. She felt lighter than she had in years, the weight of her guilt over how she'd treated Lucy finally lifted. One past mistake vanquished, only a hundred more to go.

"She's right, you know." The door to one of the stalls swung open to reveal Lexi Preston.

Julia's shoulders went rigid again. "Eavesdrop much?" She took a step toward Lexi. "I don't suppose you're going to put that conversation on the official record? It didn't make me out to be the deadbeat you're trying to convince the court I am."

"I don't think you're a deadbeat," Lexi said, sounding almost contrite. "You're not stupid, either. But I have to do my job. The Johnsons—"

"They call the shots, right? You do the dirty work for them, digging up damaging information on me and probably countless other family enemies."

"It's not personal." Lexi's voice was a miserable whisper.

Julia felt a quick stab of sympathy before her temper began to boil over. She was always too gullible, wanting to believe people weren't as bad as they seemed. It led to her being taken advantage of on more than one occasion. Not this time, though.

She had to physically restrain herself from grabbing Lexi's crisp button-down and slamming the petite attorney into one of the metal stalls. "How can you say that? You're helping them take my son away from me. My son!" Tears flooded her eyes and she turned away, once again feeling helpless to stop the inevitable outcome.

"I don't want you to lose your son," Lexi said quietly. "If I had my way…" She paused then added, "Hiding who you are and the reasons you did things isn't going to help your case. You're not the one with the big secrets here."

Julia whirled around. "Are the Johnsons hiding something? Do you have information that could help me keep Charlie?"

Lexi shook her head. "I've said too much." She reached

for the door. "You're a good mother, Julia. But you have to believe it."

Julia followed Lexi into the hall, but before she could catch up a loud crash from down the hall distracted her. She heard a round of shouts and her first thought was of Charlie.

Chaos reigned in the gymnasium as people pushed toward the exits. Julia stood on her tiptoes and scanned the crowd, spotting Joe Callahan with his arm around her mother near the bleachers. Vera held Charlie, who was contentedly spooning ice cream into his mouth, oblivious to the commotion.

Julia elbowed her way through the throng of people to Vera and Joe. "Charlie," she said on a breath, and her son launched himself at her.

"Banilla, Mama."

"I see, sweetie." She hugged him tight against her.

"Why is everyone rushing out of here?" She noticed that many older folks, like Joe and Vera, hung back.

"Big fight outside," someone passing by called. "Eddie Kelton caught his wife in the back of their minivan with his best friend."

"He's going to kill him," the man's companion said with a sick laugh. "Someone said Eddie's got a knife."

Julia grimaced. She'd gone to school with Eddie's older brother. "The Keltons are not a stable bunch," she murmured.

Joe patted her shoulder. "Don't worry, hon. Sam will handle it. I'd be out there but I don't want to leave your mom."

"Such a gentleman."

"Sam?" Julia's heart rate quickened. "Why is Sam out there?"

"Because he's the police chief." Vera spoke slowly, as if Julia were a small child.

"He's not on duty. Shouldn't they call a deputy?"

"Cops are never truly off duty," Joe said with a sigh. "But Sammy can take care of himself."

"Eddie Kelton has a knife." Julia practically jumped up and down with agitation. Her palms were sweating and clammy. Sam could take care of himself, but she couldn't stop her anxiety from spilling over. "This isn't part of the evening's entertainment. It's real life."

Joe nodded. "Being the wife of a law-enforcement officer isn't easy." He patted her shoulder again and she wanted to rip his wrist out of the socket. He pulled his hand away as if he could read her mind. "If it will make you feel better, I'll check on him. I may be rusty but I could handle a couple troublemakers in my day."

Vera gave a dreamy sigh. A muscle above Julia's eye began to twitch.

"I bet you were quite a sight," Vera practically purred.

"You know what would make me feel better? If I go and check on him." She sat Charlie on the bleachers. "Stay here with Grandma, okay, buddy?"

"Gramma," Charlie said around a mouthful.

"I'll escort you," Joe said in the same cop tone Julia'd heard Sam use. "If you're okay for a few minutes on your own?" he asked Vera.

"Be a hero," Vera answered, batting her lashes.

Julia thought about arguing but figured he could be useful. "Can you get me to the front?"

"Yes, ma'am."

He took her elbow and, true to his word, guided her through the groups spilling into the parking lot. Was it some kind of police Jedi mind trick that enabled cops to manage throngs of people?

She poked her head through the row of spectators to see Sam between two men, arms out, a finger pointed at each of them.

Eddie Kelton, his wife, Stacey, and a man Julia didn't recognize stood in the parking lot under the lights. The unknown man had his shirt on inside out and his jeans were half zipped. Julia assumed he was the man Stacey had been with. Another telltale sign was the black eye forming above his cheek.

Stacey stood to one side, weeping loudly into her hands.

"For the last time, Eddie, put the knife down." Sam looked as if he'd grown several inches since Julia had seen him minutes earlier. He was broad and strong, every muscle in his body on full alert. A surge of pride flashed through her, along with the nail-biting fear of seeing him in action.

Eddie Kelton couldn't have been more than five foot seven, a wiry strip of a man, aged beyond his years thanks to working in the sun on a local construction crew. His face sported a bloody nose, busted lip and a large scratch above his left eye. Julia gathered he'd been on the losing end of the fight until he'd brandished the six-inch blade jiggling between his fingers.

"That's my woman, Chief." Eddie's arm trembled. "My wife. He's supposed to be my best friend and he had my wife." Eddie's wild gaze switched to Stacey. "How could you do this to me? I loved you."

She let out a wretched sob. "You don't act like you love me. Always down at the bar after work or passed out on the couch." Her eyes darted around the crowd. "I found the adult movies on the computer. I want someone who wants me. Who pays attention to me. Who makes me feel like a woman and not just the housekeeper."

"I loved you," Eddie screamed.

"It was only—" the half-dressed man began.

"Shut up, Jon-o," Eddie and Stacey yelled at the same time.

Eddie slashed the air with his knife.

Sam held his ground.

Julia held her breath.

"Eddie, I know what you're feeling." Sam's voice was a soothing murmur.

"You don't know squat," Eddie spat out, dancing back and forth on the balls of his feet. "I'm going to cut off his junk here and now."

"Don't you threaten my junk," the other man yelled back. "If you were a real man—"

Sam's head whipped around. "Jon Dallas, shut your mouth or I'm going to arrest you for public indecency." He turned back to Eddie. "I do know. A few years ago I walked in on my brother and my fiancée getting busy on the kitchen table."

A collective gasp went up from the crowd and several heads turned toward Julia. "Not me," she whispered impatiently. "His ex."

Sam's gaze never left Eddie, so she had no idea if he realized she was there.

Eddie's bloodshot eyes brimmed with tears. "It gets you right here," he said, thumping his chest with the hand not gripping the knife. "Like she reached in and cut out your heart."

Sam nodded. "You're not going to make anything better with the knife. Drop it and we'll talk about what's next."

"I'm sorry, Eddie." Stacey's voice was so filled with anguish Julia almost felt sorry for her. Except for the small matter that she'd been caught cheating on her husband. "I made a horrible mistake. It didn't mean anything."

"Hey—" Jon-o sputtered.

"I love you, Eddie." Stacey sobbed.

Eddie lowered the knife but Sam didn't relax. "Drop it and kick it to me," he ordered. "She loves you, Eddie."

"I love her, too." Eddie's voice was miserable. "But she cheated."

"We didn't even do it," Stacey called, and Julia wished the woman understood the concept of *too much information*. "He was drunk. Couldn't get it—"

Jon-o took an angry step toward her. "Shut your fat mouth, you liar. I was the best—"

For a second, Sam's attention switched to Jon-o and Stacey. In that instant, Eddie launched himself forward.

He lunged for Jon-o but Sam grabbed his arm. Julia screamed as Eddie stabbed wildly at Sam, who knocked the blade out of the man's hand then slammed him to the ground. Pete Butler, Sam's deputy, rushed forward and tossed Sam a pair of handcuffs before turning his attention to Jon-o, pushing him away from the action.

Stacey melted into a puddle on the ground. "Eddie, no," she whimpered. "Don't put handcuffs on my husband."

Sam got Eddie to his feet.

"Don't worry, honey." Stacey took a step forward. "I'll bail you out. I love you so much."

Tears ran down Eddie's face. "I love you, sugar-buns."

Stacey would have wrapped herself around her husband but Sam held up a hand. "Later, Stacey." Jon-o disappeared into the crowd and Sam yanked Eddie toward Pete. "Put him in the holding cell overnight. He can sober up."

Pete pointed to Sam's shoulder. Sam shook his head, so the deputy led Eddie toward the waiting squad car.

"We're done out here," Sam announced to the crowd. "Everyone head inside. There's a lot more money to be raised tonight."

After a quiet round of applause, people drifted toward

the gymnasium. A couple of men approached Sam, slapping him on the back.

"I told you he'd handle it," Joe said proudly from Julia's side.

"You did." Julia felt rooted to the spot where she stood. Her body felt as though it weighed a thousand pounds. She couldn't explain what she'd felt when Eddie had rushed at Sam with the knife. She'd swear she'd aged ten years in those few seconds.

"Nice going, son," Joe called.

Sam looked up and his gaze met Julia's. He gave her a small smile and her whole body began to shake. She walked toward him and threw her arms around his neck, burying her face in his shirt collar. He smelled sweet, like leftover cotton candy, and felt so undeniably strong, she could have wept. She wouldn't cry. She wasn't that much of an emotional basket case, but she squeezed her eyes shut for good measure.

She willed the trembling to stop. It started to as he rubbed his palm against her back.

"Hey," he said into her hair. "Not that I'm complaining about you wrapped around me, but it's okay. It was nothing. Eddie was too drunk to do any real damage, even if he'd wanted to."

She didn't know how long he held her. She was vaguely aware of people milling about, of Joe watching from nearby. Sam didn't seem in any hurry to let her go. She needed the strength of his body around hers to reassure her that he was truly all right.

When she was finally in control enough to open her eyes, she was shocked to see blood staining his shirt near the shoulder. "You're hurt." Her voice came out a croak.

He shook his head. "The blade nicked me. It's a scratch.

I'll stop by the hospital after we finish the paperwork to have it cleaned. Nothing more."

"He could have hurt you," she whispered, unable to take her eyes off his shoulder.

He tipped up her chin. His eyes were warm on hers, kind and understanding. "I'm okay. Nothing happened."

"It could have. Every day something *could* happen to you, Sam. Drug busts, drunken fights and who knows what else."

"I'm fine."

"I'm not. I can't stand knowing you're always at risk."

He looked over her shoulder to where Joe stood. When his eyes met hers again, they were cold and unreadable. He leaned in close to her ear. "Then it's a good thing this is a fake engagement. I'm not giving up my life for a woman."

Julia felt the air rush from her lungs. "I didn't say I wanted you to." She grabbed on to the front of his shirt as he moved to pull away. "I know this is fake. Sue me, but I was worried. Heaven forbid someone cares about you, Sam. Expects something from you. Maybe I shouldn't have—"

"Forget it." Sam kissed her cheek, but she knew it was because his father was still watching. "I have to go into the station and then to the hospital, so I'll be a while. Take Charlie home. We'll talk tomorrow."

"Don't do this," she whispered as he walked away, climbing into the police cruiser without looking back.

She knew this was fake. Because she'd never be stupid enough to fall in love with a man so irritating, annoying and unwilling to have a meaningful conversation about his feelings.

She turned to Joe. "At least he's okay. That's most important, right?"

"It's hard for him to be needed by someone," Joe said,

taking her arm and leading her back toward the high school.

Julia snorted. "Ya think?"

Rotating his shoulder where the nurse had cleaned his wound, Sam stepped out of the E.R. into the darkness. His father's car wasn't in front, so he sat on the bench near the entrance to wait.

He scrubbed his palms against his face, wondering how he'd made such a colossal mess of a night that had started off so well. Julia had looked beautiful, as always, and they'd had fun with Charlie at the carnival. He'd even survived his dad and her mother meeting and almost felt okay about her relationship with Ethan.

Then he'd put his foot in his mouth in a thousand different ways when she'd been concerned about his job. Hell, he couldn't name a cop's wife who didn't worry. He'd liked that she'd been worried, liked the feeling of being needed. It had also scared him and he'd pushed her away.

Like he pushed everyone away.

He was alone. Again. As always.

"Need a lift, Chief?"

He turned to see her standing a few feet away, the light from the hospital's entrance making her glow like an angel. Not that he knew whether angels glowed. He imagined they'd want to, if it meant they'd look like Julia Morgan.

"My dad's coming to get me. Where's Charlie?"

"He's having a sleepover with Grandma." She walked to the bench and sat next to him. "How's your shoulder?"

He shrugged, finding it difficult to concentrate with her thigh pressed against his leg. "Hurts worse after the nurse messed with it than when the knife grazed me."

She bit her lip when he said the word *knife*. "You're lucky it wasn't worse."

"I guess."

"Joe's not coming to get you."

"I may want to reconsider that ride."

"You may."

"Why are you here, Julia?"

She rocked back far enough to stuff her fingers under her legs. Lucky fingers. He'd give anything to trade places with her hands.

"Just because our engagement isn't real doesn't mean I can't worry about you. I'm human. I like you. Caring about friends is what people do."

"We're friends." He tried the word out in his mind and decided he liked it. Sam didn't have many real friends.

"I think so."

He couldn't resist asking, "With benefits?"

She continued to stare straight ahead but one side of her mouth kicked up. "That remains to be seen. You're not moving in the right direction with the bad 'tude earlier."

"Would it help if I said I was sorry?"

"Are you?"

With one finger, he traced a path down her arm, gently tugging on her wrist until she lifted her hand. He intertwined his fingers with hers. "Yes, I'm sorry. I'm sorry you were scared. I'm sorry I was a jerk."

"I know you don't owe me anything."

"I do owe you. So far, I'm the only one who's benefited from our arrangement. You wouldn't let me go to court with you. I made an enormous mess of trying to get your mind off the case and now you're here picking me up. What have I done to help you? Nothing."

"That's not true."

"It is. I want to help. I'm going to the final hearing with you."

"I—"

"No arguments."

She nodded. That was a start. "We can get people to submit affidavits on your behalf," he continued. "Character references for you. The girls from the salon will do it. I bet Ida Garvey would, too, now that her hair isn't bright pink. I want to hear you agree. I can help. You have to let me."

"My LD changes everything." She looked at him, her eyes fierce. He knew this moment meant something big.

"You have trouble reading," he said slowly. "And with numbers. It caused a lot of problems but you told me you're working with a specialist."

"My brain doesn't work right." She made the statement with conviction, as if daring him to disagree.

"Is that the clinical diagnosis? Your brain doesn't work right? I don't think so, sweetie."

"Don't 'sweetie' me. I'm stupid, and Jeff and his family know it. My brain is broken. It takes me twice as long as it should to read a simple letter. Why do you think I bring paperwork home from the salon so often? I spend all night checking and rechecking my work so I don't make mistakes."

"Everyone makes mistakes."

"You don't understand. But Jeff does. He knows how badly I want this to stay a secret." She bolted up from the bench, pacing back and forth in front of him. "So much of what the attorney is talking about stems from my LD. I've hidden it for years and now they're using it against me."

"Why keep it a secret?"

"Because—" she dragged out the word on a ragged breath "—if the people around me knew how dumb I am, they could and would take advantage of me. In Brevia, I can hide it. If I really get into a bind, my mom or Lainey can help. I don't want the whole town talking about it."

Something struck a chord deep within Sam. He knew

what it was like to put on a mask so people couldn't really see what was inside of you. He knew how it felt to be afraid you wouldn't measure up. But his demons were more easily buried than Julia's. The thought of how much time and energy she'd put into hiding this piece of herself made his heart ache.

She was smart, proud and brave. She'd spent years making everyone believe she didn't care, when the reality was that she cared more than she could admit. He could see it on her face, see the tension radiating through her body as she waited for him to judge her the way she'd been judging herself for years.

He stood and cupped her face between his hands. "You're not stupid."

She searched his eyes, as if willing the words to be true. "They're trying to use it against me, Sam. To prove that Charlie would be better off with them. Not only are they ready to lavish him with their version of lifestyles of the rich and famous, they're saying that if he has the same disorder…" Her voice caught and she bit her lip before continuing, "If I've given this to him, they have the resources to get him the best help."

"*You* are what's best for him." He used his thumb to wipe away a lone tear that trailed down her cheek then brought his lips to the spot, tasting the salt on her skin.

The automatic doors slid open and a hospital worker pushed a wheelchair into the night.

"Let's get out of here," Sam whispered.

Julia nodded, and he cradled her against him as they walked to her car.

"Let me drive," he said when she reached into her purse for the keys.

"You're the injured one." But when he took the keys from her hand, she didn't argue.

The streets were quiet. Julia didn't speak, but she held on to the hand he placed in her lap. He could imagine the thoughts running through her mind as she realized the secret she'd held close for so long was about to become public. She was wrung out emotionally, and he hated seeing it. All he wanted was to make her feel better, if only for a few moments.

He pulled into his driveway and turned off the ignition.

"I should go home," she said, releasing his fingers. "You need to rest."

Rest was the last thing on Sam's mind. He might not be a master with words but he knew he wasn't going to let her go tonight. If he couldn't tell her how amazing she was and have her believe it, he could damn well show her.

He came around to open her car door and draw her out, lacing his fingers with hers once again.

"I need to go," she repeated, her voice small.

Without a word, he led her up onto the porch and unlocked his front door. He turned and pulled her to him, slanting his mouth over hers. For a moment she froze, then she melted against him, the spark between them flaring into an incendiary fire.

He kissed her jaw and the creamy skin of her throat, whispering, "Stay with me."

She nodded as he nipped at her earlobe and, not letting her go, reached back to push open the door and drag them both through. He kicked it shut and tugged on the hem of her T-shirt.

"This. Off. Now."

"Bossy," she said breathlessly. Through his desire, he heard the confidence return to her tone and was so glad for it, he could have laughed out loud.

Just as suddenly, he couldn't make a sound as she pulled the soft cotton over her head and was left bathed in moonlight wearing only a lacy black bra and jeans slung low on her hips.

Sweet mercy.

He knew she was beautiful, but he'd been with beautiful women before. Watching her watch him, though, her eyes smoky and wanting, was almost his undoing.

He flicked one thin strap off her shoulder, then the other, not quite exposing her completely but giving him a view of more creamy flesh. He traced the line of fabric across the tops of her breasts and his body grew heavy at her intake of breath.

She wrapped her hand around his finger and lifted it to her mouth, kissing the tip softly. "You, now," she commanded, her voice husky.

Sam was happy to comply, and he threw his shirt onto the nearby couch. She stepped forward and, in one fluid motion, reached behind her to unhook her bra. It fell to the floor between them. Then she pressed herself against his chest and trailed her lips over his wounded shoulder.

"If it matters," he said, his voice hoarse, "that's not the part that hurts."

He felt her smile against him. "We'll get to that. All in good time, Chief. All in good time."

From Sam's point of view, that time was now. He bent his head and took her mouth, kissing her as he reached between them to unfasten her jeans. He dropped to his knees in front of her, kissing the curve of her belly. She smelled like sin and sunshine, and the mix made him dizzy with need.

"I want you, Julia Morgan." He lifted his head so he could look into her eyes. "I want you," he repeated. "All of you. Just the way you are."

Her lips parted, and he saw trust and vulnerability flash in her eyes. He wanted that, wanted all of this. For the first time in his life, he wanted to be a man someone could depend on for the long haul.

He wanted to be a real hero.

"I'm going to take care of you," he whispered.

She smiled at him and shimmied her hips so that her jeans slipped off them.

"What are you waiting for?" she asked, and he straightened, capturing her mouth again.

Sam broke the kiss long enough to lead her the few steps to the couch. He stripped off his jeans then eased his body over hers, relishing the feel of skin on skin. She fit perfectly under him, as he'd guessed she would.

He savored every touch, taking the time to explore her body with his fingers and mouth. Her answering passion filled him with a desire he'd never imagined before tonight. He finally made her his, entering her with an exquisite slowness before his need for her took over and they moved together in a perfect rhythm.

"You are amazing," he whispered as he held her gaze.

"You're not so bad yourself," she answered, but her eyes were cloudy with passion.

"I'm going to prove how very good I am." He smiled then nipped at the soft skin of her earlobe. "All night long."

Chapter Eleven

Wow.

Hours later, Julia's brain registered that one syllable.

"Wow," Sam murmured against her hair, clearly still trying to catch his breath.

She knew the feeling. She'd had good sex in her life—maybe even great a couple of times. This night had blown away her every expectation about what intimacy felt like when it was exactly right. She wanted to believe it was because she'd been on a long hiatus.

If she admitted the truth, Sam had been worth a two-year wait. Her body felt boneless, as if she never wanted to move from where she lay stretched across him, the short hair on his chest tickling her bare skin.

The unfamiliar feeling of contentment jolted her back into reality. Their relationship was precarious enough, sometimes hot and often cold enough to give her frostbite. He challenged her, irritated her and filled her with such incredible need, she wondered how she'd walk away when the business part of their arrangement was over.

That sobering thought in mind, she rolled off him. He automatically tucked the light duvet in around her. They'd made it to his bedroom.

Eventually.

After the couch in his living room. And the stairs. The stairs? She hadn't even known that was possible, let alone that it would be downright amazing.

It was still dark and she couldn't make out much more than the outlines of furniture around the room and the fact that his bed was enormous. It suited him.

She glanced at the glowing numbers of the digital clock on the nightstand next to the bed. He shifted, propping himself on one elbow and wrapping the other arm around her waist.

"Don't go."

She tilted her head away, his face in shadow from the moonlight slanting through the bedroom window. She couldn't see his eyes and hoped hers were hidden, as well.

How did he know she was getting ready to bolt? Julia had never been much of a cuddler. The emotional boundaries she put around herself often manifested in physical limits, as well.

She looked at the ceiling. Even if she couldn't see his eyes, she knew his gaze was intense. "As fun as this was…"

His soft chuckle rumbled in the quiet, making her insides tingle again. She'd done a lot of tingling tonight.

"Fun," he repeated.

"We've got chemistry."

He laughed again.

"This isn't funny." She didn't want to make more of this than it was. She'd start talking and end up embarrassing herself with romantic declarations about how much she liked—more than liked, if she admitted the truth—being with Sam, both in the bedroom and out of it. He was the first man she felt wanted her for her, not what she looked like or an image she portrayed. It was both liberating and frightening to reveal her true self to someone.

"*You're* funny." He kissed the tip of her nose and pulled her tighter against the length of him. "And smart." He kissed one cheek. "And sexy as hell." Then the other. "I want you to spend the night." His lips met hers.

She broke the kiss. "I think we've about wrapped things up here."

He traced the seam of her mouth with his tongue. "We've only gotten started."

Julia felt her resolve disappear. She knew it was a mistake but she couldn't make her body move an inch. "Are you sure?"

"I've never been more sure."

It had been ages since Julia'd wanted to be with someone as much as she did Sam. "I guess that would be okay."

"Okay?" He tickled her belly and she wriggled in response.

"More than okay."

"That's what I thought."

She expected him to kiss her again, but instead he snuggled in behind her, smoothing her hair across the pillow.

"Sleep," he told her.

"Oh. I thought you wanted to…"

"I do. Later."

Her spine stiffened. "I've never been much for spooning."

"I can tell." His finger drew circles along her back until she began to relax. "Why did you pick me up tonight?"

"I don't like pillow talk, either," she muttered, and he laughed again.

He didn't press her for more, just continued to trace patterns along her skin. The silence was companionable, the room still and soft in the night. She stretched her head against the pillow, relishing the feeling of being surrounded by Sam. His scent lingered in the sheets, the combination of outdoors and spice that continued to make her head spin.

"Okay," she said after a few minutes, "I kind of get why all those women were hung up on you."

"What women?"

She lightly jabbed her elbow into his stomach. "Your Three Strikes Sam fan club. You're pretty good at this stuff."

"Only with you."

"I don't believe that."

"No changing the subject. I was a jerk tonight. You gave me another chance. Thank you."

She took a deep breath. "I can use all the help I can get. There's no use hiding it."

"You shouldn't hide anything," he said softly.

"I saw Lexi Preston at the carnival."

"Your ex's attorney?"

"She was there checking up on me, I think. Lots of stories to be dished from my former frenemies." She gave a sad laugh. "Lexi thinks they wouldn't be so hard on me now if they'd known what I was dealing with back then."

"Maybe you wouldn't be so hard on yourself if you told the truth," Sam suggested.

"Could be," she said with a yawn. It had been a long day. A light shiver ran through her and he pulled her closer. "Good Lord, you're a furnace." She snuggled in closer. "My own personal space heater."

"Whatever you need me to be," Sam agreed.

That was the last thing Julia heard him say before she drifted off to sleep.

She woke a few hours later and they made love again in the hazy predawn light. His eyes never left hers as they moved together, and Julia knew this night changed what was between them, even if they both acted as though it didn't.

She'd wanted him since the first time she'd laid eyes on him, no matter how much she tried to deny it. Now that she knew how good it could be, she wasn't sure how she'd ever adjust back to real life. She had to, she reminded herself, even as she snuggled in closer to him. This night was a fringe benefit of their business arrangement, and if she let herself forget that, she knew she'd lose her heart along the way.

"You're finally ready to get back into action?"

Sam ripped open a sugar packet and dumped it into his coffee. "I haven't been sitting on a beach sipping fruity drinks for the past couple of years."

"You know what I mean."

He watched his brother shovel another bite of pancakes into his mouth. Scott always could eat like a horse. Not that Scott was a kid anymore. He was twenty-nine and a good two inches taller than Sam's six feet. They both had the Callahan blue eyes and linebacker build, but Scott had their mother's olive coloring and dark hair. Sometimes a look or gesture from Scott could bring back a memory of their mom so vividly it was as if she was still with them.

"I'm glad you called me." Scott downed the rest of his orange juice and signaled the waitress for another. "I felt real bad about what happened."

"About having sex with my fiancée?"

Scott flinched. "Pretty much. Although you have to know by now I wasn't the first."

Sam gave a curt nod. "I'm still not going to thank you, if that's what you're getting at."

"I'm not."

"I didn't come here to talk about Jenny or rehash the past."

"Dad called last week. He told me you're engaged again."

Sam looked out the window of the café into the sunny morning. He'd met Scott in a town halfway between Brevia and D.C., far enough away that he wouldn't see any familiar faces. It had been almost a week since the night of the carnival. He'd seen Julia and Charlie almost every day. Sometimes it was under the guise of making their relationship look real. He'd taken them to lunch and to a neighboring playground, stopped by the salon when he had a break during the day.

He was happiest when it was just the three of them. He'd pick up dinner after his shift, or she'd cook and they'd take the dog for a walk, and then he'd help get Charlie ready for bed. They agreed if he was going to be a presence at the mediation or future court dates, it would be smart for Charlie to feel comfortable with him.

Sam hadn't expected how much playing family would fill up the empty parts of him. He counted the hours each day until he could lift Charlie in his arms and even more the moments until he could pull Julia to him.

He took another drink of coffee then answered, "It's complicated. But I'm engaged."

Complicated might be the understatement of the century where Julia was concerned. She'd opened up to him and shared her deepest secret. She trusted him with her son, her dreams for the future, and it scared him to death. He steered their conversations away from the topic of his work, no matter how often she asked about details of his day.

After the scene at the carnival, he didn't want to see

worry in her gaze or argue about the risks he took. It reminded him too much of his parents. Even so, he knew he was going to go through hell when their arrangement was finished. He'd called Scott last week and set up this meeting to talk about a new job away from Brevia, but now his purpose was twofold.

"I need some information on a family from Ohio, very prominent in the area. Dennis and Maria Johnson."

"What kind of information?" Scott asked.

"Whatever you've got. My fiancée, Julia, has a kid with their son and they're making waves with the current custody arrangement. They've got a lot of money and influence and are pulling out the stops to make her life hell. From my experience, people who want to throw their weight around like that have done it before. I'm guessing they have some skeletons from past skirmishes. I want to know what they are."

Scott nodded. "I've got a couple of friends up there. I'll make a call, see what I can find out." He stabbed another bite of pancake then pointed his fork at Sam. "This Julia must be special. You always play by the rule book. It's not like you to fight dirty."

"I'm fighting to win. There's too much at stake not to."

"I'd like to meet her."

Sam felt his whole body tense. His voice lowered to a controlled growl. "Stay away from her, Scott. She isn't like Jenny."

Scott held up his hands, palms up. "I get it. I get it."

The waitress brought a second juice and refilled Sam's coffee. Scott winked at her and she practically tripped backing away from the table.

Sam wanted to roll his eyes. "I see you haven't changed. Still chasing tail all over the place?"

"Why mess with a system that works so damn well? I'm

happy. The ladies are happy. All good. I wasn't cut out for commitment." He lifted one eyebrow. "Until I got Dad's call, I would have guessed you weren't, either."

"Dad thinks love makes the world go round."

"Dad's gone soft and it gives me the creeps."

"Amen to that."

"When you texted, you asked about openings at headquarters." Scott had worked for the U.S. Marshals Service since he'd gotten out of the army.

Sam took a drink of coffee. "You got anything?" It had been easy to imagine a future in Brevia when he'd only been the police chief, before it had started to really feel like home. Before Julia.

Scott nodded. "Maybe, but I don't get it. Why do you want to look at a new job if you're getting married? Being a cop is tough enough on a relationship. The Marshals Service would be the kiss of death. What we do doesn't compute with the minivan lifestyle."

"I told you, it's complicated."

"You're gonna run," Scott said, his voice quiet.

"I'm not running anywhere." Sam felt pressure build behind his eyes. Despite being younger, wild and reckless, Scott always had an uncanny ability to read Sam. It drove him nuts. "You said yourself the Callahans aren't meant for commitment. It may be a matter of time before she sees that. It'll be easier on us both if I'm not around for the fallout."

Scott nodded. "That's more like the brother I know and love. For a minute I thought Dad had brainwashed you with all his hug-it-out bull. Do you know he called my boss to see if he could do a seminar on using emotional intelligence in the field?"

"What's emotional intelligence?"

"Beats me," Scott said with a shrug. "But I'm sure as

hell not interested in finding out. Did you fill out the paperwork I sent you?"

Sam slid an envelope across the table. "It's got my résumé with it."

"We'd be lucky to have you," Scott said solemnly. "I'd be honored to work together."

Sam's phone buzzed, alerting him that he had a voicemail message. Coverage was spotty in this area, so he wasn't sure when the call had come in. He looked at his phone and saw six messages waiting.

"We did have some good times," he admitted as he punched the keypad to retrieve them. He wasn't on duty, so he couldn't imagine why anyone would need him so urgently.

"Here's to many more." Scott lifted his juice glass in a toast.

Sam listened to the first message and felt the blood drain from his face. He stood, tossing a twenty on the table. "I need to go."

"Everything okay?" Scott asked, mopping up syrup with his last bite of pancake.

Sam was already out the door.

Chapter Twelve

Sam was about forty-five minutes from Brevia. He made it to the hospital in less than thirty.

"Charlie Morgan," he said to the woman at the front desk of the E.R., and she pointed to a room halfway down the hall. He stopped to catch his breath then pushed open the door.

A nurse stood talking to Julia as Vera held Charlie in her lap on the bed. A bright blue cast covered the boy's left wrist.

All three women looked up as Sam walked in. Julia stood so stiff he imagined she might crack in half if he touched her. The urge to ease some of her worry engulfed him.

"Sam," Charlie said, a little groggily, waving his casted arm.

"Hey, buddy." Sam came forward and bent down in front of the boy. "I like your new super arm."

Charlie giggled softly and reached out for Sam to hold him. Vera's eyes widened but she let Sam scoop him up. With Charlie in his arms, he turned to Julia.

"Are you okay?" he asked, wrapping his free arm around her shoulders.

She nodded but remained tense. "The nurse is giving me discharge papers. We've been here for over two hours." Her eyes searched his. "I couldn't reach you."

"I'm sorry," he said simply. "I was out of cell range."

She looked as if she wanted to say more but the nurse cleared her throat. "I've got instructions on bathing him with the cast," she said, holding out a slip of paper. "Take a look and let me know if you have questions."

Gingerly, Julia took the piece of paper. She stared at it, her forehead puckering as her mouth tightened into a thin, frustrated line.

Vera rose to stand beside him. Julia looked up and met his gaze, her eyes miserable. He tugged the paper from her fingers. "Why don't you go over what we need to do?" he said to the nurse. "Just to be on the safe side. We'll take the instructions home, too."

As the woman explained the procedure, Sam felt Vera squeeze his shoulder. "Thank you," she whispered then slipped out of the room.

When the nurse finished her explanation, Julia asked a couple of questions, and then the woman left them alone. Charlie's head drooped on Sam's shoulder and his eyes drifted shut.

"I can take him," Julia said, holding out her hands but keeping her gaze focused on her son.

"I've got him." Sam tipped her chin up so she had to look him in the eye. "I'm sorry, Jules. I'm sorry I wasn't here."

"You don't owe us anything." She picked up the diaper bag from the chair next to the bed. "I want to go home."

Sam followed her into the hall and toward the elevator. She didn't say a word until they were in the parking lot. "I shouldn't have called you. We're not your problem." She took Charlie and settled him in the car seat.

"I'm sorry," Sam said again. A warm breeze played with the ends of her hair. Spring was in full swing in the Smoky Mountains. He wondered how old Charlie needed to be to hold a tiny fishing rod. There were so many things he wanted to do with her and Charlie before their time together ended. Before she figured out she should have never depended on him in the first place. He couldn't stand the thought that today might be the first nail in his coffin. "I know you were scared. I wish I had been here earlier."

She jerked her head in response and he saw tears fill her eyes. "I put the toy car together—one of those ones a toddler pushes around." She swiped at her cheeks. "I swear I followed the directions, but when he knocked it against the kitchen table, it fell apart. Charlie went down over it and landed on his arm. His scream was the worst sound I've ever heard."

Sam wrapped his arms around her. "It was an accident. Not your fault."

She let him hold her but stayed ramrod straight, obviously trying to manage her fear and anxiety. "It *was* my fault. I'm sure I read the directions wrong and Charlie got hurt because of it. Because of me!"

She yanked away from him, pacing next to the car. "Maybe the Johnsons are doing the right thing." Her eyes searched his. "I felt like an idiot when the nurse gave me his discharge papers. Do you know how long it takes me to figure out the right dose of medicine for him? How many things I have to memorize and hope I don't mess up? He's still a baby, Sam. What's going to happen when he gets into school and needs help with his homework? When he wants me to read real books to him? He's going to know his mother is stupid."

"Stop it." Sam grabbed her wrists and pulled her to him, forcing her to look up at him. "Learning disabilities don't make you stupid."

"You don't know how people have looked at me my whole life. It will kill me if Charlie someday looks at me like that." She took a deep, shuddering breath and Sam felt the fight go out of her.

"He's not going to, Julia. He's going to see you like I do. Like your family does. Like a brave, intelligent, fearless woman who doesn't let anything hold her back."

"Really?" She gave him a sad smile. "Because I don't see anyone around here who fits your description." She shrugged out of his embrace and opened the door of her car. "I need to get him home. Thanks for coming, Sam."

"I'll meet you at your apartment."

"You don't need to—"

"I'm going to pick up dinner and a change of clothes and I'll be there within the hour. For once, don't argue with me. Please."

She nodded. "Nice touch with the *please*."

He watched her drive away then headed to his own car. He had to make Julia see how much she had to offer her son. That was the key to her winning the custody battle, no matter what crazy accusations her ex-boyfriend's family threw out. If he could make her believe in herself, he knew she was strong enough to overcome any odds.

She'd win and he'd get the hell out of her life. His heart was lacking what it took to give her the life she deserved. He knew for certain that if she got too close to him, he'd only hurt her and Charlie. Just like he had today.

Sam was like a tin man, without a real heart. He might have been born with one but it had shriveled into nothing when his mother died. He couldn't risk loving and being hurt like that again.

Julia was standing over Charlie's crib when the doorbell rang. Casper growled softly from his place next to her.

"No bark," she whispered, amazed at how the dog seemed to know to keep quiet while Charlie was asleep.

She padded to the door.

"How's Charlie?" Sam asked when she opened it.

She nodded and stepped back. "Sleeping soundly."

Casper gave Sam a full-tooth grin and wagged his stubby tail. "No home for this guy yet?" Sam asked, reaching down to scratch behind the dog's ears. "You need to learn to keep your choppers hidden, buddy."

"I'm adopting him."

Sam's eyebrows rose. "Kind of a small place for a big dog."

"Charlie loves him." She didn't want to admit how much of her decision was based on her need to make something work, even if it was rescuing a stray animal. She took the carryout bag from his hand and turned for the kitchen.

Sam grabbed her around the waist and pulled her against him. "You've got a sharp tongue but a soft heart," he whispered against her ear.

"Wicked elbow, too," she said and jabbed him in the stomach.

He grunted a laugh and released her. "Why is it you don't want people to see how much you care?"

She busied herself pulling plates out of the cabinet. "I care about Charlie. That's enough for me."

"Ida Garvey told me you volunteered to do hair for the middle-school dance team's competition next month."

"Did you see those girls last year? It was updo à la light socket. I know Southerners love big hair but jeez." She set the table and took out the food. "Is this from Carl's?"

"Double burgers with cheese. Hope you approve."

"Perfect."

"I also heard you go to the retirement home once a week and do the ladies' hair."

She shrugged. "A lot of those gals were once customers at the Hairhouse, and their daughters and granddaughters still are. It's good for my business."

"It's because you care."

Why was Sam giving her the third degree on her volunteer hours? "You're making too much of it. I do things that benefit me. Ask anyone around here. I have a long history of being in it for myself."

"That's what you want people to believe."

"That *is* what they believe." She picked up a fry and pointed it at him, feeling her temper starting to rise. "What does it matter?"

He folded himself into the seat across from her. "I want you to understand you're not alone. You have a community here that would rally around you if you gave them a chance."

She took a bite of burger, her eyes narrowing. What the hell did Sam Callahan know about her part in this community? "Are you seriously giving me a lecture on letting people in, Mr. I-am-a-rock-I-am-an-island? You could take your own advice."

He frowned. "I'm a part of this community."

"No, you're not. You circle around the perimeter and insert yourself when someone needs a helping hand. No one really understands how much you give or the toll it takes on you. You're always 'on.' You're terrified of being alone with your empty soul, so you spend a little time with a woman. You get her to fall in love with you so you can hold on to the affection without having to offer any in return. People know what kind of cookies you like, so their single daughters can bake you a batch. But you're as closed off as I am in your own way."

He got up from the table so quickly she thought he was going to storm out. Instead, he grabbed two beers from her fridge, opened them and handed one to her. "We're quite a pair," he said softly, clinking the top of his bottle against hers. "Both so damned independent we'd rather fake an engagement than actually deal with real feelings."

"It's better that way," she answered and took a long drink.

"I used to think so," he said, and his eyes were so intense on hers she lost her breath for a moment. "Do you ever wonder what it would feel like to let someone in?"

She didn't need to because she already had, with him. *Oh, no.* Where had that thought come from?

It was true. Without realizing it or intending to, Julia had let Sam not only into her life but into her heart, as well.

She was in love with him.

She stood, gripping the edge of the counter as if it was the only solid thing in her world. She'd called him today when Charlie had gotten hurt before she'd even called her mother. She loved him and she needed him. Julia didn't know which scared her more.

They had a deal, and she was pretty sure Sam was the type of guy who kept his word. He'd help her get through the custody battle as much as he could, but that didn't mean… It didn't mean what her heart wanted it to.

"I don't have room to let anyone in but Charlie," she said in the most casual tone she could muster. "There's not enough of me left for anyone else to hold on to. Everything I can give belongs to him."

"I never had that much to begin with," Sam said from the table.

When Julia felt as if she could turn around without revealing her true emotions, she smiled at him. "That's why we're a perfect match. Hollow to the core."

Sam tossed her a sexy smile. "I know a good way to fill the void."

She tried to ignore the flash of electricity that raced along her spine at the suggestion in his words. "It's been a long day."

He stood and she wrapped her arms around her waist. "Really long."

"It could be an even longer night if you play your cards right."

She couldn't help the grin that spread across her face. "The only game I play is Old Maid."

"I'll teach you."

"No, thanks."

He reached out his hand, palm up, but didn't touch her. "You want to be alone tonight? Say the word and I'll go. I'm not going to push you." One side of his mouth quirked. "No matter how much you want me to."

She shut her eyes, a war raging inside of her. Letting him go was the smart thing to do, the best way to protect what little hold she still had on her heart.

"Tell me to go, Julia."

"Stay," she whispered and found herself enveloped in his arms, his mouth pressed hard on hers. Their tongues mingled and she let her hands slide up his back, underneath his shirt, reveling in the corded muscles that tightened at her touch.

"You feel like heaven," he said as he trailed kisses along her throat, her skin igniting hotter at every touch.

"Bedroom," she said on a ragged breath. "Now."

She gave a small squeak as he lifted her into his arms as if she weighed nothing. It felt good to be swept off her feet, even for the few moments he carried her down the hall.

She glanced at the door to Charlie's room. She hadn't had a man in her bed since she'd gotten pregnant with her son. It felt new and strange.

"It's going to be a challenge," Sam whispered.

"What?"

"Keeping you quiet with what I have planned."

"Oh." Her heart skipped a beat at the promise in his voice.

He laid her across the bed then followed her down, kissing her until her senses spun with desire.

"Too many clothes." She tugged on his shirt.

He stood, pulling the T-shirt over his head and shrugging out of his faded cargo shorts. Julia's breath caught again. His body was perfect, muscles rippling—actually rippling—as he bent forward and caught the waistband of her shorts with two fingers. She lifted herself to meet him as he undressed her, sliding his soft fingers across her skin.

She tried to speed their pace but Sam wouldn't have it, taking his time to explore every inch of her. He murmured endearments against her flesh, making it impossible for her to keep her emotions out of the equation.

When he finally entered her, Julia practically hummed with desire. They moved together, climbing to the highest peaks of ecstasy.

Later, as he held her, she tried to convince herself that it was only a physical connection, but her heart burned for him as much as her body did.

When she finally woke, light poured through the curtains. Julia glanced at the clock then bounded out of bed and across the hall. Charlie never slept past seven and it was already nine-thirty. Panic gripped her.

Her son's crib was empty. She heard voices in the kitchen and took a deep breath. Sam sat at the table next to Charlie's high chair, giving him spoonfuls of oatmeal.

Charlie waved his sippy cup when he saw her, squealing with delight. Casper trotted up, another big grin spread across his face.

Julia noticed the two paper coffee cups on the counter.

Sam followed her gaze. "We took the dog out to do his business and grabbed coffee and muffins. Charlie picked blueberry for you."

She dropped a kiss on Charlie's forehead. "How do you feel, sweet boy?" she asked, and he babbled a response to her. Her fingers brushed over the cast on his arm, but he didn't seem bothered by it. She sent up a silent prayer of thanks that he was okay.

She turned to Sam, who looked rumpled, sleepy and absolutely irresistible as he stirred the soupy oatmeal with a plastic spoon. "What time did he get up?"

"I heard him talking to himself around sunrise-thirty," he said with a smile.

Julia grimaced. "He's an early riser. You should have woken me."

"You were sleeping soundly. I figure you don't get too many mornings off, so…"

"Thanks." She leaned down to kiss him, and he pulled her between his thighs into a quick hug. "For everything. This morning and last night."

"More," Charlie yelled, and Sam shifted so he could give the boy another bite.

Julia stepped to the counter and took a long drink of coffee, and then she dug in the bag for a muffin.

This was too easy, she thought, as she watched Sam make faces at Charlie while he fed him, her son laughing and playing peekaboo with his cup. It felt too right. This was what she wanted, for Charlie and for herself. A family. This was what she'd never have with Sam. He'd made it clear to her that he didn't want a family. Now or ever. The thought was like a swift kick to her gut.

"I should get ready," she said, realizing her tone must have been too harsh when he glanced at her, a question in his eyes.

"I can stay while you shower," he offered.

She wanted to refuse. She knew she should push him out of her house and her life before it became harder to think of letting him go. But that would give too much away. Whether it was Old Maid or some other game, Julia did one thing well: playing her cards close to the vest.

"That would be great." She headed for the bathroom. By the time she was out, Sam had dressed, made her bed and cleaned up the kitchen. Charlie sat watching *Sesame Street,* cuddled with Casper on the couch as Sam leaned against the back of it.

"When is the next meeting?"

She sighed. "Two days from now."

"I'll drive with you."

She nodded, unable to put into words what that meant to her.

"My dad left a message this morning. He wants to take us to dinner tonight."

"I can do that."

"Along with your mom."

"Uh-oh."

"You can say that again. If those two are plotting…"

"Do you think they suspect anything?"

He shook his head. "They want to talk about wedding plans."

Julia's stomach lurched. "That's bad."

Sam pushed away from the couch. "We'll make it work. We've come this far."

He brushed his lips against hers, a soft touch but it still made her stomach quiver. "Five-thirty. Do you want me to pick you up?"

"I'll have to get Charlie from the sitter's first. I'll meet you there."

He kissed her again. "Have a good day, Julia."

He made those five little words sound like a caress.

"You, too," she muttered and stepped back.

"I'll see you later, buddy." Sam bent and ruffled Charlie's hair, the gesture so natural Julia felt herself melt all over again.

Charlie's fist popped out of his mouth. "'Bye, Dada," he said, not taking his eyes from the television.

Sam straightened slowly.

"He didn't mean anything," Julia said with a forced laugh, not wanting to reveal how disconcerted she felt.

"I know," Sam said softly.

"He knows you're not his dad. He doesn't even understand what that word means. It's something he sees on TV. A word for men. It isn't—"

"Julia." He cut her off, his hand chopping through the air. "It's okay."

But it wasn't okay. Sam was spooked. She knew by the way he didn't turn to her again. He lifted his hand to wave, and with a stilted "See you later," he was gone.

Chapter Thirteen

Sam was freaked out. He took another drink of his beer and glanced around the crowd at Carl's, reliving the pure terror he'd felt this morning.

In his career as a police officer, he'd had guns and knives pulled on him, dealt with drug dealers, prostitutes and an assortment of random losers. He didn't lose his cool or let his guard down. The danger and risk of the job never rattled him.

But one word from a toddler had shaken him to his core. Charlie'd called him Dada. Although Julia had tried to play it off, he knew that she was affected by it, too. He'd heard it in her tone. Not that he'd been able to do much talking, afraid his voice would crack under the weight of the conflicting emotions warring inside him.

Sam had never planned on being a father. Even when he'd been engaged to Jenny, neither of them had wanted kids. That was one of the things that had made him propose, even when he'd had the nagging sense something wasn't right in their relationship. It wasn't every day a guy found a woman who wasn't itching to have babies.

Sam liked kids, but he knew he didn't have what it took to be a decent father. He lacked the emotional depth to put someone else's needs before his own. He believed he was incapable of feeling something, much like his own father had been after his mother's death.

Charlie made him want to change, to be a better man.

He loved the feeling of that boy cuddled against him, his small head nestled in the crook of Sam's neck. He loved watching him follow the silly dog around and vice versa. He especially loved seeing Julia with Charlie, how happy it made her to be with her son.

He hadn't understood that bond when Charlie was a newborn. When he'd seen Julia with the small bundle after the boy's birth, Sam had run the other way. Part of him might have known instinctively how much he'd want to be a part of their world.

That was impossible. He could help her fight for her son, but he didn't have any more to give. He understood the look in her eyes when she'd thought he was in danger. He remembered the same fear in his mother's eyes each time the phone rang while his father was on duty. Her fear and worry had eventually turned into resentment.

He wouldn't give up who he was and he couldn't ask Julia to be a part of his life. He wouldn't risk what it could do to her. He knew Julia was stronger than his mother had ever been, but the life of cop's wife could wreck the strongest woman, no two ways about it.

He'd miss her like crazy, though. Already he could feel the loss of the two of them and he wasn't even gone.

"Okay, let's do this." Julia sat down at the table, her

posture rigid. Her eyes darted around as if scoping escape routes. "They're not here yet?"

Sam shook his head. "Did you have a good day?" He reached across the table to take her hand but she snatched it away.

"No use for the small talk. Save it for the audience."

Despite the fact she'd never truly been his, Sam wished for the way it had been before this morning, when she'd been unguarded and happy to be with him. He glanced around at the crowded restaurant. "There's always an audience in Brevia. Where's Charlie?"

"His sitter had an appointment, so I had him at the salon this afternoon. Lainey is watching him tonight. I thought…it's simpler without him here. We should limit the amount of time he spends with you. So that he doesn't get too attached and all." Her eyes flashed, daring him to argue with her. She was in full mama-bear mode tonight. It made him want her all the more.

Sam's gut twisted at the thought of not spending time with Charlie. "He's an amazing boy, Julia."

"He's great," she agreed distractedly. Her fingers played with the napkin on the table.

He gave a short laugh. "I didn't realize how quiet my life was until you came along."

She glanced toward the front of the restaurant. "Where do you think they are? I want to get this over with."

"My dad and your mom are coming to discuss wedding plans. You look like you can't stand to be in the same room as me." He extended his ankle and pressed it against her shin. "Relax."

She snatched her leg away, her knee banging on the underside of the table. She grabbed the water glass before it tumbled over. "I can't relax," she said between clenched teeth. "This whole thing was a mistake. You're in our lives temporarily, and now Charlie is developing feelings for you. It has to end, Sam."

He swallowed the panic rising in his throat. "You don't mean tonight?"

"Why not?" she countered. "The sooner the better."

Hell, no, he screamed inside his head.

"I don't think that's prudent at this time, Julia," he told her, his voice calm and measured. "I don't want Charlie hurt, but our business arrangement is helping all of us in the long run. You're so close to a ruling, and my dad should be heading back to Boston within the week. Stick it out, Jules. I promise it'll be worth it."

"Business arrangement," she repeated softly. "You still consider this a business arrangement?"

Something in the way she looked at him made him uneasy, but she had to know what he meant. He was doing this for her benefit—at least that was what he tried to tell himself.

"We talked about it last night. You and I are built the same way, and it isn't for emotional connections. But you can't deny our chemistry, and Charlie is a great kid. We're friends and that doesn't have to change. I provide the stability you need. Don't throw it away now."

She bit down on her lip and studied him, as if trying to gain control of her emotions. "I can't believe…" she began, but she was cut off when Sam's dad came up behind her.

"Sorry we're late," he boomed, taking Julia's hand and placing a loud kiss on her fingers. "You're looking fantastic as usual, my dear. So good to see you again."

Vera's gaze traveled between the two of them. "Is everything okay?" she asked, studying Julia.

The color had drained from Julia's face. Her eyes had grown large and shadowed. Sam wished he could pull her aside and finish their conversation. He got the feeling he'd made a huge misstep.

"We're fine," Julia said, taking a sip of water. She stood and hugged Joe then her mother. "Just working out details. You know."

Sam watched her gaze travel up and down her mother. "Are you all right, Mom?" she asked slowly.

"Never better," Vera said, smoothing her blouse.

"Why is your shirt buttoned wrong?"

Sam looked at his father, who had the decency to turn a bright shade of pink. Joe and Vera broke into a fit of giggles. Sam didn't know Vera well, but she'd never struck him as much of a giggler.

"I'll head to the little girls' room and adjust this." She swatted Joe playfully on the arm as she passed. "You old devil."

"You've got to be kidding." Julia followed her mother toward the back of the restaurant.

Joe took the seat across from Sam and gave him a hearty pat on the back. "How's it going, Sammy? Wedding stress getting to your girl?"

Sam's temper flared. "Finding out her mother is having sex with you might be getting to her."

Joe looked genuinely confused. "Really? I thought you two would be happy for us." A grin spread across his face. "Who knows, maybe we'll beat you to the altar."

"You've known Vera about a minute, Dad. That's not funny."

"Who's joking?" Joe opened his arms, lifting them toward the ceiling. "Some things are destined to be."

Sam needed a bigger supply of aspirin if he was going to continue to spend time with his dad. He pushed his fingers through his hair and took a breath. "Dad, tell me you aren't serious. I swear I'll throw you in the cruiser and deposit you at the state line if you keep talking like this. If you have an itch you want to scratch with Vera, that's one thing. But marriage? No way."

"Let me tell you something." His father leaned forward. "I'm not a young man anymore, in case you haven't noticed. I spent a lot of years sad and lonely after your mother died. Vera knows what it's like to lose a spouse. She knows what it feels like to be alone and crave something more."

"Vera is hardly ever alone." Sam shook his head. "She dates, Dad. A lot."

"From what I understand, you dated a lot before Julia. Did it make you feel less lonely?"

Sam opened his mouth then snapped it shut again. His father was right. All the women he'd dated when he first got to Brevia had just been passing time. He'd never felt connected to any of them. He'd always been on his own.

Until Julia.

"I'm going to ask her to marry me," Joe said. "It was love at first sight, and I'm smart enough not to let her get away."

"Do you think she'll say yes? I'd hope to hell she's smart enough to know not to be swept off her feet."

"What's wrong with being swept away? But don't worry. We won't plan a wedding until after you and Julia are settled. Neither of us wants to take anything away from you kids."

"That's so reassuring," Sam ground out. He scrubbed his hand over his face. "You don't have to marry her. Date for a little while. Take your time. Why rush into anything?"

"Life is short. It can turn on a dime. I'm taking every opportunity for happiness I can get. Just like you and Julia."

Nothing like him and Julia, Sam thought. This was a

disaster. His father's gushing romanticism made him look like an emotional robot.

He had to believe they were on the same page. She didn't want anything more from him than he was able to give.

Let his father rush blindly into marriage for love. It wasn't going to make him happy. If Joe hadn't learned that lesson from Sam's mother, Sam definitely had.

His plan was far more prudent. Enjoy each other but still protect his heart. It would be better for everyone in the long run.

The next day Julia cradled the phone between her cheek and shoulder as she sat in her office at the salon. She'd spent an hour staring blindly at the figures dancing before her on the computer and had made a call to an old friend to give herself a break.

"It's okay, Derek," she said with a sigh. "I'll figure it out."

"If those Southern belles get too much for you, I can always find a place for you in Phoenix. Everything's hotter out West, jewel-eyed Julia." Derek laughed at his own joke then said, "I've got to run, darlin'. My last appointment for the day just came in."

"Thanks, sweetie," Julia said, "I'll keep that offer in mind."

She hung up with Derek, a stylist she'd met years ago in Columbus. They'd both moved on from Ohio, but she still considered him one of her few true friends. For a brief moment she entertained the thought of taking Charlie and running away to Arizona. Not that it would solve her myriad of problems, but it sure seemed easier than facing everything head-on.

Julia drummed her fingers on the top of her desk, wishing she were out in the warm sun instead of stuck in the salon on such a gorgeous spring day. She needed to clear her head, and computer work wasn't cutting it.

What had started as a simple plan with Sam had gotten too complicated. She'd been stupid to think she could keep her heart out of the equation. If Julia were better at leading with her mind, she wouldn't have gotten into most of the trouble she'd had during her life. She wanted to be in control of her emotions. To be more like Sam, who could make every decision in his life based on rational thinking.

Not Julia. She was more a leap-first-then-look kind of person.

The only time that had worked in her favor was with Charlie. Now she'd even managed to mess up that.

Sam wanted to stay with her for the right reasons, at least on paper, but it felt wrong. His father and her mother were heading in that same direction on the express train. It had been torture to watch them last night at dinner, making googly eyes and barely able to keep their hands off each other.

She didn't realize it was possible to ache for a man's touch, but that was how she felt around Sam. Other than enough touching to make their fake arrangement seem real, they'd both kept their distance. Except when they were alone. In the bedroom, Sam was sweet and attentive and Julia had made the mistake of believing that meant something.

She pushed away from the desk and stalked toward the main salon. They were busy today, with every chair filled. She hoped to get the final approval on her business loan next week, needed to prove to herself and to the town and Jeff's family that she could stand on her own two feet.

Lizzy, the salon's longtime receptionist, stopped her in the doorway.

"Julia, could you take a look at this product order and make sure I didn't miss anything?" She shoved a piece of paper filled with numbers into Julia's hand.

Julia looked down as the figures on the page swam in front of her eyes. "Leave it on my desk. I'll check it over the weekend."

"I need to get it in before month end, which is today. It'll only take a minute. Please."

"I can't," Julia snapped with more force than she'd meant.

Lizzy took a quick step back and Julia noticed several customers and stylists glance her way. "Fine," she stammered. "But if we run out of anything, don't blame me." She turned away, ripping the paper from Julia's fingers.

"I'm sorry." Julia reached out to touch the woman's arm. "Lizzy, wait. I need to tell you something."

"That you're too dang important to be bothered by little details?"

Julia glanced around the crowded salon, her gaze landing on Lexi Preston, who watched her from where she sat with a head full of coloring foils. What was Jeff's attorney doing in her salon? Lexi blinked then raised one brow, as if in an odd challenge.

"I'm waiting," Lizzy muttered.

Fine. She was sick of hiding who she was, tired of working so hard to live up to her own unattainable expectations. She squared her shoulders and took a deep breath. "I have a learning disability."

"Come again?" A little of the anger went out of Lizzy's posture.

"I need time to look over the figures because I can't read them well."

"Since when?"

A hush had fallen over the salon and Julia realized everyone was waiting for her answer.

"Forever," she said, making her voice loud and clear. "I was officially diagnosed in third grade."

Lizzy looked confused. "I think I would have heard that before now. I was only a few years behind you in school."

Julia shrugged. "It wasn't public knowledge."

"Is that why you were always cutting class and getting kids to write your papers for you?"

Julia nodded. "I'm not proud of it. I was embarrassed and it made me feel stupid." She took a breath. "It still does. But I'm working on that. I hid behind a bad attitude and unkindness for a lot of years. I've changed. I don't want you to think I don't value what you're asking me to do. It just may take me longer to get it done." She swallowed down the lump of emotion crowding her throat. "That's my big secret."

Lizzy offered her a genuine smile. "My cousin was bulimic for most of her teenage years. She tried to hide that, too."

One of the customers tipped her head in Julia's direction. "My husband's addicted to internet porn."

"Oh." Julia didn't quite know how that related to her learning disability. "Well, I'll take these figures." She gently tugged the paper from Lizzy's hand. "I'll see if I can get through them this afternoon. If not, first thing Monday morning."

She looked around the salon one last time, her gaze catching again on Lexi's, and the lawyer gave her a surprisingly genuine smile. Head held high, Julia closed the door to her office. Once safely by herself, she leaned against it, bending her knees until she sank to the floor.

Her whole body trembled from the adrenaline rush that followed sharing her deepest, darkest secret with the ladies in the salon. Julia knew how the gossip mill worked in Brevia. Within hours, everyone to the county line and back would know about her learning disability.

The truth was that she no longer cared. Now that she'd talked about her disorder, its hold over her had loosened the tiniest bit. If people wanted to judge her or tried to take advantage of her, she'd deal with that. She realized she could handle a lot more when she used the truth to her advantage than when she tried to cover it up.

A little voice inside her head piped up, saying she might take that advice when it came to dealing with the custody case and Charlie's future. She quickly put it aside. Public humiliation she could risk—her son's fate she couldn't. Whether that meant keeping up the charade with Sam, or fighting tooth and nail with the Johnsons, Julia would do whatever she had to to keep Charlie safe.

Chapter Fourteen

"The Callahan brothers ride again."

Sam slanted Scott a look. "Who are you supposed to be, Billy the Kid?"

Scott grinned. "It's about time you stopped hiding in this backwater town and did some real work."

"I'm police chief, idiot. That is real work."

"If you say so. But it's nothing like being a marshal. You're going to love it, Sam. You won't have time to think about anything else."

That was a plus, Sam thought. He'd gotten the job offer early this morning. Scott had shown up at the station soon after to offer his congratulations. Sam was on duty, so they had coffee and a breakfast burrito in the car as Sam went out on an early-morning call.

His father was going to hit the roof. Joe had taken Vera down to the coast for a couple of days, so at least Sam would have time to formulate a plan before he had to explain what he was doing.

He had no idea what to say to Julia. He figured she'd understand. She'd tried to break it off last night. He knew their time together was at an end. After the custody ruling came through, she wouldn't need him anymore. Not that she ever really had. Despite her self-doubt, Julia was going to have a great life. He was the one who was hopeless.

Although he hadn't even thought himself capable of it, he felt his heart literally expanding every day with love for her and Charlie, but he couldn't make it work. He felt vulnerable, as if he was a moving target with no cover. He couldn't offer her anything more because he was too afraid of being hurt.

He'd spent most of yesterday working with Julia's attorney to file several affidavits on behalf of people around town attesting to Julia's character, her contributions to the local community and what they'd observed as far as her being a great mother was concerned. He knew she would never ask for help from anyone, let alone believe she deserved it. Once he'd explained what she was facing, people had come forward in droves to stand behind her.

He hoped that would be enough, would make up for what he wanted to tell her but couldn't find the guts to say. Instead, he was going to move on. Leave Brevia and cut his ties because that was easier than letting someone in.

"Before you go all bro-mance on me, you need to know I still think you're a jerk for what you did to me."

"You'll thank me eventually."

"I doubt that." Sam turned onto the long dirt road that led to the house he'd received the call about earlier. Strange noises, the neighbor had said. Here on the outskirts of town, Sam knew the parties could go on all through the night. He figured someone hadn't known when to let it go.

He shifted the cruiser into Park and turned to his brother. "If we're going to work together, there need to be some ground rules. The first is you stay the hell out of my personal life. It's none of your business. Even if you think you've got my best interests at heart."

"What are you going to do about the fiancée when you leave town?" Scott asked.

"I'm going to do her a favor."

"That's cold, Sam. Even for you. And I thought I was the heartbreaker. You're giving me a run for my money in the love-'em-and-leave-'em department."

"Don't make it a bigger issue than it is, Scott. She's better off without me. It's not going to work out. I'm not what she needs, after all."

"I can see why she'd be what *you* need, though. Her legs must be a mile long."

The hair on the back of Sam's neck stood on end.

"When did you see Julia?"

Scott gave him a hesitant smile. "Probably shouldn't have mentioned that."

"When did you see her?" Sam repeated, his knuckles tightening around the steering wheel.

"I drove down to have lunch with Dad last week. I needed a trim, so I checked out her salon."

"And her," Sam said between clenched teeth.

"After what Dad told me about how in love you are and the way you skipped out of breakfast to go running to her, it had me worried. I wanted to see what could be so flippin' amazing about this woman to make you all whipped."

"I'm not whipped."

"I was worried," Scott continued. "I put my butt on the line to get you this job. It wouldn't look good for you to flake before you even started. I have to admit, she'd be a big temptation. Her kid was there, too. Cute, if you're into the whole family-man scene. But I know you, Sam. That isn't who you are. Never was."

"Stay away from Julia."

"It's not like that. I told you that what happened with Jenny, I did it for your own good. Granted, I could have found a better way to handle things but…"

"You slept with her."

"I'm sorry, Sam."

Scott's voice was quiet, sincere. It made Sam's teeth hurt, because he knew his brother was sorry. He also knew that, in a warped way, Scott had done him a favor. At that point in his life, Sam had been so determined to prove that he wasn't like his father, that he could have both a career and a personal life, he'd ignored all the warning signs about how wrong he and Jenny had been for each other. She would have left him eventually. He would have driven her away.

Now he knew better, and he wasn't going to risk it again. Not his heart or his pride. He thought Julia understood him, but it was for the best that their relationship ended. As much as he didn't want to admit it, he was falling for her. He was close to feeling something he'd never felt before in his life, and it scared the hell out of him. What if he did let her in and she realized there was nothing inside him to hold on to? His heart had stopped working right the day his mother had died and he didn't know how to fix it.

Sam glanced at his brother. "Do you think about what would have happened if Mom hadn't been in the accident?"

"I used to," Scott said, a muscle ticking in his jaw. "But she would have divorced him, and the end result on us would have been the same."

"Yeah." Sam nodded. "I think Dad discovered his emotional self about two decades too late to make any difference in my life."

"You need to get out of here. Once you're working for the Marshals, you won't have time for all this thinking about your life. I'm telling you—"

Whatever Scott was going to say next was cut off when a stream of shots rang out from the house. "Stay here," Sam yelled as he jumped out of the car.

"Not a chance," Scott said, right on his heels, his gun in hand. "Call me your backup."

Sam gave a brief nod. "You go around the side," he whispered and headed toward the front of the house.

Julia dropped her cell phone back into her purse and took a deep breath. "I didn't get the loan," she said to her sister, the words sounding hollow to her own ears.

Lainey reached out a hand. The Tellett County courthouse was crowded on a Tuesday morning, and they stood near the end of the hallway, in front of a window that looked out onto the street. Julia thought it odd that the people below went about their business so calmly as her life spun out of control.

"Why not? What did they say? Oh, Jules, there has to be another way."

Julia shook her head. "They don't think I'm a good investment. It's me, Lainey. Nothing is going to change that. Everyone in the salon yesterday heard me. I told Lizzy about my learning disabilities. Clearly, the bank doesn't think I'm the right person to own my own business." She tried to smile but couldn't make her mouth move that way. "I can't blame them."

"I can." Lainey's tone was severe. "It's the most outrageous thing I've ever heard."

"Annabeth Sullivan is a vice president at the bank. I thought we'd come to an understanding and she'd forgiven me. I guess she still wants revenge."

"How long are you going to have to pay for your past mistakes? You're not the same person you were in high school. You've changed and everyone who knows you can see that. You're a good person. It's about time people gave you credit for how much you've accomplished."

"I haven't accomplished anything. The salon was my chance to make something of my life, to become more than what anyone thought I could." She scrubbed her hands over her face. "There's a reason I kept the LD a secret for so many years. It's easier to talk my way out of people thinking I'm stupid than to deal with the truth."

Lainey sucked in a breath. "Don't say that. You'll find another way. Ethan and I—"

"No. I'm not taking charity from you and Ethan, or Mom for that matter. Some things weren't meant to be. I've had enough disappointment in my life to know that." She glanced down the hall and saw Frank Davis motioning to them. "The hearing is starting."

"I thought Sam was meeting you here."

Julia swallowed back the tears that clogged her throat. "Like I said, I'm used to disappointment."

"Don't be silly. He'll be here."

Julia gave her sister a small hug. "Whatever you say, Lain. Right now, wish me luck."

"You don't need luck. You're a wonderful mother and that's what's most important. I'll be here when you're finished. We'll have a celebratory lunch."

The elevator doors opened as Julia walked past and she paused, her chest tightening as she willed Sam to materialize. When an older woman walked out, Julia continued down the hall alone.

She took her seat across from Jeff, his parents and their attorney. A small smile played around the corners of Jeff's mother's mouth. Lexi Preston didn't make eye contact, her eyes glued to the stack of papers on the table. A pit of dread began to open in Julia's stomach.

She darted a glance toward her attorney, who appeared blissfully unaware. But Julia could feel the long tendrils of impending doom reaching for her. She'd been in their grip too many times before not to recognize it now.

"Frank, what's going on?"

He looked up, a big smile on his face. "Didn't Sam tell you? He got a bunch of folks to write testimonials about your character. Really good, too. All of them."

Sam did that. For her. Then why did the Johnson family look so smug?

"Where is Sam?" Frank asked. "I thought he was meeting us here."

"Me, too." Julia swallowed. "I don't know what's keeping him."

The judge came into the courtroom. "In light of the new information given to me by both parties, I'm going to need a few more days to render my decision."

"What new information did they give her?" Julia said in a frantic whisper.

"Your Honor," Frank said as he patted Julia's arm reassuringly, "we aren't aware of any new information brought forward by the other party."

The judge slowly removed her glasses and narrowed her eyes at him. "Mr. Davis, you do know about your client's recent professional setbacks."

Frank threw a glance at Julia. "I'm not sure—"

"I didn't get the loan," Julia said miserably.

"We've spoken to a reliable source that tells us Ms. Morgan is planning to move out of the area." Lexi's shoulders were stiff as she spoke. "A colleague of Ms. Morgan's, Derek Lamb, had a conversation with her last week in which she expressed interest in a job with him at his salon in Phoenix."

Julia knew Lexi had somehow gleaned that information, as well. "I wasn't serious. I was upset about...about a lot of things, and Derek is an old friend—"

"An old boyfriend," Lexi supplied.

Julia shook her head, panic threatening to overtake her. "Hardly. I don't have the right equipment."

Frank squeezed her arm. "Be quiet, Julia."

The judge pointed a finger at her. "Ms. Morgan, your petition for sole custody was based partially on the stability of your current circumstances. Your ties to the community and your family being close were something I took into account when looking at your request."

"Her ties to the community are highlighted in the affidavits I submitted." Frank's voice shook with frustration.

"There is also the matter of her engagement," Lexi said, reaching over to hand a piece of paper to Frank.

Blood roared in Julia's head. No one could have found out her relationship with Sam wasn't real. They'd done everything right and she hadn't told a soul, not even Lainey.

Unless Sam...

She snatched the paper from Frank Davis's fingers and tried to decipher the words on the page, willing them to stop moving in front of her eyes. When they did, she felt the whole room start to spin.

"Were you aware," the judge asked, "that Sam Callahan has accepted a position with the U.S. Marshals Service in Washington, D.C.?"

Julia looked at the woman, unable to speak. Finally, she whispered, "No."

The woman's mouth tightened. "May I ask, Ms. Morgan, if you're still engaged to be married to Sam Callahan?"

Julia stared at the piece of paper in her hand, her vision blurring as angry tears filled her eyes. She blinked several times, refusing to cry in front of Jeff and his family. Refusing to cry over any man. "No, ma'am," she answered quietly. "I don't believe we are still engaged."

Frank sucked in a quick breath next to her. "In light of these new findings, I'd ask for a recess to regroup with my client."

"Yes, Mr. Davis, I think that would be a good idea. Our time is valuable, though, so please, no more wasting it. Get your facts straight and come back to me with a new proposal in one week."

"Judge Williams—" Lexi Preston's voice was clear and confident in the silence "—on behalf of my client, I'd like to request that you make your ruling today. The information that's come to light this morning is another example of Julia Morgan's inability to successfully manage her own life. It speaks directly to Jeff Johnson's concerns for his son and the reason he is here seeking joint custody."

Julia's gaze met Jeff's and he nodded slightly, as if to say "I told you so." Which, of course, he had. And she hadn't listened, convinced that this time events would work out in her favor. In large part because of Sam's confidence in her.

Sam, who'd encouraged her to go public with her learning disorder.

Sam, who'd promised to stay by her side until her custody arrangement was secure.

Sam, who'd betrayed her today.

Lexi cleared her throat. "I motion that you award sole physical custody of Charles David Morgan to Jeff Johnson."

The attorney's words registered in Julia's brain. They wanted to take Charlie from her. Completely.

She saw Jeff lean over and speak into Lexi's ear. The younger woman shook her head then glanced at Julia.

Julia felt the walls of the room close in around her. She looked at the judge's impassive face, trying to find some clue as to what the woman was thinking.

"Don't let this happen," she whispered to Frank. She needed to get back to Brevia, to wrap her arms around her son.

"We request you stay with your decision to rule next week," Frank said, his voice steady. "My client has been blindsided by some of these new developments. That in no way decreases her dedication as a parent or her love for her son."

To Julia's immense relief, the judge nodded. "We'll meet next Tuesday morning." She pointed a finger at Frank Davis. "Before that, I expect you to submit a revised proposal for custody. Remember, we all want what's best for the child, not simply what's easiest for one of the parents."

What's best for Charlie, Julia wanted to scream, *is to stay with his mother.*

She'd come into this meeting so confident. How could things have gone to hell so quickly?

She pushed back from the table. "I need to get out of here," she told the attorney.

"Be in my office tomorrow morning, first thing." His frustration was clear as he watched her. "This was a clearcut case," he mumbled. "What happened with Sam?"

She bit her lip. "I don't know." What she did know was that Sam had left her vulnerable to losing her son.

Julia would never forgive him.

Chapter Fifteen

Sam ran his hands through his still-wet hair and straightened his shirt before knocking on Julia's door.

He'd stopped home for a quick shower after the mess this morning had finally settled down. An all-night party had turned into a domestic disturbance that led to a four-hour standoff. The homeowner, high on an assortment of illegal drugs, wouldn't let his girlfriend or her two kids out of the house. The situation had eventually ended with no injuries, for which Sam was thankful. But he'd been tied up in logistics and paperwork for most of the day.

He felt awful about missing the hearing and had called and texted Julia at least a half-dozen times with no answer. He'd then called Lainey, but she hadn't picked up, either. As mad as she'd be about him missing the meeting, the character affidavits he'd helped compile had to make up for it.

Sam couldn't wait to see the joy on Julia's face now that

Charlie was safe. He wanted to hear how things went, take the two of them to dinner to celebrate her victory. Even if she didn't want to be with him anymore, he'd make her see how important it was to keep up appearances a little while longer. He told himself it was good for her reputation but knew he couldn't bear to let go of her quite yet.

Julia deserved all the happiness life could offer, and Sam wanted to have a hand in helping with that before they ended their relationship. The thought of leaving her and Charlie made his whole body go cold. But he knew it would be best for Julia and that was his priority now.

He knocked again, surprised when Lainey opened the door. Even more surprised at how angry she looked.

"You have a lot of nerve showing up here," she said through a hiss. "She doesn't want to see you. You've done enough damage already."

The confusion of not being able to get in touch with her turned to panic. "Where is she? What happened?"

Lainey went to shut the door in his face but he shoved one gym shoe into the doorway. Lainey kicked at his toe. "I mean it, Sam. You need to leave."

"I swear, Lainey," Sam ground out, "I'll push right through you if I have to but I'm going to see her. Now."

Casper came up behind Lainey, barking wildly. Sam could see the dog's teeth shining and wondered if the dog actually meant to bite him.

"Casper, quiet." The dog stopped barking but continued to growl low in his throat. Lainey studied Sam through the crack in the door. "I'd like to call the cops on you."

"I can give you the number."

She blew out a frustrated breath and opened the door. Sam went to push past. "Where is she?"

Lainey didn't move to let him by. "I'm warning you. She doesn't want to see you ever again. She's in bad shape."

He shook his head. "I don't understand. Everything was lined up. Didn't Frank Davis submit the affidavits? They were supposed to make everything better."

"Julia didn't mention any affidavits. What she did tell me, between sobs, is that you'd told her to go public with her learning disabilities. For whatever reason, Annabeth Sullivan convinced the bank that she was a bad investment for the loan."

Sam's breath caught. "No."

"The best part," Lainey said and poked her finger into his chest, "the part that really made all the difference, was the little bombshell that you've taken a job with the U.S. Marshals Service."

Sam's whole body tensed. "How did they find out?"

"You don't deny it? How could you have done that to her?" Lainey turned on her heel and stalked several paces into the small apartment.

"No one was supposed to find out until after she got the custody ruling."

Lainey whirled back toward him, keeping her voice low. "And that makes it better? You were her fiancé. A stable father figure for Charlie."

"Did Julia—"

"Oh, yes." Lainey waved an angry hand toward him. "I know all about your *arrangement*. It's ridiculous."

"I didn't mean for it to be. I wanted to help."

"You've put her at risk, Sam. At real risk of losing custody of Charlie."

"Where is she?"

Lainey stared at him. "In the bedroom," she answered finally.

"I'm going to fix this." Sam tried for confidence but his voice cracked on the last word.

"I hope you can."

He walked past her, Casper at his heels. The dog no longer seemed to want to rip off his head. Julia, he imagined, was another matter.

"I can make this right," he muttered to the animal. "I have to."

He knocked softly on the door, but when there was no response, he opened it. The curtain was pulled back, the room bathed in early-evening sunlight. Julia sat on the bed, her knees curled up to her chin, arms hugging her legs tight against her.

Sam stepped into the room and the dog edged past him, silently hopping up on the bed and giving Julia's hand a gentle lick before curling into a ball at her side. Without acknowledging Sam, she reached out to stroke the dog's soft head.

"Jules?"

Her hand stilled. "Go away," she whispered, her voice awful.

"Julia, look at me." Sam took another step into the room.

"I said go away." She lifted her head, her eyes puffy from crying, tears dried on her cheeks. She looked as miserable as Sam felt. He waited for her to scream at him, to hurl insults and obscenities. He wanted her to let loose her temper but she only stared, her gaze filled with the pain of betrayal.

Knowing it was his betrayal that had caused her suffering almost killed him on the spot. "I'm sorry," he began but stopped when she scrambled back against the headboard. The dog jumped up and stood like a sentry in front of her.

"I could lose him." Her voice was dull and wooden, as if she was in a pit of despair so deep she couldn't even manage emotion.

"You won't lose him." Sam said the words with conviction, hoping they would be true.

"You don't know. You weren't there."

The accusation in her voice cut like a knife through his heart. "It was work, Jules. I meant to be there." He sat down on the edge of the bed gingerly, not wanting to spook her or the dog.

"You're leaving."

"I thought it was for the best," he lied. The best thing that ever happened to him was this woman, but he was too scared of being hurt to give her what she needed. "That when you didn't need me anymore, it would be easier for us both if I was gone."

"I needed you today and instead I found out from Jeff's lawyer that you were taking a new job. You made me look like a fool, Sam."

The truth of her words struck him to his core. She was right. He was supposed to be there for her and he'd let her down. In a big way. It was the reason he knew he was destined to be alone: the work always came first for him. He was the same as his dad had been. It had cost his mother her life and now it might cost Julia her future with Charlie. He had to make it better somehow. "What can I do?"

She shook her head. "Nothing. There's nothing anyone can do. I have one good thing in my life. Charlie was the one thing I did right. And I've ruined that, too."

"You haven't—"

"I trusted you, Sam." As much as the words hurt, her voice, still empty of emotion, was the worst. "My mistake. I should have learned by now I can't rely on anyone except myself." She gave a brittle laugh. "And I'm iffy at best."

"Where's Charlie?"

"He's with Ethan. I couldn't let him see me like this." She ran her fingers through her hair. "I'm going to pull it together. I have to. But I needed a little time."

"We can get through this."

"There's no *we*. There never really was. You proved that today."

"I didn't mean it to end like this." He reached out for her again and Casper growled like he meant it.

Julia went rigid. "Don't touch me. I never want to see you again. I don't know what's going to happen with the custody arrangement. But I'll find a way to keep my son. He's all that matters to me now."

Sam shook his head. "Don't say that," he whispered.

Her eyes blazed as she spoke. "I thought you were different. I wanted to depend on you. I wanted to love you. Hell, I was halfway there already. It's over. I don't care what you say to your father or anyone in town about why this is ending. Blame it on me."

"This isn't over and I'm not blaming anything on you. If you let me—"

"I did let you. I let you into my heart and into my son's life and you betrayed us." She took a shuddering breath. "We're over. Whatever I thought we had is done."

"You can't be serious."

"Please go, Sam. Please."

He stared at her as she turned to the dog, petting him until he lay down again beside her. Sam wanted to grab her and pull her to him, hold on until she melted into him. This couldn't be the end.

He'd wanted to leave her happy, to do the right thing by her. Maybe he couldn't be the man she wanted but he'd been determined to see her through. To be the hero when it really mattered.

Now he was nothing more than the jerk who'd put her at risk of losing her son.

He stood slowly, his eyes never leaving her. He prayed she would look at him, give him some small glimmer of hope. When she didn't, he turned and walked from the room.

Lainey hung up the phone as he came down the hallway. "How is she?"

He shook his head. "She should never have trusted me."

"But she did, Sam. What are you going to do now?"

He thought for a moment then answered the only way he could. "I'm going to do what I do best—disappoint someone I care about."

Lainey looked as if she'd expected him to give some white-knight answer. But Sam was only good at playing the hero when the stakes didn't matter to him personally. When his emotions were on the line, he had a knack for royally messing up everything around him.

He walked out the door and into the dark night knowing he'd just ruined his best opportunity at a happy ending in life.

The image of Julia so forlorn would haunt him for a long time. Her anger and hatred might be deserved, but it hurt the most to know that he couldn't take away the pain he'd caused her.

For that, he'd never forgive himself.

Julia pushed the stroller along the plush carpet of the retirement home until she got to the common room that also served as a makeshift salon for residents.

"Good morning, Julia."

"Hey, Charlie."

Several voices called out to greet them, and she was thankful the people here were unaware of her personal turmoil, unlike most of the town. Charlie waved as though he was in a parade, which made Julia smile a bit. Her first in several days. She took a small sip of her coffee then placed it in the cup holder attached to the stroller's handle. It had been a rough week.

She tried not to show her emotions in front of Charlie, so she had spent a few sleepless nights crying in the dark hours and worrying about her future. The days were just as difficult to get through, since everywhere she went someone had a comment on her recent struggles. To her surprise, most of what people said had been supportive. Old friends and other locals seemed to come out of the woodwork to offer her a word of encouragement or commiserate on her situation.

Even Val Dupree, the Hairhouse's owner, had called from Florida to tell Julia that she was still willing to work with her to find a way for Julia to buy the salon. Julia had thanked her, but at this point she was afraid it was too little, too late. The Johnsons had so much power and she wasn't sure there was anything she could do to keep her future with Charlie secure.

Nothing mattered except Charlie.

She hadn't seen or spoken to Sam, although a couple of ladies had come into the salon specifically to tell her how they'd given him an earful about his reprehensible behavior toward her. Apparently, being screwed over by a man made you an automatic member of a certain girls' club.

If it wasn't for her constant worry about Charlie, Julia might be happy right now. For the first time in as long as she could remember, she felt as if she was a true member of the Brevia community.

But everything else faded when she thought of her son and what she'd need to do to keep him with her.

Before moving forward with her plan, she had this one last loose end to tie up.

"Good morning, Mrs. Shilling," she said as she walked into the room.

"Well, hello, dear." A gray-haired woman, sitting at the games table with a deck of cards, lifted her head and smiled.

"Hi, Iris." Julia directed that greeting to the younger woman wiping down counters at the back of the room.

"Hey, Jules. Thanks for coming on such short notice." The younger woman waved at Charlie. "Hey there, Chuckie-boy. Do you want to check out the fish while your mommy helps Mrs. S.?"

Charlie bounced up and down in his seat. "Fishy," he squealed. "Charlie, fishy."

"Thanks, Iris." Julia picked up her coffee from the stroller and pushed the buggy toward Iris. She always brought Charlie when she came to Shady Acres. The residents and employees loved seeing him.

As Iris left with Charlie, Julia turned to the older woman. "Mrs. Shilling, where did you find the scissors?" She stepped forward and ran her fingers through the spiky tufts of hair on the top of the woman's head.

Mrs. Shilling placed her hand over Julia's and winked. "In the craft cabinet, dear. They forgot to lock it after our art class yesterday."

Julia opened her bag and pulled out a plastic apron, spray bottle, scissors and a comb. "What do you think if I clean it up a little? You've done a nice job here, but I can even up the sides a bit."

"I suppose," Mrs. Shilling answered with a shrug. "When I was a girl, I had the cutest haircut, just like Shirley Temple. I wanted to look that cute again." She met Julia's gaze, her hazy eyes filled with hope. "Can you make me look like Shirley Temple, dear?"

Julia patted Mrs. Shilling's soft, downy hair. "I'll do my best." She wrapped the apron around the woman's frail shoulders. "Next time, go easy with the scissors, Mrs. S. You're beautiful just the way you are."

She usually came to Shady Acres every other week to cut and shampoo the hair of a group of residents. But Iris had called her last night to say that Mrs. Shilling, one of her favorite ladies, had butchered her hair. Julia made time to come here before she needed to be at the salon.

She used the scissors to snip a few tendrils of hair as Mrs. Shilling hummed softly.

"Everything okay in here?"

Julia turned, shocked to see Ida Garvey walk into the room.

Mrs. Shilling's face lit up. "Ida, so nice to see you here this morning. This is my friend Julia. She's making me look like Shirley Temple." She glanced at Julia. "This is my daughter, Ida. She's a very good girl." Her voice lowered to a whisper. "She still wets the bed sometimes. Has nightmares, poor girl. I let her snuggle with me until she falls asleep."

Julia gave a small smile. "Nice to see you, Mrs. Garvey."

The older woman shook her head. "I haven't wet the bed since I was seven years old. The Alzheimer's has affected my mother's memory of time."

"I figured as much. I won't be long here."

"They called to tell me she'd cut her own hair again."

"If she ever wants a part-time job, we could use her skills at the Hairhouse." Julia continued trimming the woman's fluffy hair.

"She can't do any worse than some of those girls you've got working there."

"Play nice, Mrs. Garvey. I've got the scissors."

One side of Ida's mouth quirked. "She talks about you a lot."

Julia glanced up. "Really? Me?"

"In fact, I have a suspicion she might have done this just to get you out here again."

Mrs. Shilling pointed a bony finger at her daughter.

"Children are supposed to be seen and not heard, young lady."

"I'm almost seventy, Mom."

"Still holds true," the woman said with a humph. "Besides, she's going to make me look like Shirley Temple. Or maybe Carole Lombard."

Julia smiled, something about this woman's affection lifting her spirits the tiniest bit. She was grateful for every lift she could get right now. "I was thinking Katharine Hepburn, circa *Adam's Rib*. Gorgeous but spunky."

"I'll take spunky," Mrs. Shilling agreed and settled back into her chair.

"I heard about your recent troubles," Ida said, her gaze assessing. "What are you going to do about the salon?"

"My loan wasn't approved. What else can I do? I'm not sure if I'm going to be in town for much longer, actually." She squeezed Mrs. Shilling's shoulder. "I'll miss you when I go."

The woman heaved a sigh. "All the good ones move on." She gave a watery smile to her daughter. "Except Ida. She's my best girl. Always has been."

Julia's chest fluttered at the love in the older woman's gaze when she looked at her daughter. She suddenly saw crotchety Ida Garvey in a new light. Julia knew she'd look at Charlie like that one day. She'd do anything to keep him by her side so she'd have that chance. Nothing was more important to her.

Ida gave her mother an indulgent smile, and then with her customary bluntness she asked Julia, "How did the bank deal get messed up?"

Julia pulled in a deep breath and paused in her cutting. "They didn't think I was a good investment, I guess." She paused, squaring her shoulders, and then said, "As you've probably heard, my learning disabilities are severe. Not exactly the type of applicant you'd trust to run a business, even a small local salon. Too bad, though. I had big plans."

Mrs. Shilling clapped her hands. "She told me all about it, Ida. Getting rid of that horrid name. She's going to offer spa services. I want to bathe in a big tub of mud!"

"Is that so?" Mrs. Garvey asked, looking between her mother and Julia.

Julia gave a small laugh, embarrassed now that she'd confided so much in the older woman. "My idea was to make it a destination for people traveling in the area and the go-to place for a day of pampering for women around the region. There's really nothing like that unless you head over to Asheville or down to the coast."

Ida nodded. "Tell me about it. I've put most of the miles on my car driving back and forth for a monthly facial."

Julia felt color rise to her cheeks, embarrassed she'd shared her dream now that it wasn't going to come true. "That's probably more information than you wanted for a simple question." She used a comb to fluff Mrs. Shilling's white hair. "There you are, beautiful." She handed her a small mirror. "Katharine Hepburn, eat your heart out."

The woman smiled as she looked in the mirror then at her daughter. "Do you love it, Ida?"

"I do," she agreed.

Julia removed the apron and took a broom from the supply closet in the corner. "I'll have one of the girls come out to do your hair when I'm gone." She began to sweep up the hair from around the chair.

"Ida, give her some money," Mrs. Shilling ordered.

Mrs. Garvey pulled her wallet from her purse.

Julia shook her head. "I don't charge for my time here."

Ida took out a business card and handed it to Julia. "This is the firm that handles my financial portfolio. The president's contact information is there."

Julia took the card. "Oh." She knew Ida Garvey's late husband had left her a sizable inheritance.

"If you decide you want to stay in the area and are still interested in investors for your business, call him. I see the need for the type of spa you're describing. I assume you have a business plan our loan team could review?"

Julia nodded, dumbfounded by the offer.

"Good. I don't want to pressure you. I don't know why the bank here didn't approve your loan, but I'd guess it had something to do with Annabeth. That girl isn't the sharpest knife in the drawer. But I certainly hope it wasn't because of your learning disorder. It doesn't make you a bad bet for a loan."

"Thank you for saying that."

Mrs. Shilling reached out and took Julia's hand. "Ida is rich," she said in a loud whisper. "She takes good care of me."

"You're very lucky," Julia told the woman, feeling a tiny flicker of hope that her own luck had taken a turn for the better.

Chapter Sixteen

Sam hit the mute button on the television and jumped off the couch, throwing on an old T-shirt in the process.

His heart soared at the thought that Julia could be the person insistently knocking on his front door.

He groaned as he opened it to reveal his father and brother standing side by side on his front porch. "Not now, boys," he said and went to swing the door shut again.

His dad pushed it open and knocked him hard in the chest. "What the—" Sam muttered as he stumbled back into the house.

"That's what I'd like to know." Joe's voice was hard as he stalked past Sam. Gone was the gentle emotion of his recent visit and in its place the tough, take-no-prisoners Boston cop had returned. Sam wanted to be grateful but knew what it was like to be on the receiving end of his father's temper. His own fuse felt too short to deal with that right now.

He glanced at his brother, who shrugged and stepped into the house, closing the door behind him.

"What the hell were you thinking?" Joe bellowed, slamming his palm against the wall. "You took advantage of that girl. You used her to deceive me and now you've deserted her. That's not how I raised you. I've never been so angry and disappointed in all my years."

Angry and disappointed? Even in the midst of a full-blown tirade, Joe was talking about how he felt. Sam had damn near had enough of it.

"This is your fault," Sam countered. "If you had left me alone, none of this would have happened." He squared his shoulders, warming up to the subject, needing a place to vent his own anger. "You came in here, emotional guns a-blazin', and wanted me to turn into somebody I'm not. It's never going to happen, Dad. I'm never going to be some heart-on-my-sleeve kind of guy, spouting out my feelings and crying at sappy chick flicks." He pointed a finger at his father. "You raised me to ignore my emotions. It's what you made Scott and me into after Mom died. I can't change. The mess I made of things with Julia is proof of that."

"You faked an engagement," his father interrupted, hands on hips, matching Sam's anger.

"It was wrong. I know that now. The alternative was you following me around waiting for unicorns and rainbows to come spewing out of my mouth. It ain't going to happen. Ever. Julia and I had a business arrangement and I messed it up. If I could go back and change things, I would."

"No, you wouldn't."

Sam and his father both turned as Scott spoke for the first time.

"You don't know anything about me or what I would do," Sam spat out. "Neither of you do."

"I know you," Scott countered. "I know that girl got

too close. She got under your skin, and I bet it scared the hell out of you. It sure would have me. With her big eyes, long legs and cute baby. She made you feel things and the Callahans don't like to feel." He nodded toward Joe. "Another gift from you, Dad. I don't know what she wanted or expected from you, but it's a good thing you ended it when you did. We don't do love. We're not built that way."

How could his brother be so right and so wrong at the same time? Being with Julia and Charlie had scared him. But it was because he realized he did love her even though he'd tried to ignore, then bury, his emotions. He'd fallen hard and fast, and it had made him want things that could never be.

She wanted someone to be a father to Charlie. Sam's paternal relationship was so dysfunctional it was almost laughable. How could he be a decent father with the role model he'd had in Joe?

What if he tried and failed with Julia? He was capable of love, but not in the way a woman like Julia deserved.

Suddenly Joe fell back onto the couch, clutching at his chest.

"Dad!" Both Sam and Scott were at his side in a second.

"What is it, Dad?" Sam asked.

"It's his heart, you idiot."

Joe's eyes drifted closed, and Sam moved his head and legs so he was lying flat across the cushions. "Call 911," he ordered his brother.

Scott pulled his cell phone from his back pocket, but Joe's eyes flew open and he reached out a hand. "No, I don't need medical attention."

"The hell you don't," Sam said on a hiss. "Make the call, Scott."

"My heart hurts," Joe said, his voice trembling, "because of the pain I've caused the two of you." He lifted himself to his elbows and looked from Sam to Scott. "My sons, I've failed you and I'll never forgive myself for it." He covered his eyes with one hand as sobs racked his shoulders.

"Of all the…" Sam grumbled and sank to one arm of the sofa.

Scott threw his cell phone on the coffee table and stalked to the front window, grumbling under his breath.

"Scoot over, old man." Sam sank down on the couch next to him. "You just about gave *me* a heart attack there."

"I need a drink." Scott's voice was tense.

"Make it three," Sam told him. "There's a bottle of Scotch in the cabinet next to the stove."

Joe still sat motionless, other than an occasional moan.

Sam's headache spread until his entire body hurt. "Dad, pull it together. It's going to be okay."

"Do you believe that?" Joe asked finally, wiping his damp cheeks. "Do you feel like you're going to be all right without her?"

No. Sam knew his life was going to be dark and dim, that he could spend years chasing the adrenaline rush that came with his career and nothing would compare with the excitement of having Charlie call him Dada. He felt as though he could be a hero to hundreds of nameless people, and it would pale in comparison to coaxing a real smile out of Julia.

"What choice do I have?"

"You always have a choice. That's what I didn't realize until recently. I had a choice to let your mother's death practically kill me, too, or to keep living. I didn't do a very good job of making my life count until recently. But I'm learning from the mistakes I made and doing my damnedest to make them better. You have a real chance for love with Julia. Take it."

"What do I have to offer her?" Sam asked quietly, finally getting to the real heart of the matter. His own fear. "She deserves so much more."

"I know you think that, son. But if there's even a glimmer of hope, you've got to try. Hell, you've got to try even if there isn't. Because what you have to offer is everything you are. It may not feel like it's enough but that's for her to decide. If you never put it out there, you'll spend your whole life feeling empty and alone. Trust me, that's no way to live."

What if Sam opened himself up to try? He may not feel as if he had enough to offer, but he was certain he'd work harder than any other man alive to make her happy. He wanted to see Charlie grow up, to be there for every T-ball game and skinned knee. He wanted to watch Julia hold their babies and grow old with her and everything that came between.

She was everything he'd ever wanted but was too scared to believe he deserved. He nodded as resolve built deep within him. "I've got to talk to her."

"You'd better get moving, then. She's got a head start on you."

Scott walked back into the room, balancing three glasses of whiskey. "Turn on ESPN and let's drown your sorrows."

Sam ignored his brother. "What do you mean 'head start'?" he asked his father. "Where did she go?"

"According to Vera, Julia took Charlie and headed to Ohio this morning. They caught a flight out of Charlotte. She told her mother she had some kind of a plan and needed to talk to the ex-boyfriend before the final ruling."

Sam's head spun. All he could think of was that Jeff had offered to marry Julia—some sort of business deal where Julia would come to Ohio to raise Charlie near the grandparents and they'd pay all the living expenses. Not a real relationship, but it was no better than what Sam had offered. And it would end the custody battle once and for all.

How could he have been stupid enough to let her go? What if she wouldn't take him back? What if she figured Charlie's father was a better deal?

Sam had to stop her. He loved her with his heart and soul. His life would be incomplete without Julia and Charlie in it, and he'd fight as long and as hard as he could to win them back.

He jumped off the couch and grabbed his keys and wallet from the side table. "I've got to go," he yelled to his father. "Lock up behind you."

Scott grabbed his arm as he strode past. "Don't do this. No woman is worth running after like you're some coweyed schoolboy."

"You're wrong," Sam answered, shrugging him off. "Julia is everything to me. Someday I hope you'll find a woman who makes you want to risk your heart. You deserve that. We both do. Dad's right. He messed up after Mom died, but we don't have to repeat his mistakes. I've got a chance to make it work and you'd better believe I'm going to take it."

"What if it's too late?"

"I've got to try."

Scott shook his head, disgust obvious in his angry gaze. "You have to be in D.C. tomorrow at eight o'clock sharp. You're going to make it, right?"

"I sure as hell hope not."

Scott cursed under his breath. "Idiot," he mumbled and drained his glass of Scotch.

"Sam."

Sam turned to his father. "I'm going to make it work, Dad. You know how relentless we Callahans can be."

"Good luck, son." Joe smiled at him. "I'm proud of you."

Scott snorted and picked up a second drink. "You go turn in your man card. I'm getting drunk."

Sam wanted to shake his brother, to open his eyes the way Sam's had been, but he didn't have time. His only priority right now was Julia and getting to her before she made a deal with Jeff Johnson.

"Sam?"

He turned to his father, who threw a small, velvet box in his direction. Sam caught it in one hand. "Is this…?" His voice trailed off as emotion overtook him.

"I had it sent down from Boston. Your mother would want you to have it."

He nodded. "Thanks, Dad," he said on a hoarse whisper then sprinted out the door.

"You've got a lot of nerve coming into my home uninvited." Maria Johnson looked down her nose at Julia. "Watch your child," she barked suddenly. "That's an antique Tiffany vase."

Julia leaned forward to pick up Charlie, who had toddled over to a wooden table and reached up to rub his tiny fingers on a glass vase perched on top.

"Hi, Mama," he said. His gaze went to Maria, who scowled at him, causing him to bury his face in Julia's neck.

Julia looked around the formal sitting room where a housekeeper had led her. It was cold, sterile and, like the rest of the house, totally inappropriate for an energetic boy. Even now she heard Maria *tsk* softly when she noticed the fingerprints Charlie had left around the bottom of the vase.

She'd asked for Jeff, but he was on his way back from a round of golf with his father. Unwilling to be distracted from her mission, or maybe afraid she'd lose her nerve,

Julia had insisted on being let into the enormous house. She'd known Jeff's family had money when they'd dated, but the *Dynasty*-sized home gave her a much better perspective on how rich the Johnsons really were. They clearly had unlimited resources at their disposal to get what they wanted.

Which brought her back to the matter at hand.

"I still can't believe you have the nerve to try to take my son from me," she said with a dry smile. "I guess that makes us even."

"Your case is crumbling, and you lied about your relationship status. It's only a matter of time until they take him from you. It will be better in the end. We can give him so much more than you could ever dream of. Look at Jeffrey."

"Speaking of *Jeffrey,* he asked me to marry him."

Maria didn't speak but the anger in her eyes said it all. Her face remained as smooth as marble, her expression typically blank, thanks to one too many cosmetic procedures. "Why would he do that? We don't need you to raise the child properly."

"Maybe giving a kid every material thing they want doesn't cut it. Your son is a loser, truth be told."

"How dare you! He's a respected professor with—"

"Funny, I thought that, too, when I first met him. Turns out, Jeff is a bit of a joke around campus. He does his research expeditions, conveniently funded by your husband's corporation, but little else." Julia sat Charlie on the floor and gave him several plastic toys from the diaper bag to keep him occupied. She dug through her bag for a stack of papers. "I have written documentation from the university about the sexual-misconduct charges filed against Jeff by four different undergraduates. Apparently, when he was teaching, it took a bit of extra work to get an A from Professor Johnson." Julia didn't mention that three of the incidents had happened during the time she'd been dating Jeff.

Maria tried to narrow her eyes, but they only moved a fraction. "How did you get those?"

Julia wasn't going to say where because she honestly didn't know. She hadn't even known until this moment whether the information she'd been given was real or fake. She'd been desperate, racking her brain for a way to make the custody battle go away, even wondering if she actually should accept Jeff's horrible proposal for Charlie's sake.

Then, two days ago, a package had arrived for her at the salon, containing the information about Jeff and other sordid details regarding the Johnsons.

At that moment, Jeff and his father walked into the room.

"What's she doing here?" Dennis Johnson said through his teeth.

"Julia, have you finally realized my offer's the best you're going to get?" Jeff gave her a wink and a sneer. To think she'd once found him attractive. She'd been such a fool. Charlie threw the set of plastic keys then went to retrieve them. Both men looked at him as though he was some sort of flesh-eating alien. There was no way she was going to let this family get their hands on her son for one minute, no matter what she had to do to prevent it.

"Jeffrey, be quiet." This from Maria. "Thanks to your on-campus dalliances, Ms. Morgan thinks she has some hold over us."

Jeff's voice turned petulant. "Mom, I didn't—"

"Sit down, son." Maria's voice took on a dictator-like quality and Jeff's mouth clamped shut. "You were groomed for so much more. We gave you everything." She pointed to the damask-covered couch. "Sit down and let your father and I fix this problem like we have all your others.

You've messed up things for the last time. We've got another chance with your son. I won't let you get in the way."

A sick pit grew in Julia's stomach as Jeff's shoulders slumped and he threw himself onto the couch. She'd known he didn't get along with his parents and now she understood why. She wondered how many of his problems were thanks to being raised by Mommy Dearest's twin sister.

Julia might have problems, but she knew she'd always put Charlie's best interests first in her life. Which was why she straightened her shoulders and said, "Jeff's not the only one in the family who has trouble keeping his parts in his pants." She waved a few more papers toward Dennis. "Like father, like son, from what I've discovered."

Dennis swallowed visibly as Maria sucked in a harsh breath. "How do you know that? No one has that information. I paid good money to make sure of it."

"Not enough, apparently." Julia picked up Charlie, who was grabbing at her legs. "Now let's talk—"

The door to the sitting room opened and Sam burst through, followed closely by the Johnsons' housekeeper.

"I'm sorry, ma'am," the older woman said, gasping. "He barged right past me."

Sam stood in the entry for a moment, looking every bit the bull in a china shop. Oh, how she loved him, even now. Every part of him. Julia's heart seemed to stop for a second. Charlie squirmed in her arms at the sight of Sam, squealing with delight. Julia hated that her body had the exact same reaction.

"The fake fiancé?" Jeff drawled from the couch. "Really, Julia? This is a bit of a production, even for you."

Sam pointed at Jeff. "Shut your mouth, pretty boy, or I'll come over and do it for you."

"What are you doing here, Sam?" Julia asked, her voice hoarse with emotion. She didn't want to need him. She didn't want to need anyone but was so relieved to not be fighting this battle alone, she could barely hold it together.

He looked at her and she knew he saw it, saw everything about her. He knew she had a tough exterior but was soft and scared at the core. And she knew it was okay to be vulnerable around him, that he wouldn't judge her or use her weakness to his advantage. Even with all that had happened between them, she ached to trust him. To lean on him and use his strength as her own.

"I'm here because at your side is where I belong. Forever."

"Don't bother," Maria said with a sniff. "There's no audience. The judge isn't here. No use pretending now, Chief Callahan. It's too late."

"That's where you're wrong." Sam took a step forward. "At least I hope you're wrong. Is it too late, Jules?"

"For what?"

"For me to be the man you want and need me to be." He walked toward her then bent to his knee. "For this." He pulled a small box out of his pocket and opened it, a diamond flanked by two emeralds twinkling up at her.

Julia and Maria gasped at the same time.

"It was my mother's ring. I want you to have it." He smiled at her hopefully. "I want all of it, Julia. You and Charlie and me. I love you. I want to spend the rest of my life proving how much. Proving I can be the man you deserve."

"What about the U.S. Marshals job?"

"I called today and said I wouldn't be joining them. The Brevia town council has renewed my contract for another three years. I'm there for keeps, and I want it to be with you. We're going to make this work. I'll be at your side fighting for Charlie, for our family, as long and as hard as it takes. Just don't give up on me, Julia."

Confined to her arms long enough, Charlie practically dived forward toward Sam, who wrapped his arms around him. "Hey, buddy. I've missed you."

He took the box from Sam's hand. "Here, Mama." Perched on Sam's knee, Charlie held the ring up to Julia.

She held out her hand, and the two men she loved most in the world slipped the ring onto her finger. "I love you, Sam. Always have. You had me at the car wreck two years ago."

He straightened and wrapped both her and Charlie in a tight hug then kissed her softly, using the pad of his thumb to wipe away the tears that flowed down her cheeks.

"This doesn't change anything," Maria hissed. "We've got all the time and money in the world."

"But don't forget the information I still have. I don't want to use it but I will, Mrs. Johnson. I'll do anything to keep my son safe."

"That won't be necessary." Jeff stood, looking as thoughtful and serious as Julia could ever remember.

"Jeffrey, stay out of this."

"Not this time, Mother." He took a step toward Julia and Sam. "I don't want to be a father. I never did. But I can tell you that my son deserves better than what I had growing up."

"You had everything," Dennis argued, his face turning bright red.

"He deserves a family who loves and cherishes him." Jeff's gaze never left Julia. "Have your attorney draw up the paperwork for me to relinquish custody and send it to my office at the university. I'll sign whatever you want me to."

"No!" his mother screeched.

Julia felt a lump form in her throat as Sam placed a

calming hand on her back. "Thank you, Jeff. You won't regret it."

One side of his mouth kicked up. "When it comes to funding my next research trip, I may. But I'll take that risk. Good luck, Julia." And with that, he walked from the room, followed quickly by his parents, screaming at him the entire way.

"Too 'oud," Charlie said, covering his ears with his chubby hands.

Sam's arm was strong around her shoulders. "Let's take our son home," he whispered against her ear. "We've got a wedding to plan."

* * * * *

A BRIDE'S
TANGLED VOWS

BY
DANI WADE

Dani Wade astonished her local librarians as a teenager when she carried home ten books every week—and actually read them all. Now she writes her own characters, who clamor for attention in the midst of the chaos that is her life. Residing in the southern United States with a husband, two kids, two dogs and one grumpy cat, she stays busy until she can closet herself away with her characters once more.

To the late Beverly Barton—you gave freely of your encouragement and advice the first time you read this story, and told me one day my time would come. Now that it's here, I wish I could share it with you. But I know your gorgeous smile is lighting up heaven. I look forward to seeing you again. . .

<u>One</u>

Aiden Blackstone suppressed a shiver that had nothing to do with the afternoon thunderstorm raging all around him. For a moment, he remained immobile, staring at the elaborate scrolls carved into the heavy oak door before him. A door he'd promised himself he'd never pass through again—at least, not while his grandfather was alive.

I should have come back here, Mother, only to see you.

But he'd sworn never to let himself be locked inside the walls of Blackstone Manor again. He'd thought he had all the time he would need to make his absence up to his mother. In his youthful ignorance, he hadn't realized everything he'd be giving up to uphold his vow. Now he was back to honor another vow—a promise to see that his mother was taken care of.

The thought had his stomach roiling. Shaking it off, he reached for the old-fashioned iron knocker shaped like a bear's head. The cab had already left. On a day plagued by steamy, ferocious southern thunderstorms, he certainly wouldn't be walking the ten miles back to Black Hills, no matter how much he dreaded this visit. His nausea eased as he reminded himself that he wouldn't be here for long—only as long as necessary.

Knocking again, he listened intently for footsteps on the other side of the door. *It wasn't really home if you had to wait for someone to answer.* He'd walked away with the surety that only comes with untried youth. Now he returned a different man, a success on his own terms. He just wouldn't have the satisfaction of rubbing his grandfather's nose in it.

Because James Blackstone was dead.

The knob rattled, then the door swung inward with a deep creak. A tall man, his posture still strong despite the gray hair disappearing from his head, blinked several times as if not sure his aging eyes were trustworthy. Though he'd left his childhood home on his eighteenth birthday, Aiden recognized Nolen, the family butler.

"Ah, Master Aiden, we've been expecting you," the older man said.

"Thank you," Aiden returned with polite sincerity, stepping closer to look into the butler's faded blue eyes. Lightning cracked nearby and thunder almost immediately boomed with wall-rattling force, the storm a reflection of the upheaval deep in Aiden's core.

Still studying his face, the older man opened the door wide enough for Aiden and his luggage. "Of course," Nolen said, shutting out the pouring rain behind them. "It's been a long time, Master Aiden."

Aiden searched the other man's voice for condemnation, but found none. "Please leave your luggage here. I'll take it up once Marie has your room ready," Nolen instructed.

So the same housekeeper—the one who'd baked cookies for him and his brothers while they were grieving the loss of their father—was still here, too. They said nothing ever changed in small towns. They were right.

Aiden swept a quick glance around the open foyer, finding it the same as when he'd left, too. The only anomaly was an absent portrait that captured a long-ago moment in time—his parents, himself at about fifteen and his younger twin brothers about a year before his father's death.

Setting down his duffel and laptop case and shaking

off the last drops of rain, he followed Nolen's silent steps through the shadowy breezeway at the center of the house. The gallery, his mother had always called this space that opened around the central staircase. It granted visitors an unobstructed view of the elaborate rails and landings of the two upper floors. Before air-conditioning, the space had allowed a breeze through the house on hot, humid, South Carolina afternoons. Today the sounds of his steps echoed off the walls as if the place were empty, abandoned.

But his mother was somewhere. Still in her old rooms, probably. Aiden didn't want to think of her, of how helpless her condition rendered her. And him. It had been so long since he'd last heard her voice on the phone, right before her stroke two years ago. After the car accident made travel difficult for her, Aiden's mother had called him once a week—always when James left the house. The last time he'd seen Blackstone Manor's phone number on his caller ID, it had been his brother calling to tell him their mother had suffered a stroke, brought on by complications from her paralysis. Then silence ever since.

To Aiden's surprise, Nolen went directly to the stairway, oak banister gleaming even in the dim light as if it had just been polished. Most formal meetings in the house were held in his grandfather's study, where Aiden had assumed he'd be meeting with the lawyer. He'd just as soon get down to business.

"Did the lawyer give up on my arrival?" Aiden asked, curious about why he was being shown to his room first.

"I was told to bring you upstairs," Nolen replied, not even glancing back. Did he view the prodigal son with suspicion, an unknown entity who would change life as Nolen had lived it for over forty years?

Damn straight. He had every intention of using his grandfather's money to move his mother closer to her sons and provide her with the best care for her condition, much better than he could give her personally. He'd sell off everything, then hightail it back to his business in New York City. He had nothing more than a hard-won career waiting for him there, but at least it was something he'd built on his own. He wanted nothing to do with Blackstone Manor or the memories hidden within its walls.

Having followed blindly, he abruptly noticed Nolen's direction. Uneasiness stirred low in Aiden's gut. His and his brothers' old rooms took up the third floor. To his knowledge—dated though it was—only two sets of rooms occupied the second floor: his mother's and his grandfather's suites. Neither of which was he ready to visit. His mother's—after he'd had time to prepare himself. His grandfather's—never.

The lawyer, Canton, had said James died last night. Aiden had been focused on packing and getting here since then. He'd address what the future held after talking with Canton.

He directed his question to Nolen's back as they neared the double doors to his grandfather's suite, his tone emerging huskier than he would have liked. "Nolen, what's going on?"

But the other man didn't reply; he just took the last few steps to the doors, then twisted the knob and stepped back. "Mr. Canton is inside, Master Aiden."

The words were so familiar, yet somehow not. Aiden drew a deep breath, his jaw tightening at the repeated use of Nolen's childhood designation for him.

But it beat being called Master Blackstone. They shouldn't even have the hated last name, but his mother had given in to old James's demands. The Blackstone name had to survive, even if his grandfather could only throw girls. So he'd insisted his only daughter give the name to her own sons, shutting out any legacy his father might have wanted.

Aiden shook his head, then pushed through the doorway

with a brief nod. He stepped into the room, warm despite the spring chill of the storm raging outside. His eyes strayed to the huge four-poster bed draped in heavy purple velvet.

His whole body recoiled. Watching him from the bed was his grandfather. His dead grandfather.

The rest of the room disappeared, along with the storm pounding against the windows. He could only stare at the man he'd been told had "passed on." Yet there he was, sitting up in bed, sizing up the adult Aiden with eyes piercing despite his age.

His body was thinner, frailer than Aiden remembered, but no one would mistake his grandfather for dead. The forceful spirit within the body was too potent to miss. Aiden instinctively focused on his adversary—the best defense was a strong offense. That strategy had kept him alive when he was young and broke; it did the same now that he was older and wealthier than he'd ever imagined he'd be when he'd walked away from Blackstone Manor.

"I knew you were a tough old bird, James, but I didn't think even you could rise from the dead," Aiden said.

To his surprise, his grandfather cracked a weak smile. "You always were a chip off the old block."

Aiden suppressed his resentment at the cliché and added a new piece of knowledge to his arsenal. James might not be dead, but his voice wavered, scratchy as if forced from a closed throat. Coupled with the milky paleness of his grandfather's once-bronze skin, Aiden could only imagine something serious must have occurred. *Why wasn't he in the hospital?*

Not that Aiden would have rushed home to provide comfort, even if he'd known his grandfather was sick. When he'd vowed that he wouldn't set foot in Blackstone Manor until his grandfather was dead, he'd meant it.

Something the old man knew only too well.

Anger blurred Aiden's surroundings for a moment. He

stilled his body, then his brain, with slow, even breaths. His tunnel vision suddenly expanded to take in the woman who approached the bed with a glass of water. James frowned at her, obviously irritated at the interruption.

"You need this," she said, her voice soft, yet insistent.

Something about that sound threatened to temper Aiden's reaction. Wavy hair, the color of pecans toasted to perfection, settled in a luxuriant wave to the middle of her back. The thick waves framed classic, elegant features and movie-star creamy skin that added a beauty to the sickroom like a rose in a graveyard. Bright blue-colored scrubs outlined a slender body with curves in all the right places—not that he should be noticing at the moment.

Just as he tried to pull his gaze away, one perfectly arched brow lifted. She stared James down, her hand opening to reveal two white capsules. That's when it hit him.

"Invader?"

He didn't realize he'd spoken aloud until she stiffened.

James glanced between the two of them. "You remember Christina, I see."

Only too well. And from her ramrod-straight back he gathered she remembered his little nickname for her. That stubborn *I will get my way* look brought it all back. She used to look at him that very same way when they were teenagers, after he'd brushed her off like an annoying mosquito, dismissed her without a care for her feelings. Just a pesky little kid always hanging around, begging his family for attention. Until that last time. The time he'd taunted her for trying to horn in on a family that didn't want her. Her tears had imprinted on his conscience, permanently.

"Aiden," she acknowledged him with a cool nod. Then she turned her attention back to James. "Take these, please."

She might look elegant and serene, but Aiden could see the steel beneath the silk from across the room. Was there sexy under there, too? *Nope, not gonna think about it.* His strict, one-night stand policy meant no strings, and that woman had hearth and home written all over her. He wouldn't be here long enough to find out anything…about anybody.

With a low grumble, James took the pills from her hand and chased them down with the water. "Happy now?"

His attitude didn't faze her. "Yes, thank you." Her smile only hinted that she was patronizing him. Her presence as a nurse piqued Aiden's curiosity.

His gaze lingered on her retreat to the far window, the rain outside a gray backdrop to her scrubs, before returning to the bed that dominated the room. His voice deepened to a growl. "What do you want?"

One corner of his grandfather's mouth lifted slightly, then fell as if his strength had drained away in a rush. "Straight to the point. I've always liked that in you, boy." His words slurred. "You're right. Might as well get on with it."

He straightened a bit in the bed. "I had a heart attack. Serious, but I'm not dead yet. Still, this little episode—"

"Little!" Christina exclaimed.

James ignored her outburst. "—has warned me it's time to get my affairs in order. Secure the future of the Blackstone legacy."

He nodded toward the suit standing nearby. "John Canton—my lawyer."

Aiden gave the man's shifting stance a good once-over. *Ah, the man behind the phone call.* "He must pay you well if you're willing to lie about life and death."

"He merely indulged me under the circumstances," James answered for Canton, displaying his usual unrepentant attitude. *Whatever it takes to get the job done.* The words James had repeated so often in Aiden's presence replayed through his mind.

"You're needed at home, Aiden," his grandfather said.

"It's your responsibility to be here, to take care of the family when I die."

"Again?" Aiden couldn't help saying.

Once more his grandfather's lips lifted in a weak semblance of the smirk Aiden remembered too well. "Sooner than I like to think. Canton—"

Aiden frowned as his grandfather's head eased back against the pillows, as if he simply didn't have the energy to keep up his diabolical power-monger role anymore.

"As your grandfather told you, I'm his lawyer," Canton said as he reached out to shake Aiden's hand, his grip forceful, perhaps overcompensating for his thin frame. "I've been handling your grandfather's affairs for about five years now."

"You have my condolences," Aiden said.

Canton paused, blinking behind his glasses at Aiden's droll tone.

James lifted his head, irritation adding to the strain on his lined face. "There are things that need to be taken care of, Aiden. Soon."

His own anger rushed to replace numb curiosity. "You mean, you're going to arrange everything so it will continue just the way you want it."

This time James managed to jerk forward in a shadow of his favorite stance: that of looming over the unsuspecting victim. "I've run this family for over fifty years. I know what's best. Not some slacker who runs away at the first hint of responsibility. Your mother—"

He fell back with a gasp, shaking as his eyes closed.

"Christina," Canton said, his sharp tone echoing in the room.

Christina crossed to the bed and checked James's pulse on the underside of his fragile wrist. Aiden noticed the tremble of her fingers with their blunt-cut nails. *So she wasn't indifferent.* Did she actually care for the old buzzard?

Somehow he couldn't imagine it. Then she held James's head while he swallowed some more water. Her abundant hair swung forward to hide her features, but her movements were efficient and sure.

Despite wanting to remain unmoved, Aiden's heart sped up. "You should be in a hospital," he said.

"They couldn't make him stay once your grandfather refused further treatments. He said if he was going to die, he would die at Blackstone Manor," Canton said. "Christina was already in residence and could follow the doctor's orders...."

His grandfather breathed deeply, then rested back against the pillows, his mouth drawn, eyes closed.

"Can you?" Aiden asked her.

She glanced up, treating him to another glimpse of creamy, flawless skin and chocolate eyes flickering with worry.

"Of course," she said, her tone matter-of-fact. "Mr. Blackstone isn't going to die. But he will need significant recovery time. I'd prefer him to stay in the hospital for a bit longer, but..." Her shrug said *what can you do when a person's crazy?*

Something about her rubbed Aiden wrong. She didn't belong in this room or with these people. Her beauty and grace shouldn't be sullied by his grandfather's villainous legacy. But that calm, professional facade masked her feelings in this situation. Was she just here for the job? Or another reason? Once more, Aiden felt jealous of her, wishing he could master his own emotions so completely.

But he was out of practice in dealing with the old man.

This time, Christina retreated to the shadows beyond the abundant purple bed curtains. Close, but not hovering. Though keenly aware of her presence, Aiden could barely make out her form as she leaned against the wall with her arms wrapped around her waist. It unsettled him, distracted him. Right now, he needed all his focus on the battle he sensed was coming.

"Your grandfather is concerned for the mill—" Canton said.

"I don't give a damn what happens to that place. Tear it down. Burn it, for all I care."

His grandfather's jaw tightened, but he made no attempt to defend the business where he'd poured what little humanity he possessed, completely ignoring the needs of his family. The emotional needs, at least.

"And the town?" Canton asked. "You don't care what happens to the people working in Blackstone Mills? Generations of townspeople, your mother's friends, kids you went to school with, Marie's nieces and nephews?"

Aiden clamped his jaw tight. He didn't want to get involved, but as the lawyer spoke, faces flashed through his mind's eye. The mill had stood for centuries, starting out as a simple cotton gin. Last Aiden had heard, it was a leading manufacturer in cotton products, specializing in high-end linens. James might be a bastard, but his insistence on quality had kept the company viable in a shaky economy. Aiden jammed a rough hand through his damp hair, probably making the spiky top stand on end.

Without warning, he felt a familiar surge of rebellion. "I don't want to take over. I've never wanted to." He strode across the plush carpet to stare out the window into the storm-shadowed distance. Tension tightened the muscles along the back of his neck and skull. Familial responsibility wasn't his thing—anymore. He'd handed that job over to his brothers a long time ago.

Aiden realized he was shifting minutely from one foot to the other. Creeping in underneath the turbulence was a constant awareness of Christina's presence, like a sizzle under his skin, loosening his control over his other emotions inch by inch. She drew him, kept part of his attention even when he was talking to the others. How had she come to be here? How long had she been here? Had she ever found a place to belong? The heightened emotion increased the tension in his neck. A dull headache started to form.

"You knew something like this was coming, considering your age—" Aiden gestured back toward the bed "—you should have sold. Or turned the business over to someone else. One of my brothers."

"It isn't their duty," James insisted. "As firstborn, it's yours—and way past time you learned your place."

As if he could sense the rage starting to boil deep inside Aiden, Canton stepped in. "Mr. Blackstone wants the mill to remain a family institution that will continue to provide jobs and a center for the town. The only potential buyers we have want to tear it down and sell off the land."

Aiden latched on to the family institution part. "Ah, the lasting name of Blackstone. Planned a monument yet?"

A weary yet insistent voice drifted from the bed. "I will do what needs to be done. And so will you."

"How will you manage that? I walked out that door once. I'm more than happy to do it again."

"Really? Do you think that's the best thing for your mother?" James went on as if Aiden hadn't spoken. "I've worked my entire life to build on the hard work of my own father. I will not let my life's work disappear because you won't do your duty. You will return where you belong. I'll see to that."

Aiden used his hand to squeeze away the tightness in his neck. "Oh, no. I'm not buying into that song and dance. As far as I'm concerned, this family line *should* die out. If the Blackstone name disappears, all the better."

"I knew you'd feel that way," his grandfather said with a long-suffering sigh. "That's why I'm prepared to make it worth your while."

* * *

Christina listened to the men spar with one another as if from a distance. Shock cocooned her inside her own bubble of fear.

Aiden's gaze tracked the lawyer's movements as he spoke, but Christina's remained focused on Aiden. The impenetrable mask of rebellion and pride that shielded any softer emotions. The breadth of his shoulders. The ripple of muscles in his chest and forearms, reminding her of his strength, his dominance.

Could a man that strong prevail over someone with James's history of cunning maneuvers, both business and personal?

"Why don't you just lay it out for me," Aiden said, his voice curt, commanding the immense space of the master suite. A shiver worked its way down Christina's spine. "The condensed version."

This time, Canton didn't look to James for permission. Proving he learned quickly, he cleared his throat and continued.

"Your grandfather set up legal documents covering all the angles," he said, pulling a fat pack of papers from his briefcase. "It essentially hands you the rights to the mill and Blackstone Manor."

"I told you," Aiden said. "I don't want it. Sell it."

Christina's throat closed in sympathy and fear.

"We can," Canton said. "The interested buyer is a major competitor, who will shut it down and sell it piece by piece. Including the land Mill Row is built on. And every last one of the people living in those fifty houses will be turned out so their homes can be torn down."

James joined in with relish. "The money from the sale will make a splendid law library at the university. Not the legacy I'd planned," he said with a shrug. "But it'll do."

Canton paused, but James wasn't one for niceties. "Go on," he insisted.

Canton hesitated a moment more, which surprised Christina. She hadn't cared for the weaselly man from the moment she'd first laid eyes on him, and his kowtowing to James had only reinforced her first impressions. For him to resist the old man—even in a small way—was new. Maybe having to face the person whose life he was ruining awakened a small bit of conscience.

"If you choose not to take over, Mr. Blackstone will exercise his power of attorney over his daughter to place her in the county care facility. Immediately."

A cry lodged in Christina's throat before it escaped as she envisioned the chaos this would unleash, the disruption and danger to Lily, Aiden's mother. She'd cared for Lily for five years, from the moment Christina had received her nursing degree. But Lily had been a second mother to her long before that, the type of mother she'd never had. The last thing she'd allow to happen would be handing Lily over for substandard care.

Aiden's intense gaze swiveled to search the dark recess where she stood. The shadows comforted her, helped her separate from the confrontation playing out before her. But that intense gaze pulled her forcibly into the present. His brows drew together in concern, the only emotion to soften him so far. She could literally feel every time his gaze zeroed in on her—a mixture of nerves and a physical reaction she'd never experienced before today.

But then his eyes narrowed on his grandfather, his face hardening once more. "What would happen to Mother there?"

James smiled, as his hateful words emerged from taunting lips. "Christina, I believe you've been to the county care facility, haven't you? During your schooling, wasn't it? Tell Aiden about it."

Christina winced as she imagined what Aiden must be thinking. Only someone as manipulative and egocentric as James could determine that this scenario—disowning his own invalid daughter—was the best way to preserve his little kingdom. Her voice emerged rusty and strained. "It's gotten an inferior rating for as many years as I've been a nurse, and it's had regular complaints brought against it for neglect…but very little has been done because it's the only place here that will take in charity cases for the elderly or disabled."

"How do you know I don't have enough money to take away that option?" Aiden asked, a touch of his grandfather's arrogance bleeding onto that handsome face.

Canton replied. "You can try, but with power of attorney, your grandfather has the final say."

"We'll just go to court and get it transferred to one of my brothers."

But not himself, Christina noted.

"You can, and I can't stop you," James said. "But how long do you think that case will take? Months? A year? Will your mother have that long…in that environment?"

"You'd do that to her, your own daughter?" Aiden asked James.

Having watched him since she was a kid, instinctively knowing he was even more dangerous than her own family but drawn inexplicably by Lily's love and concern, Christina fully acknowledged what James was capable of, the lack of compassion he felt for others. He'd turn every one of them out without one iota of guilt, might even enjoy it if he was alive to see it happen.

She rubbed trembling, sweaty palms against her thighs. Would Lily survive the impersonal, substandard care at that facility? For how long? Although Lily was in a coma, Christina firmly believed she was at times aware of her surroundings. The last time they'd moved Lily to the private hospital for some necessary tests, she'd gotten agitated, heartbeat racing, then ended up catching a virus from hospital germs. How long could she be exposed to the lower standards at the county facility without being infected with something deadly?

As numbness gave way to fiery pain, Christina stumbled forward. "Of course he would."

She didn't mean for the bitterness or desperation to bleed into her voice. The fire that started to smolder in Aiden's almost-black eyes sent a shiver over her, though he never looked her way.

"You son of a bitch," he said, spearing James with a glare. "Your own daughter—no more than a pawn in your little game."

Christina's heart pounded as fear battled awareness in her blood. This man, and the fierceness of his anger, mesmerized her. She instinctively knew he could introduce a whole new element of danger to this volatile situation.

James punched the bed with a weak fist. "This isn't a game. My legacy, the mill, this town, must continue or all will be for nothing. Better two people pay the price than the whole town."

Aiden frowned, his body going still. "Two of us?"

Canton raised his hand, drawing attention his way. "There's an additional condition to this deal. You can accept all or nothing."

Dragging a hand through his hair once more, Aiden moved away, stopping by the window to stare out at the heavy rain. Lightning flashed, outlining his strong shoulders and stiff posture.

Canton cleared his throat. "You must marry and reside in Blackstone Manor for one year. Only then will your grandfather release you from the bargain, or release your inheritance to you, if he has passed on."

Aiden drew a deep, careful breath into his lungs, but one

look at his grandfather seemed to crack his control. Words burst from between those tightened lips. "No. Absolutely not. You can't do that."

James's body jerked, his labored breathing rasping his voice. "I can do whatever I want, boy. The fact that you haven't visited your own mother in ten years means no judge will have sympathy for you if you try to get custody." His labored breathing grew louder. "You'd do well to keep your temper under control. Remember the consequences the last time you crossed me."

Christina winced. She'd seen more than one instance of James's consequences—they hadn't been pretty. Lily had told her Aiden's continued rebellion had cost him access to his mother, and eventually cost Lily her health.

"Why me?" Aiden asked. "Why not one of the twins?"

James met the question with a cruel twist of his lips. "Because it's you I want. A chip off the old block should be just stubborn enough to lead a whole new generation where *I* want it to go."

The cold shock was wearing off now, penetrated by sharp streaks of fear. Nolen, Marie and Lily—the other residents of Blackstone Manor—weren't technically Christina's relatives. Not blood-related, at least. But they were the closest she'd come in her lifetime to being surrounded by people who cared about her. She wasn't about to see them scattered to the winds, destroyed by James's sick game of king of the world.

Besides, she owed this family, and the intense, dark-eyed man before her. Most of all, she owed Lily. Her debt was bigger than Lily had ever acknowledged or accepted Christina's apologies for. If being used as a pawn would both settle her debt and protect those she'd come to love, then she'd do it. Christina's family had taught her one lesson in her twenty-six years: how to make herself useful.

The lawyer stepped up to the plate. "Everything is set

up in the paperwork. You either marry and keep the mill viable, or Ms. Blackstone will be moved immediately."

A strained cackle had Aiden glancing at his grandfather. "Take it or leave it," James rasped.

Christina barely detected the subtle slump of defeat in Aiden's shoulders. "And just where am I supposed to find a paragon willing to sacrifice herself for the cause?"

"I'd think you'd be pretty good at hunting treasure by now," James said, referring to Aiden's career as an art dealer, already reveling in the victory they could all see coming.

"I've never been interested in a wife. And I doubt anyone would be willing to play your games, Grandfather."

Taking a deep breath, Christina willed away the nausea crawling up the back of her throat. She pushed away from the wall. "I will," she said.

Two

"Oh, and one last thing…"

When spoken by James, those were not the words Christina wanted to hear. She eyed the door to the suite with longing. Only a few more feet and she'd be free…

For now.

"A platonic relationship between you two isn't acceptable. My goal is a legacy. I can't get that with separate bedrooms."

Panic bubbled up beneath the surface of her skin until Aiden replied with a droll, "Grandfather, you can lead a horse to water, but you can't make it drink."

Even from her new viewpoint near the door, Christina could see the twist of James's lips. "My dear boy, lead a horse to water often enough, and it will damn sure get thirsty."

The bad part was, James was right. She'd only been in the room with Aiden for a half hour and the awareness of him as a man sizzled across her with every look. But sleep with him? A man who was practically a stranger to her? She couldn't do that.

But what about Lily?

Christina noted the fine tension in Aiden's shoulders beneath his damp dress shirt. The whole room seemed to hold its breath, waiting on someone to make the next move. But it wouldn't be her—right now, she had no clue what to do, what to think. She just needed out of here.

Echoing her thoughts, Aiden turned toward her and took a few steps, only pausing for a brief glance back at his grandfather. "I refuse to make this kind of choice within a matter of minutes. Or to let Christina do so. I'll be back later tonight."

Aiden's control as he ushered them both from the room intrigued her. What was really going on behind his mask of defiance?

Christina maintained her own poise until the door to the master suite clicked shut behind her. Then she stumbled across the hall to the landing as if she was drunk. Pausing with a tight grasp on the cool wood of the balustrade, she drew air into lungs that felt like they were burning.

She'd just volunteered to become Aiden Blackstone's wife. But considering James's final requirement, how would she ever go through with it?

Startled by the shuffle of feet behind her, she tightened her grip on the wooden banister. Knowing Aiden and Canton were approaching, Christina struggled to pull herself together. She needed to get through the rest of the afternoon without the veneer cracking.

Just as she turned back to face the others, Nolen appeared at the end of the hallway. The old butler's eyes carried more than their share of worry as he approached, but he didn't say anything. He probably knew every detail of what had transpired in James Blackstone's suite this afternoon. Somehow, he and Marie always knew.

From behind her, Canton's voice rang clear. "It's early still. We can go down to the probate judge's office now and get the paperwork started. You can be married within a week."

Nolen frowned back at the lawyer, his glower making her feel cared for, protected. It was a rare occurrence for her—she was used to being the protector—making it that much more appreciated. Her heart swelled, aching with love and worry of her own. She slowly shook her head as she turned to face the men. "I need to think. Some time to think." She struggled to clear her clouded thoughts. "And I need to check on Lily."

"She's fine with Nicole," Nolen said, extending his elbow so she could take his arm. Old-fashioned to the core. Her muscles relaxed; her smile appeared. He smiled back. "But we'll stop by if it will ease your mind."

Resigning herself to his help because she knew it would soothe his concern, she slipped her hand into the crook of his arm. They crossed the landing to the other suite of rooms on the second floor. With a deep breath, Christina paused to look back over her shoulder. "Aiden, will you come see Lily?"

He watched her from several feet away, hooded lids at half-mast, hiding the only thing that would showcase his emotions. "Later," he said, short and definitely not sweet. But his still features didn't tell her whether he simply couldn't face his mother or simply didn't care. He turned to Canton. "I'm not going anywhere until I've looked over those papers and talked to my own lawyer."

With a short nod, Canton moved to the stairs and started down. Aiden followed, his stiff back forcefully cutting off any approach.

Nolen harrumphed in disapproval, but Christina ignored him. Maybe she was imagining the loneliness in that brief look from Aiden, but he seemed cloaked in an aura of solitude. With a quiet knock, Nolen let them into Lily's suite, leaving the mystery of Aiden behind her.

Here, filtered sunlight illuminated lavender-flowered wallpaper and a slightly darker carpet, the soft decor far removed from the oppressive majesty of the opposite suite. The tranquility soothed Christina's shaky nerves. They passed through a sitting room with the television turned low to the sleeping area beyond.

Nicole, the housekeeper's grandniece, sat in the overstuffed chair by the adjustable bed James had specially ordered. She looked up from the thick nursing textbook in her lap.

"Come to check on her?" Nicole asked.

Christina nodded. "How's she doing?"

"Oh, the storm did neither of us any good, but after I did her exercises, she settled right down." Nicole flashed a toothy smile, bright against her tanned skin. "Her vitals are normal, so she's resting fine now. Still a little spooky, though, seeing her respond like that."

"Oh, you'd be surprised at the stories nurses have about comatose patients. It's a very interesting area of study." Christina should know; she'd studied every case history, textbook explanation and word-of-mouth example she'd been able to get her hands on. The stroke damage had healed; still, Lily had not come back to them.

"You're gonna make a wonderful nurse someday, Nicole," Nolen said, beaming as if she were his own grandchild.

"Yes, you are," Christina agreed. She'd encouraged Nicole from the moment the girl had come around asking questions about Christina's duties. Now the young woman was a nursing student at the university forty minutes away and helped Christina with Lily on certain nights and weekends.

Christina went through the motions of checking Lily's pulse while Nicole and Nolen quietly discussed some problems she'd had with her car this week.

Christina laid her hand on Lily's forehead, noting the normal temperature, and scanned the monitors beeping nearby through habit. But there, the professionalism ended. She leaned closer to Lily's ear.

"He's home, Lily." She sighed. "He doesn't like it, but for now, he's here. I'll bring him to see you soon."

There was no indication that Lily had heard, just the beeps of the monitors. Lily's thin, pale features never moved; her eyes never opened. But Christina had to believe she was happy to know her son was back under Blackstone Manor's roof. She wouldn't be happy about her father's machinations, though. To force two people to marry... Christina shivered as she remembered the feel of Aiden's intense gaze penetrating the thin veneer with which she protected her emotions.

The housekeeper's arrival drew her from her thoughts. "So what's this I hear about a wedding?" Marie asked, marching in, still dressed in the apron printed with the words "I make this kitchen hotter" the sixty-five-year-old wore whenever she knew James wouldn't catch her.

Christina wanted to groan. How had the news spread through the house so fast? Sometimes she thought the staff had the place bugged.

"It's more of a business agreement than a wedding," Christina said, a slight wave of dizziness rushing over her at the thought. *"If* there is a wedding..." She wasn't entirely sure Aiden would go through with it, once that hot streak of defiance cooled. Could she, if it gave her the legal right to protect Lily?

But she couldn't share a bed with him. Surely, they could get around that part....

"It's unnatural, is what it is," Nolen interjected. "Two strangers entering into something as sacred as marriage."

"And those words of wisdom brought to you by a lifelong bachelor." Marie grinned. "Besides, they aren't strangers. They've known each other since they were kids."

There were flutters of panic in Christina's chest as she remembered that last face-to-face meeting with a seventeen-year-old Aiden. She'd mooned over him from afar every time she came to visit Blackstone Manor. Sometimes the hope of seeing him had drawn her just as much as Lily's company, but that day had taught her well how little he felt for her. Whenever she'd come near him, he'd demonstrated the same unpleasant endurance as her parents, who also looked at her as a pest that they wished would disappear. He'd called her *invader* many times over the years she'd hung around, aching for a bit of Lily's attention. Yes, that was definitely how he'd seen her time here at Blackstone Manor. After that final rejection, she'd stayed as far away from Aiden Blackstone as possible.

Nolen wasn't letting this go. "It is unnatural, I'm tellin' you. This isn't a good thing. James is manipulating them, and Aiden, his own grandson, into marrying for his own damnable purposes."

"And what purposes would those be?" Marie asked, her hands going to her hips.

Christina's mouth was already open, but Nolen spoke first. "Building some god-awful legacy. As if he hasn't introduced enough unpleasantness into this world. He threatened his own daughter if they didn't do what he wanted."

"Oh, I bet that's all talk." Marie looked sideways at Christina with a worried frown pulling all her wrinkles in a southern direction. "Is this true? Is he forcing you into something you don't want?"

This was getting way out of hand—and way more personal than Christina wanted. "No. I volunteered. And nothing has been decided yet." *But I will take care of Lily—and all of you.*

Marie went on, her frown softening a little. "Maybe our Christina is exactly what Aiden needs right now. These things happen for a reason, I do believe."

Christina's heart melted with Marie's sugar-scented hug, but she doubted anything she did would soften the hardened heart of the Blackstone heir.

"You never know what might happen in a year," Marie

said with a sly smile. "Besides, family takes care of their own. She'll be fine here with us."

This conversation was almost unbelievable. If Christina hadn't been in James's room, she wouldn't have believed the situation herself.

Christina's mind echoed with Marie's words. A year was a short time in some ways, a long time in others. Would she come out on the other side whole? Or with a broken heart to go with her divorce decree?

As long as Lily and the rest of her family were safe and cared for, it would be worth it for Christina. Marie was right. These people were her family, as close as she'd come to having one since her parents had divorced when she was eight. Who was she kidding? Her family had never been real.

As a child, Christina's sole purpose in life had been as a pawn in her mother's strategy to extort more and more money from her father. That's where Christina had learned what two-faced meant—her mother all lovey-dovey when Dad showed up, abandoning her at her society friends' houses when she was no longer useful. A hard lesson, but Christina had learned it well.

She'd promised herself when she'd turned eighteen that she'd never go back to that kind of situation; never again have no value outside of what she could do for another.

So was she *truly* willing to become James Blackstone's pawn?

"When are you heading back? That Zabinski woman is killing me."

He didn't want to think about Ellen Zabinski right now. He had enough problems on his hands. After a solid twenty-four hours of thinking, Aiden knew what he had to do. He still didn't want to, but this choice was inevitable.

"I'm not."

The dead silence would have been amusing if Aiden wasn't in such a bind. His assistant Trisha's silence was as rare as some of the art he imported. While he waited for her to recover, he paced across his bedroom to gaze out the back window. He compared the view of the lush country yard, the gentle sway of the grass and tree branches in the breeze, with the constant motion of the city. The very sereneness made him want to fall asleep. Not in a good way. Why would he consider uprooting his busy life, even if it was only for a few months?

A myriad of reasons not to do this rambled through his mind—work, taking a stand against his grandfather's high-handedness, a lack of interest in the mill and a whole host of other things. Then his gaze fell on the chestnut-haired beauty strolling across the lawn to talk to the gardener. Christina smiled, stealing his breath. Her stride was sure, and those hips… As she spoke, her hands gestured with elegant grace to illustrate her words.

He should be worried about his mom—not her nurse. But as Christina looked up into the fifty-year-old weeping willow in the backyard, exposing the vulnerable skin of her throat, Aiden's mouth watered.

When Trisha finally spoke again, her words were slow and measured. "What's going on?"

"Let's just say, I will be stuck cleaning up family business for a while."

She wasn't buying that. "How long can it take to get the ball rolling on the estate? He had a will, right? Why would that require you to be on-site?"

"Yes, he had a will, but that's not really helpful since he isn't dead."

A single bout of silence from Trisha was a surprise. Twice in one conversation—a miracle. But she came back with her usual snarky humor.

"So are you trying to talk me into moving to the wilds of South Carolina? Marty wouldn't care much for that."

Just the thought of Italian-born-and-bred Antonio Martinelli in Black Hills was enough to brighten Aiden's day. "No, as amusing as that would be, I was thinking more along the lines of giving you an assistant and a raise."

Make that three spells of silence, although the pause was much shorter this time. "Don't tease me, Aiden."

"I'm not kidding," he said, feeling as if he should raise his hand in a scout-style salute. "You've worked hard, sharpened your own sales skills. I'm gonna need help to pull this off. We can do a lot by conference call and video chats, and I'll make a trip up there when necessary. But the majority of first contact and sales will fall on you."

Aiden ignored the surge of misery at the thought of being away from his business for long. But he wouldn't be out of contact. And he *would not* lose the gem it had cost him years of his life to build.

"It's only temporary," he assured his assistant and himself. "Just until I can get legal custody of Mother." But watching until Christina disappeared from sight, Aiden knew his motives weren't nearly that noble.

Turning away, he gave Trisha a brief rundown of his grandfather's demands.

"Whoa," she said. "And I thought Italian-American grandparents were demanding. That's crazy. Why would you go through with that?"

"At least a wife will give me a weapon against Ellen," he said, making light of his current struggle. Shivers erupted just thinking about the barracuda with whom he'd mildly enjoyed his customary night, only to have her decide once wasn't enough. She'd spent the last month making his life miserable. "How often has she called the office?" Aiden had blocked her from his cell phone.

"Oh, every afternoon like clockwork. She doesn't believe that you aren't here. I'm just waiting for her to show up in person and force me to pull out my pepper spray."

There was way too much glee in his assistant's voice. "Don't get arrested."

"I won't…if she behaves herself—"

Doubtful. But Trisha handled most situations with tact— even if she talked tough. "Do whatever you have to do. Maybe me being out of town for several months will help. In the meantime, you can forward *client* calls to my cell."

They talked a few more logistics, and Aiden promised to be in touch daily. Balancing two businesses in two different states would not be a walk in the park, but he was determined to hold on to whatever he could in New York.

His grandfather might take his freedom, but he would not destroy everything Aiden had worked so hard to build.

Three

Aiden's uncharacteristic urge to curse like a sailor was starting to irritate him. As he snatched one of the cookies Marie had left cooling on the kitchen counter, he contemplated the grim facts. His lawyer hadn't found a way around the legal knots James had tied. There wasn't evidence to have him declared mentally unstable. He was, but then he'd always been. If jackassery could be considered a mental condition. And any legal proceedings to steal guardianship of his mother would take too long. Aiden wasn't willing to chance his mother's health and well-being. He owed her too much.

So his bad mood was justified, but when he found himself stomping up the narrow back staircase from the kitchen, the taste of chocolate chip cookie lingering on his tongue, he knew it was time to get himself under control. After all, he wasn't a schoolboy or angst-ridden teen. He was a man capable of engineering million-dollar art deals. He could handle one obstinate grandfather and a soon-to-be bride—but only with a cool head.

As a distraction, his mind drifted to other days blessed with warm cookies, spent playing hide-and-seek or sword-wielding pirates on these dark stairs. The perfect atmosphere for little-boy secrets and make-believe. He and his brothers had also used them to disappear when their grandfather came looking for them. He'd often been on a terror about something or other. They'd sneak down and out the kitchen door for a quick escape.

Aiden stretched his mouth into a grim smile as he rounded a particularly tight bend. Escape was something he'd always excelled at. Except with Ellen Zabinski.

He didn't hear the footsteps until too late. He'd barely looked up before colliding with someone coming down the stairs. A soft someone who emitted a little squeal as she stumbled. Certain they'd fall, Aiden surged forward to keep from losing his balance. Christina tried to pull back, but her momentum worked against her. Hands flailed, finding purchase on his shoulders. Her front crushed to his. Their weight pressed dead against each other, stabilizing as two became one.

Everything froze for Aiden, as if his very cells locked down. He managed one strangled breath, filled with the fresh scent of her hair, before his body sprang to life. Her soft curves and sexy smell urged him to pull her closer, so much so that his fingers tightened against the rounded curves of her denim-covered hips. The soft flesh gave beneath his grip.

He'd been without a woman for far too long. That had to be why he was so off balance. His strict adherence to his "no attachments" rule had led to a lifetime of brief encounters. His last choice had been a wrong one, a woman who wasn't happy when he walked out the door the next morning. It had soured him on any woman since.

Darkness permeated the staircase, heightening the illusion of intimacy. His and Christina's accelerated breaths were the only sound between them. They were so close, he felt the slight tremor that raced over her echo throughout his entire body. It took more minutes than Aiden cared to admit for his mind to kick into gear.

"Dreamed up more ways to invade my territory, Christina?"

He felt her stiffen against his palms, tension replacing that delicious softness. Just as he'd intended.

Before he could regret anything, she retreated, stabilizing herself with a hand against the wall. "Aiden," she said, prim disapproval not hiding a hint of breathlessness, "I'm sorry for not seeing you."

I'm not.

"And for the record, I'm not invading anything. So I'd thank you to never call me by that stupid nickname."

It was a sign of his own childhood needs that he'd resented the attention she'd received here at Blackstone Manor when they were kids, enough to tease her with his *invader* tag. There had been times he'd felt as if she *had* invaded their chaotic life, garnering what little positive attention there was to go around. How he'd resented that. To the point that, one hot summer afternoon, he'd spoken harsh words he'd always regret.

"I'm trying to help, Aiden. I really am." Her voice came out low, intensifying the sense of intimacy.

He had to clear his own throat before he spoke again. "Why? I'm nothing to you."

"And I realize I'm nothing to you, but I care very much for Lily."

He could feel his suspicious nature, the one that served him so well in business negotiations, kick in. "So what's he have on you, sweetheart?"

Christina didn't pretend not to understand. "Lily."

"Why? There are other jobs, other people in need of a nurse."

Her glare was almost visible in the dim light. He should feel lucky he wasn't smoldering under that fire. Instead, a cool brush of air drifted over him as she shifted back on the steps. "If you had hung around over the past ten years, you'd know that Lily has been like a mother to me. Ever since we were kids." Pausing to swallow, she looked down for a moment. When she spoke, her voice was once more firm and devoid of emotion. "I understand what's being required of me."

Somehow that monotone didn't make him any happier than her anger, and he couldn't resist the urge to shake her out of it. "You'd sell yourself to a stranger for what, money? Hoping ol' Granddad will give you a piece of the pie if you work hard enough for it?"

"No," she insisted. "I'm *not* selling myself, but I will sacrifice myself to do what I think is right for Lily." She reached out in a pleading gesture, but jerked back as her fingertips brushed his chest. A deep breath seemed to stabilize her control. The professional was back. "It's my belief as a nurse, and as Lily's friend, that she's conscious of where she is. This house has been her sanctuary since her car accident. I can guarantee that removing her from here will negatively affect her physical and emotional condition. Especially if he puts her in—" a shudder worked its way over her "—that place. I'll do whatever's necessary to keep Lily out of there.... Will you?"

Aiden shifted his legs, wishing he could pace despite the confinement of his surroundings. "Would he really do that to her, you think?"

An unladylike snort sounded in the air, surprising him. But Christina obviously wasn't in the mood to pull her punches. "Have you forgotten that much already? He's only become more pigheaded through the years."

"You seem to handle him pretty well," he said, remembering how she'd stared James down over the medicine.

Her brow lifted in disbelief. "He only concedes to my medical expertise because he's afraid of dying."

"He's not afraid of anything."

"Actually, Aiden, deep down we're all afraid of something." Her shaky breath told him she was afraid of something, too, but she wasn't revealing any secrets. "Death is the only thing James can't outwit, outsmart or bully into getting his way."

Though he didn't understand why, Aiden felt a strange kinship tingle at the edge of his consciousness. She might look delicate, but Christina was racking up evidence of being one smart cookie. On top of that, a common bond tightened between them: Lily. He knew the source of his guilt—his obligation to his mother. Despite her words, he knew Christina's devotion to Lily wasn't just friendship; something else lurked beneath that fierce dedication. Was it just how good Lily had been to her? Or something more? He'd find out what was going on there. She could bet on it.

The sudden silence must have become too much for her, because Christina moved forward as if to continue down the stairs. The polite thing would have been to step aside, but the ache to feel that body against his once more kept him perversely still. She slowed within a hairbreadth, tension mounting once more. "Aiden?"

"So you're really willing to do this?" he asked, almost holding his breath as he awaited her answer. What delicious torture to spend the next year with this woman and keep his hands to himself. Could he? *This was a huge mistake.*

"I don't know. I don't think I can, you know, share a bed with you."

The way her voice trailed off told him how very uncomfortable she was, which only awakened images of making her very comfortable in a bed for two. But maybe he could find a way to make this work.

"Don't worry. I'll figure out a way around that."

"Do you have any other choices for a wife?" she asked. "I didn't really give you a chance to choose."

Arguments? He had a few, but none that were effective. Excuses? A whole hay wagon full, but none he dared utter in the face of the threat to his mother's well-being. Other women? He could think of many a delectable armful over the last ten years, but none interested in anything as mundane as marriage. He'd stayed far away from the home-and-hearth type.

"No," he conceded, then stepped aside to let her pass. "I don't think I could pay my assistant enough to move to the middle of nowhere and put up with me 24/7."

"It's hardly the middle of nowhere," she said with a light tone as she scooted past, brushing the far wall in an attempt not to touch him again.

Which was just as well.

She continued, "We might not have the culture of New York City, but there's still a movie theater, nice restaurants and the country-club set." She kept that delicate face turned resolutely away as he followed her into the soft afternoon light of the kitchen. "Not something I'm that interested in, but to each his own."

Interesting. "What do your parents think about that?"

"Who knows?" *And who cares,* her tone said. Could she really brush aside what her family thought that easily? Everything he'd seen since his return made him think she was family-focused. Her graceful appearance, fierce loyalty and career choice made her seem exactly like the marriage, kids and picket-fence type. All the more reason to keep his pants zipped around her.

What were they going to do about that bed? It was long moments later before she finally turned to face him, but for once the delicate lines of her face told him nothing.

"Honestly, Aiden, I want to help. This situation is uncomfortable at best, but for Lily…"

She'll do anything. Her earlier question rang once more in his ears: Would he put aside his own selfish wants, his own desire to run far, far away for the second time, for the needs of his mother and his childhood home?

Would he?

* * *

Christina picked her way down the damp concrete steps in front of the stately Black Hills courthouse. Thunderstorms had blown through during the night, leaving a cool breeze that rustled through the Bradford pear trees lining the square. Her trembling body felt just as jostled as she followed Aiden and Canton. Were her feet really numb or was that just the shock of signing the papers?

"It's official," the probate judge had said, beaming with the pride of initiating a Blackstone marriage.

Luckily, it wasn't truly official—she still had about a week before the marriage license came in to regain her senses, but picturing Lily at home, fragile yet safe in her bed, told Christina she wouldn't change her mind.

She couldn't turn her back on the friend who'd given up so much for her.

The three of them reached the bottom just as a group of local guys approached. Cleaned up from work in jeans and button-downs, they looked like what they were—small-town guys headin' down to start their weekend with some fun at Lola's, the local bar.

"Well, look at this, boys. It's Aiden Blackstone, back from New York City."

Christina cringed inside. Jason Briggs had to be the cockiest guy in Black Hills, and had the mouth to prove it. Not someone she wanted to deal with given her current edgy nerves.

"Jason." Aiden acknowledged the other man with the single, short word. From his tight tone, Christina guessed his memories of Jason were anything but fond.

"Whatya doin' back here?" Jason asked, as if it was any of his business. "Can't imagine you showing up after all this time for a pleasure visit." He glanced past Aiden to Christina. "Or is it?"

The guys with him snickered, causing Christina to tense. While Aiden didn't seem like the "let's solve this with our fists" type, Jason had been known to push lesser men over the edge. The differences between the two were clear. Aiden was perfectly at home in his dress pants and shoes, his own button-down tucked in and sporting the sheen of a silky material. He wasn't the old-school business-suit type, but he looked like a sophisticated professional, while the dark, stylishly spiked hair and his brooding look gave him that creative edge that probably had the women of New York swooning like Southern belles.

She knew she was.

But in the midst of the other men, it was like comparing dynamite to ordinary firecrackers. Jason and his crew might be the big fish in this tiny pond, but Christina put her money on the shark invading their midst.

The metaphor proved apt as Aiden ignored their ribbing with the confidence of someone who couldn't be beaten. "I'm here to take over my grandfather's affairs, now that he's become ill," he said with quiet confidence, not mentioning the true purpose of this little visit to the courthouse.

It was Canton who stirred the waters. "Including the running of the mill," he added.

Rumblings started from the back of the group, but Jason shrugged off the explanation with a smart, "Doubt he can fix what's wrong any more than a good ol' boy like Bateman can."

"Who's Bateman?" Aiden asked.

The men simply stared at him for a minute before Christina answered. "Bateman is the current day foreman at the mill."

"Check it out," Jason said, raising his voice just a bit. "Guy doesn't even know who the foreman is, and he thinks he's gonna stop all the bull that's been going on over there."

"I'm sure I'll manage," Aiden said, cool, calm and collected. Standing tall on the steps, his back braced and arms folded across his chest, giving him the presence of a leader.

Jason held his gaze for a moment, probably an attempt to stare Aiden down, then shifted his cocky eyes to Christina. A weaker target. She fought the urge to ease behind Aiden's strong back for protection. Jason was older than she was by a few years, but that hadn't stopped him from hitting on her when they were teenagers. He hadn't appreciated her rejection, and now enjoyed hassling her whenever they met. "I guess you filled him in, huh, sweet cheeks? Is that all you gave him? Information?"

Confident he'd gotten a few good jabs in, Jason decided he was done with them. With a self-assured jerk of his head, he got the whole crew moving like the lemmings they were.

Aiden watched them go before asking, "So he works out at the mill?"

Canton replied before Christina could. "Yes. His father is in management, I believe."

"That's not going to help him if he ever talks to Christina like that again."

Startled, Christina eyed Aiden's hard jaw and compressed lips. She'd never had a champion before, at least, not one capable of doing much in her defense. That Aiden would punish Jason on her behalf…she wasn't sure how to feel about that.

Christina frowned after the departing group. Maybe she had more of her mother's tastes than she'd wanted to admit. None of the local guys had ever interested her much. Jerks like Jason who thought they were God's gift to the women of this town didn't help. But Aiden's quietly sophisticated, confident aura made her stomach tighten every time she saw him. Which was trouble, big trouble. Especially when she started looking to him for more than just that tingling rush.

Glancing back at the men, she found Aiden watching her intently. Her cheeks burned. *Please don't let him be able to guess my thoughts.*

"What's he talking about?" Aiden asked.

Was he asking her? Why not the lawyer? But the direction of Aiden's stare was plain.

"Well, I know there've been some problems out at the mill. Strange things happening. Shipments delayed or missing altogether. Perfectly good equipment breaking unexpectedly. Things like that."

"Sabotage?" Aiden asked with narrowing eyes.

Canton broke in. "Absolutely not. Just a coincidence, is all."

But Christina wasn't about to lie to the person she hoped would be able to fix it. "Some people say it is. But there's no proof of anything. Still, people in the town are starting to get antsy, superstitious, worried about their jobs—"

Canton cleared his throat, shooting her a "shut your mouth" glare. "Everything will be fine once they realize a strong Blackstone is back at the helm."

Still, Aiden watched her, assessing as if he were cataloging her every feature. But then his gaze seemed to morph into something more, something she couldn't look away from as heat spread through her limbs like seeping honey. When was the last time a man, any man, had truly seen her? Gifted her with a moment of intense focus?

But Aiden's silvery-black gaze didn't hold desire—at least, not the kind that shivered through her veins. No, his eyes appraised her, calculating her value. Their shared look allowed her to see the moment the idea hit him.

Yes, she could be useful to a lot of people, but to Aiden in particular. She knew this town in ways he didn't anymore. And Jason had just proven that taking over the town's biggest source of income wasn't going to be easy. Small-town Southerners had long memories, and little tolerance for outsiders coming in to tell them what to do.

He didn't have an easy road ahead of him, but she had a feeling she'd just been chosen to pave his way.

Four

Christina enjoyed reading to Lily. Sometimes she would indulge in short verses from a book of poetry, magazine articles or a cozy mystery. Today the words from a story set in a small town like theirs eased over them both, until muffled bumps and bangs erupted from the adjoining room. She cocked her head, hearing more thumping sounds. A quick glance reassured her Lily was okay, so she set the book down and hurried through the dressing room.

The noise grew as she approached the door that led from Lily's dressing room to Christina's bedroom. What was going on?

Opening the door, she found herself facing a…wall? A mattress wall?

Going back through Lily's suite to the other exit into the hallway only gave her time to get good and angry. Nolen stood outside Christina's room, arms crossed over his chest. His closed stance matched his expression.

"What's going on?" she asked.

Nolen shook his head. "That boy. Master Aiden always was one to get something in his mind, and that's all she wrote…."

Alarm skittered through Christina. What was he up to? One step inside the disarray told her it was no good.

"Why are you rearranging the furniture in my room?" She didn't care that her voice was high-pitched and panicked. He could not do this. He could not simply move himself in without permission.

Furniture had been shoved aside, her bed taken apart and general chaos reigned. In the midst of it all, Aiden stood, legs braced. He wore almond-colored cargo pants and a blue button-down, sleeves rolled up to expose muscled forearms with a sprinkling of dark hair. A masculine statue in purple girly land.

He nodded to the delivery guys. "I think I've got it from here."

Christina practically vibrated as she waited for them to clear the room. Her eyes rounded and her throat tightened as the men took her old mattress with them.

"Thanks, Nolen," she heard Aiden say before the door clicked closed. Then he resumed his autocratic stance nearby.

"Don't you think we should have talked about this first?"

His insolent shrug matched his nonchalant attitude, which only upped her panic for some reason. "Why? You said you would go through with this for Mother."

She wanted to scream, but held on to her control for a moment more. "Yes, but not sharing a bed."

He was silent so long that she shifted uncomfortably. Finally, he said, "James will get his way—you said that yourself."

"But if we give him the marriage, maybe—"

"He doesn't want this half-done, Christina. You know that. But I'm not going to force you to do something you don't feel comfortable with."

She raised her brows, pointedly surveying her disheveled room. "It seems like that's exactly what you're doing. I'm definitely not comfortable with *this*."

"We each have a side. I'll keep my clothes and stuff upstairs, out of your way. This doesn't have to be any more intimate than two people sleeping beside each other."

She wanted to study his face, see if he really believed that, but she couldn't scratch up the nerve. Instead, she concentrated on maintaining what small modicum of grace she still possessed.

"Look," Aiden said, "if we're gonna do this, we've got to be all in. Either that, or get out now."

Christina glanced at the door to Lily's room. "No. I'm in," she conceded. But as she turned back to measure the queen-size mattress dominating her small room, she had to ask, "Couldn't you have bought two twins?"

His grin should be illegal. "Where's the fun in that?"

Christina shoved leaden limbs through the armholes of her nightgown and dragged it on. The day had been long, and an even longer, probably restless night lay ahead. Her emotional turmoil was compounded by worries over Lily, James's health, the bargain she'd agreed to and Aiden... always Aiden. Nicole had testing to keep her away for the next two days, but Christina looked forward to the nonstop vigil Lily's care required. Sometimes she wished taking care of Lily were a bit more labor intensive. It might help her think a whole lot less.

Her sigh echoed around her tiny bedroom. Soon she'd be the wife of Aiden Blackstone. The cocktail of fear, desire and worry bubbling through her veins might just be enough to keep her awake until then.

But hopefully not. She stared at the new queen-size bed that consumed more than its fair share of real estate. Great, another worry. How in the world could she share a bed with Aiden Blackstone?

Long moments spent unable to imagine such a thing convinced her to worry about it another day. Instead, she settled in and let lethargy weigh her into the mattress. *Please, just a few hours of oblivion.*

But before she could drift off, she heard a sound from

Lily's room. Christina's heavy head lifted. Again, that shuf-fling sound. Muffled by the dressing room that connected her to the suite, but there nonetheless. Had Nolen or Marie come to check on Lily before retiring?

A grimace twisted Christina's lips as she pulled her-self out from the warm nest under her covers. In the two years since Lily's stroke, she'd often heard noises from her friend's room. Sometimes the others came to say good-night. Sometimes a branch from the oak tree outside had scraped against the window. Sometimes she heard just the creaks and groans of a house that had seen a lot of living.

Each time, a small part of Christina's heart hoped it was her friend. That Lily had woken up and would walk in here to gift one of her gentle hugs and tell Christina she was okay. That she wasn't responsible for what had happened.

But it never came to be—and that broke Christina's heart.

A muffled voice sounded through the partially closed door of the dressing room, and Christina slowed, not want-ing to interrupt. As she paused, the words "Hey, Mom," barely floated in and her feet rooted to the floor. Aiden? To her knowledge, he hadn't been to see his mother since he'd come to Blackstone Manor. But she'd hoped. Someday.

She knew she should leave, give him some privacy. In-stead, she found herself easing up to the door and peeking through the opening into the room beyond.

Aiden hunched forward in a chair just on the far edge of the faint illumination from the night-light. Even in the deep shadows she recognized his long, solid build. His head hung low, and his shoulders slumped, as if a weight of emotion dragged him down. He remained silent for long moments, not moving, almost not breathing. It was hard to reconcile him with the virile man who had confronted her on the stairs days ago. Or who'd stood his ground against the derision of Jason and his crew.

Her thoughts cut off as he looked up, gifting her with the sight of his strong features and stubble-lined jaw. It intrigued her, that small sign of weariness, that little mark of imperfection on a man usually so perfectly groomed. Would it scratch her skin if he kissed her? His deep-set eyes barely glittered in the darkness, lending to the mystery, the hushed intimacy of the moment.

"I screwed up, Mom," he said, surprising Christina with not only his words but his matter-of-fact tone. "I left here a kid, full of anger and pride. I had no idea what that would cost me, cost us. But especially you."

He ran a hand through his hair, leaving it in spiky disarray instead of sculpted artistry. "You didn't blame me then, and you probably don't blame me now. That's the kind of person you are. But I blame me. Boy, do I—"

The small choking sound tore Christina's heart. She saw no evidence of tears, but the depth of Aiden's sorrow reached out from across the space separating them. She wanted to go to him, hold him and tell him his mother understood. Her foot moved before she realized what was happening and only by locking down her muscles could she stop herself.

Invader. Aiden wouldn't want her comfort. And if he knew the role she herself had played in Lily's accident, hers would be the last face he'd want to see right now.

"But I will make up for it. I promise you, you will stay in this house for the rest of your life."

I'll do my best, too, Christina thought.

He stood, hands fisted at his sides, but he made no move to approach the bed holding the ever-silent woman. "Grandfather thinks this is some kind of game, with him in the role of chess master. But it's not. It's an act of penance. After all, you'd just been to see me when you had the accident. Coming to me because I refused to buck the old man and come to you. Resisting him was more important to me than you were." Long moments elapsed when Christina could only hear the pounding of her heart.

His final words floated through the air. "I'm sorry, Mom."

He remained still for the length of one breath, then two, before he turned and walked away.

Christina didn't move. Couldn't leave, couldn't continue forward. She stood frozen, held by the realization that this might be a game to James, but Aiden was more than a willing player. His investment was deeper than she'd thought, and if he ever found out her involvement in Lily's accident, she would become the biggest loser of all.

Five

Almost a week after making his pledge to his mother, the marriage license arrived—and Aiden was royally screwed.

Oh, he would go through with it. In his gut, he knew this was the last thing he could do for his mother, one thing she could be proud of him for. She'd made her home here, been highly involved in the community, and she'd want him to care for it, too.

He couldn't promise her he'd stay. But he could get her safely settled and make sure the town remained secure. Still, his confrontation with Christina on the stairs taunted him. And the fire with which she'd argued with him in her bedroom—soon to be their bedroom—tempted him to enjoy everything she might have to offer. Which made it imperative to lay out some ground rules with his future bride, so they both knew what to expect—from this situation and each other.

Following Marie's directions, he found Christina in the back garden among his mother's irises, which were in full, royal purple bloom in the spring sunshine. She was sitting on a wood and wrought-iron bench, a truly genteel resting place in the shade of a small dogwood tree.

He marched up beside her and dug right in. "Look, Christina, in terms of this marriage, we should start with—"

"Good afternoon, Aiden," she said, squinting up at him in a way that wrinkled her delicate nose. "Won't you please join me?" She motioned to the matching bench opposite her own.

He frowned. "Christina, this is a business arrangement. We should treat it like one."

"Aiden," she said, her tone a mocking version of his own stern one, "we don't do business like that in the South. Or have you forgotten? Now stop being a jerk and sit down."

Her words brought on a mixture of irritation and amused admiration, but it was the haughty stare that cinched the deal, that had his blood pounding in all the inappropriate places. It was the same implacable look she'd given James, though this time, that arched brow almost dared Aiden to defy her.

So be it. He was a New Yorker now, but he hadn't forgotten how Southern hospitality worked. He forced himself to take the offered seat and studied his bride-to-be. "And how are you this afternoon, Miss Christina?" he asked with a cheeky grin.

His Southern-gentleman routine coaxed a laugh from those luscious lips, which emphasized the shadowy circles under her eyes. For the first time, he wondered just how much of a burden this marriage was on her. Did her family approve? He didn't remember much about them, except that his mother hadn't cared for either parent. They'd divorced when Christina was quite young, he thought.

Had they changed at all, like their daughter? He remembered her as a needy, clinging girl, always hanging around, begging for attention with soulful eyes that could rival a puppy dog's. Or maybe those memories were colored by his resentment that she actually got the attention, the positive attention he'd wanted.

Now there was nothing needy about her. The calm, capable woman before him was both admirable and frustrating. Still, he wanted to break through that mask and see the real woman underneath, the one he'd caught glimpses of when she'd defended his mother and insisted on doing what was right. That attitude was more than just the picture of Southern hospitality. She possessed Southern grit. He wanted to dig deeper, to learn whether her dedication to those around her could be transferred to a sorry SOB like him.

He shook his head. Nope, not gonna happen. When he finally walked away from here, he wanted it to be a clean cut. It was the way he lived his life: no attachments—not even to the woman he planned to marry.

That didn't mean he shouldn't learn more, if only to guide him through the next year. *Yeah, right.* But he pushed, softening his tone. "Are you ready?"

"I guess so," she said, though her gaze slipped away to the irises dancing in the slight breeze. "I doubt even real brides are ever really ready."

You're a real bride. Even as the reassurance leaped to his lips, he forced it back. "It'll be over soon. Before long, everything will be settled, I'll return to New York, and you'll be free again."

Those dark eyes, sporting depths that made him uncomfortably curious, swung his way. "What do you mean?" she asked, her brow creasing.

"Isn't it obvious?"

"Not from my side of the equation, it isn't." Her body angled toward his despite the carpet of green grass separating them. "How can it all be over? How can you take care of your mother and the mill from New York?" Those gorgeous brows lifted high. "And not break your end of the deal, because James isn't about to let you out of it."

Aiden put out a hand in a soothing gesture. "Calm down. I'll get Mother settled and a good manager in to take care of the mill. I know how to follow through—"

"But not how to follow the letter of the law?"

"James is playing dirty. I don't think I should be expected to stay spick-and-span."

"Your mother would expect it."

Her words shot an arrow of emotion through him that he couldn't name. But she was right. His mother had always expected them to take the right road, not the easy one. "Don't worry. By then I'll have found a way to break the agreement and clean up this mess."

For once, he caught just a glimpse of hurt on a face that was normally schooled with graceful care. "Thanks," she said with a dry tone.

"Would you please stop analyzing every word and just trust me?"

"I don't really know you. Why should I do that?"

"Because I know what I'm doing. Or I will—" Eventually, but until then… "My grandfather certainly thinks he can outwit the two of us. He's making us marry each other."

"Actually, he's only making you," she said, reminding him once more of the picture burning in his mind of her stepping from the shadows of his grandfather's bed. The echoes of her words still rang in his head.

"But are we going to let him continue to drive this boat?" Aiden asked. "I'd much rather be at the wheel."

She nodded, slow at first, but then stronger, as if she'd come to a decision. "Exactly what do you propose?"

"A partnership, a business partnership with a few key goals. No pressure for anything else." This arrangement would be more for his sanity than hers. As much as he knew he should not get on more intimate footing with this woman, he wasn't a saint. But he wouldn't be alone in that bed. And sex would only complicate his leaving all the more.

No woman should get married in scrubs, even if the wedding wasn't real.

There'd been no time to change when James had summoned her to the study earlier. She'd thought he wanted to talk about Lily or his health, but walked in to find a local judge with ties to James. Now she stood self-consciously, waiting for this drama to be over.

Aiden, on the other hand, looked much more put together in casual khakis and a slick black polo shirt. Even his hair was styled in perfect little spikes, while hers was pulled back in a thick ponytail because she'd been finishing up Lily's exercises. One could almost be forgiven for hating a man for being so beautiful.

As the judge's benevolent gaze fell on her, she felt a twinge of conscience. She knew it was nerves, but she wasn't quite sure what to do with it. Especially since there weren't any acceptable options she could think of to stop this wedding from happening.

Screaming as she ran from the room wouldn't be appropriate bride behavior. Lily had taught her to act like a lady. Maybe it was her mother's crazy genes trying to break through?

She avoided meeting anyone's eyes by cataloging the one room in Blackstone Manor she'd rarely been in. James's study. Tradition seeped from the woodwork, adding to the gloom. What did James so love about this oppressive place? Maybe that was it...the atmosphere only added to the power he wielded here.

Dark, mahogany shelves were loaded with perfectly placed leather-bound volumes. Heavy green drapes framed the three sets of windows in the room, the color of the material meant to reflect the landscaping outside. There was an impression of money and masculine strength, but not in a good way.

The lingering feel was one of suppressed power and manipulation, as if the meanness exhibited here had soaked into the wood, though maybe that stemmed from the similarities to her own father's office. He'd delivered many a harsh punishment from behind a desk similar to the ornate mahogany one dominating the far corner.

Suddenly, Aiden appeared in front of her, blocking everything from view but his silvery gaze. "Christina," he murmured, those mobile lips drawing her attention down, making her wish this was all real, even though she knew she shouldn't.

"You good?" The furrow between his brows deepened. "I mean, we don't have to do this right now if you don't want to."

Oh yes, they did. Before the nausea in the pit of her stomach got the best of her. The slight hope in his eyes made her sad. His face wavered for just a moment. "No, I'm fine," she murmured.

Nolen appeared over Aiden's shoulder. "Anyone you want to be here, Miss Christina? I could make a call."

She couldn't tell if the look of surprise crossing Aiden's face was because Nolen asked or because she might want someone here. The last thing she needed was one of her parents showing up. Her brother would consider this a waste of his precious time. Besides, the fewer people to know, the better.

At least for now. The truth would get out soon enough. It always did in a town the size of Black Hills.

She closed her eyes tight, letting the darkness shut out all the watching faces, then centered herself from the outside in. By the time her lashes lifted, she was back on track. "No, Nolen," she said. "All the family I need is already here."

Her eyes met Aiden's. "I'm ready."

As they settled into place, Judge Harriman studied her for a moment, as if he knew all the secrets she was trying so desperately to cover up. Not that everyone wouldn't eventually guess, once they knew she'd married the Blackstone brother no one had seen in ten years. Her pride was worth Lily's comfort.

"Let's get a move on," James fussed from his chair behind the desk. Christina could hear the shuffle of Nolen's and Canton's feet behind her.

For Lily...

"Dearly beloved, we are gathered here today to join these two people in holy matrimony..."

For Lily...

"Since it is your intention to marry, join your right hands and declare your consent. Do you, Aiden, take Christina to be your lawful wedded wife to have and hold from this day on, for better or for worse, for richer or for poorer, in sickness and in health, as long as you both shall live?"

Christina struggled not to wince. *For Lily...*

"I do."

Was it her imagination or did Aiden's voice echo through the room?

"Christina, do you take Aiden to be your lawful wedded husband…"

For Lily... "I do."

"With this ring, I thee wed…." Instead of looking at the plain gold bands that came from she knew not where, Christina started making a mental list of all the things she needed to do for Lily this afternoon. And tomorrow. And the day after that.

Finally, Judge Harriman put her out of her misery. "As you have pledged yourselves to each other before God and these witnesses, by the power vested in me by the state of South Carolina, I now pronounce you husband and wife. You may kiss your bride."

She hadn't allowed herself to think about this part. Luckily, Aiden had more sense than she did. His hand lifted to her chin as he turned to face her. Her mind registered the smallest details: how surprisingly rough his fingertips were, the difference in their heights as he leaned down, the first soft brush of his lips against hers….

For me.

Finally, her brain shut down, leaving only the feelings. The sharp tingle she hadn't expected, and the heat she had. But it was the urge to curl up against him that had her jerking away.

"Not as bad as you thought it would be, huh, boy?" James cackled.

The room righted itself, giving her a clear view of the disgust on Aiden's face as he stared James down—then licked over his lips. "Sweet," he said, though his expression was neutral. "Something you wouldn't understand, Grandfather."

All Christina felt then was the sting of the embarrassed flush creeping over her cheeks.

If the judge was surprised by the exchange, it didn't show. For once he ignored the old man. Pulling some paperwork out of his briefcase, he said with a grin, "Let's get this signed all official-like." Christina added her signature, which looked quite ladylike next to Aiden's masculine scrawl. Then the witnesses and the judge signed. They'd just tied everything up in a neat little legal bow when the door opened.

"Surprise," Marie said, wheeling in a tray with a three-tier—oh, dear—wedding cake!

Christina rushed over on the pretense of helping. "Marie, what are you thinking?" she asked, her overblown mind barely registering the chocolate and teal colors swirling over the layers like waves.

"What was I thinking? What were *you* thinking? Couldn't you have at least worn a nice blouse?" Marie tsked.

Christina tried to ignore the criticism, but found herself straightening the hem of her scrub shirt, anyway.

"Every wedding's a reason to celebrate, my dear," Marie said loudly, then continued under her breath. "Unless you'd like Judge Harriman telling people otherwise. There's a good reason Mr. James picked the judge with the most gossipy wife in town."

Christina nodded, but didn't answer. Her shredded nerves wouldn't allow it. She just cut cake and smiled, hoping she was making Lily proud. And safe.

No one pushed for the traditional "smoosh cake in each other's faces" move, thank goodness. Christina eased as far from Aiden Blackstone as she could get without raising eyebrows, but his warmth remained temptingly close. She wanted to lean in, share some of his strength, his outward calm.

Another kiss. But no. Not even while they were sharing that big ol' bed in her room. She would not get intimately involved with this man. It would mean nothing to him, and she knew herself well enough to know it would mean a whole lot to her.

How did people endure those long receptions after their weddings? It had only been twenty minutes of cake, and Christina was done. She gathered plates, helping Marie clean up while the men spoke in low voices. She was slicing cake for storage when she heard someone at the outer door of the house. Nolen had barely managed two steps toward the open doorway of James's study when a man filled it.

Luke Blackstone. Aiden's younger brother. He was known to be laid-back. He always had a big grin both in personal situations and when being interviewed on national television as a race-car driver. Cameras didn't faze him. He was always cool under pressure. And he'd become a sort of adopted older brother in the years Christina had been here. Among the three brothers, his visits home were the most frequent, allowing their childhood friendship to continue into adulthood.

"So." He grinned his trademark lady-killer smile. "What are we celebrating?"

He took in Christina, the cake, Marie and then the group of men at the far side of the room. His aqua eyes widened when he noticed his brother standing there. It took only moments for him to put two and two together. He was pretty, but he wasn't stupid.

Seconds later, he was storming over to his grandfather's desk. Hands planted on the mahogany monstrosity, Luke paid little attention to the papers sliding to the floor as he loomed over James. "What the hell did you do?" he growled.

Christina wanted to cry. Would the wedding-day horrors never end?

Six

"Now, explain to me one more time why we're at a bar on your wedding night?"

Luke might be a hotshot who had every woman in this bar sneaking a peek at what the tabloids described as his "dreamy" eyes, but all Aiden could think of at the moment was coldcocking him. Or shipping him back to Charlotte in his souped-up sports car. "Apparently, my wife thinks being here will keep her from having to face the new bed I moved into her room."

"Dude, if you're having to track down your wife, then this is gonna be one rough wedding night. Are you sure this marriage is real?"

"Oh, it's real." And more tempting than Aiden wanted to acknowledge. "And it's only temporary, but that doesn't change the requirements."

Luke's teasing turned serious. "I'm still trying to wrap my head around this. That's all. Make sure Christina is being taken care of, not just used."

"Thanks for worrying about *me,* your own brother," Aiden said.

"Oh, you're a big boy. You can take care of yourself, though obviously not very well."

The narrowing of Aiden's eyes should have warned him just how on edge his brother was, but Luke smirked it off. "Besides, if you wanted our help you would have called.

Jacob and I would have been on the first plane here. Why didn't you?"

"And have both my brothers witness my personal defeat? That would have been a fun family reunion."

"Still," Luke said, his gaze sobering even more. "We would have been here, you know that."

Aiden nodded. To add to his troubles, he could hear that asshat, Jason, running his mouth off at a table behind them. The young woman serving as bartender kept glancing in that direction with a worried frown, but Aiden had too much class to engage in a bar brawl with someone so, frankly, beneath him.

The difference in their stations had nothing to do with money, and everything to do with class. Jason had none. Aiden's parents had instilled the habits of proper public behavior from an early age. Aiden had refined himself even more as he moved among the highest circles of New York, and even international society. Besides, someone known to run his mouth in public was only going to damage his own reputation. Eventually no one paid people like that any attention.

As long as Jason kept it general and not too personal, Aiden would overlook it. He didn't want to start his tenure at the mill with the firing of a prominent, vocal citizen. But he had a feeling the time would eventually come when Jason would have to be dealt with—and Aiden would be more than happy to do it.

They thanked the bartender as she set Luke's beer and Aiden's Scotch before them, then sampled their drinks. "You hearin' much of that?" Luke asked with a jerk of his head in Jason's direction.

"Oh, there's plenty of insinuations and comments whenever I run into him and his little posse in town. He's careful not to be too direct. Everyone else just stares. No outright confrontations, but then again, Jason thinks he's big stuff because his daddy is on the management track out at the mill. I'm going to have to remind that guy of his place on the food chain. Soon."

"Let me know when that happens. I'm right there with ya." Aiden shared his brother's grin and fist bump. "But seriously," Luke said, "I haven't had any trouble the times I've come home and I haven't heard of Jacob having any, either."

"Yeah, but you didn't announce to them that you were taking over the main source of support for the entire town. I did. And I'm sure it spread like wildfire."

"So Granddad is really gonna let you do it? Take over the running of Blackstone Mill?"

"It's already done. I've been wading through paperwork for days and have a meeting set up with the day foreman next week."

A waitress rounded the curve in the bar with a full tray, pausing behind them. As she set their plates down, Luke asked, "Where's KC? I haven't seen her in a while."

The waitress's flirty smile faded into an oddly uncomfortable look. "Oh, she's been out of town for a bit."

Luke nodded and the men turned back to their food. As they dug in, Aiden's gaze was drawn again and again to a particular spot. He and Luke sat at one corner of a bar that formed a square in the middle of the room. Tables and booths filled the rest of the space, except for a small dance floor at the far end and a worn stage where a DJ mixed records. From where he sat, Aiden had occasional glimpses of some tables clustered together in the far corner near the dance floor, and who should be seated at one of them but his lovely bride.

Weren't they a pair? A real honeymoon should involve a bed and a shower for two, in Aiden's opinion. Instead, they were in the local bar. Separately. But then, this wasn't a true marriage, so he should leave all thoughts of a true honeymoon far, far behind him.

Still, as much as he wanted to deny it, saying those generic vows made possibilities available, intimate possibilities they shouldn't indulge. But the tantalizing options still lingered in his brain....

Being forbidden didn't stop him from watching, from imagining. She looked way too classy for this joint, even in a simple sundress that gave him a conservative glimpse of her creamy skin. But she seemed to fit, gifting that gorgeous smile to her girlfriends at the table and to the many who stopped by to chat. She was obviously well liked, just as he'd expected, and her generous nature made everyone feel welcome. Though he knew he shouldn't, he wished he could have a small amount of that genuine welcome spill onto him when he was in her presence. Instead, she guarded herself well, including running away on her wedding night. Not very far, but still—way to make a guy feel rejected.

"So what is the plan for the mill?" Luke asked. "If Jason is any indication, taking the reins might be a bumpy road. But I can guarantee in the end you'll be liked better than ol' James. Once they get to know you, of course."

Aiden grinned. "Would that really take much?"

"Nope."

Aiden didn't think so. "I haven't worked out the full strategy yet. Currently, I just need to solve whatever hoodoo is going on over there and install an overseer. Then I can hightail my ass back to New York City and get on with my real life."

"So you're going to win their trust, all the while planning to get out while the gettin's good?"

Well, when he put it that way... "No, I'm going to gain their trust so I know exactly what needs to be done to protect the town—from itself and any sharks that might want to come in. A strong management will keep everything on track, maintain the area's prosperity, and shut yahoos like Jason out. Then I'll know the right man for the job and ev-

eryone will get what they want." He tilted his Scotch glass
in his bride's direction. "Christina will be helpful in getting
people to accept me. Look how well she's liked."

"Yeah," Luke drawled, "people here love her. But for
her to help, you'd have to persuade her to stay in the same
room with you."

Aiden took a moment to indulge in a slap against the
back of Luke's head—an older brother's privilege. Across
the room, a waitress stood chatting with Christina, her
empty tray tapping against her bare calf. "That table's been
a revolving door tonight. All classes, too. That's hard to do
in a small town."

"Especially *this* small town," Luke agreed. "But it's not
gonna help you any if you're over here and she's over there."

Aiden glared.

Luke calmly licked some wing sauce off his fingers.
"Just sayin', bro."

Was it time? Christina hadn't noticed him. He'd chosen
this spot specially to watch her without detection. Give
himself a feel for what she was really like, the side of herself she wouldn't show him. Now he couldn't stop looking
that way, watching her sexy smile and the light glittering
off her bare shoulders. How sappy was that?

After tonight, the whole town would know they were
married. He was actually surprised it had taken this long.
Despite his hard-nosed attitude about business, he wasn't
a complete ass. He knew people needed to think their marriage meant something. At least while he was here. He
stood, telling himself he was doing this because it was the
best thing for his future. *Yeah, keep telling yourself that....*

"Go get 'em, tiger."

This time Aiden indulged in a harder slap on his brother's shoulder. "I will."

Leaving his brother rubbing the sting away, Aiden
stalked across the room. He found himself ultra-aware of

the eyes following his progress to the group of women in the far corner. Despite the music being louder here, he could almost hear the crowd suck in a breath and wait.

Finally, Christina's gaze stumbled on him…and stayed. *That's right, sweetheart. Found ya.* That baseline arousal, now becoming so familiar when he was in her presence, kicked in. His heart picked up speed. His muscles tensed. He could have been readying for a high-price negotiation or fast-paced auction, but the prize here could be so much more pleasurable if he let it.

Which he wouldn't.

He leaned in close, letting the end of a pop song cover his words. "Christina, would you care to dance?"

Panic widened her eyes and tightened her features for a moment before she shook her head. He didn't repeat himself. Glancing around the table at the women seated nearby and several more hovering, their avid interest unmistakable, he then let his gaze fall to the bare ring finger of her left hand. "You sure about that?" he mouthed.

This time she placed her hand in his, allowing him to help her up. He led the way to the far side of the small dance floor, away from the now-whispering women. This side of the room was more sparsely populated, offering a small amount of privacy. The music had switched to a rare slow song, so he simply pulled her close and swayed. The point wasn't for them to dance, and the place didn't lend itself to fancy moves. He simply wanted them to be seen together, talking together, jump-starting the community's acceptance of them as a couple.

This had nothing to do with holding her. *Nothing.*

Unfortunately, Christina wasn't cooperating. Her back remained stiff, the muscles under his palm tight. He drew her a touch closer, trying to ignore the brush of her body against his. As if that was a possibility. He lifted their clasped hands to the crook of his shoulder. *God, she felt good.*

"You can loosen up, Christina," he murmured. "We are married, after all. And this is our first dance."

Which should give him the right to touch all the silky skin within reach. But it didn't. He needed to remember that.

Her fingertips dug into his palm. When she spoke, she was all politeness and concern. "I'm sorry. It's not you. I just haven't danced much."

He studied her, even as she refused to tilt her face up toward him. Instead, she stared into the distance over his shoulder. "So, why don't you tell me why you're spending our wedding night at a bar...without me?"

She shook her head. "It's not a real wedding night."

That bed says differently. "Is that what you want them to think?" he asked with a nod toward the bar.

"No." She stumbled a bit, brushing against him for a deliciously brief moment. "I just...I don't know."

Interesting. "Why did you come here tonight?" Of all nights...

He could feel her slight shrug.

Which wasn't really an answer, but he wouldn't press. He shouldn't want to know. He really shouldn't, but he could guess. After all, sharing a bed with an almost stranger couldn't be very comfortable. For her. It had been his M.O. for years, but the thought of Christina on that queen-size mattress felt nothing like the one-night stands that populated his history.

He found himself lifting her hands to his shoulders, guiding her where to place them. Then bringing her flush to his body. His arms encircled her easily, one hand resting just on the edge of the material of her sundress. Giving him his first true feel of the skin he'd been coveting.

Her eyes widened, but by degrees her body softened, inch by slow inch, as if she were sinking into him. It shouldn't feel so good.

"That's better," he said, his voice deepening, relaxing with her. "We don't want anyone to think you don't like me. After all, our news will hit the gossip mill any second now."

The luscious depths of her eyes were revealed by the gradual lift of her lashes, as if she was surfacing from a dream. "It would have already hit if Judge Harriman's wife wasn't out of town visiting her sister."

Aiden couldn't help but grin. "That's small-town life for you."

"Yeah," she said, sharing his amusement. "James didn't time his plan very well. But a woman has to see her sister every now and then."

As her grin matched his, he marveled at how natural it felt to hold her like this. To look down on her, shelter her against him. Warning signals were a muted clang in the back of his mind, overpowered by the blood thrumming through his veins. Of its own volition, his hand inched upward, sampling the bare skin along her spine, tunneling beneath that wealth of hair to find the sensitive spot at the nape of her neck. Her eyes lost focus as he stroked there. What would it be like to repeat this morning's searing kiss?

No. Not going there. James would be thrilled for them to get busy, make this a real marriage and provide him with another generation to control. But Aiden had no intention of sticking around long enough for that to happen. No matter how tempting his new wife might be. And no intention of letting his grandfather completely control his life ever again.

"Look, Christina," he murmured against her hair, "you don't have to be afraid of me. You don't have to do anything you don't want to. I know you didn't want the bed, but someone had to make the decision. I'm just trying to fulfill James's requirements and let you remain near Lily."

He felt her sigh against his throat. "So you were trying

to be gallant by moving a mattress in without my permission?" she asked.

He couldn't help teasing. "It's a comfortable mattress, isn't it?"

She pulled away enough to glare at him. "This isn't a joke, Aiden."

He paused, staring solemnly into those chocolate eyes. "I promise I will keep my hands to myself." Letting loose a little of the lust thrumming through his body, he added, "Unless you ask me not to."

Her lips parted, but no words came. Her expression was conflicted, and Aiden totally got that she couldn't decide whether to scold him…or take him up on the offer.

Lucky for them both, the song ended. The dance floor flooded with patrons ready to line dance, but "Boot Scootin' and Boogie" would not save either of them from the long night ahead.

Seven

Christina stared at the cabin she had completely forgotten existed. The last time she'd been this far from the house, shoulder-high weeds had curbed any exploration.

But the adult Aiden had been hard at work on the little cabin Lily had ordered built for him when he was a teenager. The immediate vicinity had been freshly cleared and lengths of unfinished two-by-fours had been used to replace the sagging porch. Old-school rock blared from inside. As she came around the corner, she saw a brand-new AC unit blocking the side window.

So this was what was holding Aiden's attention the past few days. Christina had been avoiding her husband, and memories of that embarrassing confrontation in the bar, for almost a week. Nights had been even more excruciating, but one or the other of them seemed to weasel out of being in the room at bedtime and wake-up time. Christina curled into a ball on her side to keep herself from brushing against Aiden in her sleep. Aiden, on the other hand, was more of a sprawler.

But she'd do anything to avoid a repeat of their wedding night. Aiden had entered the room just as she left the bathroom. He'd allowed his gaze to sweep over her sleep shorts and overlarge T-shirt with uncomfortable speculation. She'd scurried over to the bed and claimed her preferred side. But closing her eyes like a squeamish spinster had left her listening to the rustle of clothes as he undressed, her mind whirling with heated questions about just how much he'd left on.

Needless to say, she wasn't getting a lot of sleep. The days were only a little better. While Luke had been here, he'd served as a bit of a buffer, but she'd been glad when he went back to North Carolina because the speculative looks were killing her—she got enough of that when she dared go out in public. Considering the complicated web they were now living in, she couldn't blame Aiden for planning to spend a lot of time here. He probably needed one place that was solely his own. She wished she had one.

Noting the fence line indicating the end of Blackstone Manor's property and the beginning of mill land, she couldn't help but notice this was as far away from her as he could get. The realization lowered her confidence.

She knocked, then waited a moment or two. The music blared loudly enough to pound inside her head. After another knock, she forced herself to grasp the knob and turn.

Stomach churning, she stepped inside. Aiden stood in the far corner with his back to her. A back so smoothly muscled her mouth watered. His shirtless torso was magnificent. Sweat meandered down the indention of his spine and disappeared beneath the waistband of his loose khaki shorts. Muscles bunched and shifted in his arms and back as he wielded a chisel and hammer.

Before him rested a block of some kind of stone that he chipped away with focused intent. To her surprise, several other half-finished sculptures sat on other waist-high tables as if awaiting their turn. A cabinet in the middle of the room had various tools scattered across the top. Christina took it all in with a sense of wonder. She'd known Aiden powered a very successful import/export art business, but had no idea he created pieces himself. A twinge of sadness streaked through her that he hadn't shared this. But then, why should he? Just because she wished she knew him, didn't mean he felt the same.

Watching him move was like art in motion, the clench and release of his body mimicking the orchestrated roll of the ocean. Feeling awkward, she called, "Aiden." No response. Not even a twitch. She called his name again, raising her voice above the blare of Nirvana, but he still didn't turn.

She walked over and placed light fingertips on his bare shoulder. It was just meant to be an "I'm here" touch, but her fingers trailed down the slick skin of their own volition.

He glanced over his shoulder, his eyes faraway in a haze of glittering darkness. Several moments passed before he turned toward the stereo to shut it off. The slight frown between his brows confirmed her fears.

Her cheeks flushed, guilt creeping in as if she'd done something wrong. Not that she had, but words rushed out, anyway. "I called your name, but—" She gestured toward the player.

He set the tools on the table in front of him, then turned to give her a full tempting view. The chiseled muscles weren't confined to his back. His chest and arms suggested he was capable of some serious work without the bulk of heavy weight lifting, while his stomach gave washboard abs a new meaning.

She hadn't realized what those sophisticated clothes had been hiding…. She swallowed, drawing her eyes up before they strayed too far.

"No problem," he said, his voice even, reserved. "What can I do for you?"

She glanced around, distracting herself from all that skin by perusing the cluttered work surface.

"I, um, Marie needed to get a message to you, but she said there's no phone in here." She glanced back at his still features. "Didn't you bring your cell?"

He shook his head, reaching for a clean towel from a stack. "Too distracting."

He wiped the sweat from his face with a towel, then started on his arms. She swallowed hard, once again inspecting the tools and blocks of rock.

"I didn't know you sculpted. Lily never mentioned it."

He reached around her for the tools, putting them into a nearby box. "She's never seen my work. I didn't start until after her accident. It's great stress relief."

And Lord knew this was extremely stressful for them both.

She turned away from his intense stare, attempting to hide her trembling. She motioned to the horse he'd been working on. "I'm no art expert, but these look professional to me."

She felt, rather than heard, his approach. "It is. I sell my own work as well as other artists'."

He gestured at the blocks. "I had these brought over from the quarry so I could work until my assistant and I can arrange for a shipment."

Ah, a forceful reminder that he'd had a life before he came here. Unlike her. She should cut him some slack. Adjusting to a resented future was difficult. Even knowing that, she couldn't stop thinking he was standing awfully close....

"I'm glad you've got this..." She gestured forward. "I want you to feel at home—"

She clamped her mouth shut. That made him sound like a visitor. He wasn't. And she didn't want him to be. But after a lifetime of trying to appease and put people at ease, she simply had a hard time turning it off. And with him standing next to her, half-naked, she was only capable of reacting on autopilot.

"I'll never feel at home here." He shifted away, leaning

back against another workbench, putting himself unknowingly on display. "But I'm finding ways to make it work."

Did he mean his sculpting? Something of his own, uniquely his, to help him relax, relieve tension? Or something more? She should be thrilled that he was trying. Staying despite circumstances he hated.

Aiden broke into her thoughts. "What was the message?"

"What?"

"You said Marie had a message. From?"

Even those thick brows, simply raised in query, aroused her. "Bateman, the day foreman, called the house. He'd like to meet with you about things at the mill," she said.

"Did he really?" Aiden asked. "When?"

"This evening after shift."

His finger started tapping against his biceps. "So he wants to do this at the mill?"

She frowned at the odd note in his voice. "Yes."

The tapping accelerated. He was so different today. Normally, he walked around with emotions boiling beneath the surface like a volcano, but today he seemed to have mastered all that volatility. What was he keeping so locked down?

She found herself wanting to know more, to push deeper to places he'd say she didn't belong.

"The blocks," she said, grasping a subject from thin air. "How do you know what to sculpt? Client choice?"

She crossed to a half-formed block of black rock with goldish flecks. The top of a human head, thick with hair, had been roughed out, but for now all the fine details appeared below the chin. No features graced the face, granting no life to the form.

Reaching out, she traced the outline with her fingertips, noting how cool the rock was despite the heat in the room as the air conditioner slowly lost its battle. The texture was rough, but she could imagine the smoothness of such an elegant medium and form when it was complete.

Aiden had taken so long to answer, she thought for a moment he wouldn't. When he finally spoke, his voice seemed gruff.

"It's easy, really. You just have to listen."

She looked over her shoulder to find him watching her, or rather her hands. "Listen? To the stone?"

He trailed his gaze up her body before meeting her eyes. That turbulence of his seemed to be making a return. "Sort of. It's different for every artist. Most of the time I have a general idea of the goal. But the details change with the stone's intricacies and composition."

By now, she was sampling the textures with both palms. She could imagine Aiden chip, chip, chipping away, studying the angles until he found just the one that worked for him. The same way he approached life.

He wasn't the type to listen and work with an outside element. She smirked, her hands stilling. Of course, this was an element he had ultimate control over.

Suddenly, she was aware of that masculine heat at her back, blocking her in. Aiden's hands slid down her arms to cover her fingers where they curved around the rock.

His breath accelerated, stirring the hair lying heavy against the back of her neck. Tingles of fear and excitement made her heart race.

People might say he was a stranger, but he didn't feel like one. The aching need she felt around him had grown familiar. She'd spent long days thinking about him, long nights beside him feeding her fascination. Dangerous as it was, she didn't want to stop.

He leaned forward, trapping her between his hard length and the workbench. His arousal was unmistakable, subtly rubbing against her backside. She barely restrained herself from arching back against him. The need to respond grew despite her fears.

He pressed closer. With a groan, he nuzzled through the thickness of her hair, his movements slow, as if he acted against his own will.

The reluctant need echoed inside her, pulling down more of her barriers. She let her head tilt away, exposing vulnerable skin to his questing lips.

She shivered as moist heat slid along her neck, his open mouth sucking and nipping its way down. She lifted onto her toes. She was no longer thinking, just aching. For more feeling, more sensation, more Aiden.

His arms encircled her stomach, increasing her sense of security in the face of danger. Reaching the crook between her neck and shoulder, his teeth joined in play, his bite teasing, gentle. She jumped as the sensation shot straight to her core. Her body melted in surrender.

His hands slid upward, pausing just inches below her breasts.

Please, please don't stop. She wanted to cry out, but bit her lip, not quite ready to voice her desires. Her nipples tightened in anticipation. When he didn't move, she shifted, rubbing herself against him, an age-old move conveying her willingness for more.

Abruptly, his hands clamped onto her hips, holding her still. Her body and spirit froze in his grip as she realized it stemmed from something other than desire, despite the hardness still nestled against her.

All movement ceased except their breath. Christina fought the urge to move. As his mouth left her shoulder, she tracked his breath to her ear. Somehow, she knew she wouldn't like what he was about to say.

"Christina." Just her name in his rough tone sent shivers chasing across her skin. What would it be like if they were naked?

"Christina, you need to go." He shook his head against hers. "Now." More breathing. "Go. Now."

His hands tightened once more before freeing her, but she couldn't move. He might have told her to leave, but his body still cradled hers. He couldn't move away, either.

She should be humiliated at his rejection, but the evidence of his arousal bolstered what little feminine power she had buried deep down inside. Even knowing he would leave her far behind when given the chance, she wanted to risk getting burned, if it meant he would make her feel. She wanted him to let go and love her in a way she hadn't let a man do in, well, ever.

She turned her head and gathered every last ounce of courage to whisper, "What if I don't want to go?" Long moments lingered as her heart pounded in her ears.

Finally, he pulled away. "Then I have to be strong enough for the both of us."

Aiden drove to the outskirts of town in silence, Christina seated next to him in the cab of the estate's pickup truck. The awkwardness of their near miss in the studio earlier clouded the atmosphere between them.

But they both ignored it as he followed the newly installed signs pointing the way to the massive factory. Though mill property adjoined the grounds of Blackstone Manor, the roads leading there wound around and through the miles of land owned by the family. The drive took them along Mill Row, a sort of subdivision built on the border of mill land with houses for workers to rent, then through the fields behind Mill Row, which were used to grow cotton that provided a large portion of the mill's raw materials.

The closer they came to the actual plant, the slower Aiden drove. He'd dreaded this moment from his first step back inside Blackstone Manor. But he wouldn't allow himself to think about why. He certainly wouldn't explain his reluctance to the woman sending questioning glances his way. She had too much power over him already.

Besides, explaining his trepidation would require explaining why he'd asked her along. And what man wanted to be viewed as a wuss who couldn't face the site of his childhood traumas?

There were changes since he'd last been here. The parking lot had been widened and repaved. A new chain-link fence enclosure had been installed, along with a guard shack. But Aiden still viewed the metal buildings and now nonfunctioning smoke stacks with anger. To him, they would forever embody the oppression of his grandfather, even if they did keep the town viable.

They paused at the shack, but were waved through by a man Aiden didn't recognize. He didn't miss the surprise on the guard's face.

Once he had parked the truck, Christina got out and started forward but Aiden hung back. Each step was an effort of will. Either his body or his mind did not want to enter the massive building before him, but he refused to examine the source too closely.

Christina glanced back, her own steps slowing. "Aiden, are you okay?"

He didn't answer, but focused on moving one of his concrete-block feet one step at a time. He shouldn't stop, because he might not start walking again. But then his steps slowed to a standstill, anyway. His gaze strayed to the office building adjacent to the factory. His mind screamed at him to be quiet, but Christina's soothing, questioning presence pulled the answer from him.

"I haven't been here since the day my father died."

Her quiet voice reached him through the whirl of turbulence inside his brain. "I think you'll find a lot of people here remember your father. He did great things for the mill."

He would want you to do the same. Aiden gradually

picked up the pace, forcing himself to focus on his purpose. Not the images from the past crowding into his brain.

As they stepped through the entrance, they were met by a welcome committee of two. A man in a black jacket, looking more like a scientist than factory worker, stepped forward. "Mr. Blackstone, Mr. Bateman sent me to meet you. If you'll follow me, sir, I can drive you to his office."

Aiden waved him aside. "That's okay. We'll walk," he said, wanting to get an updated look at the operation. If this postponed his trip to the other building, that was no one's business but his.

The man blinked behind his round glasses as if he didn't know how to proceed now that his plans had been thwarted. At least he didn't seem inclined to argue.

The female half of the duo stepped calmly forward with her hand out. "Welcome, Mr. Blackstone. I'm Betty, Mr. Bateman's assistant. If you want to walk the mill floor, I'd suggest some earplugs."

Aiden accepted two pairs, handing one to Christina, who smiled at Betty in thanks. Then Aiden led the way out onto the mill floor, Christina, Betty and the little man trailing behind. The skin across Aiden's back tightened as he felt the eyes of their audience tracking their progress. He hadn't been out enough around here to realize he was living in a glass bowl. Christina's uneasiness reminded him that she was now living there with him.

But he forced himself not to hurry, strolling along the floor, occasionally asking questions of Betty. He spotted a production line undergoing some maintenance and spoke extensively with both employees about it. After exiting the factory floor, they wound through corridors for quite a ways. Aiden felt himself tense as they journeyed from the main action to the second story of the administrative building.

"This was built while my father was here," Aiden said, trying to moisten his dry mouth.

Betty answered, surprise in her tone. "Why, yes it was."

As soon as they crossed the heavy double doors into the administration building, Aiden felt his body's stress ratchet up a notch. His shoulders stiffened. He stared straight ahead, not looking down the little corridors they passed on each side. Finally, they reached the glass door marked Management. Betty led them through an outer office into a bigger room with casual office decor.

"Aiden, Christina, thank you for coming," Bateman said, shaking their hands.

Aiden watched as his wife was met with a warm hug, but his own greeting was more reserved.

"Betty had someone radio that you were walking the mill floor. What did you think?"

Aiden detected a note of pride, but also concern in Bateman's voice. "Everything looks good. The equipment has been updated."

Bateman nodded. "In the long run, it's more cost-effective to do so."

Aiden nodded, consciously tightening down on the grief hovering at the back of his mind. "How long have you been in charge?" He'd met a lot of men during his time here with his father, but Bateman's face wasn't familiar.

"Twelve years. I apprenticed under the man who took over from your father."

Aiden's shoulders tightened once more at the mention of his father, but he made a conscious effort to relax, stretching his neck to loosen up. "You've done a good job. The lines are running well."

Bateman indicated a sitting area. Hardly aware of what he was doing, Aiden guided Christina to the small love seat and tucked her close against him as they sat. Though he hated to admit it, the warmth where her thigh met his kept him focused. The tremors deep down inside receded, leaving him enough space to breathe. Contrary to his earlier actions, he needed her close, and for once his need had nothing to do with sex.

They chatted for a minute—Aiden well remembered Christina's lesson on polite behavior—then he got serious. "Before we start, there's something I'd like to address," he said. "As I'm sure you know, I've run my own business for several years now. An art import/export business out of New York."

He took close note of the defensive straightening of Bateman's back in the chair opposite them. Betty leaned casually against the edge of the desk in case she was needed.

"But a factory, especially a working mill, is outside of my experience," Aiden continued. "I've been studying my grandfather's reports, but I would appreciate it if you could fill me in on a few logistics of this type of operation."

Asking questions first rather than jumping in with orders appeared to be the right start. Bateman relaxed back into his chair, arms stretched along each side rest.

"The mill runs at full capacity eighty percent of the year, with some holiday and annual maintenance shutdowns. You may remember we carry out all production from the raw cotton bales to midgrade linens, so it is a large-scale operation."

He went on to explain about profits, which had declined the previous year due to drought, but were improving. Aiden listened attentively, but remained cued in to every subtle shift of the woman at his side. This split awareness was new to him. Normally, business always came before pleasure. But Christina could not be ignored. Pretty soon he wouldn't be sleeping at all. Her effect on him only grew. Good or bad, it simply was.

"Any financial concerns in the immediate or near future?" Aiden asked.

"No, sir. You'd have to ask accounting for specific numbers, but thanks to the long-term equipment upgrade schedule your father initiated and the profits reinvested, we've weathered through pretty well." Bateman's chest expanded a bit. "Our sales force has worked hard to establish a stable, loyal client base. We have no worries for the near future, outside of the normal business concerns in today's economy." A frown slid across his face. "No financial worries, anyway."

Aiden sensed they'd come to the purpose for this meeting. Christina must have, too. She leaned forward to join the conversation. "Is there something we need to know?"

Bateman's face was a guarded mask, as if he was deciding how much to say. He studied Aiden for long moments, until Christina spoke again. "It's okay, Jim. We wouldn't be here if Aiden wasn't going to do his best for the mill *and* the town."

Aiden wondered where her confidence came from, but didn't add his own reassurances. Bateman would have to take him on faith until he could prove his intentions himself.

When the older man spoke, each word came quicker than the last. "There is something off around here. Random problems cropping up. No pattern that I can tell."

"How long?" Aiden asked. The news wasn't unexpected, but he wanted details.

"Maybe a year," Bateman said, a frown of concentration on his face. "Little things, at first. But then the problems gained momentum, the worst happening most recently. A major supplier canceled at the last minute. One we'd been working with for a few years. Like everything else, it was an annoyance. But when they refused any further orders for no reason, it became a suspicious annoyance. It meant we had to delay a large delivery to an established client."

"If the mill gets a reputation for that sort of thing, it

could hurt sales," Aiden filled in what Bateman wasn't saying outright.

The other man exchanged a look with his assistant. "Did you show him?"

Betty nodded.

"We had a problem with one of the lines this past week," Bateman explained. "A delay because of equipment malfunction, but the tech came straight to me with his report. He thinks the failure wasn't an accident."

Aiden asked, "Any guesses as to who would do that?"

"Not the tech," Bateman said with a sad grin. "It could have been any employee with access to that area –part of the maintenance crew, or even the cleanup crew. I hate to think about it being any of those, really."

Aiden felt Christina straighten as the significance finally hit her. "You think it was an inside job."

Bateman nodded. "Unfortunately, yes. It was more an annoyance than anything, but I worry about the next time, if the source is who I think it is—"

"Why don't you just spell it out for me," Aiden said, absently laying a soothing hand against Christina's spine.

"About a year ago, a man named Balcher made an offer on Blackstone Mills. He's well-known in the industry for buying out the competition at rock-bottom prices and taking them apart, piece by piece, until eventually the plants just close."

"Eliminating the competition."

"Exactly. Only Blackstone isn't hurting. Yet. But if the safety standards are compromised on the equipment…" Bateman rubbed his balding head until what little hair was left stood on end. "I'm afraid someone will get hurt. Then we'll have more than our financial standing to worry about."

Aiden cursed. This must be the potential buyer Canton

had mentioned. The one who would destroy Black Hills, unless Aiden kept the mill viable. "Any suggestions?"

"Increase nighttime security?" Bateman said. "I'm worried about causing a panic, but I thought I'd tell the line managers so they could be more vigilant and strict about safety."

Aiden frowned. He didn't have much pull around here, but said, "I'll see what I can do about getting some authorities involved."

Bateman's face echoed his own worry. "I'm afraid it is time for that, though all I have is the tech's word. No real proof."

Aiden stood, shifting on the balls of his feet like a boxer. His mind worked over the puzzle. "If he's hiring inside personnel to sabotage the plant's effectiveness, you might not like what you find."

Still, he felt the surge of competitiveness rush through him. The grin he let slip out wasn't a nice one. "Too bad for Balcher, I'm not a pushover."

The tension in Bateman's shoulders and face eased, telling Aiden he'd gone up in the man's estimation. Good. They were going to have to work together on this. Teamwork? The loner Aiden balked at the idea, but this was bigger than just him and his own survival.

Though he knew he should be cursing a blue streak over this complication, instead, his energy surged. His competitive nature looked forward to taking Balcher on....

And winning.

Lost in his own thoughts, Aiden didn't realize Bateman was watching him with a speculative gleam in his eye. "Tell me," the other man said, "why are you doing this?"

"What do you mean?" Digging into motivation wasn't something Aiden enjoyed.

Bateman arched a gray-sprinkled brow. "You haven't set foot in this town since you were eighteen years old.

I'm smart enough to know you aren't here because you want to be."

"Then you are a smart man." Aiden dropped into a chair this time, letting his eyes drift shut against the glare of the fluorescent lights. He didn't want to focus too much on his surroundings and the memories they evoked. He didn't want to think about how alone Christina looked, seated there without him. He especially didn't want to think about how much he missed her warmth against him.

But Bateman wasn't finished. "You know, I was in upper management when your father took over direct supervision from James. I saw him in action on a daily basis. No matter why he came in the first place, your father stayed for one reason and one reason only. The people."

Aiden's eyes shot open, giving him a too-clear view of the white ceiling tiles. He wished he could throw out some quick, sarcastic remark, but his normally agile brain remained blank. "So what are you saying?" he asked, instead.

"That the two of you are a lot alike."

Aiden was ashamed to realize they weren't. He'd been so caught up in his own wants, desires and rebellion that he had hardly thought about others since that first afternoon at James's bedside. His father wouldn't be proud of the man he had become. Not at all.

As the realization threatened to close his lungs, Aiden knew he had to get out of there. Fast.

Eight

Christina had been so fascinated watching Aiden work, seeing his mind process the problems, that she wasn't prepared when he made excuses and motioned to the door. Her gears didn't change quickly, but the quivering urgency beneath his polite facade propelled her out the door ahead of him.

He turned the opposite direction from which they'd arrived, and his steps picked up speed.

"Aiden," she called. "Aiden, where are you going?"

She struggled to keep up, trailing behind by several feet. His steps were quick, and he never looked back. Her heart pounded. A seriously wrong vibe made the fine hairs on her arms stand on end. She followed him around twists and turns in the long hallways. Where was he going?

Finally, she rounded a corner to find him stock-still, arms and legs spread as if he'd jerked to a halt. His rigid stillness kept her silent, but she couldn't deny the impulse to get close. As she neared, she noticed fine tremors vibrating along his muscles. From the rigidity or something more?

Hesitant, she slowly extended her arm. This wasn't her place. He'd made it clear that she had no right to pry into his issues. Still, some inner need to heal, more intense than she'd ever known, urged her forward.

Just as her fingertip grazed his shoulder, he turned, blindly plowing back the way he'd come. And right into her.

He managed to keep her from falling on her tush. They danced a few steps until they collided with the wall. Their bodies came to a full halt, Christina's back braced, Aiden's arms on either side, facing her. His harsh breathing stirred her hair, awakening the urge to stroke her hands down his back until he calmed. Until he talked to her...

"Aiden," she said, aiming for a no-nonsense tone. He wouldn't appreciate emotion. "What is it?"

"I have to get out of here."

His voice was so strained, tight. She almost didn't hear him, he was clenching his teeth so hard. "Then let's go back through—"

"No."

She listened to his breathing a moment, searching for guidance. His straining lungs, tight fists and taut body told her he was seriously fighting for control over whatever was happening on the inside. Beneath the surface, something powerful was wreaking havoc.

"Why?" she whispered, her voice full of sympathy, coupled with something deeper, darker.

"I can't." He drew in a breath, flattening her chest against his. He kept his head facing away, shoulders crowded so close she couldn't turn to see. Finally, his voice came again, slow and reluctant. "I can't go back there. But I can't be here."

She wanted to understand, but felt as if she was navigating in the dark. So she did the only thing she knew how.

Reaching up, she placed her hands on each side of his waist, where his upraised arms left him vulnerable to her invasion. Her fingers traced the steeliness of his body under the thin cotton as she ran her hands over his ribs, then around to the bowstring muscles of his back.

Let me hold you.

For a moment, he ceased to move, to even breathe. Closing her eyes, she mentally sent out sympathy and peace as she'd learned to do long before her nurse's training. She could only hope to somehow restore his inner equilibrium through touch, physically and mentally.

He drew in a deep breath, easier this time, giving her hope that she might have reached him.

She inched closer, aligning her body with his, focusing solely on his breath as her hands slid around him. The intimacy of their position, of this situation, softened her voice to a caress. "Tell me what's wrong."

He held out, jaw tightened to trap the words inside. Her healing hands splayed across the small of his back. Her head tilted until her forehead rested on his chest, next to his pounding heart. Once again she sent the energy out, hoping for some kind of breakthrough.

"What's wrong?" he finally said, anger and bitterness giving the question bite. "I'll tell you what's wrong."

He twisted to point to the hallway he'd run from. "He died down there." She felt him shudder. "He simply stepped out of someone's office and fell to the floor."

She spoke despite her tight throat. "Your father?"

Aiden's nod shattered her control. She gazed into his taut face, darkened eyes, and felt the tears he refused to shed spill onto her own cheeks.

James certainly was a bastard. She'd thought he'd trapped them in a marriage they didn't want. She had no idea he'd sent Aiden back into his worst nightmare.

Aiden had little recollection of finally finding the exit door and getting to the truck. He wouldn't want to remember, even if he could. At least he hadn't blubbered like a baby. Running like one had been bad enough.

He'd just been sitting there, listening to Bateman talk about his father, and it had all become too much. He'd known if he didn't get out of there right then, things would get out of hand. Fast.

Before he'd come here, he'd gone days, sometimes weeks, without thinking about his dad. But now, everywhere he turned were memories of his parents, chipping away at the emotional control he'd built up all these years. Something he couldn't afford to lose.

Especially in front of Christina.

The familiar rhythm of tires on pavement, the mindless task of driving back to the manor, and the darkness helped him regain control. It didn't even slip when Christina spoke again.

"You were there…when he died?" He could hear the tears in her voice and wanted to tell her not to cry for him. But he didn't.

Surprisingly, he could answer without that gripping sensation returning to his chest. "He often took me to work with him that summer. I'd become too much of a handful for Lily at home, bucking James at every turn. She had her hands full with the twins, too. So he made me work down there as a runner for him."

He slowed down and pulled into the Blackstone estate, turning on the wipers as an evening drizzle started to fall.

"He'd just come out of a meeting when I met him in the hall. 'Hey, son.' That's the last thing he said before his heart attack."

Pulling around back, Aiden parked on the gravel lot outside the garage. The soft ping of water on the hood and windshield grew louder when he turned off the engine. Neither he nor Christina made any move to get out. The intimacy of dusk and the falling rain loosened his tongue.

"My father always had time for me, before we came here. He was a business-management professor for a small college. But James wanted Lily closer, and I guess my father felt he couldn't refuse the salary he was offered to manage the mill."

Put that degree to some real use, he remembered James

saying. But James had insisted on his old-fashioned ways and constantly found fault with the methods used by Aiden's father.

"Betty pointed out quite a few improvements your father made," Christina said. "Seems he was a good manager."

"I hope it was worth it," Aiden said, bitterness tightening his grip on the steering wheel. "The long hours and stress probably killed him."

They sat for long minutes in silence. Aiden's eyes drifted closed. The rain seeped down like the good memories, washing away those last dreadful moments: his father lifting him high in the air, explaining some kind of economic concept with apples and bananas, and grinning when one of the workmen praised Aiden. That's how he should remember his father.

It wasn't until his grip relaxed and his eyes opened that Christina spoke, "Ready to make a run for it?"

He grinned, his mood lifting as he caught the mischievous glitter of her barely visible irises. They'd had a bumpy road, but she had a way of soothing him. She seemed to know exactly what others needed in a given moment, and provided it if it was within her reach. It was so good, even while it scared the hell out of him.

He nodded, and they both opened their doors. Jogging out from under the trees, the rain fell harder. He hadn't realized how heavy it was until he was out in it. With his long legs, he could have easily outdistanced Christina, but he paced himself, only pulling forward enough to get the door open for her without breaking stride.

The kitchen was dark, the house quiet except for rain on the roof. They stood facing each other in the back mudroom, clothes dripping on the utility carpet, both looking like drowned rats. Christina's eyes met his. He couldn't resist a small grin at her soaked hair and the thin shirt now plastered over her very interesting curves. Her hands plucked at the clingy material, then she started laughing. Not the polite, amused titter of some of the society women he'd met.

Not for this woman. It was a deep, rolling belly laugh, doubling her over, making it hard to catch her breath. He couldn't help but join her, reveling in the lightness after the storm of his emotions. God, she was gorgeous. Even now.

"Marie is going to have a fit if we drip all over her kitchen floor—" she said.

"And the stairs."

She stuck her tongue out at his teasing tone. "You have farther to go than me, since your clothes are still on the third floor."

Even though *their* bed was on the second. And that's when it hit him. He was going to play, even though he knew he shouldn't—

"Not a problem," he boasted. Then he held her gaze for as long as possible before his shirt cleared his head. He dropped the material to the floor with a splat. Watching her closely, he noticed the smile had disappeared, and her gaze had moved down from his face. Even though his pants weren't nearly as wet, his hands went to the zipper. "You gonna join me?"

Her head was shaking before he even finished.

"You sure?"

Her gaze traced his pants' fall to the floor then traveled back up to devour the boxers he was left standing in. There wasn't any hiding his reaction to her interest.

"What's the matter, Christina? Scared?"

She stared at him, as if she was unsure how to take his question. Then she inched her bare feet—he'd missed her slipping off her shoes—toward the doorway. "No, I'm good."

Before he could stop her, she'd turned away. Her dripping clothes left a trail as she hightailed it for the stairs.

But she wasn't getting away that easy. His heart raced with anticipation as he followed. She was going to taste so good. So much better than the bitterness he'd forced down today.

His feet found the stairs, his legs propelling him after her. He heard her gasp right before he rounded the corner to meet her once more.

His voice growled from a throat tight with need. "These stairs hold the best surprises." Twisting her around, he pulled her off balance to meet him like the last time. His breath hissed through his teeth as her cold clothes pressed to his bare chest, but he didn't care. He was too busy anticipating her taste.

"Chilly?" she teased, but it didn't hide the way her body trembled beneath his hands. Then he was hit with her scent—jasmine or lavender, so soft he could breathe her in forever. Every centimeter of his body stood up and took notice.

He stared through the gloom. The wealth of hair—now curling in the humidity—hiding the vulnerability of her neck. The thin shirt outlining the soft rounds of her breasts. The pale skin of her collarbone. The awareness he'd been fighting since that first night exploded like a sizzle beneath his skin, loosening his control inch by inch.

Cupping her face between his hands, he whispered, "Not anymore," then drank from her mouth, letting the force of his desire push him beyond thinking.

Her lips parted. Her tongue met his, stroke for stroke, fueling the fire to an inferno. The feel of her delicate hands exploring his chest pulled a groan from him. "I need you, Christina. Now."

"Yes," she gasped.

Before he could lose himself in the feel of her body against his, he swept her into his arms. This was happening; nothing would stop it now.

His quick stride took them to the third floor and into his

room in precious seconds, leaving the chance of interruption far behind. Laying her on the dark navy comforter, he stripped her shirt off. The contrast between her pale blue bra and the dark background caught his attention; itches of possession tingled along his nerves.

With shaking hands he stripped her, uncovering the pale mounds of her breasts, which were more than a handful. Then he came to the silky slimness of her stomach, leading to rounded hips and the soft dark curls between her thighs. He moved to spread her long, toned legs, but she resisted.

"No," she whispered.

It took him only a moment to realize her fears. "Do you really need to hide from me, Christina?"

Her troubled gaze slowly zeroed in on him until he could see the moment she made her decision. This time he pressed firmly against her knees, not allowing her to hide. Exposing the softness between, he buried his lips against her. The greedy sounds of passion escaping from her throat ignited a heat under his skin. All thought ceased.

His whole being focused on bringing her pleasure. On the slick evidence of her passion. The silky lips of her sex. The tight arch of her back. The jerk of her hips as he concentrated in that most important spot.

All it took was one gasp, one short cry as she came to make him desperate to be inside her. Pulling back, he planted his knees in the mattress, forcing her even wider. As his body crowded over her, his mouth retraced his steps. He lapped at the delicate ring of her belly button, then along the line of ribs that heaved with her gasps for air. But it was her hands that pulled him higher. "Please, Aiden," she begged.

He made her wait a moment more while he drank deep and long from her lips, satisfying the thirst that had been building within him since the day he first saw her.

Her wicked hands explored his chest, nails scraping lightly over his skin until urgency rode him hard. "Now," she demanded, her voice strained with need. He wasted no time fitting his body to hers and pushing deep inside. Her soaked passage rippled around him, tight and unbearably hot. He could only savor her.

Don't think. Only feel.

For this moment in time, there was only the two of them working together. The lift of her hips driving him deeper with each stroke. The push of his thighs driving them both to a pleasure previously unknown.

He glanced down, and her wide-open stare caught him, the chocolate depths of her eyes holding untold secrets. As his body pounded into hers, that gaze wrapped chains around them that tied his soul to hers. He saw beauty, acceptance and the promise of rapture. She reached up to cup his face, fingers tangling in his hair as he burrowed deeper. Her eyes lost focus. Anticipation squeezed his lower back, his body pulling inward, readying for the leap. But it was the wonder in her eyes that sent him over.

With a groan, the tension exploded outward, leaving him shaken and useless. As if sex between them had drained every last ounce of rebellion and frustration, stripping away his starch. Limbs limp and sated, he sank over her and savored the long moments of quiet peace. Of relief.

A small jerk of her hips brought him back to the present. Reality flooded his mind in a rush: the quietness of the house around them, the darkness held off by the single lamp beside his bed, the unevenness of her breathing. The greedy gasp of the flesh surrounding his own.

Again his body hardened at the feel of the silken skin surrounding it, no barriers to dull the sensation—

No barrier!

With a mighty pull, Aiden separated from Christina and sprang from the bed. Her surprise slowed her reaction, granting him a glimpse of trembling breasts, pale skin marked by the rough touch of his fingers and the dark center where he'd found a peace unlike any he'd experienced before. Too soon, she jerked upright, reaching to push her thick, dark hair back from her face. He wished he could ignore her confused expression.

"What's the matter?" she asked.

Underneath the panic flooding his veins, his logical brain knew he was going about this all wrong. But when had he ever handled anything emotional right? He should be holding her, bringing her to another climax, not sinking into the depths of his own anger and fear.

"Condom," he said, passion still straining his voice. "I didn't use a condom."

Stalking to his closet, he yanked on underwear and then pants. "I can't believe I did that. What the hell was I thinking?" He jerked a shirt on in hard, short pulls. He'd spent his adult life avoiding commitment—especially a lifelong one like parenthood. As images of a pregnant Christina muddled up his brain, his voice gathered volume, "Tell me you are on the pill. Tell me."

His movements ceased abruptly when he glanced over his shoulder and spied the woman huddled in the middle of his bed. Her chin was tucked against her neck, her gaze pointedly fixed on the navy comforter she had wrapped around her naked body. The body he had just made love to, then left without so much as a thank-you-very-much. But he couldn't stop the freight train of his panic. "Tell me you are taking the pill," he insisted again.

He didn't catch her mumble. Striding across the carpet, he placed a firm hand under her chin, guiding it up until he could look once more into the gorgeous depths of those dark eyes.

She didn't even have to speak. He could tell by the way she shied away from his touch that she wasn't protected in any way. "Damn," he muttered, stumbling back on suddenly shaky legs.

"What is the matter with you?" she asked.

"This isn't what I planned. It isn't what I wanted," he said, more to himself than her. His brain shut down, as if it had been dealt one too many shocks over the last few weeks.

Hearing a rustle, he turned to find her standing beside the bed, gathering the length of the comforter around her curves. Her back was straight and tense, those tight shoulders reminding him of the time they'd first met as adults. The only contrast being the sight of smooth, pale skin that tempted him to throw his panic to the winds and reenter forbidden territory.

She walked to her pile of clothes and started gathering them up in her arms.

"Okay then, is this a bad time of the month to conceive?" he asked clinically, his nerves demanding some form of reassurance.

"It's a bad time of the month," she replied, though her voice sounded robotic as she tucked the damp clothes against her.

Allowing her a small modicum of dignity, he waited until she was almost to the door before pressing for more information. "Are you serious or are you just saying what I want to hear?"

She turned to face him, giving him a head-on look at the misery in her eyes. "Is being a jackass genetic for you?" Without another word, she turned away. He grabbed her bare arm, sucking in a breath at the chill on her skin.

"Christina, please. I know I started this, but I didn't mean to leave either of us with a child we don't want."

"How do you know I wouldn't want it?"

Shock held him immobile for a minute, then heat blazed across his body. And not the good kind. "Are you saying you *want* me to get you pregnant?"

"No, Aiden," she said, her voice steadier than before.

"I'm just saying I've always wanted children of my own. But you don't have to worry. I'll take care of everything."

He wouldn't have to worry? "I don't want children. Ever. When this is over, I'm heading straight back to New York. Not staying because I gave James another weapon to use against me. I have to get away." He would smother if he knew he was only here because his grandfather had tied his hands.

Her eyes closed for a moment, then that tight, haughty look slipped over her face once more. A mask that was achingly familiar.

She held herself away from him, preserving a few inches of space between their bodies. It only served to remind him of those moments just past when there'd been no space between them at all.

"I understand, Aiden. Believe me, I do. You'll get your wish. I promise."

Would he? Did it really matter in the aftermath of what they'd just experienced? Shame rolled over him as he watched her walk out of the room with quiet dignity, somehow graceful despite the improvised wrapping and his selfish commands. As his body demanded he follow and his mind demanded he stay away, he had to wonder what it was he really wanted.

Nine

Christina grasped the banister extra hard to keep herself steady. Walking with her head high down the main staircase, she forced one foot in front of the other. She refused to hide in Lily's suite, as much as she might want to. Hiding was for sissies. She would face Aiden like the strong woman she wanted to be, not the scared rabbit she'd been so often in the past.

Memories from the night before didn't make her walk to breakfast any easier.

From the moment his mouth had met hers, she'd been lost. All the heat, excitement and passion she'd craved her entire life had been contained in that kiss. It had been like coming home and finding all the holidays her family had neglected being celebrated all at once. Every nerve ending in her body had lit up, and thinking had become a thing of the past.

The part that had truly gotten under her skin had been the moment his gaze met hers. While his body drove deeper than deep between her thighs, his eyes had locked with hers for moments on end. She'd seen the man underneath, the same need for love and acceptance she had. The need to prove himself—not just to the world around him, but to himself. As she'd struggled to keep her eyes open, her gaze locked on his; she'd felt their souls touch in an intangible way she'd never experienced before.

Hell, birth control had been the last thing on her mind, even considering the complications of not using it. She'd known only the burn of Aiden's hard flesh inside her. Obviously, he'd come to his senses a lot quicker than she had.

And *she* was the one feeling awkward now. He hadn't come to bed last night, so she'd gotten a reprieve until morning. Still, she took a deep breath and walked through the door with even steps. Aiden was already seated at the table, sipping coffee and reading a newspaper. Business as usual. At least she wouldn't have to suffer as the sole focus of his attention.

Nolen hovered near the door to the kitchen and gave her a knowing look as he stepped forward to pour her coffee. *Dang it.* She'd love to know how they found out about things. Her cheeks heated. It didn't matter that she wasn't the one who'd stripped by the back door. She'd never have sex in this house again.

Aiden glanced over as she sat down. She ignored him, focusing on Nolen as he poured her coffee. "How about some waffles, Miss Christina?"

The thought had her stomach roiling, but even a nibble would be better than sitting there in strained silence. "That would be lovely, Nolen. Please tell Marie thank you for me."

With a nod, he left. Christina carefully poured cream then sugar into her cup. Today was for full leaded, not a halfway commitment. Waffles and sweet coffee. Screw her waistline.

"Christina, about last night—" Aiden began.

Of course he couldn't leave her in peace. Where was the fun in that? "Don't worry about it. It was a mistake. No problem."

"Of course it's a problem. I'm sorry—"

She wasn't sure if it was her angry glare or Nolen's reappearance that stopped him, only that she didn't have to hear more about what a problem she was. At least for the moment. Nolen lingered, to her appreciation, making sure she had everything she needed before reluctantly easing back over to the door. "I'll be nearby if you need me," he said, his tone strong, a little louder than it needed to be.

Her protector. She'd never had one before, but it sure felt nice.

Aiden studied her as she smothered the warm waffles with butter and heated strawberry preserves. The fruity aroma should have been tantalizing. Still, she forced herself to cut a bite and lift it to her mouth. Aiden spoke again as she chewed.

"Look, you're right," he said, much to her surprise. "I did say all the wrong things last night. I kind of freaked out—"

"Kinda?" she mumbled.

"But I want to make this right. We will be seeing each other a lot over the next several months—"

Not as much as she'd seen of him yesterday.

"—and I don't want things to be awkward between us."

Too late.

"So I propose—"

"You ungrateful, sorry excuse for a grandson!"

The interruption came from the hallway this time, leaving Christina disconcerted. At first, she had the horrible suspicion that James had found out about her sleeping with Aiden. Then she realized what he'd said. Why was he so upset?

Her stomach tightened. Confrontations had happened frequently when she was growing up and never ended well. James preferred his arguments loud and long.

Leaning heavily on a cane, he came through the door. "You think I'm already in the grave, boy?"

Aiden switched gears pretty quickly. "Hardly," he said, letting a wry amusement stretch the word. He'd turned toward James, but as she watched, he deliberately relaxed back into his chair.

"Oh, but you can ignore me, act like I don't exist, while you conduct my business right under my nose?" In his anger, James was unusually flushed and agitated. Christina's senses tingled as his left arm jerked a few times.

"Did you think I wouldn't hear about that little visit to the mill?" James winced, but he didn't take a step toward one of the empty chairs. "Don't you think you should have asked permission from the actual owner of the mill? Or are you trying to get in good with that day foreman while I'm too sick to stop you?"

"Why would you want to stop me? You told me to take over. That's what I'm doing, abiding by the *letter* of your law."

James grabbed Aiden's left arm, hard. Christina's sensibilities kicked into overdrive. "James—"

"By cutting me out of the loop?" James gripped his cane tightly, seeming to sway on his feet. "Taking meetings behind my back? I'm still in charge here."

As she stood, Christina felt an unnatural calm come over her. Gone was the frightened child witnessing one argument among many. The nurse took over, reminding her not to ignore her instincts. "James—" His color was pale but his cheeks burned red. He was definitely unsteady on his feet, but then he had been since his last attack.

Aiden found his feet, too, meeting his grandfather on equal ground. "You won't be in charge for long. Remember?"

When James's hand reached to press against his chest, Christina was around the table in seconds.

"Please, James. The doctor said you needed to stay calm. Let's just quiet down—"

"You!" James's focus finally shifted her way. "You're helping him take everything away from me. You should be grateful for all I've done for you. Instead, you're plotting to ruin me."

Christina wasn't sure where the paranoia was coming from. She didn't care. Right now, he needed calm and his medicine. But his next words halted her in her tracks.

"I should have known you weren't good enough for this job. Convenient, yes, but those scheming genes of your mother's had to show up sometime."

Christina swayed as all the blood drained from her head.

"Enough." Aiden's voice echoed off the painted paneling. "Bateman asked to meet with us at the mill. We went. If you want a report, I'll have it to you by this afternoon."

James looked like he wanted to say more, but winced, instead. Christina rushed forward, pushing everything aside but her training. "James. We'll get your doctor out here to look over you. Nolen!" she yelled.

James gasped, and panic spread across his face. "It'll be okay," she soothed. "Nolen, let's get him to the study and call an ambulance."

But James was having none of it. "No. Just take me back to my room. Dr. Markham can come."

"But, James—"

"No. No hospitals. If I'm gonna die, I'll do it at Blackstone Manor."

Two hours later, his wish came true.

Aiden stared at the monstrosity of a monument James Blackstone had erected for himself before turning away in disgust. He walked away from the crypt and the bronze coffin, leaving Christina behind as she greeted those still lingering at the graveside. Practically the whole town had attended the funeral, which made sense. The Blackstones were known by all. James would have expected the town to pay homage to him in his death.

Aiden just wished he could ignore the twinges of guilt James's death had given him. Those final words, spoken in anger, left him feeling lower than low. Which was just what James would have wanted. Aiden's emotions made no logical sense, but his grandfather had left him with more than one unwanted legacy.

As Aiden walked up the hill to the far corner of the cemetery, he shed the fake gratitude for fake sympathy that had soaked the last few days. Some of the ungodly tension he'd felt since he first walked back through the door of Blackstone Manor drained away. By the time he joined his brothers at his father's graveside, he felt marginally lighter.

James Blackstone was dead. For real, this time.

As much as he hated to celebrate a death, without James, Aiden would be free to do as he wanted, no interference allowed. Lily's guardianship would pass to him or one of his brothers, so James's instrument of punishment was removed. Aiden could legally start a trust and care for his mother, and find a stable management team for the mill. No one would be left hanging. Then he'd be free to return to New York and his business there.

If part of him cringed at the thought of never tasting Christina again, he refused to acknowledge it. Just like he wouldn't think about the last lonely nights back in his own room. In the long run, this was better for both of them.

"You hangin' in there, brother?" Luke asked as Aiden approached.

Aiden nodded, then turned to hug Luke's twin, Jacob. He had flown in as soon as Aiden contacted him about James's death. As the chief operating officer of a major manufacturing company in Philadelphia, he was as steady and by the books as his twin wasn't. The two men stood facing each other, looking like mirror images with their blond hair and suits. But Aiden knew the similarities ended there. Each twin was an individual, with his own strengths and talents, his own weaknesses. Today, dressed alike, with Luke's hair trimmed for the occasion, the differences didn't show. But they were there.

Blackstone Manor hadn't been home for him in a very long time. But anywhere his brothers were, he counted as his home. Despite living in separate cities, they came together for several days three to four times each year. Aiden and Jacob had dinner once a month or more, since they lived about two hours apart.

Aiden glimpsed his father's tombstone over his brothers' shoulders. How he wished he could talk to his dad one more time—get some guidance on where to go from here. His major instincts screamed at him to run, but he was more and more reluctant to do so. And that scared him.

He told himself he'd grown a soul. That leaving the people of Black Hills high and dry just wasn't what his mother would have wanted. But he feared his real motivations were much more complicated than that.

"Luke has been catching me up on all the drama," Jacob said. It wasn't surprising that the task had been left to his younger brother. Aiden had been running like a chicken with his head cut off since James's death. "Married, huh?"

Aiden nodded. "Not for long, I hope."

"I thought the deal was for a year. Besides, Christina is a lovely woman," Jacob said.

Luke snorted. "Damn straight."

"The deal was for a year while James was alive." Aiden mentally crossed his fingers, and refused to think about just how lovely Christina was—his brothers didn't need to know how far things had gone between him and his wife. "I'm hoping now that he's gone there's some way to untangle this whole situation. We'll meet with Canton tomorrow for the reading of the will, then I'll get my lawyer on it."

Jacob nodded slowly, his hand rubbing at the back of his neck like it did when he was thinking. He stared past Aiden at the gathering below them, but Aiden had a feeling he wasn't seeing much. Jacob was the problem solver of this little group. He'd been the one to find ways around

James's rules when they were kids, and viewed a multi-million-dollar problem as a simple brainteaser. So many times over the past month Aiden had picked up the phone to call him, ask him to get him out of this mess, but had always hung up.

This wasn't Jacob's problem; it was his.

"And what's the plan?" Jacob asked.

"I'm not sure about long-term care for Mom yet. The guardianship should transfer to one of us. I figured, when the time came, we could talk to Christina about options." And pray she didn't spit in his face when he walked away. As unsettling as the thought was, he was determined to go through with his plans. He didn't belong here. And he was quickly realizing that Christina deserved a lot better than the deal she'd gotten with him. "Without James here, I can visit Mom often, check in on her just like you all do."

He turned back to watch the remaining visitors clear the cemetery, leaving Christina standing with Nolen and the funeral director. A slight, warm breeze blew the silky black material of her dress against her legs, displaying an outline of full hips and thighs. "I'll need help finding someone to put in charge of the mill. With all the questionable stuff going on, we need someone smart enough to get ahead of the problems and hard enough to tell Balcher we'll never sell—and make him believe it. Someone who will work well with Bateman. Getting it done before someone gets hurt is my major priority at the moment." He'd worry about the personal issues later.

"I think I might have the man for you."

Aiden turned back to look at Jacob. "Already? Seriously, dude, you are scary sometimes."

"Not really. I want the job."

Aiden stared at his brother. Out of the corner of his eye, he saw Luke doing the same. "Why?"

"I've been thinking about moving back here for a while."

"And leave a successful career where you're making millions? Again I ask, why?"

Jacob shrugged. "It's personal, okay? I just want us to talk about it, see if that's an option."

"Is it? Of course. But I want you to be very sure." Aiden's arms crossed protectively over his chest, where hope was starting to form. If Jacob came home, Aiden could return to New York without any worries. Everything would be taken care of. Everything. *But what about Christina?* "I don't want anyone stuck where they don't want to be."

Luke pushed his way back into the conversation. "You mean like you?" he asked, eyes narrowed in a way that made Aiden uncomfortable.

Again came that twinge of uneasiness. Aiden ignored it. He'd made his intentions very clear to Christina from day one. "Damn straight."

Ten

Aiden pushed open the study door with anticipation sizzling through his veins. An older man stood at the far window. When Nolen had told him who was waiting, Aiden had been surprised. Leo Balcher's background and business had been an obsession since the trip to the mill. His showing up at Blackstone Manor and asking specifically to see Aiden was a stroke of luck. Whether good or bad remained unclear.

But it could give Aiden a chance to face off with the competition on home turf. He observed Balcher for a moment. The man's chubby hands curved around the carved wood borders of the shelves on each side as he surveyed the farmland as if he already owned it.

He was in for a rude awakening.

He turned as Aiden closed the door behind him, a too-jovial smile on his round face inviting Aiden to treat him like a good ol' boy. Unfortunately for him, Aiden hadn't bought into the old Southern traditions men had for interacting with each other before he left, and he wasn't about to schmooze and pat backs with Balcher. Having fought to earn his own way in a precarious profession, Aiden judged other men by the same standard of effort.

Comparing Christina and her sacrifice to some of the socialites he'd left behind in New York had him extending that thought to women, too. They might be on uneasy footing at the moment, but she was a woman worth more than many of the men he'd met. Including this one.

But Aiden wasn't above using Balcher's expectations against him.

Balcher crossed the room with his hand extended, his too-tight navy suit in stark contrast to Aiden's polo, khaki pants and hair still wet from the shower. Seeing Balcher eye his informal attire, Aiden barely suppressed a grin. Under normal circumstances, Aiden would never attend a business meeting dressed like this. But he was still more put together than the crew they'd met on the courthouse steps the other day. Wearing a lot less cologne, too. But Balcher probably counted on him being a pushover, someone who had no interest in professional behavior, when the truth was he'd been caught at an inconvenient time.

But Aiden wouldn't disabuse Balcher of his misconceptions. He'd use whatever advantage he could get.

"Mr. Blackstone. Nice to meet you."

"Please, call me Aiden," he said, enduring the man's hearty handshake. *Not really working, old man.*

"This is a beautiful place, Aiden," Balcher said, once again surveying his surroundings with possessiveness, only this time focusing on the dark, oppressive interior of the room Aiden had taken over as his office since moving back.

Taking in the heavy wood, curtains and ornate mirror, Aiden realized he really should gut this place and start over.

His lack of response unnerved Balcher, whose flashy smile was a little strained, giving Aiden a glimpse of too many teeth. He finally broke the silence on his own. "I hope the family is faring well, given the circumstances."

Aiden dropped into the creaky leather chair, leaning back to clasp his hands together over his stomach.

"Thank you," Aiden said with cool politeness…as close to chummy as he could manage. "We're doing our best. As you can imagine, there is a lot going on at the moment. Is there something I can do for you this morning?"

"I would have thought James mentioned me in some fashion, and my interest in Blackstone Mills."

He hadn't directly. Aiden had to find that out on his own. Bateman was right—Aiden's research showed Balcher loved to take the competition apart, piece by piece.

"I assumed this had to do with the mill, though I'm surprised you'd be here to talk business this soon after my grandfather's death."

The other man plopped his corpulent figure into one of the curved leather chairs facing the desk, adjusting his tie as if it was suddenly too tight. "No need to be so blunt, my man. Business should have its niceties. I simply prefer to get the ball rolling before other interested parties start moving in."

Aiden leaned forward, resting his forearms on the desk, and almost grinned as he echoed Christina's words. "Blunt is the way I deal—take it or leave it."

Regardless of his thwarted desire to settle the mill quickly and walk away, Aiden wouldn't have ever sold it to this man. Balcher wasn't being polite for manners. No, his attitude had a slickness and Boss Hog–style that spoke of greed, of consumption to the detriment of others. Besides, Aiden didn't believe in handing the lives and livelihood of people depending on him to someone he disliked on sight.

"Well, then, I'm sure your grandfather informed you of our discussions over the purchase of the mill and everything connected to it—"

"Marie told me we had a visitor, so I thought I'd bring along some refreshments," Christina said, easing sideways through the door. She carried an old-fashioned tea tray with a teapot, cups and some fancy-looking cakes. Aiden greeted her arrival with reluctant fascination.

He could look at her beauty all day, but he'd rarely seen

her since the funeral. Every room he entered she was just leaving. She'd taken most of her meals in Lily's suite, leaving him alone with his brothers. If she didn't relent once Jacob and Luke were gone, he'd be stuck eating alone.

And whose fault was that?

Having her here with her gracious movements and flattering smile was only going to distract him from besting Balcher. "That won't be necessary, Christina. Mr. Balcher won't be here long."

"Oh." She looked at them with dark eyes so guileless he immediately knew she was up to something. "Are you sure you won't have one of Marie's petit fours? They'll melt in your mouth, I swear."

The look in Balcher's eyes made Aiden wonder whether he was craving a cake, or Christina. Something dark and hungry rose in Aiden, taking him by surprise. He didn't need her here. She was a distraction from his true purpose, both professionally and personally. Was he hard enough to send her away?

"I don't believe we've met," the man said, clearing a spot on a side table so Christina could set down the laden tray. "I'm Leo Balcher, the owner of Crystal Cotton."

Hands finally empty, she extended one to their guest with all the graciousness of an antebellum hostess. "Hello, I'm Christina. Aiden's wife."

Eyes widening, the man looked from one to the other. "I was under the impression that all the Blackstone boys were single. Where'd he snag a pretty filly like you?"

Aiden's irritation kept growing, but he couldn't decide if it was directed at Balcher or at her. Or himself. He'd been on edge since the moment he'd left his bed with her in it. The days of deprivation since then hadn't helped.

What the hell was she up to? "Christina's a local," he said, watching her closely.

The man seemed to think the gracious Christina might

prove to be an ally. "Oh, well, I was just discussing the purchase of the mill."

She shot a quick glance in Aiden's direction, finally cluing him in. The woman who had dedicated her life to taking care of Lily and Marie and Nolen was concerned enough to take the weight of an entire town on her shoulders. He'd told her they'd work together, but instead of calling for her, he'd walked into this meeting alone.

Leaving *her* shut out.

Boy, he just kept being a bastard, didn't he?

"Balcher," Aiden broke in. "My grandfather is barely in the ground, and you are coming around to talk business? What was that about observing the niceties?" Aiden asked with a sardonic twist.

Out of the corner of his eye he saw Christina's shoulders relax, as if she realized he wasn't going to send her away anytime soon.

The man wiggled back into his chair, the joints creaking under his weight. "Well, now, you haven't been around these parts much," he said, his eyes shifting away from the intensity of Aiden's stare. "I heard there wasn't any love lost between you two. No reason for you to take over such a huge burden. After all, I doubt after living in New York City you'd be interested in settling down in the back of beyond." He smiled again, as if his rudeness made perfect sense.

"You're right. There wasn't any loyalty between my grandfather and I. Quite frankly, he was a sorry excuse for a dictator."

Balcher's facial muscles stiffened. Aiden hoped the other man was getting an idea of who he was dealing with now. Not an old man at the end of his life, but a young businessman at the top of his game. Though Aiden didn't want to tip his hand too quickly.

Maybe Christina would play the game, as well. She had trained her wide eyes on Balcher and was blinking as if confused. "What in the world would you want another mill for? You should have more than enough by now."

The little vixen! Digging for information on her own. He was perfectly capable of telling Balcher the deal would never happen and escorting him to the door. When the time was right.

She didn't trust him to do that.

Not that he blamed her. She had a huge stake in this venture. This town was her home; the people here meant a lot to her. She was justified in her interest. He just hoped she didn't steer the conversation away from where he wanted it to go.

"Well, my dear," Balcher was saying, matching her tone. Aiden began to feel like a drama was playing out before him, only the subtext was more interesting than the dialogue. "Competition is competition. It's a tough market, leading to tough decisions. Every mill can't stay in operation."

As Balcher's gaze inventoried the room once more, Christina eased farther into the background. Aiden's libido kicked into gear as he saw the emotions shift on her face. The same wave that had washed over her when she was defending his helpless mother. She was so passionate when it came to protecting others. Or when she was so pissed off that she forgot to be a polite little lady.

The temper churning in those chocolate eyes should not turn him on. Luckily, Balcher couldn't see it.

"But I understand Blackstone Mills is special." Balcher said, a small grin stretching his full lips. "And this house would fit me just perfect. I figured, after everything I heard about Aiden, we could come to some sort of compromise."

"I see," Aiden said, not giving the other man any clues. "What sort of compromise did you have in mind? After all, I think the manager, Bateman, is getting a little suspicious."

"Suspicious? What's there to be suspicious of? This is business, pure and simple."

Aiden saw Christina, now angled slightly behind Balcher, open her mouth to protest. He knew what she was thinking. That this wasn't business, it was people's homes and lives. *He* understood. But he needed to get information more than he needed to make a point Balcher wouldn't get.

He shot a warning glance in her direction before he said, "Well, you know that and I know that, but others don't. I can't stop Bateman from getting the authorities involved for long."

Balcher shifted his bulk from one side to the other. "Authorities?"

Maybe Aiden could push a little harder. "Well, you aren't exactly known for clean tactics, but equipment tampering could actually get someone hurt. If proof got into the papers, it could be seen as going too far. By some."

Aiden honestly thought Balcher's eyes would bug out of his pudgy, round face as he shot to his feet, but he slowly regained control. He thought hard for a moment before he said, "I don't know what you're talking about, but if this little problem gets to be too much for ya, I'll be happy to take it off your hands." He glanced out the window, absently rubbing his belly as if he was hungry. "It and all the perks that come with it."

"That's a shame, because it's not in the best interest of the mill or Black Hills for me to sell to a man like you." He grinned as he remembered something. "Oh, I'm sorry you've wasted your time." *There, niceties observed.*

Just as he made his way around the desk to escort Boss Hog to the door, it opened, and Nolen appeared. Was everyone listening in on this conversation?

"I'm just asking you to consider—" Balcher blustered as Aiden crowded him toward the exit.

Aiden must not have made his point clear. "I know what you want. We're not selling. Now get out."

Aiden didn't miss the satisfied expression on Christina's face. He only wished he'd had a more intimate role in putting it there. Too bad they shouldn't sleep together. Ever. Again.

But Balcher recovered fast. Reaching out, he offered Aiden a business card. "Well played, son. But you'll change your mind soon enough, when the problems only get bigger...and more expensive. Here's where you can reach me."

Aiden didn't hesitate. The card easily tore in half.

"I see," Balcher said. His eyes narrowed, his frown and frustration slipping through the good ol' boy facade. He turned slowly to look at Christina where she stood near the opposite window. Then he turned back to Aiden, the smile once more firmly planted on his face. "Just figured family would be the most important thing to you right now. Not some ol' business."

This time Aiden's inner alarms blared. Was that a personal threat? Was Balcher willing to get filthy dirty in order to get what he wanted? He glanced at Nolen, who had narrowed his gaze on their visitor.

Christina seemed to sense something, too, and all her sugary sweetness melted away. "Just what is that supposed to mean?" she demanded as she stalked closer, glaring with the same quiet stubbornness she'd used on James in his sickbed.

"Nothing, ma'am," Balcher said, all flashing teeth and concerned appearance. "I just know a brand-new husband like yours would be in full protection mode, that's all. I just figured he'd want to do what's best for y'all, town be damned."

Aiden wasn't buying the false concern. That hint of steel underneath Balcher's facade might make him harder to shake than he'd thought.

"I am," Aiden said, deciding he'd had enough formalities to last him an entire summer. "But I can protect my family *and* keep these people's jobs. Instead of turning the plant over to someone who will shut it down and sell it off as scrap metal."

Christina added, "Just like you did to the Athens Mill. Last year, wasn't it?"

Balcher didn't deny it, though he looked a bit startled.

The businessman ambled slowly to the open door, ignoring Nolen. Maybe he was tired of beating his head against a brick wall. Or maybe he'd decided to retreat and reassess his new opponents, opponents who seemed to have done their homework. But before disappearing, he glanced back at Aiden. "There may not have been any love between you and your grandfather, but you've got a lot of the old man in you, I think."

Anger and denial roared through Aiden for long moments after the door closed on that parting shot. When the haze finally cleared, Aiden swung back to face Christina. "What the hell was that? Waltzing in here with tea and cakes like this was social hour?"

Again that wide-eyed guilelessness, though Aiden detected a hint of uneasiness around the edges. "I don't know what you mean. I was simply being polite."

"You were spying. On me."

"Don't be ridiculous."

Some part of Aiden warned him he was taking his emotions out on an innocent, but he was tired of thinking when it came to Christina. He stalked closer, backing her up against the bookshelves. The soft smell of some kind of flowers wafted over him, but he ignored its soothing scent in favor of the anger driving him. Or was it something more, just as aggressive, but not as destructive?

"Let's get one thing straight, little girl," he said, resorting to the derogatory tone from that long-ago, childish conversation. "I won't be spied on, I won't be manipulated and I won't be played with. I got enough of that from my grandfather. I won't tolerate it from a wife."

For a moment, he could have sworn he saw a hint of that same emotion he'd seen so many years ago. Like a lost puppy being run away from a place she'd thought to call home. But whatever he'd seen disappeared in the flood of something far more potent.

Within seconds she was pushing back, practically standing on her tiptoes to get in his face. "Then don't be someone I have to spy on. Be open like you were at the mill. Work with me like you said you would."

Something primitive inside him sat up and took notice… of the dilation of her eyes when he leaned closer…of the uptick in the pulse at the base of her throat…of the tongue that sneaked out to wet her lips. *Careful.* It would be all too easy to slip back into her arms.

You did promise. Aiden wanted to ignore the thought, but he couldn't. Because he wasn't like his grandfather— no matter what Balcher thought. With a deep breath, he purposely moved their conversation in a safer direction. "I guess we do have a passable good cop/bad cop shtick goin' on."

Her eyebrow arched skyward, affording her a superior look that told him she still didn't trust him. She spoke in a low tone, but her words carried straight and true. "You could have sold it. Easily."

"To that guy? Unnecessarily cruel, I think." Aiden knew he should step back. Move away. But he couldn't.

She searched his face, probably hoping for reassurance, but as with Bateman, she'd have to learn to trust him from his actions. He just needed to give her something better to work with. Of course, if the reading of the will went according to his expectations, there wouldn't be a lot of time for her to learn. It was the reminder of the separation that was coming upon them so quickly that finally forced him to turn away.

As he walked back to the desk, she murmured, "The servants aren't the only ones good at figuring out what's going on around here."

"Don't you trust me?" Aiden could have smacked himself. He'd just decided trust was up to her, so why was he begging like a dog at the dinner table?

He barely heard her reply. "Should I?"

With those two words she conjured up memories of things he should definitely forget. Warm skin. Eager hands. Willing flesh. Everything he needed to stay far away from.

She glanced at her watch. "Look, I need to check in on Lily."

Something deep inside him protested. This might be his last chance to have her to himself. After their meeting with Canton… "What about you? Are you okay?"

She turned her head toward him by slow increments. "Are you worried about me? Or whether I'll make things more of a hassle for you?"

"These past few days have been crazy," he deflected. "They're about to get crazier."

"Why?"

"Now that James is dead, we can get this all sorted out," he said, gesturing between them. "Behind us."

He could tell the moment she realized what he was talking about. Not because of the emotion on her face, but because all expression disappeared. She nodded. "You'll be glad to get back to New York."

"It's where I belong."

She studied him for the course of several breaths. "Are you sure about that?"

Eleven

Christina stalled as she entered the study. She was the last to arrive, thanks to lingering with Lily and Nicole for longer than she planned. Avoiding the inevitable, as if that was possible. After all, will or not, Aiden would leave. His smooth good looks and smoldering intensity had seduced her into forgetting that. Too bad his temperamental attitudes weren't enough to cool her newly awakened libido.

She paused beside Nolen, whom she'd been worried about since James's death. "How are you holding up, Nolen?"

The butler rested sad eyes on her. "I know it was his time, Miss Christina. But this will be a big change."

"Yes." A delicate shudder shook her body. "Yes, it will."

Aiden moved closer, pausing nearby as if he wanted a word with her, but she studiously ignored him. The meeting with Balcher had been an emotional roller coaster, with another one directly in front of her. Coping with Aiden one-on-one wasn't a good idea right now.

As Canton gathered the papers out of his briefcase, Christina made her way to the couch and chose a seat next to Luke, who smiled in welcome. Let Aiden think what he would. It was way past time for her to stop caring.

Only family was there—or what Christina would consider family. Each grandson, herself, Nolen and Marie. No outsiders. Her stomach tightened. Did that mean the will was James's way of controlling them still? Had he refrained from airing their dirty laundry to others? Suddenly, her fears for the future were magnified.

She'd never trusted him—never in life, and not in death. It was a chronic issue with her and the Blackstone males, it seemed. But with Lily as a factor, there was no way to turn her back on whatever was coming their way.

Lily was all that mattered now. Not Christina's breaking heart, nor Aiden's damnable pride. Only Lily—the woman who'd sacrificed everything for those she loved.

Chatter continued at a low volume until Canton tapped his stack of papers against the desk. "As you can imagine from your dealings with him in life," Canton began, "James left extensive instructions about how things will continue after his demise."

Christina's sense of unease escalated, growing even worse as those around her shifted in their chairs. Whatever was coming, Canton knew. The knowledge shone in those beady little eyes behind his glasses. Christina got the impression he was about to have a taste of the power he'd been hungering for while James was alive.

She sure hoped that power was short-lived.

"Would you like me to read the will verbatim or give you an overview?" The little weasel's chin tipped up.

"Just tell us how we can unravel this tangle James created…my mother, the mill, this marriage," Aiden demanded.

Christina tried not to care about being classified as part of a *tangle,* especially since she could understand why Aiden felt that way. Besides, people had viewed her as a complication her entire life. So she pretended it didn't hurt worse than all the other times before.

"Divorce proceedings are easy enough to initiate," Jacob said.

Christina sensed Aiden shift forward in his chair. "Yeah, but that could leave Christina in an awkward position when all is said and done," he said.

She breathed deep. This discussion had to happen, even if it hurt her. She'd rather it be in public than privately between just her and Aiden.

Luke chimed in. "What about one of those annulment things?"

"Would be even easier," Jacob agreed.

"Yes," Canton said. "An annulment would be easy enough, provided you qualify."

He turned his gaze to her, staring as if he could tunnel beneath her cracking facade. In that moment, it felt as if every eye in the room shifted her way and heat flashed over her face. She wasn't sure where her protest came from, but she wished she could take the little sound back with all her heart.

Canton raised a superior brow, satisfaction in his small smile. "But I'm assuming the requirement that the marriage not be consummated makes this no longer an option…"

Mortification burst over her, forcing her to lower her lashes. Having her sexuality discussed in this room full of seething testosterone was not at all what she wanted.

"What about something to do with coercion?" Aiden asked.

That brought Christina's head up. Surely, he wasn't inferring that she— But then he continued. "After all, James coerced me into this. Even though Christina volunteered, she was simply trying to help me, to help Lily. We'll go at it from that angle."

She should thank him for thinking of her. If only he wasn't fighting for something she wasn't sure she wanted.

"It doesn't matter," Canton broke in. "James wanted everything to continue as is. If you'll just allow me to continue—"

"Spit it out," Aiden demanded, his voice sounding like a growl.

Jacob and Luke nodded their agreement. Christina remained silent. She wanted nothing from this will. Nothing except to be left alone to care for her friend. If deep down she had hoped to have a chance to hold on to Aiden just a little bit longer, then she'd bury it under the shame of his abandonment and pretend it never existed.

"James changed his will after Aiden's return and his subsequent marriage."

Christina didn't turn to look as Aiden mumbled curses under his breath. Luke's sigh was an indication that all the men realized this probably wasn't a good thing.

"He wished the marriage—and your presence—to continue the full year. He also expressed his certainty that you would disregard his instructions should he die."

Christina's stomach twisted, forcing bile up the back of her throat. James had known Aiden all too well.

"So what's the threat this time?" Aiden asked, exasperation tightening his voice. "He can no longer use Mother as leverage. Between us grandsons, money isn't an issue. So what is it now?"

Canton's grin was reminiscent of the man Christina had both feared and loathed while he was alive. She had a notion those feelings were about to kick back into gear.

"Who said Lily was out of the picture?" he asked.

Christina gasped, jerking forward as pain shot through her. She barely noticed the warmth of Luke's hand against the small of her back. Her entire focus was on the weasel behind the desk. "What are you saying?" she moaned.

"I'm saying you will stay here and take care of Lily, and Aiden will stay to take care of the town. Just as James wanted."

That should have made her feel better, but it didn't. "Why?"

"Because Lily's guardianship now reverts to me. As does control of all Blackstone funding."

Curses rolled from the men around her as they jumped

to their feet, but Christina remained frozen on the sofa. Her breath stuck in her throat so long she thought her chest would explode. Fear let loose like a runaway train—for Lily, for her future....

But a small part of her brain—the part she refused to acknowledge—whispered, *He can't leave just yet...*

"Everything will remain as is, for as long as Mr. Blackstone wished. At the end of the year, all inheritances will be dispersed and Lily's guardianship will revert to Jacob."

That was very little comfort to Christina. A lot could happen before the end of that year.

Aiden stepped forward beside her, staring Canton down as if he could force his surrender with a singular glare. "What reason could you possibly have for controlling a woman who can't defend herself, keeping her from her family and threatening her health. Much less threatening the demise of an entire town's way of life?"

"You can't get away with this," Jacob added. "When it comes to protecting our mother, we won't hold back. We'll find a way to stop you."

"According to this will," Canton said, shaking the papers in his hands, "I can. You can fight it, but again, it will take time. More time than the year in which Aiden and Christina are to carry out the conditions. If they stick to James's instructions, your mother will be perfectly safe from me."

"Wait," Christina whispered, pulling to her feet. "Did you say all inheritances?"

Canton's gaze leveled on her once more. "Yes."

"Since they're present, I assume Marie and Nolen receive something, as well? You're saying they have to wait until we fulfill these requirements before you will give them their portions?"

"It isn't me, my dear. It's the will. If his wishes are not carried out, James left instructions for his assets to be liquidated, Lily to be moved and no one to receive anything further. Guardianship will eventually go to Jacob, but the only inheritance will go to the university. The mill will shut down completely."

No, no, no. "That inheritance is Marie's and Nolen's retirement," she said. After everything they'd been through with James, they more than deserved the means to live out their lives comfortably. Not struggle day in and day out on a lifetime of counting pennies.

So instead of lowering the bar with his death, James had upped the ante. He was threatening not just his daughter and the town, but anyone who meant anything to Christina. Too bad he wasn't here for her to take apart piece by piece.

Christina forced herself to speak, though the words would barely move past the tight muscles in her throat. "So if we don't do this, everyone loses? You're okay with carrying out those instructions?"

Canton inclined his head in that condescending way of his. "I am."

The horror of what he was saying sank through the fog in Christina's brain. "Why?" she murmured.

"Money." Aiden spat the word out in disgust. "Why else? Did he make it worth your while, Canton?"

Once more the weasel gave that regal nod. "Very much so. But as James Blackstone was my client, I am obligated to honor his wishes."

"I'll bet," Luke said.

Canton's face took on a stony edge. "Again, you are welcome to bring in lawyers, but it will take time. Better to just continue as planned."

Seeing Aiden practically vibrating with anger, Christina figured the plans had pretty much been blown to hell and back.

Aiden could have done without dinner at Black Hills's local country club, where the elite of the entire northern county considered it a privilege to be seen. Give him a sophisticated restaurant in New York any day. This was simply people eating overpriced food for the chance to be ogled.

Right now, he preferred solitude.

But his brothers had insisted on a nice dinner before they both left. Luke would be away for quite a while as he got ready for racing season. Jacob was headed out to start preparations for moving back home. It would take him some time, but the move was a definite. The will said nothing about Aiden hiring someone to run the plant, so he was still abiding by the letter of the law.

James's law. The cause of all the tension, especially between him and Christina. The wife he'd tried at the first opportunity to get rid of after persuading her to have sex with him.

Brilliant.

How could one woman make him feel so out of control and alert at the same time? He was always trying to guess what she'd do next—when she wasn't driving him crazy with desire. Amazing. Christina was everything *but* amazed by him. They'd gone back to avoiding being in the same room except for meals, where Nolen kept a close eye on Aiden.

He was surprised Luke had been able to convince her to come with them. Yet here she was, seated on his left between him and Luke around the circular table.

The rich gold of the walls and amber lighting highlighted the dark brown color of her hair and emphasized the creaminess of her skin and the shadow along the neck he'd been itching to explore for days. He kept glancing her way, which was dangerous. He knew that. Still, he couldn't stop.

Which was how he noticed the light in her eyes as she talked.

"Y'all remember how much fun the fair was growing

up? At least, I really enjoyed the few times I got to go. And the kids at school always made a big deal about it. I think it's a great idea."

Wait. "What?" Aiden asked.

"Where have you been, dude?" Luke ragged him.

Mooning over a woman. "Just thinking about some work stuff. What's going on?"

Jacob chimed in. "Christina has a great idea for building morale in the community. You know, considering all the changes and stuff going on, it might help to foster some goodwill. Show everyone you aren't the same as old Scrooge, I mean, James."

Aiden glanced toward his wife with a raised brow, causing her to shrug with a sheepish grin. "Women think about these things," she said. "I was just considering how to signal to the community that you are trying to keep everything together, bolster sales and stuff, instead of prepping the mill to sell. It would be nice to do something totally unrelated to the mill that would just be a nice gesture for the community."

Aiden leaned back in his chair. As an art dealer with his own company, he tended to work alone more often than not. He wasn't really familiar with fostering a community's goodwill; the extent of his charity thus far had been monetary contributions. But he could see her point, and Christina knew these people a lot better than he did. "So the idea is…"

"We could bring in a fair. Do a bunch of competitions with prizes, games, food, hire a carnival with good rides. We could even use the proceeds to sponsor something like new equipment for the playground downtown."

As the others bounced ideas around, Aiden couldn't take his eyes off Christina's excited expression. It struck him hard that this woman had a seriously underused talent. He'd never known someone who could bring people together so easily and created a bond that snapped into place as seamlessly as LEGO pieces. Yet she continually remained on the outside of the circle.

Even though he wanted to resist, his brain couldn't stop asking why.

Watching her so closely allowed him to catch the brief grimace that twisted her lips before her face resettled into the smooth calm that she constantly showed the world. He wondered what she was hiding beneath the surface. For once, he was going to find out.

"What's the problem?" he asked.

She glanced around the table, then back at him. "What do you mean?" she asked when she realized he was talking to her.

Luke and Jacob tuned in, but Aiden ignored them. "I mean, why did you frown like that? What's the matter?"

He could see the why-do-you-care expression form as she took a bite of her bread. Her standoffishness was getting old, even though the fault lay solely with him. He leaned closer. "It's not nice to make me drag it out of you. Just tell me."

Her pout was quickly squashed. *Good girl.* Because he wasn't afraid to make a spectacle of himself. These people meant nothing to him, but he and Christina would be spending a lot of time together—another ten months, as a matter of fact. He wasn't going to be miserable the whole time, and he didn't want her to be, either.

"My father is sitting near the French doors," she said with a tilt of her head.

Luke scoffed. "He barely qualifies for the title."

"How would you know?" Aiden asked.

Luke sized him up for long moments, while Jacob simply watched the play from the sidelines. Finally, Luke spoke, "I actually talk to her, that's how. Conversations have a way of revealing things like that."

Ouch. His brother had been a bit touchy since the reading. Apparently, the aggravation ran a bit deeper than worry over his new race car. But it couldn't compare to Aiden's being schooled in front of the woman he—wanted. A lot.

Aiden chose to ignore his brother. "Do you talk to your family at all, Christina?" he asked.

Her shrug gave the impression that she didn't care, but the teeth steadying her lower lip spoke otherwise. "Not if I can help it. But that's okay. They aren't much on talking to me, either. When they do, it's more *at* me than anything else."

Aiden looked over and noted that the woman seated at the table with Christina's father was young enough to be her sister. Which reminded him to ask, "What about your mom?"

"I talk to her more often, usually when she calls."

"To check on you?"

"Not really."

Not wanting this to become a grill session, but anxious to keep her talking, Aiden asked quietly, "Then what for?"

Christina was silent for too long. Aiden was on the verge of pushing when Luke answered, instead. "She wants money."

Huh? "I thought your parents had money," Aiden said.

He should be irritated at her for rolling her eyes, but it was kind of cute. "My dad does. My mom falls into the genteel poverty category."

"Ah, she's always calling for a handout."

"No," she said, drawing the word out. "After the first year of my stint with Lily, she learned I meant no when I said it. I'm not even really sure why she bothers calling anymore." She crumpled the last of her bread onto her plate, tearing tiny pieces off at a time.

"They divorced when you were…"

"Eight. The split between them was ugly. Very ugly."

Christina shuddered over memories he could only imagine. "Of course, my mother gave him a lot of ammunition to work with. Affairs. Alcohol abuse. That sort of thing."

"And he left you with her?" Aiden couldn't imagine leaving a child of his in that type of situation. Apparently, James had been a walk in the park compared to Christina's childhood.

"Wealthy businessmen have a lot more on their minds than child rearing, or so he said."

That must have hurt. Especially to a girl of eight.

"He basically paid Mother off to take me, giving her a generous amount of child support, though he stinted on the alimony in view of her numerous affairs. That didn't stop her from asking for more, telling him I needed uniforms or new books for school, dental work, anything to con more money out of him. Sometimes she made stuff up, just to see if it would work."

He eyed the polished man across the room. "Did it?"

"Not as often as she would have liked. Which made me more trouble than I was worth. Not a lot has changed since then, for either of them." Christina moved her salad around on her plate. "Can we talk about something else, please?"

As the last of her earlier excitement faded from her eyes, Aiden's guilt kicked in. People looking in from the outside probably saw her as privileged. He saw a hard childhood, a complicated life, and he hadn't made it any easier. "How does she support herself without your income now?"

"Same way she did then. Always on the hunt for some wealthy man to support her bad habits. There have been quite a few, even another ex-husband, though it's getting hard as she ages. I get calls for money every couple of months. Honestly, enough of my expenses are paid at Blackstone Manor that I have the extra money to spend on her, but…"

"It would just be wasted."

She nodded. "Exactly. Instead, I've opened a money market account that I add to every month. Mother doesn't even realize she has a retirement fund, without any of the work to go along with it."

Acting on an unexpected desire, Aiden stretched his hand across the space between them. He didn't hold Christina's hand, but simply stroked his fingers along the back of it, once again savoring the smooth feel of her skin.

She shifted, uncomfortable with either the conversation or his touch. Christina didn't talk about herself much. In all actuality, she didn't put herself forward a great deal, only when she was advocating on behalf of someone else. Though she often complicated his own plans, forcing him to see all sides of the story, he couldn't help but admire her motives.

The only other truly selfless woman he'd known had been his mother.

Aiden couldn't help but compare Christina's childhood to his own, at least before they'd come to live at Blackstone Manor. His father had been an attentive man, balancing his work as a professor of business management with an active family life. He'd generously lavished attention on his wife and children, which had made the move to the manor that much more unpleasant. After that, his father's time had run out. He'd come home from work late every night exhausted, and left early in the morning before the boys were out of bed. Aiden had missed him with an ache that had been unbearable sometimes. Unfortunately, his mother had borne the brunt of his bid for more attention. Something he deeply regretted now.

He stared at the woman beside him, one who seemed so together and on top of things, and wondered what she had done to gain attention as a teenager. And instead of making those years easier, Aiden had tried to run her off from the only home she'd been able to create. Boy, he was a bastard.

She had taken her life in a much healthier direction than a lot of girls in her situation would have. It was just one more thing to admire her for; if only it didn't make him feel like even more of a screwup. No amount of success in his work had ever made that feeling go away.

Which meant keeping his distance from her was all that much more essential. Developing any kind of relationship with her was crazy, but the simple truth was he couldn't stay away. Deep down, he didn't want to. He knew himself well enough to realize he couldn't keep his hands to himself for the next ten months.

The question was, what should he do about it?

Twelve

Christina didn't pull her hand back as quickly as she should have, but knowing that simple touch was the only thing she'd ever have from Aiden made it hard. Still, watching her father walk toward her table evoked more emotions than she could handle. Nerves and resignation churned in her stomach, not mixing well with what she'd had for dinner.

How, after all these years, could the man who had biologically sired her still make her want to shrivel up into a tiny ball to escape his notice?

George Reece paused next to their table, drawing all eyes to him. His presence was commanding, much the same way as James's. Money, self-confidence and a hard personality would do that for a man.

Christina's brother brought up the rear. His height and thick, dark hair matching his father's, Chad was a couple of years younger than she was, but according to George, he might as well have been an only child. He didn't have his father's presence, instead putting off the I-don't-care vibes of a young man with no responsibilities and even less drive. His gaze flickered around the table, before sliding away to assess if any of his peers were in the dining room.

Rounding out the trio was Tina, Christina's stepmother. Or rather, the woman her father had married. After all, she was only twenty-eight to Christina's twenty-six. With her stereotypical big blond hair and tan, she had the lithe fig-ure of a woman who worked hard on her body, the blank stare of a woman who didn't care about her brains and the fake boobs to crown her the ultimate trophy wife.

George never had liked 'em smart.

His gaze roamed the table before coming to rest on Christina. "Well, girl, aren't you going to introduce me?"

Her muscles jerked, instinct urging her to hop to her feet and make introductions, but she resisted. Instead, she rose with carefully controlled grace and inclined her head. "Daddy. How are you?"

Approval drifted through his distinctive dark eyes, so like her own. She wished she felt some positive emotion, but truthfully, she never had. Self-preservation would do that to a girl.

"I heard through the grapevine you've been busy."

But he couldn't be bothered to call and find out for sure, could he?

Tina giggled.

Aiden stood as well, hopefully distracting everyone from Christina's reddening cheeks. His full height only topped her father's by an inch, but to Christina it could have been a foot. Her father's condescending glare lost a little power when he had to look up. "I apologize for not recognizing you, Mr. Reece. It's been a long time," Aiden said.

"I'm sure living in New York for so long has dimmed your hometown memory," George said, though his tone gave the impression he didn't understand how anyone could forget him. "Luke, Jacob." He nodded to each man in turn.

Finally, he zeroed back in on Christina. "It would have been customary to invite us to the wedding. Especially when you were marrying a Blackstone. Ungracious of you."

Behind her father, Chad smirked. Her father enjoyed his social position. It never occurred to her that her marriage would be the one thing guaranteed to garner his approval.

Jacob and Luke rose as one, but Aiden spoke before they could. "Considering my grandfather's health, we thought it prudent to keep the ceremony *very* private."

"Yeah," Luke drawled. "I didn't even know about it until it was time to cut the cake."

Christina flushed as the memory flooded over her, despite Luke's surreptitious wink.

George didn't acknowledge the men's excuses, but they seemed to put him in a better mood. "It's about time you started making choices worthy of your heritage. Acting like the lady you should be, instead of somebody's servant."

Tina couldn't help but add her two cents. "Well, it did help her snare a rich husband."

Luke mumbled something that sounded suspiciously like "You outta know," distracting Christina from the coming lecture. When he could be bothered, her father had criticized everything from her clothes to her reading material since she was born. Her nursing career was a particular sore spot.

Even more humiliating was that this should happen here, in front of Aiden. But in the same way it was hard to warn a speeding train of an impending collision, she saw no way to stop the man determined to see the worst in her.

"Christina's not a servant. She's based her career on helping those in need. But I'm guessing you're not fond of doing unto others." Jacob drawled. She thought he was echoing her thoughts, then realized he was referring to her father's last statement.

"Why should I be?" George asked. "What good does it do me?"

She could almost feel the men jerk in surprise. Not her. She knew her father better than he probably realized. He was all about getting ahead, and dropping everything that didn't help him do that by the wayside. Like the child he hadn't wanted.

Aiden let her father's comment slide. "Well, her care has certainly kept our mother alive all these years. We're grateful to Christina for that."

She managed a weak smile, then chastised herself for glancing at her father for his reaction.

"And again I ask, what good has that done her?" George didn't slow down even though Christina could feel anger spark in the men around the table. "Years spent at an invalid's bedside, when she could have been earning her place in South Carolina society. But that's where she'll be in the end, thanks to her bloodline and now her marriage. In time, people will forget her common laborer background and see her as they should, as the wife of the Blackstone heir."

Christina gasped, his expectations cutting through the hard-earned self-respect of taking care of herself and others since college.

Before she could gather herself, Aiden was around the table and towering over her father. "All that hard work did gain her something—a family that cares about her, unlike the people who donated the sperm and the egg. You aren't a father—it's a father's job to protect his children, not tear them down."

Unused to being dominated, George opened his mouth. But Aiden didn't give him a chance to speak. His mouth split into a predatory grin as he stared her father down. "So run on about your business. Christina *is* well taken care of, all without any effort on your part. And don't expect any invitations to the manor. We prefer to keep our environment…pleasant."

The roar in her ears covered up George's response, though it must have been weak considering the grins shared between the brothers. Aiden had defended her with a knight's loyalty. As the Blackstone men surrounded her, tears welled for the first time since she'd seen her father across the room.

Her defenders. Her protectors. Her comrades. Finally, family had found her.

* * *

Christina flopped onto her empty bed, stretching out as far as her body would let her. Nicole had a few night shifts for the next few days, allowing Christina the luxury of sleeping uninterrupted. She planned to enjoy it, no matter how lonely it might be. Curling over onto her side, she lay quietly in the glow of her bedside lamp. Though her mind craved rest, her body wouldn't shut down, even after the hot bath she'd taken.

The gentle drip of the soft rain outside should have calmed her, but instead, her mind spun. She wasn't even sure what it was about Aiden that made her crave him so much. Those rare times when they worked together to solve a problem made her mind sing. His confession about his father and his attempt at reaching his mother made her heart ache. Even arguing with him had her adrenaline humming. More than anything, his smile, his touch, made her heart come alive. And his defense of her against her father's criticism—she'd never forget it.

Thoughts of him were always there, like a lingering presence at the back of her mind. But she'd distracted herself all afternoon by planning for the upcoming fair. She'd roped in some women to help her, made tons of phone calls, lists and plans, and then saw Jacob and Luke to the door when Aiden took them to the airport.

He'd watched her all day, his gaze stroking her body as if his hands wished to do the same. He didn't touch her, and he hadn't since that last time. Yet she'd known his focus on her was carnal. He wanted her. Her body knew it and that knowledge left her tingly and aching. What would she do if he joined her in this bed once more, if he reached out for her?

The response of her body was answer enough. If he came to her, she would take whatever he was willing to give. He was an addiction. As much as she wished he could love her, she would settle for less, just to have him one more time.

Sad as that might be, it was the truth.

From the time she was young, she'd dreamed of having someone who would want her for herself. Not because she fulfilled a role as their daughter. Not because of the money she could provide. Not because of the services she had to offer. Someone who wanted Christina, well, just because.

Aiden wanted her for a lot of reasons. But when he held her in his arms, she *felt* as if he wanted her for herself. She simply wanted to feel that one more time. There were too many reasons why she couldn't have him forever.

A knock sounded on the door to the outer hallway. Christina stared at it for a moment, a feeling of inevitability settling over her. Just as she rose up on her elbows, the door opened. Aiden stepped inside, then closed the door with a firm click.

His posture looked relaxed, his unbuttoned dress shirt showcasing the tight muscles along his abdomen and the rise and fall of his chest from his rapid breathing. Then he stalked forward, one slow step at a time. His hooded eyes bored into her, leaving her breathless and shaking.

"What are you doing here?" she asked, jumping to her feet.

"Don't you know?"

Forcing herself to push out her arm, she stopped him at arm's length. "Aiden, we need to talk about this. I can't—" she swallowed hard "—I can't go back and forth. I need to know what we're doing here."

Reaching out, he brushed her thick hair behind her ear, caressing his finger over the skin. A shiver worked its way over her neck and down her arms.

"I'm not playing games, Christina. We both want each other. I, for one, cannot ignore it anymore."

She stared at his face, straining to see something, some

answer to what was driving his passion. "So I'm just convenient. Is that it?"

"Far from it, sweetheart. The way you make me feel isn't convenient at all."

His glittering black eyes didn't falter. Christina had a choice: she could take a risk or play it safe. With slow steps, she skirted the bed until she stood before him. Lifting to her tiptoes, she brushed her lips across his. Her sighing breath mingled with his.

"I want you, Aiden," she whispered, tucking her fear deep down inside where no one could see. Not even her.

"And I want you, Christina. More than I ever thought possible." He gently pushed her back onto the cool cotton of the comforter and crouched over her. "Remember, we're in this together."

She was half-prepared for him to change his mind and pull away. He always pulled back from her, always found a way to distance himself. He would this time, too, somehow. But she was done holding back.

"Please," she whispered, giving herself permission to reach for him. "You are what I need."

With a growl, he drove forward, taking her mouth once more, sinking his tongue deep. He went from zero to sixty in a few seconds, as if he'd thrown off restraint along with his shirt. She could fight no more. Need was all-consuming. She had to have him, no matter what the aftermath.

Aiden devoured her mouth with skill and devastation. First he rimmed her lips with his tongue, then delved deep to explore. He didn't rush like the last time they were together. Instead, he lingered at her mouth, his body crowding over hers, his fists digging into the mattress on each side of her head. Like a gentle trap, his hold left her little freedom, but all the sustenance her soul could possibly need.

He nibbled her lower lip, moaning low in his throat. Christina's entire body came to attention, instantly taut from her chest to the soles of her feet. The ache to once more feel his hands on her skin was overwhelming.

She returned his kiss with all the intensity building inside her. When that wasn't enough, she arched her back, her body meeting his inch for inch. After long minutes he pulled back until they were barely touching, yet close enough for their breath to mingle.

"I'm going to take you so, so slow, Christina, until I touch every part of you." His breath brushed along her cheek. Though fear lingered, she forced herself to look him in the eye. She found his complete and total focus on her, as if whatever barrier he'd been holding up between them had been shattered.

Excitement locked her breath in her throat for a moment, then it rushed back as her barriers completely collapsed. With both hands, she tunneled into his thick, brown hair and pulled his mouth back down to hers. If this was the only place he would touch her, that's what she would take.

Giving in to her demands, Aiden's hands glided along her bare arms, savoring her skin in long strokes. He touched her over and over, as if he couldn't get enough. Moving his hands up and along her neck to cup her jaw, he cradled her face once more for his kiss.

"I have to feel you, Christina. I have to feel more of you," he said, reaching for the hem of her tank top. Impatient, he pulled it over her head in one swipe, leaving her torso naked beneath his hot stare. She stretched, shamelessly offering herself to him, desperate for his touch.

He gave it to her. His large hands cupped and shaped her breasts, teasing her nipples unmercifully. Stroking from her ribs up to the tips, she felt them tighten just for him. He rewarded her with licks and gentle bites until she couldn't hold back the cries building in her throat. She craved warm skin and soft hair. Every touch filled the empty well inside her, the space that had been abandoned for so very long. Her hands weren't enough. With no more inhibitions, she circled his lower back with her legs, trying to pull him down.

As if their minds were linked, he bent to rub his bare chest along hers. She cried out in pleasure, arching in an attempt to keep contact with as much of him as possible. Her hands clutched at his back, savoring the feel of flexing muscles and hard ribs.

With a growl, he stood. His gaze held hers as his hands moved to the zipper of his pants. She wanted to look as he revealed himself, eager to enjoy his body in all its glory, but she couldn't tear her gaze from his. All that intensity, all that focus, for her.

Rising to her knees, she sealed her mouth once more to his. He pulled her close while his hot hands caressed her back, traveling down to slip beneath the waistband of her pajama pants. The feel of him cupping and shaping her melted her all the way to her core. Before there had been fire; now she was an inferno.

With a soft push, he tossed her back onto the bed and stripped off her pants. Her thighs spread wide, eager for attention. She thought he would enter her quickly, but that would have been too easy. Bending at the waist, he once more buried his face against her core to wreak havoc.

Obliterating what little control she had left.

Tongue and fingers played with devastating skill, driving her to the brink before Aiden pulled back. Her face burned as he reached for the little foil packet from his pants pocket, sheathing himself with ease.

No family, no matter how much she might dream.

Flexing his leanly muscled arms, he hooked his hands underneath her knees and pulled, dragging her to the edge of the bed, positioning her perfectly for his entry. His strength left her at once vulnerable and powerful. His urgency spoke of a desperate need. For her. For Christina. For the satisfaction her body could bring him.

A satisfaction she was more than willing to give.

For once uninhibited, she opened her legs wide, bending her knees to rest her heels on the edge of the bed. He leaned forward, guiding his hardness to her liquid heat. Eager, she lifted her hips, anxious for that first touch.

It came too soon and not soon enough. He hissed as his flesh met hers, clenching his teeth. He pushed slowly inside, an inch in, then out again. Feeling every bit of pressure and fullness as he stretched her, Christina struggled to remain still. She wanted to feel every inch. But her core wouldn't listen. Her inner muscles clenched around his invading length, stroking it with welcome.

Aiden's breath changed. He panted out her name, lungs struggling to keep up. Christina's control shattered. Within minutes, her head thrashed from side to side, her hands grasping the sheets beneath her.

Aiden's lower body rocketed into overdrive, thrusting heavily within her, setting off explosion after explosion as sensation built to a fever pitch. All the while his lips clung to her nipples, multiplying the riot along her nerves a thousandfold.

Within seconds, her orgasm burst through her, captivating her body and roaring through her mind. His hands clamped onto her shoulders and he buried himself as far as he could, then froze with an expression of stunned ecstasy. His groan drowned out her heartbeat as she savored every breath, every touch.

Pride and satisfaction drifted through her euphoric state. Aiden collapsed across her stomach. Her fingers trailed along the heaving muscles of his back as she counted his heartbeats. Here was what she had craved for so long: this man, this moment, this passion.

All had been more than she'd ever hoped for.

Thirteen

Aiden lay spooned around Christina's back. He had never been the cuddling type. But he'd been drawn here with no other explanation than that…it felt right. The whole time they'd lain together, his hands had been moving like a slow, lazy river, stroking over whatever skin was within reach—her arms, back, hips, thighs, even demanding access to her breasts and stomach. He couldn't stop.

Beneath his touch, a fine tremble ran through Christina. Like a purring kitten, her body showed its appreciation, maybe even without her permission.

He shouldn't be lying here with her. Hell, he should never have come to her room. There was a certain practicality in his argument, but the bare truth? He couldn't control himself. He'd never run into that with another woman. He'd always been able to walk away the day after. But now that he'd told himself he could have her, there was no going back. Despite the circumstances, he couldn't wait to have her *again*.

Her softly spoken words distracted him from the surges of lust in his veins.

"What changed your mind?" she asked.

"About what?" The deep notes of satisfaction in his voice were unfamiliar.

"About being with me?"

He could tell from her hesitation that she didn't really

want to pursue this line of conversation, so he admired her for sticking to her guns. If they were going to be intimate with each other, she deserved to know some of what he was thinking. Better to know the why of it and that it would end, than to get her heart all tangled up in something that wouldn't last.

He sighed, his long fingers squeezing her hip before moving up to rest at her waist. "Haven't you learned anything about me yet, Christina?"

"What do you mean?" she asked, stiffening against him.

Not that he blamed her. "I'm one of those unpredictable types who flies off the handle and lives to regret it later." Like the first time they'd been together. "What happened between us last time wasn't your fault and wasn't my fault. It was a product of this attraction between us."

As if eager to demonstrate, his hips surged against her, making very clear that the attraction he referred to hadn't diminished in the slightest. If anything, he felt hungrier than he had half an hour ago.

Lifting up, he let her fall to her back so that he crouched over her upper body. She bravely met his gaze, turbulent eyes looking both afraid and exhilarated. Aiden didn't do things by half measures. He could be controlled, as in his dealings with Balcher, but he wouldn't apologize for the passions constantly churning beneath the surface, just waiting for an opening to burst free.

"We're going to be here, in this house, together, for a while yet. Despite how this all came about, we have the same goals—to take care of Lily and make sure the mill remains viable. There's no way I can ignore the way I feel around you in the meantime. So unless you tell me this isn't what you want, I think we should just accept this as a connection we both can benefit from in a bad situation."

Breath catching in her throat, Christina went very still for long moments. Aiden was being honest, something that wasn't always appreciated. They were both eager to protect themselves, but there was no reason why they couldn't enjoy the desire between them while it lasted.

He would just have to keep it from going any deeper than that.

Christina jerked awake from a deep sleep, her heart racing, body poised to run. The suspicion that she'd forgotten something important pounded through her brain. What was it? What was the matter?

She glanced toward the clock, only to find the view blocked by a bare chest with a sprinkling of hair. As she watched, Aiden rolled to his side, his dark eyes blinking languidly in her direction. "Morning, beautiful," he murmured.

Was it the sleep-roughened voice or the morning stubble that melted her all the way to her core? Or simply the fact that it was morning and he was still within touching distance? What a way to wake up—

Morning! Sitting up, Christina spied the late hour on the bedside clock and shot out of bed.

"Christina, where are you going?"

"I'm late," she said as she closed herself in the bathroom. She didn't allow herself more than a quick swipe of the brush through her hair and use of her toothbrush before she was back out again.

Aiden had migrated to the edge of the bed as she swept past. She thought he would ignore her in favor of lying back down. Instead, he followed her to the dressing room. Besides a cabinet of gowns and bedding for Lily, the dressing room now served as Christina's closet. She pulled out a set of scrubs and struggled not to blush as she changed her panties.

"I can't believe I slept so late," she said, trying to take the focus off what she was doing. Which was very difficult, considering she'd never had a man watch her dress, much less one who stared with the intensity of a painter memorizing her curves.

"It isn't surprising," Aiden said. Just as she turned to ask why, he teased, "After all, I did keep you up pretty late."

That was an understatement. He'd come to her room after ten last night, and had woken her up twice more after they'd turned out the lights. Not that his insatiability bothered her. She'd been willing and just as eager.

No, every bit of tiredness was worth the incredible experience of last night. Except now her blush suffused not only her cheeks but her entire body, as well. But really, was there any point in being shy about it? What had happened between them in her bed wasn't something she'd willingly give up.

So she chose to tease back, instead. "And I'm pretty sure you aren't sorry in the least," she said with a saucy grin. "No matter that I won't be good for much today."

"Nope," he conceded, but his smile faded as she rushed to the opposite door.

She paused with her hand on the knob and glanced at him over her shoulder. The sadness creeping over his grin made her ache. To her knowledge, he hadn't been to see his mother since that midnight conversation she'd overheard, but she couldn't force him. He had to make this decision for himself. "I have to go to work," she said.

He nodded, smile long gone. She forced herself to turn away, not to linger or reach out to him in any way. But the disappearance of their earlier connection still hurt.

When Christina entered Lily's suite, Nicole glanced up from where she was packing her books. "I was just coming to knock on your door," she said.

Thank goodness she hadn't planned to just walk in like usual. Nicole always had been a smart girl. "Sorry I'm running late. Ready for your quiz today?"

"As ready as I can be…" Nicole's voice and gaze trailed away, causing Christina to glance behind her.

Aiden stood in the doorway to the dressing room, having pulled on his khaki pants, but nothing else.

Turning back, Christina found a big smile plastered on Nicole's face and an approving look in her eyes. Again with the damn blush! Though Nicole would have heard through the grapevine about Aiden's mattress-moving strategy, Christina wasn't used to parading her love life in front of others.

"Thank you, Nicole," Christina said, her voice quieting. The other woman left the room as Christina turned to the bed, going through her usual motions of checking Lily's pulse and temperature.

She was aware of Aiden as he came into the bedroom and leaned against one of the chairs near the doorway. The same chair he'd sat in before. But she had a feeling he wouldn't let his guard down enough to do so today.

She studied him through her lashes as she talked to Lily in a low, soothing tone.

"You doing okay this morning, sweetie? Nicole takes good care of you, doesn't she?"

Aiden maintained his distance, his posture closed off, arms crossed over his chest. The sunlight filtering through the curtains glinted off the spiky points in his chestnut hair, but didn't illuminate his eyes. She tried not to notice the tight strength of his thighs as he stood there.

His complete lack of movement amazed her. He didn't so much as fidget. Ordinarily, his shut-down expression might have indicated disgust or lack of caring, but she suspected it was more a product of caring too much.

It hurt him to see his mother like this.

Which was the very reason he'd avoided this room. She'd seen it so often, she wished she could tell him he wasn't the only one, but didn't want to risk scaring him off by getting too deep. She settled for, "You haven't spent much time in a sickroom."

His eyes widened slightly before his face resumed an emotionless mask. "Does it show?"

Sighing, she sank into her chair on the opposite side of the bed. Why had she thought he would make this easy on either of them?

She smiled down at Lily, the woman who'd become a surrogate mother to her before the older woman's accident. Her heart ached with the guilt of her involvement. "It's often hard for family and friends in situations like this. Not only does it hurt to see her sick and unresponsive, but it is an awkward situation."

She cast a tentative smile in his direction, wanting to connect, but fearful of rejection. She wasn't going to mind her own business, even if he was Lily's son. Lily had talked so much about him—his drive to succeed, his interest in art, his independence, his loneliness. She had truly loved him.

And now he was Christina's husband. She needed him more than he'd ever understand.

"It's much easier for nurses, who have charts to check, exercises to perform and chores like dressing and bathing. We have a purpose, a job to do. We can be—" she swallowed "—useful to both the patient and their families."

And useful she'd proven to be, as always. Far more so than she'd ever intended, despite her resolve never to travel that path again. She'd been useful to her mother for a while. James, too. Her father had rejected her because she was not of use to him. Which side would Aiden fall on?

"How long have you worked here?" Aiden asked, relaxing enough to stroll to the window and glance out. Was he remembering this room, the view from his childhood years here?

She had continued to spend time with Lily during high school and university, eager to have someone in her life who cared whether she succeeded or failed. "Almost five years." Something she was very grateful for, since it also allowed her to give back to Lily after her accident. Their relationship had deepened before the stroke rendered Lily comatose. "I was here visiting Lily one day when James called me to the study. He offered to give me a job taking care of her if I would come live here with them."

"He asked you?"

"Yes." She'd been happy, but Lily had been ecstatic. Only later did she realize how tough it was being a live-in nurse of someone she loved and knowing she'd probably never recover.

Aiden went on, "You weren't looking for work?"

"My father gave me a small trust fund that helped me through college, so I hadn't planned to actively search out work until the next semester," Christina said. "My last one."

She thought she heard him mumble "Very clever," under his breath, but she kept speaking as she absently rubbed Lily's arm.

"As soon as my degree was completed, I came here to live, assisting Lily with her daily activities, exercises and stuff. The years before her stroke were good ones, despite the paralysis from the car accident."

The words seemed so mundane compared to the reality. She'd built a life here, loving Lily, Nolen, Marie, Nicole and the rest of the staff as a family. She couldn't have enjoyed them more if she'd handpicked them. Despite her awkward childhood, she finally had girlfriends who lived in town, women she could talk to on the phone and shop with. Blackstone Manor wasn't just a place she worked. It was home.

"Good years," she whispered, turning watery eyes to Lily's quiet features. Her hand shook a bit as she reached out to smooth the coverlet. The last few weeks had left her way too emotional.

Aiden surprised her by speaking from the foot of the bed. When had he moved so close?

"How can you handle seeing her like this?"

Christina turned to face him, startled by the turbulent emotions so evident after his earlier composure. So she'd guessed right. He hadn't avoided his mother because he didn't want to see her, but because he wanted it so badly. To see her as she was before the accident had changed her. He wanted to avoid the painful emotions stirring inside him.

Something she could relate to but not condone. "Because I love her."

His gaze shifted to Christina and he stared intently, as if anxious to verify her words. They were true. Even without their history, Christina would have loved Lily's peaceful acceptance of her situation, pride in her children's accomplishments and graceful offer of friendship.

Christina only wished she could have begged Lily's forgiveness before the stroke had separated them forever.

"What if it was your fault that she's lying there?" Aiden asked.

The muscles around Christina's heart squeezed down hard. She couldn't move, couldn't breathe. It was her greatest fear laid bare before her very eyes. One hard thump reverberated in her chest, then another, until everything returned to its normal pace.

But Christina would never be the same. "What do you mean?" she forced out.

His hand shook slightly as he indicated his mother in her hospital bed. "I mean this. It's all my fault."

Christina should not have been relieved.

"Why?"

"She'd come to see me because I was too selfish to bow to James's demands and come to Blackstone Manor. We'd spent a few days going to art galleries and shows. She loved the creative side of New York City." Without his seeming to notice, he'd reached down to wrap his hand casually around Lily's foot. Christina held her breath, but he continued on. "I don't know if you remember the day of her accident."

Christina remembered, all too well. The bad weather, the storm warnings.

"She assured me she wanted to get home, not wait for it to clear," Aiden said. "After all, the sun was still out." He gazed at the headboard but his eyes were fuzzy with memories. "But it got bad. Really bad. Why didn't she stop?" He squeezed his mother's foot again. "I should have made her wait. It's all my fault."

Lily's foot flexed. Her heartbeat, so steady on the monitor up until now, picked up speed. Aiden jerked back, his hands flying wide. He stared at his mother as color drained from his face.

He's gonna pass out. Christina rushed to his side. A little unsure, she snuck up against his body, leaning in to keep him steady. "It's okay, Aiden."

This close, she could see him swallow hard. "What… was…that?" he asked.

"Remember me saying that Lily's coma isn't a constant state? Coma patients can rise through the stages, then sink back down."

He nodded, even though she wasn't sure if he was comprehending.

"Sometimes it means they respond to things like weather, temperature, touch. Sometimes they can even sit up and open their eyes, but then they sink back down into the coma minutes or even hours later."

"Has Mother ever…?"

"Sat up?"

He nodded again.

"No." She stroked her hand up and down Aiden's arm. "I've often wished she would. Sometimes I think these little episodes are her way of letting me know she's still here, but in truth they may only be an involuntary physical reaction. I choose to think of them as the former, despite my nursing degree telling me it's just the body's way of releasing energy."

To her surprise, his arms went around her, hugging almost too tight. Neither of them acknowledged what prompted the embrace, just settled into it for long, long moments.

When he finally pulled away, she decided to give Aiden what he most needed right now, whether he knew it or not. Placing a hand on one sculpted arm, she whispered, "I'm sure, no matter what it is, that she'd love the fact that you are here with her. And she's perfected her listening skills over the last two years." She smiled, even though he didn't return it. But at least he didn't look whiter than white any longer. "Why don't you start with 'Hello, Mom'?"

Ignoring the ripple of his muscles under her fingertips, she let go and walked away. Gifting him with the chance to heal the rift between himself and his mother was the least she could do for both of them. She just wished she could keep him when all was said and done.

Fourteen

"We're a little too early for a harvest festival, which is what we put together for the high school last year. How can we fine-tune this summer fair, ladies?" Christina asked.

Surrounding her was a group of women who loved working together for the good of the community, and were known as the go-to choice for getting things done. They weren't from the country club like Tina's set, who simply threw money at a charity to be seen doing it. Just good women who worked hard and had fun.

"I'm so excited," Mary Creighton said, clapping her hands together like a kid. "It's been a long time since we had a *true* country fair. Or anything more than that rinky-dink carnival set up in the high school parking lot."

Jean Stanton jumped in, too. "And the fairgrounds are still in really good shape. We'll easily have enough room for anything we want to do. It'll be nice to have something to look forward to after all this—"

A hard look from the other woman had Jean closing her mouth quick, but Christina had already tuned in.

"It's okay, Mary. I need to know these things. Jean, go ahead."

Jean shrugged, setting her dangly earrings into motion. "It's just been tough with the economy and worry over what might happen to the mill after Mr. Blackstone got sick. Then our men started talking about what was going on at the mill and all..."

Christina hadn't been aware that the disturbing incidents were common knowledge. Obviously, the workers had taken note and had ideas of their own. "I know, Jean. And trust me, Aiden is working closely with Bateman to put a stop to that nonsense."

"That's good, especially after that equipment failure last week," Avery Prescott added. "Having him involved takes a load of worries off all of us about working out there. She just means it's a good time to have some fun, blow off steam…even better than a night at Lola's."

Mary's brows shot up. "Do you honestly think anything is better than a night at Lola's?"

"I can think of a few things…" Jean snuck in, leaving everyone laughing.

"Now, about the fair—" Christina prodded.

"The carnival is already contracted. A really good one, with a great safety record," Jean said. "Why not have a couple of those blow-up waterslides for the kids, too? And a watermelon-eatin' contest."

Christina hurried to scribble notes as the ideas flew fast and furious.

"A bouncy castle for the little ones."

"A cake walk."

"A petting zoo."

Mary leaned forward. "Too bad KC isn't in town. She's always good for fun adult-only ideas," she said with a waggle of her eyebrows.

"Hmmm…maybe some eye candy? I was thinking of asking Luke to come home that weekend," Christina said. "He could bring the car for display, sign autographs… I'm pretty sure both the men *and* the women will like that."

The youngest of the group now that KC Gatlin had moved away, Avery quickly chimed in. "What about a kissing booth? Would he be willing to do that? Because that man is hotter than a sidewalk in the South in July."

The other women quickly agreed. "And in his racing suit," Mary elaborated, "that man has buns tighter than—"

"Are you ladies talking about me?"

As Aiden's voice rang throughout the room, a flush encompassed Christina's entire body. The women around her froze, staring at one another with wide eyes until giggles escaped one by one. Christina tried to maintain her cool beneath Aiden's sexy grin, but her mind betrayed her with images of Aiden, naked in her bed.

Oh, that so didn't help anything.

"Aiden, these are the ladies working with me on the fair."

"Very nice," he said. "I can't thank you all enough. I know it's a lot of hard work, but we really appreciate it."

The charm came on, and every woman in the room melted into pliant goo. Even Christina. Especially Christina. He'd taken to her lessons on Southern hospitality way better than she could have imagined.

She didn't get to see this side of him often, and intense Aiden was just as attractive, but when he went out of his way to make someone feel valued, it really worked.

Determined to stop blushing, Christina tuned in to the murmurs of approval wafting his way. When her gaze followed, she found him watching her. The smoldering look in those dark eyes sent a shiver down her spine. In this room full of people, they might as well have been alone.

And deep inside, the fragile hope that he would stay burst into full bloom. She'd been fighting for so long, aching for too long… For once, the simple wish to keep someone she loved close to her overran practicality.

He turned and walked away with a small wave. Christina knew he'd be in her room when she went upstairs. Their room. She only hoped she could survive waiting that long.

Mary fanned her forty-something face. "Oh, girl. That one's a hottie, I have to say. Runs in the family. You are one lucky woman."

Christina just sat there, her face getting warmer and warmer, while the other women enthused over her new husband's traits.

"So tall. And all that dark hair."

"And those dark eyes." Avery shivered. "So intense."

"Did you see the muscles in his arms?" Jean asked. "Talk about carry me away."

Christina refused to squirm, but something of her thoughts must have revealed themselves on her face, because the laughter tapered off.

"Oh, honey," Mary said, rushing over to pat her arm. "Are we embarrassing you?"

Christina wanted to yell *yes!* but bit her tongue, instead. Her inexperience and confusion were not their fault.

"Oh, course you are," Avery said.

Mary's concern coated her every word. "We didn't mean to, Christina. Honest."

Christina smiled her understanding. Avery put her arm around Mary and said, "We know you didn't. You just can't help it."

"Me and my big mouth, my husband always says." Mary shrugged. "I can fit both my size nines inside."

Christina smiled up at her. "No harm done."

Relief softened Mary's face. "Good."

Luckily, at that moment, the door cracked open once more, this time to reveal Nolen and a tray of goodies. He smiled over his obvious welcome and led the group to the farthest end of the room where he set up the refreshments on the table.

When she moved to join the others, Avery motioned for her to stay. "You okay, Christina?"

"Sure," Christina said. Avery had been a good friend to her. They hadn't been close when they were younger, but had reconnected when Avery had returned to town after getting her training as a physical therapist. Both were single, around the same age, with no interest in the party scene, so they had a lot in common and could talk easily about almost anything.

Avery also encouraged her to take care of herself and have fun every so often, thus the frequent invitations to Lola's.

Avery glanced at the table of women who were now moving on to other things. "That Mary is something else."

Christina nodded. "Yeah. I know she was just playing around. I just—" Christina twisted her fingers together "—haven't figured out how to respond naturally."

Avery took a drink, but her blue eyes remained calm and steady on Christina.

"I feel like everyone knows why we married and is going to judge everything I say." Christina looked to her friend for comfort.

Avery didn't disappoint. "They are not judging you," she said, reaching out to still Christina's hands with her own. "Most of them are thrilled, because the marriage gives them a sense of stability."

Christina frowned. "For their jobs?"

Avery nodded. "And for their future. Whatever the reason behind it." She leaned forward to look directly in Christina's eyes. "And that's no one's business but yours. One of the Blackstone grandsons having a permanent reason to stay here means the mill will continue to be run by the family. And if that happens through an arranged marriage— well, those have been happening all over the world since the beginning of time." She leaned back. "People in town feel they can trust the family not to abandon them, to have their best interests at heart."

Christina felt slightly sick to her stomach. If only they knew. "That's what baffles me. They don't really know Aiden at all. Not the man he is now."

Avery shook her head. "Doesn't matter. He's familiar, which is always better than the unknown."

If Christina had anything to say about it, he wouldn't disappoint. Since he possessed a mind of his own, there were no guarantees. But oh, how she wished there were. He'd worked hard for Black Hills so far. If only he would stay...

"I'm not going to pry," Avery was saying, "but you know I'm here to talk if you need me, right?"

Christina smiled. "Thank you."

Avery shrugged, then steered the conversation on to more mundane topics, helping Christina relax. This was exactly what she needed. Calm. A project to focus on. Friends to distract her.

No worries about the future. No challenging conversations. No brooding, attractive male to turn her inside out and upside down.

Life often moved in directions Christina never expected. She had spent a lifetime going to movies and restaurants alone, hanging out in coffee shops and bookstores on her days off. But as she looked around the dinner table a month later, she finally understood that she was no longer alone.

That's what family was for. And she had claimed the people around her as hers, for as long as they would let her.

"I have an idea," she said, gaining the attention of the table. Everyone was in their usual places, one end full now that Jacob had rejoined them and Luke had been able to clear a brief few days for his appearance at the fair. Nolen and Marie peeked through the door from the kitchen. "I think we should go to the fair. Together."

"Fair?" Marie said with a grin. "I haven't been to one of those since I was a kid."

Christina was glad to see some enthusiasm. "I was out there working last night and it looked so exciting. I've always wanted to go to one."

"You've never been? Not even to the county fair as a kid?" Jacob asked. "Then you definitely have to check it out. Cheap thrills for all."

Nolen, who had entered the room carrying a tray with their after-dinner coffee, threw out a word of warning. "It isn't safe for you to go alone, Miss Christina. You men should take the ladies."

Luke agreed. "I wouldn't miss it."

But there had to be a fly in the ointment. "I've got reports to finish," Aiden said, accepting his usual cup of black decaf from Nolen. "But Luke over there never met a roller coaster he didn't love."

"The Scream Machine is my favorite," Luke said, waggling his brows in a suggestive expression. "But seriously, I'd love to have some fun before I have kissing duty tomorrow night."

Aiden just snorted, which started the ball rolling.

Luke pounced. "Ah, big brother here just doesn't want everyone to know what a wuss he is."

Aiden's growl of warning was accompanied by Christina's chant, "Tell us! Tell us!"

"Luke," Aiden said, his voice deepening in warning, "I will hurt you."

A mock expression of fear covered Luke's face, drawing a laugh from the women. "In that case, I won't tell them roller coasters make you puke like a girl."

Aiden lunged for his brother, knocking him out of his chair and onto the dining room floor. The sound of male grunts and wrestling crowded out the formal atmosphere of the room. Christina stood, watching the men twist back and forth on the oriental carpet with a sort of breathless wonder. The boys had been physical as kids—at least when James hadn't been around—and Christina had watched them on her visits with a mixture of fear and fascination. She'd certainly never expected this kind of frivolity as adults. These wild antics shocked and delighted her.

Nolen calmly stepped around the writhing mass to place Christina's hot tea on the table. Jacob simply moved away, watching his brothers with an amused expression. The contrast boggled her brain. When a draw was finally called— or rather, both men claimed to have won—they stood up and continued talking as if nothing had happened. Well, that wasn't quite true.

Luke smoothed his hands over his dark blond hair then jerked his button-down shirt back into place. Aiden, on the other hand, left the evidence of their fight, for once not caring about his scuffed look. The mussed hair, red, roughened chin, and twist of his T-shirt brought naughty thoughts to Christina's mind. Her heart thudded as she imagined pulling that shirt off and adding to his breathless state.

A quick walk around the table took her to his side, where she slipped under his arm. Tucked up against him, palm resting on his heaving ribs, she met his gaze with a teasing look of her own. "We'll just check out the atmosphere. How about that?"

As Aiden's laughter faded, Christina became aware of the hushed silence in the room. She suddenly felt every inch of Aiden pressed against her, the heavy weight of his arm around her shoulders. Though the others knew they shared a bedroom, even after James's death, she and Aiden had never taken their intimate relationship farther than the privacy of that room. She knew beyond a doubt she'd inadvertently signaled to the others living in the house that their relationship was much deeper than the expected convenient marriage. Embarrassed, she drew back, only to have his arm tighten around her.

Looking up, she found his eyes trained on her face. The look he gave her wasn't angry or irritated, but still sparking with amusement and adrenaline from wrestling with his brother. He squeezed her arm. "I think that sounds like a great idea."

Her body automatically relaxed and she returned his smile with relief. Everyone else turned away, moving toward the door with excuses about preparing for their night out.

But Christina and Aiden remained locked together. She swallowed, her heart beating in excitement. Which was ridiculous. To anyone else, this would be the smallest thing imaginable, barely significant in the whole scheme of things. But her heart knew Aiden didn't make gestures, big or small, lightly. And he wasn't done amazing her tonight.

He leaned down as if to kiss her, but stopped just short of her parted lips. "So, Christina…will you go to the fair with me?"

She swallowed hard, struggling to keep her tone teasing like his. "Are you asking me on a date, Aiden?"

"I believe I am," he said, moving the final distance to brush his lips across hers. Once. Twice. "But I have to warn you that my intentions don't involve letting you kiss me good-night at the door."

Christina's heart thudded. If only this could be real. Forever. But she hid her hopes and grasped this opportunity with both hands. Because the truth was she could have now, and all the other memories they created, to keep her through the lonely days ahead.

After a lingering kiss of her own, she said, "I think I can live with that."

She held on to that mantra over the next few hours. Through dusty fairways, caramel apples and threats to ride the Sidewinder. At one point she stumbled, and Aiden steadied her at her elbow. As they continued on, his hand slid down to hers. And stayed. In the twinkle of carnival lights, Christina's heart filled with the gesture.

She wasn't a logical woman. Practicality came naturally

with her profession, but getting attached to others was in her nature. Closeness was actually a craving for her. Aiden filled that need as no one else ever had. That he was willing to do it with the whole town watching meant even more.

With one squeeze of her hand, she was lost. And happy about it.

"Mrs. Blackstone, will they make enough money for the new playground?"

Christina paused at the high-pitched voice, smiling over at Bateman and his family. She looked down at their kindergarten-aged granddaughter. "I sure hope so, sweetheart. It will be a lot of fun to have a new one, wouldn't it?"

"It sure would," Bateman's wife said. "Give me something to do with these young'uns while their mama is at work."

"I wouldn't know," Bateman said with a grin, which grew bigger when his wife swatted his arm.

"Come on, Susie Q," his wife said. "I'll let you try to win me that teddy bear."

"No, the teddy bear is for me, Grandma."

"Are you sure?" she asked as they walked away. "I could have sworn it was for me."

"This was a great idea," Bateman said. "Everyone is having fun."

Christina agreed. "And Jean is excited to keep moving the counter up on the fund-raising scoreboard. I really think the new playground will be a go."

Bateman extended his hand. "Thank you, Aiden. We needed some fun right about now. Someone to invest in our community."

Aiden shook the hand, but corrected Bateman. "It wasn't my idea. You can thank this one," he said, lifting his and Christina's clasped hands. "I just provided a little labor and encouragement."

Much to her dismay, Christina wanted to preen under

his praise. She shrugged, instead. "Getting through tough times is easier if we do it together."

Bateman smiled his approval. "As long as things stay quiet at the mill, then I think all this talk will die down. Maybe that little chat with Balcher did the trick?"

Aiden frowned into the distance. "I don't know. He doesn't seem the type to give up after a simple slap down. I feel almost as if there's a time clock ticking down to his next move."

"Let's hope not," Bateman said.

Amen. If things could stay the same, for herself and the town, Christina would be a happy woman. She used to long for something different, but now she held her breath, praying nothing would ever change. Unrealistic, but true.

Fifteen

"Are you coming inside?" Aiden asked.

Christina had been strangely silent on the way home. She got that way sometimes, and he'd learned to give her space to think. In fact, he'd taken a few unnecessary turns on the drive. The late summer night enclosed them in patchy fog, and a cool breeze blew through the open windows. It had been so long since he'd been at ease with anyone, especially in that kind of silence, that he hadn't wanted it to end.

Yet here they were, looking at each other through the open window of the truck. Luke, Jacob and Marie had long ago returned to the house, which was silent and barely lit. Aiden wanted to scoop Christina into his arms and carry her to their room, but something held him back. It was almost as if they'd moved into a new stage, and he should once again ask her permission before introducing intimacy.

Logically, he knew only his feelings had changed. But what about her?

"I'm not sure," Christina said. She still sat inside the truck, staring at him in the dark as if searching for something, but he wasn't sure what. "Aiden…"

His throat constricted in anticipation. "What is it?"

"I'm afraid."

The words barely registered. He wanted to wipe away her fear with some pat little phrases, but he couldn't. Obviously, she felt this, too. But they both had to embrace it for it to go anywhere. "I know," he finally said. "I'm a risk. But most of the things we want in life are scary. It's up to you how you deal with it."

Unwilling to coerce her decision with his presence, he turned away. The side expanse of green lawn was still damp from the dew, along with the outer ring of azalea bushes. As he approached the weeping willow tree, he heard running footsteps behind him. Turning back, he watched as Christina ran across the lawn and barreled into his chest. Together they burst through the curtain of swaying tree limbs. He wasn't quick enough to brace himself, so her momentum knocked him off balance, and they tumbled to the ground in a tangle of bodies.

But when they came to rest, Aiden found himself in a win-win situation, with Christina's toned legs straddling his thighs and her breasts snug against the hard wall of his chest.

His body surged to instant hardness, the fullness punching the back of his zipper in an attempt to reach her skin. He arched against the sensation, pressing deeper into the V of her thighs.

She glanced around them, and he let his gaze follow, then smiled. The thick fall of branches from the fifty-year-old tree isolated them from the world outside. It was a veil enclosing them in the magical discovery of each other. Christina braced her hands on his shoulders to keep him from bucking her off, but her own hips tilted, rubbing her most private of parts across his length in one long, slow slide. Aiden's heartbeat burst into overdrive.

He needed her. Now.

She crouched closer, her lips meeting his in an all-out assault. Her mouth open, tongue delving deep. He met her with everything he had to give.

He explored, tracing the inner curves of her mouth, the moist heat stirring an ache to bury himself inside her. They couldn't linger long. Aiden knew Christina's hunger grew with his own by the way she kneaded his chest and nibbled his bottom lip. Her breathy pants brushed his skin, increasing his urgency for more.

With a jerk, he had her button-down shirt open and gaping, so he could explore her smooth skin and the lace of her bra. Leaning back, she delved between her thighs for the button to his khaki pants. Her fingers fumbled for a moment before she released him, inching back so she could get the zipper down. The condom wasn't far behind.

He lay on the hard ground, barely noticing it, his hands gently squeezing her lace-covered breasts, while his wife prepared to ride him for all she was worth. And he was in heaven. The only thought pounding through his brain was a refrain of more, more, more.

She stood to shuck her own pants, and it was all he could do not to jerk her back against him. He wanted everything. More of that delightful mix of shy and brazen. More of the woman who comforted him and wasn't afraid to point out when he was wrong. More than anything, he needed her to complete his soul.

If he hadn't already been shaking, Aiden would have started. Pulling his wife back onto him, he fitted himself at her entrance and guided her down. It killed him to go slow, but suddenly, she arched her back and slid herself home.

Stealing his breath away.

Unable to sit still, to remain at her mercy, he gripped her hips, forcing her into a counterrhythm with his own body. They ground together. Aiden savored every breathless cry straining from her throat. In the darkness, he caught the swing of her hair as she moved, the curve of her jaw silhouetted against the lighter backdrop of leaves.

As he fought for completion, only one thought remained: mine.

With that, he drove himself as deeply as he could, allowing her body weight to aid him. Her cry mingled with his. Her body contracted around him as she slammed into her peak, dragging him along in the undertow.

For long moments he knew nothing but the warmth of her flesh, the pounding of his blood and the need to never let go.

Before he could stop it, his first coherent thought emerged from his hazy brain. *I don't think I can live without this.* But separation came soon enough. Christina simply slipped to the side and onto her back, her head pillowed on his biceps.

"I need to get up," she said, "but for some reason my muscles won't move anymore."

He chuckled, feeling the sound vibrate through his chest under the very spot where her hand rested. "You need to be careful. I think I could get addicted to you ending every date this way."

He heard her smile in her voice. "Oh, I think I can live with that."

And as he helped her to her feet and into her clothes, he knew that he could, too. Because damn if he wasn't in love for the first time in his miserable life.

Christina brushed the grass off her pants before pulling them back on. She should be ashamed, or embarrassed, or something…but she wasn't. Aiden didn't even give her time to put her shirt on before he was pulling her across the lawn and into the back door. She couldn't help but giggle as they raced up the stairs. "This is becoming a habit," she said breathlessly.

"This is a habit I can most definitely live with," he said with a grin.

Christina slept deep, secure in the knowledge that Aiden was curled around her, but it ended with the harsh reality of a ringing phone. She woke at the loss of warmth, her euphoria slowly fading, and listened in the predawn gloom as Aiden spoke.

"Yes?"

Amazing that his sleep-scruffy voice could still give her shivers.

"What happened?"

The murmur of the voice from the other end sounded feminine, but urgent. His assistant from New York?

"Was anything damaged?"

That had Christina sitting up.

"How many of the paintings did it ruin?"

As he listened to his assistant's answer, a thrum of anxiety hummed along Christina's nerves. What would he do? She felt selfish worrying about it, but couldn't stop the circle of thoughts in her head. What if he left and didn't come back?

Finally, he pushed the end button. The muscles of his naked back flexed as he leaned over to set the phone on the nightstand. Her mouth watered. She wanted nothing more than to trace those sleek plains with her fingertips. Last night she wouldn't have hesitated. Today everything had changed.

Aiden twisted her way. "Hey," he said, one low word reaching through her confusion. "Sorry to wake you."

"No problem." She pulled the comforter tight around her, wishing she wasn't naked. The protection of her clothes would be a big comfort right now. "What's going on?"

"Water leak at the warehouse. The alarms alerted Trisha pretty quickly, but there's still some damage. I'm gonna have to make a trip up there."

Her throat went dry. Even though she knew her fear was irrational, it still built within her. "Why? Hasn't she already got a handle on things?" At least, her report had seemed kind of lengthy.

"Do you honestly think I'm the type of guy to let someone else handle my problems for me?"

No, he wasn't. She knew better. But the thought of him leaving brought so many fears.

She didn't answer, and he didn't wait for one. He was already pulling pants and underwear out of the drawer. "I'll get a shower and pack. Find out when I can get a flight. Jacob can drive me to the airport."

"What about the mill?" she asked. Standing, she reached for a robe to wrap tight around herself.

"Jacob is catching up on things, anyway. No reason why he can't jump right in." His clipped tone told her all the questions irritated him, but she couldn't seem to stop herself.

She took a step toward him. "Don't you think you should, you know, ask Canton before you do this? What kind of provisions are there for trips? Duration, things like that."

Aiden's shoulders straightened, his jaw growing hard. "No." The single word was sharp and forceful, telling her this was the wrong question to ask. "I don't have to ask anyone for permission to do this. That business is my life and I won't lose it over some stupid game my grandfather thought he would play. Got it?"

"Even if others get hurt?"

Aiden stalked closer, his stare boring into her. "Are you insinuating that I'm not holding up my end of this bargain?"

"Are *you* insinuating that what happened here is nothing *but* a bargain?" she demanded, waving her hand over the bed.

Again, the wrong thing to say, because all emotion disappeared from Aiden's face. His guarded expression took her back to those first days together. "I'm going," he said.

With those two words, all the anger drained from Christina. Her gaze dropped to the floor at her feet. She'd blown it, letting her insecurities push Aiden farther away. Not that it mattered if he viewed their relationship as, well, not really a relationship. "Fine. I get it."

They stood in silence for long moments, but she refused to look up again, afraid that if she did, Aiden would see the devastation breaking her apart inside. He would leave, regardless. Why she'd thought she might be a reason to at least proceed with caution was ridiculous. What she wanted would never matter. It never had.

Finally, he mumbled, "I've got to shower," and stalked back through the door to the bathroom.

Wilting all over, Christina hurried to the dressing room, lingering until she heard Aiden dress and leave. An hour later, she was showered and dressed and seated at Lily's bedside, forcing herself to read aloud to her friend when she really wanted to give in to the tears threatening every second. She'd heard the house start to stir—the voices of the men as they went up and down the stairs and finally, luggage being bumped on the steps as Aiden and Nolen spoke in quiet tones.

She ignored it all. But her focus on Lily was shaky at best, especially as footsteps stopped outside the suite door. Looking up, she spied Aiden in the shadows of the hallway. Their eyes met, but she quickly looked back down to the book, unwilling to display her feelings and give him the opportunity to dismiss them.

He moved inside slowly, almost hesitant as he stepped across the threshold until he reached the foot of Lily's bed. He didn't wait for Christina to look up. He simply spoke in a tone much softer than before. "I'm leaving now. I'll call and let you know when I'll be back once I see what needs to be done."

She nodded, using every last ounce of strength to keep her expression neutral. She'd been the one who screwed up, demanding something unreasonable out of fear. But this had simply reinforced the many years life had taught her that people, relationships, weren't something she could keep. She might as well get used to it now as opposed to later.

"Do you understand what I'm saying, Christina?"

She forced her throat to work. "Sure."

"Look at me." He didn't raise his voice, but the quiet command had her aching to obey.

With a deep breath, she met his gaze with her own. "Yes?"

"I understand what's at stake here."

Do you really?

"I know the town needs me. I know Lily needs me." He paused for the span of a long breath, then continued, "I will be back. I promise."

But what about me? She ignored her thoughts and simply nodded her head.

Still, he stared. His phone started to ring, but he ignored it. With each second that ticked by, her internal shields cracked until she knew one single push would have her squalling like a baby.

"Is there anything you want to tell me, Christina?"

Her mouth opened, drawing in the breath that would push out the words *I love you*. Words he most definitely would not want to hear. So she simply shook her head.

"I'll always come back. I promise."

"Lily said she would come back, too." And she had, but the results had been disastrous. Would Aiden's return be just as devastating? Once he had another taste of New York, would he realize how much he hated being here?

"What are you talking about?" Aiden asked, his tone hardening once more. "I realize I'm responsible for her accident. That I left Mother all these years instead of setting aside my pride to see her again. I don't need you to point my responsibilities out to me, Christina."

Christina's head shot up. "That's not what I meant at all."

"Then what did you mean? Because I won't be guilted into staying here."

Once more, the ringing of the phone filled the room.

"Guess you should go, then," she said, turning back to the impersonality of the book and the quiet atmosphere of the sickroom. Things she could control. Things she couldn't screw up. She wished she could start this morning over and tuck all her ridiculous emotions inside so she couldn't complicate things.

With a curt nod, Aiden did just that, leaving her behind. Just like everyone else in her life.

Sixteen

Christina's bare feet ghosted over the back lawn, damp from the evening's dew. She couldn't stand being cooped up in the house anymore. Aiden had been gone five days. The amount of time Canton had informed Jacob he was allotted to be away. After tonight, they would be in violation of the will. Aiden hadn't contacted her personally, so she had no idea if he planned to be home by morning…or not.

She wished she had the option of escape, even if only for a few hours. Instead, she'd waited until Marie headed out for Wednesday night church. The sympathetic looks were more than she could handle.

She must have been out of her mind. Or totally blinded by the situation they'd found themselves in. How could she have been so desperate for love as to trust her heart to a man who'd told her outright he wouldn't stay?

Something inside drew her to Aiden's studio, as if by being there she could once again be close to him. She had a moment's trepidation when she reached the porch. Aiden kept the little house locked, but the single key hung with the other keys in the mudroom. She just had to be here. The door opened easily beneath her shaky fingers.

She let herself into the darkened room, reaching out her hand to feel for a light switch. Instead, her arm brushed a lamp that she suddenly remembered was sitting on the table near the door. Tracing down, she located the switch.

The soft glow that sparked to life revealed the work space Aiden prized so much.

If she were her mother, she'd put the sledgehammer she found to good use in here. She'd seen her mother pitch many a fit on her father's things before they'd divorced. She'd even keyed up his brand-new car one time. But destruction had never been Christina's thing. Guilt had. She'd spent more than her fair share of her life living with guilt.

Guilt from Lily's accident. Guilt over not preventing the stroke that had taken her beyond Christina's reach. And guilt over not being able to pull her mother from the destructive life she was determined to pursue.

Guilt was everywhere, and yet nowhere. Because it came from within Christina. Although sometimes external things fueled a person's guilt. Just as Lily's stroke had hers. Logically, as a nurse, Christina knew she had no control over that. But she'd been determined to make up for it ever since.

Hoping to distract herself from her never-ending thoughts, Christina stepped over to the shelves to check the progress of the marble pieces she'd seen on her last visit. Despite how close she'd thought they'd become over the past few months, Aiden had never invited her here. She'd trespassed only the one time, but hadn't returned. It just seemed too personal, too presumptuous on her part to invade his most private retreat, his source of solace and peace. Until he wanted her here.

Maybe he hadn't wanted her to get to know this part of him? After all, those times when he had confided in her had been times they'd connected on an intimate basis. Maybe he'd never had any intention of going any deeper than sex with her.

She wandered idly about the room, gliding her finger along his tools, resting her palms against half-finished sculptures. Until she reached the final statue in one corner. It took her a moment to make out the dark contours in the dim light. The last time she'd been here, the block of black rock streaked with gold had been carved into a slight curve along the top, and the straight edges chipped away from the sides. Now the rough stone at the bottom remained the same, but out of the rocky ground rose the silhouette of a woman. Christina. Her gaze traced the curve of her own jaw to the slight point of her chin, her abundant waves of hair and a gentle expression she couldn't place.

Reaching out with hesitant fingers, she skimmed the contours of the face, amazed at the smoothness of the stone. The hair actually had texture; she could feel the lines and waves that gave it movement.

Why would he create this incredible work of art featuring her, of all people? Though she'd hoped he felt something for her, he'd thrown it aside the first time she hadn't lived up to expectations. At least it felt that way. Her life had been about not making waves. But that morning, she'd gone over the top emotionally. Aiden getting angry and walking out had just confirmed her failure.

So what could he find so fascinating about her that he had to capture it in stone?

Christina started as footsteps pounded on the porch. Twisting around, she stared anxiously at the door, waiting for Aiden to walk through it and find her inside. Her stomach cramped. Had he returned? Would he be angry she'd invaded his special space?

The footsteps traveled across the boards, then stopped, giving Christina the impression that whoever it was had gone on around the side of the house.

Crossing quickly to the window, she stood to one side and cautiously leaned over to look out. She was just in time to get an impression of young men running toward the dirt track that led to mill property.

Two stood for a moment in the yard, talking, giving her a look at their faces. She recognized both: one she didn't know personally but had seen around town. The other was Raul, one of the part-time groundskeepers at Blackstone

Manor. Puzzled, she watched as they both turned away and trotted around the fence, until she lost sight of them in the woods edging the property.

A shiver worked its way down her spine as she thought of being alone inside with the men around the house. Why, she wasn't sure. She'd known Raul for over a year now. He wasn't the most personable employee, but he'd never been rude or lazy. Still, something about them upset her.

Should she wait until they were long gone before leaving? Or risk them seeing her by leaving now? What if they watched from the woods?

Turning toward the door, she decided to risk it. She'd moped around here long enough. Plus, she'd seen the guys disappear into the woods, so she should be able to get back to the house undetected.

When she was about five feet from the door, she noticed the smoke. She paused, her mind not quite understanding what the gray wisps leaking under the door meant.

As comprehension burst over her, so did a sheen of sweat. She stared, panic licking along her nerves. She shook her head to clear it, but her breath sped up no matter how much she tried to stay calm.

Numb shock cocooned her, but she was still able to acknowledge that those men had set the studio on fire. With her inside it. She didn't know how far the flames reached, but she had to find a way out. Now.

She glanced back at the only window not blocked by the air conditioner. The building wasn't that big, and by design, neither were the windows. It was a basement casement-type window, set head-high in the wall. Even if it would open all the way, she didn't think she'd fit through.

The smoke pouring in under the door grew thicker, warning her that her decision couldn't wait. She marched forward. This might not be the best option, but the door seemed to be the only exit left. She reached out, tapping the metal of the handle to test its temperature. Definitely warm, but not skin-searing yet.

Though her heart pounded and her eyes watered from the smoke, she forced herself to act. Grabbing the handle, she drew a deep breath and twisted the knob. Using the door as protection, she eased it open with slow caution.

Too late, she realized her mistake. The door swung in with a whoosh, knocking her backward. Pain exploded through her head. She tried to lift up. *What happened?* But her body refused to move. Sinking back down to the floor, she felt something trickle across her forehead.

Through the now-open doorway she could see the firelight eating away at the porch. Low on the doorway, flames inched up each side. *Move. Now.* But nothing happened. The vision before her wavered, causing nausea to rise. Closing her eyes, she tried to think.

She needed out. She couldn't move. What should she do?

Aiden jerked from automatic pilot as he caught a glimpse of a weird flickering light somewhere on the west side of Blackstone Manor. Nearing the gates, he turned in, then punched the gas. The closer he got, the more a cold grimness settled over him.

Shoving open the door so he could jump out of the truck, Aiden found himself staring at a rising plume of smoke from the vicinity of his studio. With a curse, he remembered clear as day Balcher telling him to watch out. Aiden was too careful and too familiar with studio work for this to be a result of his use of the building, and he'd had all the electrical lines checked out. Had the rival businessman decided to strike at the Blackstones a little closer to home?

Anger tightened his chest. If the man wanted to send a message, he'd sent it to the wrong person. Aiden would make sure Balcher paid for this little stunt, and paid dearly.

Rushing out of the truck, he jogged to join Jacob and the others on the lawn. "What happened?"

Jacob pointed back at the house. "I saw the flames as I passed by a window and alerted Nolen. We've called the fire department, but it will take them a bit to get this far out."

"How long?"

"At least another ten minutes," Nolen answered. "We're getting some hoses to hook up to the outdoor faucet in the well house down there, but I don't know how much good it will do. I'm sorry, Master Aiden."

"I know, Nolen." He turned his back, looking over the small group. Marie watched from a little farther away, a shawl draped over her nightgown. Nicole stood with her arm around her grandmother. Luke and the gardener, who had an apartment over the garage, came around the corner of the house dragging hoses. The only ones missing were Lily and—

"Where's Christina?"

The men looked at each other, then around the back lawn. Aiden's whole body tightened.

"I guess she didn't come out," Jacob said. "She must still be in the house."

Nolen was already shaking his head as Aiden spoke. "Have you ever known her to not be involved in something with this household?" He turned to sprint toward the cabin, adrenaline surging through his veins.

"I thought the cabin was locked," Jacob yelled from beside him as they ran.

It seemed like forever before they reached the clearing now dusky with smoke. A quick glance back showed the other men were headed their way, loaded down with hoses and buckets. Just as the heat burned a little too close, Aiden heard a faint noise. He stopped short, trying to slow his breathing so he could listen. "What is that?"

"Someone calling for help," Jacob said around his panting breaths. "She's inside."

Looking around, Aiden noticed the porch was pretty well engulfed in the flames. He wouldn't fit in through the window. But he needed in, quick. Darting around, he faced the steps to the porch.

"Aiden, don't," Jacob called, but Aiden couldn't listen. If he thought too long, it would be too late, and he couldn't leave Christina inside. That simply wasn't an option.

The fire was heaviest along the wall, less so among the new boards on the porch. Aiden closed his mind off to the sensation of heat, pulled the collar of his shirt up over his nose, and dashed across the porch, praying the boards held under his feet. He'd barely breeched the doorway before he stumbled over Christina on the floor.

Oh, Lord. Please no. His heart resumed its pounding as her head lifted slightly. "Come on, baby. Let's get out of here."

"Aiden?" she asked in a cracking voice then immediately started coughing. Lifting her up and over his shoulder, he turned back toward the door. It was hard to see for all the smoke, but it looked like someone was spraying water onto the fire. Aiden made straight for the lower flame and raced back outside, welcoming the cool shower in the midst of the blistering heat.

He cleared the stairs to find the gardener and Nolen manning the hose. Jacob and Luke helped him get Christina laid out on the grass. She continued to cough, rolling over onto her side.

That's when Aiden saw the blood.

"Get that hose over here," Jacob commanded.

They sprayed both Aiden and Christina down, making sure no lingering embers were on their clothes, then returned to their attempt to keep the fire from spreading.

Aiden wiped at the blood covering one side of Christina's face. "Luke, what does this look like to you?" he asked, knowing that his brother had first-aid training for his racing profession.

Luke shined his flashlight on Christina's face. She flinched, letting her eyes squeeze tightly shut. Her teeth started to chatter, interrupted by more coughing.

"I think it's just a cut, which isn't surprising. Head wounds bleed a lot. But there'll be paramedics with the fire trucks. Definitely want this looked at."

Aiden was grateful help was on its way. He didn't care about the studio, or his work and tools inside. Only this woman. If anything happened to her, he'd be lost for sure.

Not much later, the back lawn of Blackstone Manor was filled with vehicles and flashing lights. Three volunteer fire trucks had arrived minutes after local police officers. The ambulance, and even some county officers, were now on the scene.

Christina was being treated. She hadn't looked at him, hadn't asked for him. There was only that single time she'd called his name. That might haunt him for another twenty years or so.

Aiden had allowed the paramedics to treat the larger of his wounds, then he'd dismissed them to check out the other men. Instead of hovering, Aiden searched until he found his brother standing with the fireman in charge, two police officers in uniform and Bateman, who had on a volunteer firefighter jacket. Silence fell as he approached the group.

"Do we know what the hell happened yet?" he asked, his voice deep, harsh.

The men glanced at one another, then focused on Jacob, who nodded at one of the policemen. He introduced himself to Aiden. "From what we've been able to gather, right as the sun went down, five male individuals took it upon themselves to burn the building down. The burn patterns indicate they spread an accelerant, then lit various spots around the building."

"Five males? Do we know any of them?"

Jacob nodded. "Raul, one of the gardeners."

"So you have them in custody already?"

The policeman shook his head. "Not yet, but we've put out APBs for them. They won't get far."

Aiden looked out across the chaos of the back lawn. "If you haven't caught them, how do you know who it was?"

"Your wife was able to ID two of them—"

So much had happened, Aiden was having a hard time comprehending. "So she saw them as they set fire to the building?"

"She saw two of them clearly, and identified the gardener," the officer said. "The others she just saw running into the woods. It wasn't until she approached the door that she realized what had happened."

How terrified she must have been to know the building was on fire, yet be afraid to go out the door. Bile rose in the back of Aiden's throat, forcing him to swallow. "What was she doing in there?"

Jacob shook his head. "I'm not sure."

Guilt shot through Aiden. He should be with her. But would she want him? Another hard swallow helped him regain his equilibrium. But he wasn't sure how long it would last.

The lights surrounding them lit up Jacob's face in flashes of red and blue. Aiden clearly saw the other man's jaw tighten. "Somehow she hit her head and went down as she opened the door. I guess she thought she had no choice but to jump through the flames off the front porch."

Dizziness raced through Aiden. Though he thought he might go down, he managed to stay upright by sheer will and tightening his grasp on his brother. Clenching his jaw kept him from screaming his frustration.

Intellectually, he knew he would care about anyone who'd gotten hurt, but his emotions were ricocheting all over the place. Though they'd left things on rough footing, his week away had only confirmed his feelings for his wife. He didn't know what would happen, but in this moment, it didn't matter.

He had to be with her. Right. Now.

Jacob trailed behind as Aiden made a beeline for one of

the ambulances, where a paramedic stood talking to Marie. A second paramedic was packing up the equipment. "How is she?" Jacob asked as they approached.

Marie turned to them with worry clearly stamped in her furrowed brow and the tightness around her mouth. "Better, I think."

Aiden pushed forward for a glimpse into the interior of the vehicle. Christina lay on a gurney. The dim lighting allowed him to see her body tucked underneath a white sheet, the paleness of her skin against the tangle of her dark hair, and the oxygen mask against her mouth. Blood was still smeared in haphazard streaks along the right side of her face.

Aiden turned to the paramedic near him. "How is she, really?"

The man met his gaze head-on, reassuring Aiden somewhat. "She has lung irritation from extended smoke inhalation. We're going to take her to the hospital so they can watch her lungs for a little while. There are a couple of small burns we've treated where her clothes caught on fire. The cut on her forehead will need stitches."

Aiden's jaw tightened at the picture the other man's words sent to his brain.

"But all in all, she's very lucky."

Aiden glanced back at the woman who was his wife, whom he'd refused to contact over the last week as he'd vacillated between irritation and need. Regret pushed to the forefront of the emotions swirling through him.

"Sir, we really need to get you checked out, too."

Aiden nodded in acknowledgment, not trusting himself to speak. Another medic let them know he was ready to drive Christina to the hospital.

Aiden's first instinct was to insist on riding in the ambulance so he could be there with Christina. But she had yet to open her eyes. He wasn't sure if she was asleep or just avoiding him.

Unsure of his welcome, Aiden turned to Marie. "Could you and Nolen possibly follow them? She'll want someone with her, and I need to finish up a few things here." Not anything that he couldn't delegate to his brothers. But then again, hadn't he spent his entire life off-loading his responsibilities onto them?

Marie nodded. "I'll keep you boys up-to-date on what's happening. Until you can get there, that is."

Quite frankly, he might be the last person Christina wanted to see. No harm in letting them run the preliminary tests, so he'd have some information by the time he got down there. "Let me know the minute they tell you anything. I'll be there as soon as I've sorted out some of this mess."

The ambulance closed up. Nolen led Marie to his truck. Within minutes, they were both on the move, the ambulance siren blaring a warning to anyone who got in the way.

Aiden turned back toward the chaos of cars, people, and trampled plants that now constituted the back formal lawn. He took in the rubble that was now his studio, once the roof had caved. He couldn't imagine Christina, resourceful as she was, fighting her way out of that building. The very thought terrified him.

As Aiden stared at the activity before him—the firemen spraying the collapsed building, Luke and Nicole handing out cups of coffee and snacks, the policeman standing with his notepad, jotting down his thoughts from the interviews—a familiar sense of guilt wavered through him.

But for once, he would not let it keep him away from those he loved. Not this time. Not ever again.

Seventeen

Drawn to the woman he loved like a puppet on a string, Aiden approached her hospital bed with caution. Sitting in the chair beside her wouldn't do it. He needed to be near, to touch her and assure himself that she was okay. The doctor said they only wanted to monitor her oxygen, but the need remained.

Her body was so still. Was she sunk deep in the healing sleep she so desperately needed? Or was she pretending to sleep so she didn't have to deal with him at all?

Taking a chance, he settled on the space beside her in the bed. There was just enough room for him to sit, his thigh resting along the curve of her back as she faced the opposite wall. Testing his welcome, he lay his hand on top of her hip. Sure enough, her body jerked, though there was nowhere for her to go.

"Christina," he said, the soulful sound tinged with pain and regret.

She didn't respond, but her muscles tightened under his touch. Though he regretted the rejection, at least she knew he was here, was aware, even if she didn't like it.

"Are you all right? Is there anything I can get you?" Aiden made a sucky nursemaid, as evidenced by his inability to even set foot in his mother's room, but he had a lot to make up for here.

Christina didn't respond, but he heard a slight catch in

her breath. His eyes drifted shut, letting his senses focus solely on her, instead of the shadows from the light of the television in the far corner of the room.

"Christina, I know I screwed up, honey, and I'm sorry." He paused to see if any response came. But she seemed to curl in on herself even more than before. His hand rubbed absently along the curve of her spine. Up. Down. Savoring the feel of her delicate bones beneath his palm.

"Christina, I know I blew up the other day." He paused, searching for the right words, even though he knew he was going to screw this up big-time. "I got angry. You know more than anyone how easily I fly off the handle when I feel like I'm being manipulated, even if it's from the grave."

He thought he felt a catch in her breath. Was she crying? He didn't hear anything. The thought of her lying there, silent tears tracking down her face, stole his breath.

"I'm sorry for leaving like that."

This time her quavering breath was more distinguishable, but he plowed on while he could hold himself together enough to talk.

"I know I didn't call you this week, but I was trying to figure out how to apologize, and how to undo all the… crap…everything. In case you haven't noticed, I act before I think sometimes. When something means a lot to me, it takes a while for my head to catch up."

Aiden took comfort from the warmth of Christina next to him, and the darkness that hid his shame. So many times in his life his mistakes had hurt those he loved. Was he forever doomed to be defined by his mistakes?

He bent closer to her. "I'm so sorry, Christina. More than I can ever say. I know you can't forgive me right now and I can't prove to you how very sorry I am. But someday I will, Christina. I'll make it up to you. Someday."

Aching to feel her, he twisted around, lying down on the bed with his front curved against her back. They lay there in silence for long minutes before her body gradually relaxed into his.

Aiden couldn't sleep. He thought of the fragile woman in his arms, and how—just this once—he wanted to slay all her dragons. Never let anyone make her feel unwanted again. He only hoped she gave him the opportunity before it was too late.

Three days later, one very weary Aiden made his way into the local police station to meet with the deputies handling the arson case. He received some good news and some bad.

"We think we've rounded up everyone now, five in all, just like Christina said. The gardener was the last one, because he ran as soon as the others started getting picked up. Officers from the next county brought him in today. Would you mind confirming that this man was your employee?"

Aiden nodded.

As he stood in the viewing room, staring at the man who'd worked at the manor for a year at Nolen's last count, he wondered how someone could make such a grievous mistake.

"According to the other perpetrators," the officer said, "the basic plan was to burn the building down. They had no idea anyone was inside. They checked, since a single lamp was on, but didn't see anyone. This one—" he gestured to the gardener with a nod of his head "—was the ringleader. He riled them up, saying you didn't deserve to take over, and they would all eventually end up without a job. Trying to run you off, they claim."

Aiden was far from convinced. "Why? There was no proof of that. He had to be working for someone else." The question was, who? The man who wanted Aiden's company? A local upset over new management? Or some other unknown threat?

"We're hoping to get this guy to crack, but it doesn't look good. He's been tight, whereas the others opened up like the proverbial can of worms. But with our other boys ratting him out, it might give us some leverage to bargain for a name. It all depends."

Aiden inclined his head, watching the man through the one-way glass. Something about his eyes, cold and hard, told Aiden they would have to wield any leverage they had very carefully. This wasn't some punk running the streets or a teen led astray. According to the cop, he suspected the guy had done time in juvie, though he couldn't prove it. And he carried a look like he didn't care what happened to him. Balcher could have promised him a lot of things, including paying more if he kept his mouth shut. If the price was right, this one just might hold out.

"Did you find anything to link him to Balcher?" Aiden asked. He'd mentioned his conversation with the rival businessman the first time he'd talked with the officer.

"No. He was at a convention and received an award in front of five hundred people the night of the fire. And the gardener's phone records show no link to Balcher."

As the detective went on, Aiden felt his frustration grow. He wanted Balcher responsible because it made the most sense, and he wanted this over for Christina. She'd been shut down ever since the fire. Not just with him, but with everybody. He didn't want her worried about her safety. But Aiden had a feeling that, until they could find out who was truly behind this, none of them would be safe.

"Let me know if you find out anything."

The detective nodded. "We will. And I'd just like to say, for the record, that we do appreciate all you're doing to keep the mill going. It can't be easy uprooting your life, but it means a lot to the people of this town."

Aiden shrugged away the thanks, uncomfortable in his role as savior. "You can thank Jacob when you see him next. Having someone who's better versed in this stuff has made all the difference."

"But you will be staying, right?"

Aiden nodded slowly. "I will." *If Christina still wants me to.*

The other man nodded, and they exchanged a few pleasantries before Aiden made his way out to the car. He paused beside it, staring up into the bright sunshine under a cloudless sky. Honestly, the last thing he wanted was to go home. Back to Blackstone Manor, though the mere fact that he'd begun to think of it as home had come as a huge surprise to him.

Maybe he was growing up after all, he thought with a smirk. The place was crowded with his family now, though Luke didn't make it back as often. Still, having his brothers around both eased his own burdens and was a whole lot of fun. The camaraderie they'd shared on those visits as adults continued, even though they saw each other more now. Aiden had even been talking to a contractor about having a new studio built, along with a warehouse to move his base of operations here instead of New York.

The only fly in the ointment was Christina. Seeing her looking so calm was upsetting. That made no sense, except Aiden knew the facade was fake. And he had a feeling she was restless because she wasn't working, too. They'd hired a temporary caregiver for a couple of weeks to take over Lily's care, because Christina had been told to take it easy while her lungs and wounds healed. Aiden insisted on sleeping with Christina, using the excuse that he could listen out for Lily at night, but she kept herself stiffly on her side of the bed.

Except every morning they woke up in the same position: Aiden curled around her with their legs tangled together. She never mentioned it. Neither did he. But that was about to change.

Aiden feared if he wasn't able to break through the wall Christina had erected to protect herself, he'd lose her for good. She'd been neglected too often in the past to forget, so he'd been trying to give her time. Instead, she seemed to be slipping farther from his grasp with each passing day.

If she'd just give him a chance, they would have a future together. Right now, that's what Aiden wanted more than anything else in the world. More than his business. More than tearing up James's will.

Even more than his freedom.

Eighteen

She was crying over shoes. Christina knew she was in a pitiful state, but this was more than even she could condone. Shoes were shoes. And as Christina sat in front of her open closet, she knew she shouldn't make any decisions in this frame of mind.

Because choosing which shoes to get rid of should not make her cry.

In reality, her over-the-top emotions had nothing to do with shoes and everything to do with Aiden. He was always busy, but until today, always within reach. The problem? He treated her like a delicate figurine that would break with a simple touch.

She missed how he threw himself into everything, right or wrong. She missed arguing and the comfortableness of working together. The connection that she'd felt when they'd talked about his father. The awe she'd felt when he stood up to her father. Above all, she missed the intensity of his passion, and the feel of her soul mingling with his.

The days were torture. The nights were devastating.

They went to sleep, each on their respective sides of the bed. Some nights, lying there feeling useless and empty, Christina thought she'd give anything to have him curled against her back like he had that night in the hospital. Sure enough, by morning they would be tangled together, and her heart broke all over again. Something had to give soon because having him close but not having him for real was killing her. If she was braver, she'd ask him to stay. Why didn't she just ask?

She couldn't force herself to face any more rejection in her life.

Knowing he had left her without trying to understand her fears told her everything. All of those precious memories lay around her, shattered like broken glass. She had to escape, couldn't stand one more day moping around, wishing for things she couldn't have. But the inhabitants of Blackstone Manor had become her life; how could she possibly go?

So here she was, cleaning out her closet and crying.

As if conjured by her infernal wishing, Aiden slipped through the door. Twisting around, she stared up at him from her seat on the floor. "When did you get back?"

"Just a few minutes ago." He hesitated for a moment before speaking again. "The police now have all five of them in custody."

Christina grimaced. Just thinking about her glimpse of those men outside the cabin window gave her the shivers. She forced herself to shrug it off. "Will I have to testify?"

Aiden shook his head. "I doubt it. They have confessions out of four of them. It's a done deal. They just can't find anything that ties Balcher to the crime, and they have no other leads to who would have put them up to this. And we've found nothing more at the mill that could help."

Christina let that pass, not wanting to think about someone who was willing to destroy property to scare people away. Thugs didn't deserve her attention in any way.

To her surprise, Aiden approached with measured steps across the carpet, then knelt down beside her. She glanced up at his face but quickly looked away. He was just too beautiful for her to watch without giving away the pain she was feeling.

"Christina, what's the matter?"

Christina could feel herself close down. She wiped the tear trails from her cheeks. Experience had taught her that men didn't like messy, emotional women.

When she didn't move, he joined her on the floor. He turned her as if she were a doll so she was facing him. She couldn't quite reconcile the sophisticated, sexy businessman she knew with the casually comfortable man before her now. Instead of a T-shirt with his khakis. His hair was still tousled, but more from running his fingers through it than from gel.

Whether dressed to the nines, sweaty from sex or sitting on her bedroom floor, he was still the most attractive man she'd ever seen.

And here she was in yoga pants and a tank top, her hair pulled up in a large clip. He'd definitely gotten the raw end of their deal.

Still, he didn't move, and that waiting expression told her she better start talking. The last thing she wanted was Aiden prying into her feelings, so she chose the safest topic. "I'm struggling," she said with a shrug. "I just want things to be normal again." She gestured to her closet. "This is just so useless." *Pointless.* And it was true. Having no real purpose to her days gave her no reason to get up, no reason to do anything. Too much time to think, to mope. To feel unwanted and unneeded.

"You know we just want you to be able to heal, right?"

"Yes, Aiden. I know. But I'm fine." *I need to get back to work.*

"You don't act fine."

A quick peek from beneath her eyelashes showed that same searching expression in his eyes that had been there for a week. She didn't want to be a puzzle he had to figure out. She wanted to be a partner. In a burst of clarity, she realized he was right. She wasn't acting fine. She was moping around, hoping someone would fix all the problems, instead of taking charge.

When had waiting for someone else to make the first move done her any good? The only times she'd been happy in her life had been when she stepped up to the plate, taken on the challenge of doing what fulfilled her. Time to make something happen instead of waiting for it to happen. But what was the right step?

"I'm more than ready to take care of Lily again." That much she knew for sure. "I can't lie around here feeling useless while someone else does my job."

"Useless?" The disbelief on his face was hard to understand. But he wasted no time enlightening her. "Christina, you go out of your way to help everyone—this town, Nolen, Marie, Nicole. You sacrificed yourself to keep Lily safe—"

"Stop." She jerked to her feet. "Don't do that."

He stood, stalking closer. "Christina—"

"No." She could feel the trembling start along her nerves, fingertips to shoulders, toes to tummy. Needing to move, she paced past him. Soon she'd be an allover mess, but she had to get this out. "I didn't sacrifice myself for Lily. I love her, but I volunteered to marry you because of guilt. I *owe* Lily."

That stopped him cold. His voice, when he spoke, was softer than she expected. "What are you talking about?"

She almost wished she was facing the angry Aiden. This would be so much easier if he wasn't being so nice. "I caused her accident," she whispered.

Aiden shook his head. "No. She was coming home—"

"Because of me. You'd told her to stay an extra day to wait out the weather. But I'd gotten sick. Really bad appendicitis. I was in the hospital after having my appendix removed. Marie called Lily, told her my mother had left me there alone. Heck, she barely even stayed long enough for me to get out of recovery."

She swallowed hard, her stomach churning at the memories. "Lily came home in spite of the weather to be with me. So I wouldn't be alone. I didn't find out about the accident until I was released from the hospital."

"Oh, my God, Christina." Aiden's voice rose. He stalked forward, hands settling on her upper arms to give her a little shake. "Don't you know Lily would never feel that way? She would never blame you for what was very much an accident."

"But I blame myself. Just like I blame myself for you having to come back here, to stay here. You want to be in New York, I understand that. But instead, you're here, with me."

"That is not your fault. That's James's doing. He put us in this situation...."

"But I want you to stay."

The silence that filled the room drowned out the pounding of her heart. Had she really just said that out loud? Fear kept her from looking at him for a reaction. There was no going back now.

"You are only here because you have to be, Aiden, but I want you with me. Permanently." *I'll make it up to you.* His words from the hospital haunted her, but she had to take a risk. Could she really do this?

A hard swallow helped her continue. "I love you. Whether you're here or in New York, I will love you. But I'd much rather you be here. I'm sorry if that makes me a clingy, desperate woman. I don't want you to have to choose between being tied to a place you hate just because you slept with me, and going back to the life you love. I just...want you."

"Who says I have to choose?"

Surprise shot along her nerves.

"Christina, I've been waiting a week for you to reach for me. To need me. But you never did. I thought I made myself clear at the hospital. I'm not here because I have to be. I'm here because I want to be with you, with Mother, with my family."

Her brain churned over the words, but comprehension was slow in coming. "What about New York?"

"Who says it has to be either/or?" His grin was self-deprecating. And charming. Always charming. "Yes, I realize I've made it out to be just that. But this trip did teach me something. I can have it all. The business I've built. The family I love. *And* the woman I need."

He approached her with measured steps, as if afraid she'd run. He paused near enough for her to feel the warmth of his body, so temptingly close, then threaded his fingers into the hair at her temples. He cupped her face, raising it to his. Lovingly restrained, there was no out. "Christina, you light a passion in me that…well, it's the only thing that's ever topped my art."

She could feel herself drowning in his touch, in the depths of those dark eyes.

"Since I came back to Blackstone Manor, I've made more than a few mistakes. I didn't want to be here, so I fought with everything in me to break away. But there was one tie I don't want to fight. Haven't been able to since the first moment you challenged me to do what was right."

His arm encircled her waist, bringing her body flush against his. The same security she felt every night in his arms immediately flooded over her.

"You challenged me. You fought with me. And you loved me."

Her heartbeat jumped, then resumed at a faster speed. "Aiden—"

"Let me finish, because I'm not sure if I can keep this up," he said with a wry twist of his lips. His thumb stroked along the line of her jaw. "I am, beyond a shadow of a doubt, a better man for it. Your warmth reminds me I'm not alone.

Your passion ignites my own. Your purpose points me in the right direction. Your forgiveness keeps me sane. I don't need demands to keep me here. I'm selfish enough to want it all—and I hope that you'll give it to me."

The tears spilled unchecked down her cheeks. Leaning forward, he brushed his lips back and forth over hers before pulling back a finger's breadth. "Let me stay with you," he murmured against her lips. "I will make mistakes. I'm just hoping you'll love me, anyway."

Finally, she reached out to him, sliding her arms up over his shoulders, and around the back of his neck. "Oh, Aiden. Don't you know I love everything about you? You're passionate. Creative. Hardworking. I'll take whatever part of you you'll let me have."

"Then you can have it all, too, because I'm not whole without you. I love you. Marry me…again."

Her breath catching in her throat, Christina pressed her lips to his, reveling in his quick control of the kiss and breach of her lips.

Then she knew beyond any doubt that her heart had finally found its home. Not because she was needed. Not because someone demanded it. For the first time in her life, she was wanted for who she truly was inside, flaws and all.

Just as she wanted Aiden. Forever and always.

* * * * *

THE UNEXPECTED HONEYMOON

BY
BARBARA WALLACE

Barbara Wallace is a lifelong romantic and day-dreamer, so it's not surprising that at the age of eight she decided to become a writer. However, it wasn't until a co-worker handed her a romance novel that she knew where her stories belonged. For years she limited her dreams to nights, weekends and commuter train trips, while working as a communications specialist, pr free-lancer and full-time mum. At the urging of her family she finally chucked the day job and pursued writing full-time—and she couldn't be happier.

Barbara lives in Massachusetts with her husband, their teenage son and two very spoiled, self-centred cats (as if there could be any other kind). Readers can visit her at www.barbarawallace.com and find her on Facebook. She'd love to hear from you.

To my fellow writers,
Donna Alward, Wendy S. Marcus, Julia Broadbooks,
Abbi Wilder and Jennifer Probst, without whom I
could never have gotten this book written. Thank you
for showing up every morning and pushing me to be
productive. You ladies are the absolute best!

And, as always—Pete and Andrew, you're my heroes!

CHAPTER ONE

"BUENOS DIAS!"

Having grown up in the hospitality industry, Carlos Garcia Chavez thought he'd seen everything. But nothing prepared him for the blonde standing in the doorway of the Presidential Villa. With her tight white dress and messy halo of platinum blond hair, she looked like she'd stepped out of a black-and-white newsreel. So much so, he half expected to hear her call him Mr. President in a husky stage whisper.

What he got was a big, overly bright smile that sent awareness shooting through him. Something else he was unprepared for. He adjusted his grip on the wine bottle cradled in his arm and pushed the unexpected reaction aside.

"Buenas tardes, Señorita Boyd."

"Oh, right, you say *tardes* in the afternoon. My bad. I'm still on East Coast time. I'll catch on eventually."

Carlos refrained from pointing out that East Coast time would place her later in the day, not earlier. After all, the guest was always right, no matter how wrong they might be.

Meanwhile, this particular guest leaned. She leaned a hip against the door frame, a position that drew further attention to her curves. "So what can I do for you, Señor…?"

"Chavez. Carlos Chavez. I'm the general manager here at La Joya del Mayan."

"Did you say *general manager?* Damn. I knew this was too good to be true."

"There is a problem?" he asked. Carlos tensed. Errors were the kiss of death in the hotel industry. Mistakes led to bad reviews. He had enough on his plate keeping La Joya's current woes under wraps; he did not need to add to his troubles.

"Lucky for you, I haven't unpacked yet." He followed, trying not to stare at the way her bottom marked her steps like a white silk pendulum. "I mean, Delilah and Chloe might be generous, but seriously, this? Doesn't matter if they are married to millionaires. Well, Del's married to one. Chloe and her boyfriend aren't married yet, although anyone with two eyes in their head can see they're going to be. They're absolutely crazy about each other. Do you want some champagne?" She lifted a bottle from the coffee table.

"No, thank you." Judging from her rambling friendliness, she'd had enough for both of them. "You said there'd been an error?"

"I've never had Cristal before. This stuff is really good."

"I'm glad you approve."

"Oh, I do." She took a long drink, nearly emptying the glass. "I definitely do. I should have served it at tomorrow's night—I mean tomorrow night's reception."

"We can upgrade the menu if you'd like."

She snorted, for some reason finding his suggestions amusing. "Little late for that."

"Not at all. We can make changes right up to the last minute. So long as you're happy."

"Because everyone knows, it's the bride who matters, right?" A shock of blond curls flopped over one eye. She swiped them away with a sloppy wave of her hand. "Long live the bride."

Her groom was going to have his hands full tonight. Come to think of it, where was her groom? According to their records, Señorita Boyd booked one of their famed wedding packages, but the front desk said she'd checked in alone. Most guests arrived either as couples or with a gaggle of family and friends.

Only unhappy brides drank alone.

Stop it. The señorita's drinking arrangements were none of his business. For all he knew, she wanted to be alone. Her accommodations, however were his concern, and so he repeated his original question. "Is there a problem with your room?"

"Only that I'm here. That's why you're here, isn't it? To tell me I have to move?"

So that was her worry. His shoulders relaxed. "Not at all."

"Seriously?"

"I handled the upgrade personally." In fact, her friend, Señora Cartwright's, phone call had been one of the few positive highlights of his first week. "For the next week, consider this villa your home away from home."

"Really? Wow. I have the best friends." She looked down at her glass, her eyes growing so damp that for a moment, Carlos feared she might cry.

"If I recall, Señora Cartwright said you'd admired the photos in our brochure," he said.

The comment did its job, and distracted her. "More

like drooled. This place is amazing. More than amazing, actually."

"I'm glad you approve."

"Oh, I do." Draining her glass, she reached for the bottle again. "So, Señor… What did you say your name was again?"

"Carlos Chavez."

"Car-rrr-los Cha-a-a-vez. I like how it flows off my tongue." She gave a tipsy grin. "You sure you don't want anything to drink?"

"Positive."

"Then why are you carrying a bottle?"

The Cabernet. In all the distraction, he'd almost forgotten the point of his visit. "My desk manager told me you talked with the Steinbergs while waiting to check in."

She drew her brows into a sensuous-looking pout. "Who?"

"The couple from Massachusetts who were staying at the Paradiso."

"Oh, right, Jake and Bridget. They'd walked up here from the beach. I told them they were wasting their time getting married at the Paradiso. I researched every destination wedding location in the eastern hemisphere, and none come close to being as romantic as this place."

Given his family's outrageous investment in creating said romance, Carlos certainly hoped so. The Chavez family prided itself on owning the most exotic, most enticing resorts in Mexico. "Apparently your enthusiasm was contagious because they placed a deposit for next spring."

"I'm not surprised."

She paused to wipe champagne from her upper lip with a flick of her tongue that left Carlos gripping the bottle a little tighter. He didn't know whether she always moved with such sensuality or if the alcohol unleashed some hidden sexuality gene, but he found himself re-acting in a most unwanted way.

"They said they stopped by on a whim, but no one hikes four miles along a beach on a whim. Besides, Bridget had that look, you know? After five minutes, I knew she'd made up her mind. Can you believe the front desk wanted to send her away with nothing more than a brochure?"

Yes, Carlos could. "Unfortunately, we are between wedding coordinators at the moment," he told her. No need to explain the disaster he'd been sent to fix. "Thankfully, you were there to speak on our behalf. I wanted to come by and personally thank you for as-sistance, and to give you this with our compliments." He presented the bottle. "Cabernet from Mexico's own Parras Valley."

"How sweet. Mexican wine." She reached to take the bottle from him, only to stumble off balance and fall against his chest. Champagne sloshed over the rim onto his shirt, but Carlos barely noticed as he was far more focused on the hand pressed against his chest.

"I like how you pronounce *Mexico*." There it was, the husky whisper. Carlos's body stirred instinctively.

"Perhaps you and your fiancé can toast to a long life together."

Gripping her shoulders, he righted the señorita and thrust the bottle into her grip. A bit rougher than nec-essary, perhaps, but he wasn't in the mood to play sub-stitute. The force caused her to stumble backward, although thankfully, she managed to catch her balance without assistance. Giving a soft "whoops," she smiled and swayed her way to the writing desk. "Nice thought,

Señor Carlos. Unfortunately, he's off having a long life with someone else, and I don't feel like toasting that."

"Pardon?" She had booked a wedding package, hadn't she?

"My fiancé—ex-fiancé—decided he'd rather marry someone else."

No wonder she was drinking. He felt a stab of sympathy. "I'm sorry for…" Did one call a broken engagement a loss? No matter, he hated the phrase. *Loss* was such an empty and meaningless word. Having your world implode was far more than a loss.

"You're here alone, then," he said, changing the subject.

"Honeymoon for one." She raised her glass only to frown at the empty contents. "Wow, this stuff goes down way too easily."

"Perhaps you ought to…"

Blue eyes glared at him. "Ought to what?"

"Nothing." Wasn't his place to monitor her behavior. She was a guest. His job was to make her happy.

"Do you know what he said? He said I cared more about getting married than I did him. Can you believe it?"

"I'm sorry." What else could he say?

"Yeah, me, too." She swayed her way back to the coffee table. "Like it's a crime to be excited about getting married. News flash: It's your wedding day. The one time in your life when you get to be special."

Hard to believe a woman who looked like her needed a specific day to feel special, but then as he knew all too well, there existed women who needed constant reassurance, despite their beauty. Perhaps the señorita was one of those women.

"Besides, if Tom was that upset, why didn't he say

something sooner? He could have said, 'Larissa, I don't want a fancy wedding,' but *nooo,* he let me spend fifteen months of planning while he was busy having deep 'conversations' with another woman, and then tells me I'm wedding obsessed.

"Seriously, what's so great about having deep conversations anyway? Just because I don't go around spouting my feelings to anyone who will listen, doesn't mean I don't have them. I'll have you know I have lots of deep thoughts."

"I'm sure you do."

"Tons. More than Tom would ever know." Turning so abruptly, the champagne yet again splashed over the rim of her glass, she marched toward the balcony.

He should go, thought Carlos. Leave her to wallow in peace. But he didn't. Instead, something compelled him to follow her outside to where she stood looking at the Velas Jungle, her shoulders slumped in defeat.

"I would have listened to him, you know," she said, the energy depleted from her voice.

"I'm sure you would have."

He joined her at the rail. It was the view that made La Joya famous. Across the way, snowy egrets had taken up their nightly residence in the mangroves, their noisy calls reverberating across the lagoon. The water rippled and lapped at the tree roots, creating a blurry mirror for the green and blue above.

The champagne glass dangled from her fingertips. He was debating reaching for the glass to keep her from dropping it into the water when she asked abruptly, "Are you married, Señor Carlos?"

The word *yes* sprang to his tongue, same as it always did. "Not anymore."

"Divorced?"

"Widower."

"Oh." Downcast lashes cast shadows on her cheek. "I'm sorry."

Again with the meaningless words. "It happened several years ago," he replied.

"My problems must seem really silly to you."

Her remark surprised him. Normally, people relaxed when they heard his answer, assuming the passage of time meant less pain and mistaking his numbness for healing grief. To hear her express sympathy, left him off balance. "I'm sure they don't seem superficial to you."

"But they are," she said with a sigh. "They're silly. I'm silly."

She was sliding into self-flagellation, dangerous territory when combined with alcohol. Old warning bells rang in his head. "Why don't we step back inside?" Away from the railing. "I'll get you a glass of water."

"I don't want water," she said, but she did push herself away from the rail. "I want more champagne."

As long as it moved her off the terrace. He stepped back, expecting her to turn around, only to have her cup his cheek. Her blue eyes locked with his and stilled him in his tracks. "I'm sorry for your loss," she said with far more sincerity than the word merited. Behind the kindness, Carlos recognized other emotions in her eyes. Need. Loneliness.

A spark passed through him, a flash of awareness that he was alone with a beautiful, vulnerable woman looking for reassurance. The similarities between now and the past were far too many, forming a dangerous rabbit hole down which he swore he'd never go again.

"Our staff is here for anything you need," he told her, breaking contact before other, more disturbing memories could rise to the surface. When it doubt, turn to business. The rule served him well these past five years. "We'll do our best to ensure you enjoy your stay, regardless of the circumstances."

"You're sweet."

On the contrary, he put an end to sweet a half decade ago.

After leading her inside, he made sure to lock the balcony door. With luck, she would curl up on the sofa and fall asleep. To be on the safe side, however, he made a mental note to have security keep an eye on the villa.

Images of a lifeless body floating atop water flashed before his eyes, stopping his heart.

Housekeeping, too. You could never be too careful.

The sun still beat strong on the sandstone walkway when he stepped outside. The beach side of the resort always remained sunny long after the lagoon settled in for the night. Guests enjoyed what they considered two sunsets. They would gather on their balconies or their private docks, margaritas in hand, and watch the shadows spread across the lagoon. A short while later, they'd turn their attention westward in time to see the sun slip behind the ocean. One more of the many perks that came with vacationing in paradise.

Personally, Carlos liked this time of day because the resort was quiet. Gave him time to walk the perimeter and ferret out any potential problems. There were always problems. Creating paradise took work—more work than people would ever realize. He'd been here six weeks now, not yet long enough to know all the resort's idiosyncrasies. Much of his time, thus far, had been consumed by cleaning up his predecessor's mess. Misused funds, unpaid accounts.... His predecessor's managerial incompetence knew no bounds. And of course, there was Maria. Stupid woman was supposed to plan weddings, not run off with the philandering idiot. A decade's worth of reputation in jeopardy because of two people's recklessness.

Rashness led to nothing but disaster.

"Whoops, excuse us." A pair of newlyweds cut around him to duck under the southwest archway, their arms filled with beach bags and each other. Carlos stepped aside, heaviness tugging at his heart as he watched the young woman playfully swat her husband's hand from her bottom. He'd been that way once himself, romantic and naive, believing the magic would last forever. Before a pair of needy brown eyes sucked him dry.

He wasn't an idiot. He was well aware there was more behind his family sending him to La Joya than righting managerial mistakes. They hoped that his tenure at La Joya might lighten his heart. As if being surrounded by romance would be enough to revive the man he used to be. What his family failed to realize was that man died. Destroyed by his own romantic illusions and desires, he could never be resurrected again, no matter what his surroundings.

No, Carlos's days of romance were over. Best he could do was let others enjoy the illusion while it lasted. Or, in the case of Señorita Boyd, help reality sting a little bit less.

Who turned on the lights?

Even with her eyes closed, the brightness stabbed at Larissa's right eye. If she could cover her face, maybe she could eke out an hour or two more of sleep. She reached to her right only to swat at empty air. Same when she reached left. Whoever was trying to blind her had also stolen her pillows and shrunk her bed.

Prying open one eye, she found herself face-to-face with a royal blue wall. Her bedroom was beige-and-brown. Whose bedroom was this? More importantly, how did she get here?

Bit by bit, reality worked its way into her brain. Mexico. Sometime during the night, she'd decided to stare at the stars, and stumbled her way to the terrace. She must have fallen asleep on the divan because she lay on her stomach, the side of her face smashed against a royal blue throw pillow.

How much did she drink? Too much, seeing how her tongue felt like it'd been wrapped in cotton socks. And her head… Thinking made the pounding at the back of her skull worse. Damn Delilah and Chloe for sending her that champagne.

"Why? We weren't the ones filling your glass," her friend Chloe would say, and sadly, she'd be right. Larissa did the pouring all by herself. Seven hundred fifty milliliters of champagne and half a bottle of Spanish wine worth. She gagged, contemplating the volume.

Wouldn't Tom be thrilled to see her now? After all, wasn't she to blame for everything? Their breakup, his cheating. *She challenges me, Larissa. Makes me think about things. All you talk about is the wedding. It's like you don't care about anything else.*

Apparently he missed the part where planning a wedding was a lot of work. Too busy having deep conversations with the other woman, no doubt.

Letting out a groan, she pushed herself to an upright position and stumbled to the living area, praying the powers that be included an industrial-strength coffeemaker. She still couldn't believe Delilah and Chloe paid to upgrade her to the Presidential Villa. The place was astounding, albeit filled with way too much sunshine at the moment. One glass wall looked out over the ocean, the other onto the lagoon. The entire villa was a glass box with curtains. Ironic since the resort boasted complete privacy.

Where did she put her sunglasses? She could have sworn she had them on her head when she checked in. Without them, her head was going to explode.

Oomph! She forgot the living room had a sunken conversation area. Missing the step, she lost her balance and pitched forward. Fortunately, her hand managed to catch the edge of the sofa. As her fingers curled around the cushion, a memory made its way into her head. Sad brown eyes with thick lashes that sent odd spiraling sensations down her back. *They'd talked about relationships. He said he was a widower. She said she was sorry for his loss and...*

And she touched him.

Oh, Lord, please say she did not come on to a complete stranger last night. A quick look at the open wine bottles said it was entirely possible.

A knock on the door sliced her head open. "Room service," an accented voice called out.

Peering through the peephole, Larissa spied a cart laded with silver serving pieces as well as—heaven help her—another bottle of champagne—and groaned. The wedding day breakfast package. She must have forgotten to cancel.

"For the bride," the server announced when she opened the door. He very diplomatically pretended not to notice her appearance, but Larissa caught the sideways glance as he wheeled the cart inside. Whatever. No different from the looks she got checking in. Single definitely stuck out at La Joya. Combing her fingers through her hair, she smiled brightly, as if she woke up wearing yesterday's clothes and smelling of stale wine every morning. Damn, but those sunglasses would definitely come in handy about now.

Dish by dish, the server unveiled the contents of each platter. Fresh strawberries. Whipped cream. *Huevos motulenos* with plantains and peas. Their aromas mingled together into one fruity, spicy fragrance. Larissa's stomach rose in her throat.

"Is there coffee?" she interrupted before the man could unveil the final dish, which she was pretty certain would be bacon. The greasy scent would send her right over the edge.

"I can serve myself," Larissa continued when he reached for the thermal pot.

Her upright quotient was nearing its end, and she didn't want to waste what little standing ability she had left on some elaborate presentation. Scribbling her room number on the bottom of the bill, she thrust the paper in the man's hand and hoped the generous tip would balance out her curt behavior.

"Please tell the chef everything looks wonderful." She swallowed hard to get the words out. "Exactly as advertised."

"I'm glad you think so," a new voice replied. Before she could reply, the man from her memories strolled into the room. Tall, dark and way too crisp-looking.

Her vague memories didn't do him nearly enough justice. Broad shoulders. A hard, lean body. Her fingertips tingled recalling the feel of his torso all too clearly. Especially the way her palm spread against the taut muscles.

It was his face she'd forgotten. Hidden by the distraction of sad eyes was a face marked by character. A strong jaw, a prominent nose. Skin the color of burnished gold. It was a rugged, masculine face, carved to capture both attention and respect.

He greeted her with a polite nod. "*Buenos dias,* Señorita Boyd."

Dammit, she'd forgotten his name. He wasn't the kind of man a person forgot, either. Maybe if she smiled brightly enough, she could fake her way through the conversation until it came to her. "*Buenos dias.* How are you doing this morning?"

"I am fine, señorita. A more important question is, how are you?"

"Right as rain," she lied.

He arched his brow, proof she wasn't fooling anyone, but chose to turn his attention to the room service cart. Larissa couldn't help but notice the server's nervousness regarding the inspection. Señor Whoever-He-Was must run a tight ship.

"You're having the bridal breakfast, I see," he said finally.

"Yes, I am."

"Interesting choice. Did you mean to?"

An odd question, although she'd been kicking herself over its appearance herself. She waited until he'd dismissed the server before asking, "What do you mean?"

"Only that considering your circumstances, I'm surprised you're interested in having the full bridal morning experience."

Was he referring to her hangover or the fact she was no longer a bride? His diplomatic description made it hard to tell.

He uncovered the bacon. A big mistake. Larissa started to gag.

"I'm looking forward to it," she replied, swallowing

her stomach back into place. Easier than swallowing her pride, apparently. "No sense letting a good meal go to waste."

"I applaud your attitude. Personally, I wouldn't be able to look at food, let alone eat so much."

Okay, so they were talking about her hangover. "I have an iron stomach."

Again, he raised his brow, unconvinced. They both knew she hammered herself into oblivion last night. Only a fool would insist on pretending otherwise. Call her a fool then. And would have to salvage pride where she could. Especially considering her only clear memory from last night involved falling against that hard, lean chest.

"You have a far better constitution than I do," he remarked. "Cream and sugar? Or do you prefer your coffee black?"

What she would prefer would be if he—and the breakfast cart—left her alone so she could collapse. "Black, please."

"I have to warn you, Mexican coffee is brewed stronger than American. Many of our guests are taken by surprise."

"I'm willing to take the chance." Anything to hurry him out of her room. What was he doing here anyway? Her fingertips started to tingle again. Oh, no. Maybe she did come on to him, and he was here because he thought she wanted some kind of Mexican fling.

"While you are here, you must try our version of *café de olla*. We brew the coffee with cinnamon and *piloncillo*. It's sweet, but not overly so. The secret is in using the right pot."

"Uh-huh." She was far more interested in getting through this cup of coffee. Those stainless steel covers didn't do much to contain aromas, did they? His nattering on about brown sugar didn't help. Between the two, her stomach was pretty much ready to revolt. If she didn't know better, she'd swear all his talk was on purpose, to test how long she could hold on before cracking.

"Do all your guests get such personal service from the general manager, or am I one of the lucky ones?" Assuming he was the general manager; she could be promoting him in her head. Drat, why couldn't she remember his name?

His chuckle as she snatched the cup from his hands was low and sultry, making her stomach list. Well, either the sound or the champagne. "I suppose you could consider yourself lucky. Normally, our wedding director meets with our bridal guests."

"But you don't have one," she replied. Another piece of last night's conversation slipping into place.

The coffee smelled horrible. Apparently, the resort considered *strong* a synonym for *burnt*. Holding her breath, Larissa lapped at the hot liquid. The acidy taste burned her esophagus before joining the war in her stomach.

Check that, the coffee was still debating whether it wanted to join. She put the cup on the desk.

Meanwhile, her dark-suited guest was helping himself to a cup. "That's correct," he said. "We are in between coordinators at the moment. Which is why I'm making a point of working with our VIP customers personally. I want to make sure their experience with us is exactly as they anticipated."

"Little late there," Larissa replied. This trip already wasn't what she expected.

Realizing his *faux pas,* the manager cleared his

throat. "That is why I decided to visit you first. I noticed—"

Carlos! His name rushed back. Unfortunately, so did the coffee. Larissa grabbed a nearby waste bucket.

And promptly threw up.

CHAPTER TWO

"ARE YOU FEELING better yet?" The voice on the other side of the door rolled far more gently than Larissa's stomach.

"Yes," she managed to croak. After her embarrassing display with the waste bucket, she wasn't about to admit anything else.

Happy Wedding Day to me. Her big day. The moment she'd dreamed about her whole life, when the world would see that she, little Larissa Boyd, found her Prince Charming. No more pinning sequins on someone else's wedding gown or standing in the sidelines.

Never, in all her dreams, did she see herself sprawled on Spanish tiles with her head propped against a walk-in shower.

Dammit, Tom.

"Do you need anything?"

Something to put her out of her misery might be nice. "I'm fine. I need a few minutes is all."

"Are you sure?"

"Positive. There's no need to for you to hang around. I'll be fine."

She listened for sounds of his departure, but heard none. You'd think he'd take advantage of her locking herself in the bathroom to get as far away from her as possible. Was he that afraid she'd pass out and bang her head?

Struggling to her feet, she wobbled to the sink. Shaky as her mind was, she was still able to appreciate her surroundings. The room was so large, you could fit three of her bathroom back home—one in the sunken tub alone. Needless to say, at the moment she could do without all the sunlight. What was it with this place and windows? Brightness poured in from all angles, bouncing off the glass accessories in near blinding proportion.

Too bad she couldn't keep her eyes closed forever. Crawl under the covers and start the day over. One look at her reflection, however, and she wondered if simply starting the day over would be enough. No wonder the room service guy looked at her askance. She looked like a rabid blue-eyed raccoon. Grabbing a tissue, she swiped at her eyes, succeeding only in spreading the smudges to her temple.

"Señorita?"

On top of everything, he wouldn't leave. Señor Chavez. No way she'd forget his name again. Although she'd bet he'd like to forget hers. In less than a day she'd gotten drunk, flirted with him and gotten sick in the wastebasket.

So much for being a VIP guest.

Clearly he wasn't going away until she showed her face, so she might as well drag herself outside. With a heavy sigh, she gave one last useless swipe at her mascara, and reached for the door.

Señor Chavez stood looking out to the lagoon. Meaning his back was to the room, thank goodness. She needed to work her way up to looking him in the eye. As it was, his black-suited presence filled the room with an awkward tension.

Interestingly, she could no longer smell the food. Her breakfast had disappeared.

"I moved the service cart outside," he said. "I know how overwhelming certain aromas can be when you're feeling under the weather."

And yet, he'd made a production of serving her coffee. She'd been right; her little pretense didn't fool him one bit. If she weren't about to die, she'd be annoyed.

"And the waste bucket?"

"Outside as well. Housekeeping will bring you a fresh one later today."

"Thank you," she said, annoyance taking a back seat to manners. Whether he'd been testing her or not, she had no one to blame but herself for her condition, and they both knew it.

He glanced at her from over his shoulder. "Your bag rang while you were indisposed as well."

Took a moment to realize he meant her cell phone. "My friends checking in to make sure I arrived safely." Had to be. Delilah and Chloe were the only two people in her life who cared. Grandma was gone and Tom... well, like he'd call.

"The same people who paid for your upgrade?"

"And the champagne." The enablers. "I don't normally drink so much," she told him, figuring she should at least try and explain her sorry state. "Let alone on an empty stomach. It's just that last night, I was sitting here..."

When it struck her, she was on her honeymoon alone. What back in New York seemed like such a grand gesture of independence suddenly felt pathetic. And so she figured, why not indulge in a good old pity party?

"I guess I was feeling vulnerable," she told him. "Today was supposed to be my wedding day."

"I know. You told me last night."

"That's right, I did." She always did over share with strangers when she'd had a little too much to drink. Chloe used to tease her about how she practically shared her life story the day the two of them met, and that was after a few glasses of wine in a bar after their corporate orientation. Who knew what a bottle of Cristal made her babble? "Did I say anything else?"

"You don't remember?"

"For the most part I do." A small white lie. She remembered thinking the space didn't feel quite so empty once he arrived, and the way his five o'clock shadow had felt rough against her fingers. "There are a couple blank spots, though. I didn't do anything…embarrassing, did I?" Like come on to him? A flashing image of brown eyes looming dangerously close set her stomach to churning again.

"I left the coffee in case you needed the caffeine," he said. A neat change of subject that was answer enough. Inwardly, Larissa cringed.

"Would you like me to pour you a fresh cup?"

"No, thank you." She couldn't take the burnt smell for a second time. "I think I'm better off with something cold. Maybe one of those twenty-dollar colas from the mini-bar." A few dozen pain relievers would be nice as well, she thought, combing her fingers through her hair. "I don't suppose these rooms also come stocked with aspirin."

"Next to the coffeepot."

Sure enough, a bottle of pills sat on the desk, next to the thermos. They hadn't been there before. "I suspected you might need them."

"Thank you."

"You're most welcome. We strive for nothing less

than one hundred percent satisfaction from all our guests. You said cola, correct?"

"That's not…" Before Larissa could utter a protest, she'd crossed the distance between terrace and cabinet. "Necessary."

"Of course it is. You're my guest. It's my job to make sure you're happy."

Although Larissa knew she was but one of a thousand guests, his lilting tone made the comment sound far more personal. As though she were the only one getting such hands-on treatment. She blamed her condition for the nervous fluttering in her stomach. "Even the hung-over ones?"

"Especially the hungover ones," he said popping open the can.

Larissa felt her cheeks flush. "My friends always did say I was high-maintenance."

"Are you?"

Good question. It always struck her funny, how her New York circle gave her that reputation. Growing up, she'd perfected the art of staying out of the way. Expensive dresses and "sticky kid stuff" didn't mix, according to her grandmother. If she was going to live there, Larissa had better learn to be careful.

"I prefer the term *particular,*" she replied.

Naturally, the universe decided to deflate her argument by tangling their fingers when Larissa reached for the soda can. The contact shocked her, so much so she jerked the can from his grip with a gasp. "I—um." She looked up in time to catch something—a light but not quite a light—flashing in his brown eyes. One blink and it disappeared. Hidden behind a polite, distant shade. Didn't matter. Even if she hadn't seen anything, the way his body stiffened at the contact was message enough.

She did them both a favor and stepped back. "Are you sure I didn't do or say anything stupid last night?"

"Nothing that bears repeating."

But something, nonetheless. Enough that her proximity made him uncomfortable. Great, she thought, cringing. Probably best that she not to press for details. "I'll do my best to stay under the radar for the rest of my visit. In fact, you'll barely notice I'm here," she added, taking a drink. Raising the can blocked her from seeing any skepticism.

On a positive note, the cold fizz felt wonderful on the back of her throat. Didn't completely wash away the cotton sock taste, but helped.

"Speaking of your stay, Señorita…" Reaching into his breast pocket, he removed a neatly creased sheet of paper. "I had some questions about your itinerary, now that your original plans have…"

"Bitten the dust?" Larissa supplied. "And please, call me Larissa. Formality seems a little silly at this point, don't you think?"

A hint of a smile played at the corner of his mouth. "Very well, *Larissa*. According to our records, you booked a number of activities for while you're staying with us."

Larissa remembered. The wedding coordinator made everything sound so wonderful over the phone. Unable to pick one or two, she selected everything. *You only get one honeymoon,* she'd rationalized. Why not make it as romantic as possible?

"I'm assuming you are no longer interested."

"You assume correct." Moonlight dinner cruises and couples massages weren't exactly solo activities. "The only activity on my schedule this week is following the angle of the sun." And hopefully figuring out what caused her perfect engagement to implode so spectacularly. *See, Tom, I am capable of introspection.*

Out of the corner of her eye, she caught the manager looking at his paper. "What? Is there a problem?"

"Not at all. I'll make sure all your previous events are canceled. Although you realize, by canceling at such short notice, you are respon—"

"Wait, wait, wait. Short notice? I canceled everything weeks ago."

He frowned. "Not according to our records."

"Well, your records are wrong." It would take more than a couple bottles of wine to erase that phone call from her memory. "What did you think I was going to do? Marry myself?"

"I assumed you didn't realize the wedding was off last night."

A logical assumption. Wrong, but logical. "I spoke to your wedding planner six weeks ago."

"Six weeks." He inhaled deeply. "Are you sure you spoke directly with Maria del Olma?"

"Positive, and she assured me canceling wouldn't be a problem."

Except apparently it was, if his quivering jaw muscle was any indication. "It appears there's been a miscommunication. Maria never noted the cancellation in your records."

"Well, I'm noting it now."

"I don't suppose you have written confirmation."

Larissa started to say yes, only to snap her mouth shut. Come to think of it, Maria didn't send any follow-up. Normally, Larissa would request a letter for her files, but she'd been so upset she must have let it go. Plus, Delilah was getting married, and Chloe was having relationship drama. Following up slipped her mind.

Could she start this whole trip over? Please?

Turning on her heel, she stomped onto the terrace. Sunshine and brightness be damned; she needed fresh air. In keeping with the morning's theme, she bumped into the lounge chair, stubbing her toe on a piece of plastic. Her missing sunglasses skidded across the floor. Score one positive. She shoved them on her face as she limped toward the railing.

At least the view remained as beautiful as she remembered. Unlike in New York where activity reigned 24/7, the day had yet to get started. The lagoon's surface was an aqua-green mirror, the only sign of visible life a solitary egret stalking the opposite shore. Occasionally the leaves in the upper canopy would rustle as an unseen bird, or monkey maybe, alighted from a branch. After four years of city living, Larissa forgot such serenity existed.

She remembered when she decided to get married at La Joya. The photos online looked so gorgeous, she'd fallen in love at first sight. What could be more romantic than getting married in paradise? Delilah and Chloe always teased her when she said stuff like that. *You think everything's romantic,* Delilah would say. Then they'd joked and call her a Bridezilla because she changed the venue three times.

She loved her friends, but they didn't understand her any more than Tom did. She'd been planning her wedding day since she was six years old, and spied on her first dress fitting through the crack in her grandmother's accordion doors. When the bride stepped out of the fitting room all white and sparkly, it was like a princess in real life. So pretty, so…special. Standing there, surrounded by faded yellow wallpaper, she glowed. They all did. All the brides, all the prom queens. Delilah did, too, when she married Simon. So much so, it took her breath away. All Larissa wanted was to glow like that. To have one day where she was the princess.

And she'd come so close. She could still remember how excited she'd been when Tom proposed. Handsome, successful, stable Tom Wainwright wanted her. All those years dreaming a man would fall in love with her, and whisk her off into the sunset and finally her dream had come true. Or so she'd thought.

A soft cough reminded her she wasn't alone. Señor Chavez had moved to her elbow. "I'm told our former wedding coordinator was quite distracted toward the end of her tenure with us. Her abrupt departure has caused more than a few loose ends."

"Let me guess. She left six weeks ago."

"I'm afraid so."

Figures. How much did Larissa want to bet she took off shortly after their phone conversation?

"I'll personally take care of canceling all your obligations. However, there is one problem."

Say no more. Larissa made her living typing advertising sales contracts. An agreement was an agreement. Without evidence she actually spoke with Maria del Olma, it was her word against the computer system. "You're telling me I'm liable for the expense. How much?" She tried to remember the terms of their agreement. Technically, she gave them fewer than twenty-four hours. Which meant…

There was a pause. "The entire amount."

Oh for crying out loud. "Seriously? The whole thing?"

"I am afraid so."

"Even though you guys are the ones who made the mistake." She shook her head. If she ever found Maria del Olma, she would slap the woman. No way Tom would pony up any of his share, either. She could hear him now. *This was your obsession, Larissa, not mine.*

"You know this is completely unfair, don't you?"

"I'm sorry."

"You can't take something off the bill?" After all, it was his staff member's error.

"Please?" she asked, lowering her glasses. She could tell from his expression, he was struggling with a response, the need to recoup costs clashing with his desire to make the guest happy. Might as well throw a little hangdog-inspired guilt in to tilt the scales in her favor. "What if I pay half?"

He sighed. "Best I can do is reduce the cost by thirty percent."

"Only thirty?" This was so not helping her headache. "What about the fact that I brought in business? Didn't you say those people signed a contract?" In her opinion, she deserved half off for that alone.

A shadow crossed the railing as he appeared at her elbow. Looking right, she saw him studying her with an arched brow. "I thought you didn't remember last night."

"I remember the reason for the Cabernet." In fact, she was pretty sure she toasted the couple's health and happiness once or twice.

"The Steinbergs are the reason I'm willing to go as high as thirty."

"Oh."

"You have to understand, space was blocked off, food has been specially prepared. The bridal cake alone…"

"No need to explain. I get it." She'd heard the sales department make similar arguments every day. Legal contracts didn't care about your sob story.

"I am sorry."

Not as sorry as she was. "What's going to happen to everything I ordered?" The custom-colored linen, the custom spa arrangements. Her headache doubled as she thought of all the little extras. She couldn't begin to list everything.

"What can be returned to venders will be returned, the rest, like the food, will be served through the restaurant or sadly, thrown away."

"Including the cake?" Her beautiful, three-tier white chocolate cake with raspberry mousse filling.

"I suspect it will become tonight's dessert special."

"Well, isn't that peachy? I can order my reception dinner and pay twice. I might as well go ahead and have the reception anyway."

He stared, clearly trying to read whether she was serious. "Aren't we being a bit extreme? It is, after all, only a dinner."

"Only a dinner?" No, chicken in a bucket was only a dinner. This was fifteen months of work and planning. "We're talking about my wedding reception."

"Which, had it taken place, would have had you marrying a man who was unfaithful."

Larissa winced. "Thanks for reminding me."

"Better to see things clearly now than stay lost in a romantic haze only to discover the truth five months later," he replied. "Trust me, a dinner is a far easier price to pay."

"Reception," Larissa corrected under her breath. There *was* a difference. Clearly, he thought her as silly as everyone else. Maybe they were right, and she was silly and overly romantic. Didn't make today sting any less.

"I think I'm going to lie down," she said with a sniff. "My head feels like it's going to explode."

"Of course. I'll make sure housekeeping doesn't

bother you," he said, moving toward the door. "Again, I am sorry for the miscommunication."

"Thirty percent sorry, anyway," she replied.

A small smile tugged at his mouth, but was quickly reined in. "I hope you feel better."

"Me, too," she told him, turning back to the view. Paradise had suddenly become very expensive.

So help him, if Maria del Olma or her boyfriend ever stepped foot on resort property again, he would strangle both of them with his bare hands. Teeth clenched, Carlos let out a low growl, and wished he was farther away from Larissa's front door so he could growl louder. He knew his predecessor and the coordinator left the resort in chaos, but he'd thought they'd caught the worst of the errors weeks ago. Apparently he thought wrong.

At least housekeeping did its job and spirited away both the waste bucket and room service cart while he was having his awkward discussion with Señorita Boyd. Guests might want to overindulge in Mexican paradise, but they didn't want to see the morning-after evidence. Señorita Boyd's—Larissa's—villa wouldn't be housekeeping's only stop. There would be a number of guests looking for dry toast and aspirin this morning.

But only one had the aspirin delivered personally by the general manager. Then again, none of the other guests invaded his thoughts all night long, either. He couldn't shake the image of her alone in her suite, drinking away a broken heart, to the point that when he woke up this morning, the first question in his head was how she fared.

The answer was about as he expected. The results of an alcohol-fueled pity party were never pretty. She looked like death warmed over, yesterday's sex appeal all but obliterated. To her credit, she tried, pretending her skin wasn't turning green while he talked about coffee. She lasted longer than he thought she would. Then, to work up the energy to negotiate her bill, as well. Admirable.

Too admirable seeing how he agreed to absorb thirty percent of her expenses. What came over him, making such an agreement? There were concessions and then there were concessions.

You know exactly what came over you. You looked into those big blue eyes and wanted nothing more than to make them sparkle.

Nonsense. He felt sorry for the woman, that was all. He knew all too well the pain of waking up and realizing you'd been living a delusion. And to have the covers ripped from your eyes so quickly… His own disenchantment unfolded slowly, and that pain was bad enough.

What would have happened if he'd realized the truth about Mirabelle from the beginning? Would he have still spent so much energy trying to make her happy? Probably. He'd been such a stubborn, romantic fool back then. Quick to fall, slow to let go.

Thank goodness he'd learned his lesson since then.

"Hola, primo! I've been looking all over for you."

His cousin, Jorge, jogged toward him. Like Carlos, he wore a black suit, although in Jorge's case, the jacket fit snugly around his barrel chest, a fact his cousin, an American football player at UCLA, took great pride in. "You do realize the resort has a perfectly good boat launch that allows you to cover the ground in half the time," he said, wiping the dampness from his upper lip.

"The boat launch doesn't allow me to see the beach

side of the resort. You might want to consider walking this route yourself. You're out of breath."

"Because I've been walking all over the property looking for you. Where have you been? You missed morning coffee."

"I was meeting with a guest."

"At this hour of the morning? Don't tell me you're picking up Rodrigo's bad habits."

Upon hearing his predecessor's name, Carlos's muscles tensed. "I was meeting with La—Señorita Boyd—regarding her wedding plans."

"Boyd. Isn't she the woman who checked in by herself yesterday?"

"She is. Maria forgot to cancel her wedding ceremony."

"You're kidding."

"I wish I was," Carlos replied with a sigh. "It appears she was too busy sneaking around with Rodrigo to let catering know. I had to break the bad news to Señorita Boyd this morning."

"You're not charging her, are you?"

"What choice do I have? Everything was ordered, and you know as well as I do the resort isn't in a position to eat those kinds of costs right now. I gave her as much of a discount as I could."

That he even had to conduct such a negotiation made him want to rip his hair from his head. "Sometimes I don't know who I want to strangle more. Maria for being so careless or Rodrigo for mismanaging the resort into financial crisis."

"I thought that's why I came aboard. To give you an extra set of hands so you could strangle both simultaneously."

This was one of those rare days when Carlos wanted

to take his cousin's joke seriously. "I need you to have someone go through every event Maria booked. Call the people and update their contracts. I do not want a repeat problem."

"I'll take care of it soon as we get back to the office."

"Thank you. Meanwhile, let's hope the wedding co-ordinator candidate I'm interviewing this afternoon is more levelheaded."

"He's male, so at least we won't have to worry about the two of you running off together."

Carlos ignored the remark. Wouldn't make a difference if the candidate was male or female. His days of losing his head were long gone and they both knew it. "Have you checked on the Campanella arrangements yet this morning?" he asked instead.

His cousin nodded. "Everything's running on schedule."

"Bueno."

"The señor and the señora did ask if you'd be willing to make a toast. Apparently someone they know was toasted by the captain of a cruise ship."

"And they would like something similar." Carlos thought of Larissa asking about her cake. "So many silly details. As if any will matter six months or even six hours later."

"It would mean a lot to them."

"Then I'll be there." Whatever a guest wanted. Especially guests like the Campanellas who seemed the type to leave online critiques. He wondered if Larissa Boyd left critiques? What would she say? The general manager efficiently provided aspirin?

"What's so amusing?"

He didn't realize he'd chuckled aloud. "Nothing.

"Uh-huh. Is everything all right, *primo?* You seem distracted this morning."

"Of course I'm distracted. I thought we were finished mopping up Rodrigo's and Maria's messes. Instead I had to bill a jilted customer on her wedding day."

"Better you than me. I would have caved completely out of sympathy."

Carlos didn't say how close he came to doing that very thing. The two of them fell into step back to the office. Although only midmorning, the sun already hung hot in the cloudless sky. Sunbathers, eager to turn their skin to Aztec gold, crowded both sides of the walkway. A mosaic of body shapes sprawled towels and chaise longues. Some of the more cautious tourists staked their claims on the popular cabana beds scattered strategically around the resort. He wondered, would Larissa Boyd find her way to one of them to sleep off her hangover or would she prefer the privacy of her terrace? Pale skin like hers would definitely burn if exposed too long.

"I have to admit," Jorge continued, "now that you tell me the wedding was canceled weeks ago, I'm surprised she's here. She must have had nonrefundable airline tickets."

"Or perhaps she simply needed to get away." He understood. After a while, all the well-meaning comments and sympathetic looks started to eat at your soul. It was either scream at people to go away or lose yourself in a place full of distractions. "Whatever her reason, ours is not the place to judge."

"The staff is fascinated by her. She made quite a memorable impression yesterday."

Blue smudged eyes and rat nest hair came to mind. Memorable indeed. Wonder what Jorge would say if he saw her this morning.

Interestingly, he was beginning to think this morning's version might be more memorable.

Mirabelle used to worry incessantly about her appearance, obsess over every hair, every ounce on her frame. As much as he reassured her that she would be the most beautiful woman in the world to him, his reassurances fell on deaf ears. Fell, and fell, and fell.

Something in him wanted to hope Larissa Boyd was different. Stronger.

"I don't think we've ever had a guest stay solo before." Jorge's voice saved his thoughts from traveling down a dark road.

"Of course we've had single guests," he replied.

"Single, yes, but always as part of a group. I can't remember ever having someone attend completely alone before. Certainly not a woman on her honeymoon."

"There's a first time for everything. Perhaps Señorita Boyd will spark a trend."

"Wouldn't that be nice?" Jorge grinned, his smile white and even. "We could become the new singles hot spot on the Riviera."

"You'd like that, wouldn't you? A hotel full of heartbroken women."

"What is it the Americans say about getting back in the saddle? Perhaps our señorita could use a stirrup."

The idea of his muscular cousin touching pale American skin stuck hard in his chest, giving him heartburn. "The señorita came to nurse a broken heart. I doubt she's interested in riding lessons."

"You never know. Not everyone—"

"Not everyone what?" Carlos whipped around.

"Nothing."

As if Carlos didn't know what he was going to say.

Not everyone grieves forever. Of anyone in the family, he expected Jorge to understand.

"It's just…" His cousin's voice softened. "It's been five years. Don't you think Mirabelle would want you to move on?"

"My days of giving Mirabelle everything she wanted died with her," he replied. Fitting, really. Given all the times he failed her in life, why should his grief be any different?

Besides, he thought, looking out to the Atlantic, if she'd wanted him to move on, she should have left his heart intact. "The only people I care about making happy these days are our guests. In Señorita Boyd's case, that means protecting her privacy."

"Were you worrying about her privacy when you had security checking on her last night?"

Carlos stopped short. He should have known Jorge would hear of his orders. The hotel staff was a small community, and nothing escaped notice. "She'd been drinking. I thought it a good idea to watch out for her."

"Old habits die hard, do they?"

Some did anyway. He thought about arguing the point, and blaming liability for his behavior, but Jorge would see right through the excuse. After all, his cousin knew all about Mirabelle. More, he'd been there the day they found her.

"I didn't want to take any chances. There were too many similarities." More than he wanted to admit.

Before he could say anything, the two-way radio on his cousin's waist began to crackle. The first sentence was all Carlos needed to hear. "Housekeeping emergency, Presidential Villa."

CHAPTER THREE

"I'M NORMALLY NOT this squeamish. I mean, I live in New York City. I've seen things." But this wasn't some scrambling little roach or scurrying sewer rat.

The maintenance man grinned. "Tarantula," he said.

No kidding, it was a tarantula. One the size of her fist and it was clinging to the bathroom wall next to the bathtub. Larissa shivered, thinking how she'd been sitting on the floor while it had been crawling around. For all she knew, it could have crawled right by her foot. Or her hair. Heebie-jeebies ran across her skin.

All she wanted to do was take a nice long bath, thinking a whirlpool and a jungle view would be exactly what she needed to shake off her pity party and start fresh. Nowhere did her plans include sharing her tub with a man-eating creature.

She looked over from her place atop the double vanity. "Can you get rid of it?"

"*Sí.*" Taking a hand towel, the man brushed the offending creature to the floor. Larissa squeaked and tucked her legs beneath her. How was that getting rid of anything?

Suddenly commotion sounded outside. "What happened?" Señor Chavez burst into the bathroom.

Oh, great, he was back. Was the general manager

going to witness every embarrassing moment she had this trip? This time he brought a friend along, as well. A second dark-suited man pulled up behind him.

"The radio said there was an emergency." He looked Larissa up and down with a scrutiny that made her wish she was wearing more than the complimentary robe. She tugged at the gap, making sure the cloth covered her legs.

"There was an emergency. I had an unwelcome guest," she replied, pointing toward the floor. The maintenance man had laid the towel on the ground, and the tarantula was crawling onto the cotton surface toward the middle. "I called to have someone get rid of him."

"I'm afraid tarantulas are an unfortunate byproduct of sleeping so close to the jungle," the other man replied with a smile. In comparison to Señor Chavez's scowl, it was positively blinding. "Our staff does its best to sweep them off the property, but every once in a while one makes its way into a room. I'm Jorge Chavez, the assistant manager, by the way."

"Pleasure to meet you." Larissa watched as the maintenance man scooped up the towel and spider. "What's he going to do with him?"

"Pedro will release him away from the property. Don't worry, he won't be back."

"I'm more worried about whether he has friends."

"I doubt there are others, but we'll sweep the villa to make sure. Of course, if you're truly uncomfortable, I can arrange for you to move to a different suite."

"No, that won't be necessary." With the spider gone, she was feeling a little braver. Not brave enough to move off the vanity, but braver. "As long as there are no others."

"I'll check the property myself."

"Thank you." She looked to the general manager, who hadn't said a word since bursting on the scene. At first, she blamed the silence on annoyance, but now that she looked closer, she saw that he'd gotten lost in thought. Distance allowed her to see past the shutters, revealing the haunted sadness she remembered from last night. A sympathetic ache curled through her stomach. He didn't seem the kind of man who would look so lost, and yet at the moment, *lost* was exactly the word she'd use.

"I didn't mean to cause a big scene," she said, raising her voice. Partly to let Jorge hear her and partly to shake Chavez from his thoughts. "When I called housekeeping, I didn't expect an entire army to show up."

"We were in the area."

"They said it was an emergency."

Both men spoke at the same time. Because it was the first Señor Chavez spoke since entering, Larissa turned her focus to him. He'd shaken off whatever ghost captured his attention and returned to scrutinizing with such ferocity you'd think she'd committed a crime, rather than been a victim. "It was an emergency to me," she said, defensiveness rising. "You all might be accustomed to finding poisonous spiders in your bathrooms, but I'm not."

"Contrary to popular belief, tarantulas aren't deadly. At best, you'd get a slight fever."

"Good to know. I'll sleep much better knowing if one does decide to bite me, I won't die." His blunt tone surprised her. What happened to the exceedingly polite, do-anything-to-please-the-guest manager she met this morning? This man seemed far more intent in glaring at her. She didn't understand the change, since she swore when he first burst into the room she saw real live fear on his face.

"No sign of any hairy friends," Jorge announced, returning to the doorway. "I'll have Pedro do a more thorough search and wash down the outside walls to make certain. I'm sorry for your discomfort."

"Me, too. Now I'll be looking everywhere for creepy crawlies my entire vacation."

"We can still switch you to a different suite, if you'd like."

"That really isn't necessary." A new room wouldn't stop her from tiptoeing every time she stepped through the door. A thought occurred to her. "Although, I wouldn't complain about having something taken off my bill. I mean, since my ability to relax has been compromised." Laying it on a bit thick, but seeing how she was in the hole for seventy percent of her wedding, every little bit helped. She arched a brow in Señor Chavez's direction, hoping he'd take the hint.

Instead, the man turned and spoke to his assistant in Spanish. Larissa didn't understand a word of their conversation, but she noticed Jorge's expression soften as he touched his boss's shoulder.

"I'm going to find Pedro," Jorge said after a moment. "If there's anything else we can do to make your stay more comfortable…"

"I'll let you know," Larissa replied. She had a feeling she'd be able to parrot the phrase by the end of the week.

"Guess I'm not doing well when it comes to being low-maintenance," she quipped once Jorge left.

The manager didn't crack even the hint of a smile. "I'll take another ten percent off your reception bill."

Looked like she owed the tarantula a thank-you note. "Too bad his friends weren't around. I might have gotten the costs knocked off the bill completely. I'm joking," she added at his continued glare. "Nothing would be worth having five or six of those suckers crawling on my walls. One was bad enough."

"You do realize you were never in any real danger. There was no need to tell housekeeping you had an emergency."

"I didn't." Was that why he was angry? Okay, so her voice might have been high-pitched and panicked-sounding, and she might have asked that they get to her room "right away," but she never used the word *emergency*. "It's not my fault your housekeeping staff takes panicked tarantula calls seriously. Is that why you came back? Because you thought I was in danger?"

"I was told it was an emergency."

A point he seemed incredibly intent on repeating. "*Emergency* could mean anything. It could mean a broken water faucet. What made you think something happened to me?"

He didn't answer. Rather he strode to the large window on the far end of the bathroom. Hands clasped behind his back, he looked out the large window at the mangrove trees waving in the breeze. For a moment, Larissa thought he'd pulled inward again. "How's your headache?" he asked.

"Better. Manageable." What did that have to do with anything?

"And your mood?"

"Well, until Hairy the Spider showed up, I was planning on soaking myself into a better one. Why?"

"You were pretty upset when I left."

"I was annoyed because I'm stuck paying for a wedding I'm not going actually have. Wouldn't you be? I still don't get what that has to do with—" Seeing him wash a hand over his features, a horrible thought hit her. "Don't tell me you thought I—"

"To be honest, I wasn't sure what to think," he said, turning from the window. "When I left you were shaky, upset, stumbling around. Any number of things could have happened. You could have slipped and fallen, cut yourself on a broken glass...."

"Thrown myself off the balcony."

"It's not funny," he snapped. "Distressed people behave unpredictably."

So they did. But, considering his over the top reaction, Larissa had also managed to touch a nerve. She regretted the remark. "I'm sorry."

"I am the one who should be sorry, Señorita Boyd. I overreacted. Hotel managers never like hearing there's an emergency situation. The word is somewhat of a hot button, I'm afraid."

Something about his expression, the way he avoided looking in her direction, said Larissa wasn't getting the complete answer. "Have you ever had a guest... you know?"

"A guest? No."

But someone. He'd avoided her gaze again. Larissa suddenly felt very, very bad about giving him a hard time. "I thought we decided you were going to call me Larissa."

"So we did. And you should call me Carlos."

"Fair deal. Thank you for saving me from the big mean spider, Carlos."

"Housekeeping saved you, but you're welcome anyway," he replied with a smile. Finally. While he didn't look completely relaxed, the shadows had receded from his features. Larissa was surprised to feel her own spine loosening as well.

Suddenly, it dawned on her that she'd held this entire conversation while curled up on the bathroom vanity. Slowly, she straightened one leg at a time, wincing at the stiffness in her kneecaps.

"How long have you been sitting there?" Carlos asked.

"Awhile. I was afraid to move past the spider, so I climbed up here to call housekeeping."

"Tarantulas don't jump."

"I didn't want to take any chances." She swung her legs, trying to get back her circulation. Her joints clicked with the movement, sending sharp jolts across her kneecap. "Looks like I'm going to need that soak more than ever now."

"Would you like some help getting down?"

"I've got it." She scooted her bottom forward, so that when she dropped, she wouldn't land with much force. When she reached the edge, her feet still dangled six inches or so from the floor. "Funny, I remember jumping up with far less issue," she said before sliding to the tile. No sooner did her toes touch down, than her ankles, numb from her sitting on them for so long, turned, causing her to wobble. Carlos immediately grabbed her elbows. They ended up standing hip to thigh. Larissa felt the roughness of summer wool against her skin, a reminder of how exposed she was beneath her robe. One little movement in either direction and the terrycloth would gap open. Warmth rose from the small space between their bodies. It joined with the coolness of his breath at the hollow of her throat, causing goose bumps.

"Are you steadier now?" he asked.

Larissa nodded. "Looks like you were right to worry. I'm not as steady as I thought." More disturbing was the rush of awareness coiling through her system. She couldn't remember ever reacting this strongly to a man's proximity before, not even Tom's, and here she'd reacted to Carlos twice. Afraid of what he'd think about her burning cheeks, she dropped her gaze to the floor.

"Perhaps after your bath," Carlos began.

"Perhaps." She wasn't so sure. Relaxing her muscles when they were already like jelly didn't seem like a smart idea all of a sudden. The solidness of his grip disappeared. Larissa reached back to hold the vanity.

"I'm sorry I gave you a hard time a moment ago. It was very kind of you to be concerned."

"No more than I would do for any guest."

Right. Because his job was to keep guests happy. She didn't know what had her thinking she was any different. "Still, it seems as though you're forever finding me in a bad way. Hopefully from here on in, I'll be—"

"Lower maintenance?"

"Exactly."

"We can only hope." With a curt nod, he turned and left her alone. As quickly as possible, Larissa noted.

One of these times, he was going to leave with a good impression. Thus far, she hadn't done a very good job.

In the meantime, she planned to soak away her hangover. Having indulged in her pity party, it was time to clear her head and figure out how she let things with Tom go so far south.

But, it wasn't Tom who came to mind as she sank into the lavender-scented water. It was a pair of deep brown eyes she'd known for less than twenty-four hours. And a strong touch she could still feel on her skin.

"You have no idea how much this means to me. To us." Paul Stevas played with the straw hat which, until five minutes ago, had covered his auburn curls. "Linda and

I didn't get to have a traditional wedding and there's nothing I'd like more than to give her the wedding she always dreamed of."

Carlos studied the man sitting across from him. Kid, really, as he couldn't be more than twenty-one or twenty-two. The young man corralled him as he was crossed the lobby, and asked for help marking his first wedding anniversary. "We're delighted to help," he said. "I promise, this will be the anniversary celebration of a lifetime."

"Linda's going to be so excited. I was afraid because I asked so last-minute…." Carlos swore the boy's eyes were growing moist. "I didn't want to say anything to her until you and I spoke, in case things didn't work out."

"Last minute is never a problem at La Joya. Our job is to make sure you and your wife have the perfect vacation. Give us a day to pull together a basic proposal package for you to work off of, and we can go from there."

"Fantastic." The young man pumped Carlos's hand. "And don't worry about the budget. Money's no object. I want her to have anything and everything she wants."

He better have a big line of credit, then. Granting his true love's every whim could get expensive. And in the end, it wasn't always enough.

Carlos kept his thoughts to himself. Business was business. If Señor Staves wanted to run himself into debt in the name of love, La Joya would gladly take his business. Served as a nice change of pace to rearranging the accounts to keep their vendors happy. Or negotiating bills with sexy blond guests.

He walked Señor Stevas to the lobby, the young man thanking him effusively every step of the way. "You made our vacation," he repeated, enthusiastically pumping Carlos's hand one last time before leaving.

"Nice to see such a satisfied customer."

His shoulder blades stiffened. Silly to think he could avoid Jorge forever. He could only imagine what his cousin thought about the way Carlos rushed to Larissa's villa. Over a spider, no less. What had he been thinking? Contrary to what he told Larissa, he'd heard the term *emergency* used countless times in his career. Never had he rushed to a room the way he did hers.

Not in five years anyway. When he was married to Mirabelle, he rushed everywhere for fear something might have gone wrong.

"Carlos?"

Turning, he saw his cousin helping himself to one of the complimentary water bottles kept at the front desk. "Those are for the guests."

His cousin's reply was to hand him a water bottle as well. "You didn't answer my question. What did you do to make his vacation?"

"I promised him a vow renewal ceremony to end all ceremonies."

"Sounds simple enough."

"Would be, if we had a decent wedding coordinator."

"I take it this afternoon's candidate failed to impress you?"

Busy drinking his water, Carlos could only shake his head. *Impress* was such a subjective term. While qualified, the man lacked imagination. Anyone could slap together menus and hang decorations. La Joya's reputation required someone with passion. Whose events sang with magic and romance and all the other intangibles people were willing to pay top dollar to experience. Thus far, he'd yet to find such a person.

Ironically, once upon a time he would have been that person. Pre-Mirabelle, of course, when he saw everything through a romantic lens. Those days seemed so long ago. When he was young and willing to do anything—be anything—for the woman he loved. He'd fallen for Mirabelle on sight, and from that moment on nothing mattered but making her happy.

Little did he know he'd taken on an impossible challenge. Mirabelle could never be happy, at least not for long. Her demons—and did she have demons—needed, needed, needed. Right up to the end, when, sensing his heart had no more to give, she shattered it to pieces.

Perhaps his past was the problem. Here he was relying on his gut to find a wedding coordinator when he'd used up all his romantic instincts years ago. He hadn't so much looked at another woman since Mirabell's death. Even if his heart were whole, why put himself at risk a second time?

"So what are you going to do?" Jorge's question brought him back to the issue at hand: Paul Stevas's request.

"Have catering pull together a proposal and hope that it's magical enough to please our young guest and his wife."

"Seeing his enthusiasm, I think you're safe."

"Let's hope. He did say money was no object."

"Well, if that's the case, perhaps you should steal Señorita Boyd's ideas. I took a look at her file when reviewing our bookings—which by the way, appear to be in order—she and Maria pulled together quite an extravaganza. Too bad, it won't be taking place."

"Too bad indeed, seeing as how we're now stuck paying for nearly half of it."

"Tarantulas happen. We'd have given the same deal for any other guest."

"Hmm." Carlos tossed his empty bottle into a wastebasket. Did he run to the other guests' rescue?

"Did Pedro spray her foundation? I would prefer we not have to make any further concessions."

"Juanita called it an emergency. You had no way of knowing—"

"Did he spray?" While he appreciated Jorge's effort, he wasn't in the mood to discuss what happened.

"Si."

"Good."

"He also checked her room again. As I suspected, this morning's visitor traveled solo. Although, if you'd like, I could double check myself."

"No." The vehemence with which he spoke embarrassed him. "I think we've wasted enough of our time on Señorita Boyd's tarantula."

"Right. I'll leave well enough alone, then." His cousin gave him a long look, full of smug double meaning that left Carlos feeling so exposed, he wanted to smack the man.

Instead, he said, "Thank you," and headed back to his office.

He spent the rest of the afternoon with his nose stuck in occupancy reports, desperately hoping to push the morning's escapades from his brain. He didn't like how Larissa Boyd had captivated his attention. The hold made him uncomfortable. At the same time, he couldn't stop thinking about her. If anything, the harder he tried, the more ingrained she became. How sexy she managed to look curled on that vanity. How, when she slid to the floor, her body came so close he'd felt the belt of her robe brushing against his pant leg. The way her lips parted in surprise…

Maldita! What was wrong with him? Larissa Boyd was but one attractive woman in a resort full of attractive women—a woman who'd been nothing but trouble, he might add. Why the sudden fascination? Had he been living so long as a monk that her innate sensuality had an extra strong grip?

Whatever the reason, he might as well forget getting any paperwork done. It was time for his evening walk anyway. Who knows what emergencies crept up while he was behind closed doors? Half the time, his inspection found the problems before the staff did.

Thankfully, after six weeks of robbing Peter to pay Paul, the resort appeared back on financial stable ground. The last thing they needed was a rash of bad reviews. But then, wasn't that his job? To anticipate and erase problems before guests ever had a chance to complain? Lucky for everyone, guests were the one class of people he could keep happy.

The lobby was quiet when he opened the door. He must have been lost in thought longer than he realized. Gone were the sun-worshippers and sightseers. The soft flop of sandals had been replaced by the click of high heels. Guitar music and laughter drifted through the terrace porticos. The bar was in full swing. Both restaurants would be, as well. Nighttime had arrived. He gave a few parting instructions to the night manager, and with Paul Stevas's proposal tucked under his arm, set off for the day's final inspection.

He wasn't looking for Larissa Boyd, he told himself as he passed the hotel's open air restaurant. He wasn't. If he was scanning the tables at the open-air restaurant, it was simply to double-check service. Her presence leapt out at him purely by coincidence. How could a man not notice her? She was the only woman dining alone.

What a difference from the woman he left this morning. Gone were the smudged makeup and floppy hair, replaced by a thick blond bob. The strands brushed just below her jawline, the restaurant lighting turning the color silver. Perhaps the lighting was why her skin looked more radiant, as well. The waitperson said something, and she smiled with such enthusiasm, Carlos swore her face glowed.

Before he realized, he was halfway across the dining room floor.

She was gazing out the window when he approached the table. Mindlessly sipping from her champagne glass. A fringed shawl, so delicate a strong breeze would carry it away, covered her shoulders. Every time she raised her drink, the material would slip, revealing a sliver of white shoulder. Not much. Only enough to make you want to see more. Reminded him of the morning's terrycloth robe, modest and tantalizing at the same time. Like this morning, his body reacted appreciatively.

His voice was uncharacteristically hoarse when he spoke. "Enjoying your dinner?"

She turned quickly, liquid spilling over the rim of her glass. "Señor Chavez! You startled me."

"*Lo siento.* I didn't mean to sneak up on you," he said, retrieving the handkerchief from his breast pocket. "And if I'm to call you Larissa, you should call me Carlos."

It dawned on him she was the only guest he'd ever suggested use the familiar term. Oddly, the suggestion felt completely natural. "I take it, our view has claimed another victim."

"Afraid so. I thought my villa cornered the market on beautiful, but I was wrong."

"Paradise through every window."

"For once, the advertising brochure doesn't exaggerate." She slipped the cotton from his fingers with a smile, a little shyer than the one she gave the waiter, but bright nonetheless. "You must think I'm a horrible klutz. Every time we meet, I'm stumbling or something. I swear I'm usually more graceful. Not much, but definitely more than you've seen."

"This spill I'll take the blame for. The others we'll blame the champagne."

"Oh, I blame the champagne for a lot of things, including not seeing my hairy visitor sooner. Cristal definitely does not come up as smoothly as it goes down." His eyes must have flickered to the glass because she hastily added, "Sparkling water. My drinking alone days are finished."

Good to know. Perhaps now she'd stop occupying his thoughts so much.

Or perhaps not, he thought, scanning her length. Worry certainly wasn't what he was thinking at the moment. "You certainly look like you've recovered from your ordeals."

"I have, thank you." She handed back his handkerchief, now damp. "Amazing what a long soak and a five-hour nap can do for your psyche. I'm ready to start this trip fresh."

"I'm glad. I hope your stay is everything you envisioned."

"Well, that ship sailed six weeks ago, but I do plan to make the most of it. Who knows when I'll get back to paradise?"

There was that smile again. The muscles in Carlos's

cheeks tightened, making him realize he was smiling broadly in return. "Well, let's hope it's not too long between trips."

This was the point where he normally moved on, to greet another set of guests, to complete his perimeter check. "By the way, if you haven't ordered yet, I recommend starting with the *ceviche*. It is Frederico, our head chef's, specialty."

"Oh, I intend to. Along with the *sopa de lima* and the *pollo ticul.*"

He recognized the menu immediately. "You're having your reception dinner."

"Of course. I planned it. I'm paying for it. By God, I'm going to eat it."

"You're a woman on a mission, then."

"Damn straight. And after dinner, I plan on having two pieces of my cake. Diet be damned."

Just as he hoped, she was stronger than she first appeared. Carlos's appreciation grew stronger. Did she had any idea how attractive a quality resilience could be? "In that case, I hope the meal is everything you hoped for. *Buenas noches.*"

Finally, his legs moved and he took a step toward the next table.

"Carlos, wait." Her fingers brushed his cuff, stopping him in his tracks. Turning, he caught her peering up through downcast eyes, the blue still vivid in spite of the mascara curtain. Her lower lip worried between her teeth. Simultaneously erotic and shy, the gesture turned his entire body alive with an awareness he hadn't felt in half a decade.

"I don't suppose you'd like to join me?" she asked.

CHAPTER FOUR

"Just for a little while. A drink."

Larissa could feel her cheeks getting hotter by the second. She was handling this all wrong. After this morning's "moment" in the bathroom, he probably thought she was hitting on him. His tense expression said as much.

"It would give me the chance to pay you back for all your kindness the past twenty-four hours," she continued, hoping the reason was enough to erase any hint of a come-on. She didn't know why his opinion mattered so much to her, but it did. This morning's tarantula incident clearly touched a nerve, and she hated being the one responsible for bringing up bad memories. She'd spent a good chunk of the afternoon dwelling on the horrible impression she'd made.

When she wasn't flashing upon the way his hands felt gripping her elbows, that is.

Why that moment caused such an intense wave of attraction to begin with was a mystery. After a long soak, she decided to blame a hazardous combination of exhaustion, alcohol and adrenaline. Along with a dose of old-fashioned female appreciation. He was a handsome man, after all.

"There is no need to pay me back for anything," Carlos said. Larissa blamed the tightness she heard in his voice on her imagination. "I was only doing my job."

"I disagree. You went above and beyond, and I'd like to say thank you. Please." She gestured to the empty seat across from her. "Word on the street says the kitchen has an abundance of chicken."

"Well…"

She could hear him weighing the option in his head. "Seeing as I do own thirty percent of the chicken…."

"You mean forty percent, don't you?" she corrected. "Don't forget, I earned an additional ten percent thanks to Hairy the Tarantula."

"Of course, forty percent. How could I forget?" His comment held a hint of humor, however, and he took a seat. Instantly, a waiter appeared with a place setting.

"Wow, I didn't even see him watching the table," Larissa noted.

"You aren't supposed to. We train our staff to be as discreet as possible."

"So as not to disturb the moment."

"Precisely. Our guests like their privacy. Although—" he paused while the waiter poured a glass of water "—there are moments when our staff has been too good at their job."

"I don't understand."

"Put it this way. While my staff members might be discreet, our guests don't always follow the same rules."

Larissa got the picture. "I suppose love and paradise will cause people to get carried away."

"Yes, they will," he muttered into his glass.

Great, she'd gone and said the wrong thing again. Quickly, she rushed on, hoping to erase whatever bad thoughts she'd churned up in his mind. "Luckily, your staff can relax where I'm concerned. There are absolutely no indiscretions on my agenda."

A hint of a smile played on his lips. "Back to practicing low-maintenance, are we?"

"Hey, it wasn't my fault a man-eating spider decided to vacation in my tub."

The waiter reappeared with their appetizers. "I've often heard Americans call *ceviche* the Mexican sushi. Interesting that you picked so many traditional Yucatán dishes for your reception," Carlos remarked as he set down the plates of spiced fish. "Most of our American guests insist on American staples for their big day."

"American food didn't go with my destination theme. I figured why travel all this way and not completely embrace the culture? Consistency makes for a far more memorable event."

"You sound like an expert."

"Nah, just something I learned from my grandmother. She was a seamstress, and always telling brides 'you don't want one bridesmaid sticking out like a sore thumb and ruining the photo.' I figured the same advice applies to the rest of the wedding."

"Interesting logic."

"Thank you." Larissa decided to accept his remark as a compliment, whether he meant it as such or not.

Almost twelve hours since she saw him last, and, with the exception of his five-o'clock shadow, he looked as darkly perfect as he did this morning. The wear and tear of the day enriched his appearance. The wrinkles in his suit added depth; the stubble gave him a feral edge.

He ate with the same predatory grace that dominated all his movements. The prongs of his fork slipped neatly between his teeth, disappearing as his lips sealed shut, only to slip free a moment later. Larissa had never paid much attention to how a man ate before, but now she found herself following every bite.

"Is something wrong?" he asked suddenly. "You've barely touched your appetizer. Don't tell me after all your effort, you don't like the dish?"

"The fish is delicious. I—" *I was too busy staring at your mouth to eat.* She speared a piece of fish with her fork. "I was thinking how nice it is to have someone to talk with. Privacy is great, but when you're by yourself, things can get a little dull. Let's face it, there's only so much introspection a woman can do." Not that she'd done much at all yet.

Quiet settled between them, as they chewed their food. "Do you mind if I ask you a question?" Carlos asked after a moment.

You had to commend him for politeness. Most people would have gone ahead and asked, the question was so obvious. "You want to know what I'm doing here by myself in the first place."

"Far be it for me to downgrade my own resort, but La Joya is a couples getaway. If you wanted to spend time in the sun, there are dozens of quality Mexican resorts that cater to single guests. Why come here, especially considering you and your fiancé planned...?" He let the question drift away.

"You mean, why pour salt in the wounds by showing up at the same resort where I planned to be married?"

"Exactly."

Where did she start? Setting down her fork, Larissa folded her hands in front of her and tried to put her thoughts in order. Since she'd given the same speech to Delilah and Chloe, the answer should have come easily, but her mind didn't seem to be working the same way today as it had been the past six weeks. "Six weeks ago, I would have said the same thing. Why come here. In fact, I had my hand on the phone the next day, planning to cancel everything. Plane tickets and reservations included."

"What made you change your mind?"

"Michael D'Allesio."

"Who?"

Goodness, but she hadn't said that name in almost nine long years. "He was a boy I knew in high school." Pimply-faced Mike D'Allesio who played trumpet in the band and worked Saturdays at the ice cream shop. He'd always smiled at her when she went to his window to order. "I asked him to go to the prom, and he said yes, only to take Corinne Brown instead."

"He canceled?"

Larissa shot him a look. Clearly he'd never been an unpopular chubby girl. "More like never followed through."

"You mean, he stood you up?" A foreign concept to someone like him, who lived and breathed etiquette.

"Turns out he only said yes because I put him on the spot and he didn't know how to say no."

"So did you go by yourself?"

"No. I sat home and stuffed my face full of cream cheese brownies while wearing my prom dress." She could still see herself, mascara streaking her face, crumbs spilling onto her lap. Such a pathetic scene. The memory left her sick to her stomach.

"I'm sorry."

"It was eight years ago," she said, shrugging. "Anyway, I had the telephone in my hand to cancel this trip when I saw the picture of my wedding gown I stuck on my mirror and I said, 'screw it.' I wasn't sitting home again. At least here I can sit around and stare at palm trees

"Plus I had nonrefundable airline tickets," she added, seeking to lighten the moment. There was only so much pathos a woman could take.

Across the table, Carlos choked on his drink.

"What?" she asked.

"The part about the airline ticket. Jorge suggested that very same reason this morning."

"You and he were talking about me?"

"I talk about a lot of my guests."

"Oh." She felt a tiny thrill anyway. "Jorge… That's the man who arrived with you this morning, right?"

Carlos nodded. "My cousin."

"I wondered when I heard you two had the same last name. I figured you were either related or Chavez is the Mexican version of Smith."

"We came here together about six weeks ago, shortly after the general manager left."

"I thought you lost your wedding coordinator."

"We lost both," he said in a sharp tone. "They ran off together."

"Oh, my gosh, you're kidding. My friend Delilah just married our boss. They fell in love on a business trip."

"I doubt your friend's relationship and this one are the quite same. Unless your boss also left a wife and an infant son behind."

Oh. "I didn't realize. The poor woman." Larissa's heart went out to her. "And here I thought Tom blind-sided me."

"I'm sorry, I shouldn't have said anything. That was inconsiderate of me."

"No, it's okay." At least now, she understood his comments from this morning. "You were right, when you said it's better I found out before the wedding.

"Funny thing is, I didn't stop to think there might have been a wife when you said they ran off. I assumed they were soul mates."

"More like partners in crime," he said, signaling for the waiter.

"Or both."

"You're joking."

"Look, I'm not saying they were right or even that they're nice people, but love is unpredictable. The heart wants what the heart wants."

"You're far more generous than I am. Considering your own story, I would have thought you'd be far more bitter."

The waiter arrived to clear their plates. Grateful for the interruption, Larissa watched silently as a copper hand lifted away her half-eaten plate. Carlos's comment tapped a can of worms she wasn't ready to deal with yet, including the fact she had yet to feel any real heartache over Tom's leaving.

"What's done is done, right?" she said, when it was once again the two of them. It was the best answer she could muster at the moment. Everything else required deeper explanation, such as accepting that maybe Tom hadn't been the man of her dreams after all. "We can't go back and change the past."

"Unfortunately, we cannot."

Sharpness coated his words, reminding her, too late, that he'd lost his wife. Now it was Larissa's turn to regret her words. She opened her mouth to apologize, only to be stopped by a couple rushing the table.

"We're sorry to interrupt your dinner, Señor Chavez," the man said.

"It's my fault. Paul told me about the vow renewal and I was so excited, I had to say thank you in person."

Carlos introduced them as Paul and Linda Stevas, guests at the resort. "Señor and Señora Stevas want to host a vow renewal ceremony at the end of the week to celebrate their anniversary."

"Congratulations," Larissa said.

Looking at them, she couldn't believe they were old enough to get married, let alone renew their vows. The woman was so waifish and thin, she belonged on a runway. Both her legs together wouldn't make one of Larissa's thighs. Her eyes, which along her lips, took up most of her face, glowed with enthusiasm.

"Thank you," she replied. "I can't wait to hear Señor Chavez's ideas. Paul tells me they're amazing."

"No, I said I'm sure they will be amazing," Paul corrected. "I mean, look around. How can they not, right?"

"Like I told your husband this afternoon, we'll do everything in our power to make sure your anniversary is everything you wish it to be."

Based on the young woman's squeal, neither she nor her husband noticed that Carlos's smooth-as-silk answer lacked enthusiasm. She clapped her hands together. "You have no idea how awesome this is, Señor Chavez. It's, like, a dream come true. I mean, it *is* a dream come true."

"I told you she would be thrilled."

"I'm glad you're both happy," Carlos replied. "We want nothing less here."

"Oh, trust me, we are beyond happy," she assured

him. "I don't know if Paul told you, but we didn't have a real wedding…"

"Linda, baby, I don't think we need to go into all that now. We're keeping Señor Chavez from his dinner."

The young woman was so pale, her blush looked crimson in comparison to the rest of her. "When I get excited, I tend to babble."

"I do the same thing," Larissa told her. "No worries. And your husband's right. There's no way you can go wrong with any event you hold here. Whatever you do, make sure you book a private moonlight cruise on the lagoon. The two of you alone under the stars, the smell of mango in the air. It'd be great way to end your trip. Like a repeat wedding night."

Linda blushed again. "That does sound wonderful."

"Can we do that?" Paul asked, looking to Carlos.

"I don't think that will be a problem," Carlos replied.

The pair grinned, then Paul slipped his arm around Linda's shoulders. "Come on, baby. We've taken up enough of Señor Chavez's time. We'll talk more tomorrow."

"They're so sweet," Larissa said after they'd walked away. "Sounds like they're really excited to renew their vows."

"Hmm."

"Is there a problem?" So far as she could see, Paul and Linda were dream guests, eager to spend money and enjoy everything the hotel had to offer. Plus, she did find it sweet the guy wanted to give his wife a fancy anniversary celebration.

"Excuse me. I'm sorry to interrupt again." Paul suddenly appeared back at their table. "But that midnight cruise thing you suggested. Pull out all the stops. I want to make it a night Linda won't forget."

"Of course," Carlos replied. "We wouldn't give you anything less."

"Okay," she said, once Paul was out of reach. "He just became doubly sweet. Doing all this to make his wife happy."

"I only hope he finds everything worth the trouble."

"Why wouldn't he? You saw his wife's face. She's thrilled."

"Tonight. What about tomorrow? Or the week after the ceremony? And if he has to go to this much bother for their first anniversary, what will he have to do for the second to make sure the smile stays on her face?"

"Wow, could you be any more cynical? The two of them obviously eloped, and now the guy wants to indulge his wife. What's wrong with that? You were married. Didn't you oblige your wife now and then?"

"Now and then," he replied.

"See? I rest my case."

"So you do." An odd look crossed his face and Larissa couldn't help but wonder if his concession was more to avoid an argument than because of any point she might have made. There'd been a definite edge to his voice that suggested as much.

"I'm sorry," he continued. "I'm afraid I'm not cut out to be an event coordinator. I was brought here to handle the financial issues, not plan weddings."

There was more to his outburst than being uncomfortable with the job, Larissa was certain of that. She was beginning to think that, for some reason, he had a deep dislike for weddings in general. Rather than press the issue, however, she allowed him his excuse.

"Don't you have a catering manager who can handle these kinds of events for you?"

"You saw what kind of mistakes Maria left us to deal

with. My catering manager is already overcommitted handling the events on the books. Asking him to plan a last-minute ceremony in addition to everything else he's doing might cause him to quit. Then where would I be? I will take care of planning Paul's and Linda's event myself."

Larissa nodded at the manila folder that lay by his bread dish. "So is that the work you're bringing home? Their ceremony?"

"It is. I plan to write their proposal after supper."

"What do you have planned?" Like Linda, Larissa found herself eager to hear his ideas. Probably not for the same reasons, but eager nonetheless.

"Does that include the moonlight cruise you sold them on a second ago?" Carlos asked.

"Yes."

Her request had to wait, because the waiter chose that moment to bring out the next appetizer. Two bowls filled with a pale green broth. *"Sopa de lima,"* he announced. Larissa stirred the mixture with her spoon, letting the citrus smell wash over her. "Tom thought all these details were a waste of money, too."

"I didn't say I thought it a waste of money."

"But you don't think much of all the planning, either. And don't say that's not true," she said, shaking her spoon, "because it's obvious you don't."

She could tell he was choosing his argument by the way he hesitated. "So many people…they spend all this time and effort creating the perfect memory, and for what? So they can pick apart the event after the fact, and focus on the mistakes? Every day, my managers bring me complaints. The food wasn't what they expected. The temperature in the room was set incorrectly. The service wasn't discreet enough. The service was too discreet. The list is endless.

"Makes me wonder why people even bother," he added, stabbing at his bowl with his spoon. "Especially when no matter what you do, you can't make them happy."

Larissa refrained from comment. The acerbity accompanying his last comment suggested their conversation had crossed from theoretical to personal. Very personal, in fact. She thought of their other encounters. His exaggerated concern this morning, his shuttered expression. Didn't take a detective to realize her host carried some dark, heavy baggage.

Curiosity pushed her to find out what, but she held back. This vacation was about focusing on her own issues, not distracting herself with someone else's. No matter how much someone else's issues cried for her attention.

"Unfortunately for you, Paul and Linda *are* bothering," she said, pointing out the obvious instead. "And from the sounds of things, Paul's looking for spectacular."

"Unfortunately, yes, he is, and if you have any spectacular suggestions, I am more than willing to hear them."

"I am the last person to ask for suggestions. Chloe and Delilah said I was a regular Bridezilla when it came to planning mine."

"Pardon?"

"You know, a wedding monster." One of those very people he'd just described.

For the first time since their conversation began, a small smile tugged at his mouth. "I know," he said, sipping his soup. "I read your proposal."

If she weren't so distracted by the way his lips covered the spoon, Larissa would have been insulted. Damn, but he turned eating sexy. "There's nothing wrong with wanting perfection." She'd given the same argument to Tom and her friends dozens of times.

The smile tugged wider. "If you say so."

"I wouldn't expect you to understand." No one else did. Her ex certainly hadn't.

She turned to stare at the beach. The long silver-white path that stretched to the horizon. "Did you ever dream of something your whole life only to have it suddenly come true?" she asked. "When that moment does finally come, you want to create this perfect sliver of time. A memory that stands up to all the dreams and wishes. Because you only get one shot at making fantasy reality. If you don't go all out, you'll spend the rest of your life replaying the memory and wishing you'd had."

Her cheeks grew warm realizing how much she'd rambled on. "Anyway," she said, turning back, "that's why people get crazy about their weddings."

Across the table, Carlos was studying her with an indistinguishable expression, his brown eyes sharper than she'd ever seen them. "Go ahead and tell me I'm over the top," she said, tugging her shawl over her exposed shoulders. After all, Tom said that and worse when they broke up. *Over the top, superficial, caught up in the unimportant.* The can of worms she didn't want to open—the one in which Tom might have a point—threatened to raise its lid again.

Eyes yet to leave her, Carlos leaned back in his chair. His long fingers tapped at the file on the table. "So what would you do if you were planning the Stevases' ceremony?"

"Well, to begin with I would…" She stopped when she caught him looking down at the file. "Are you trying to pick my brain for ideas?"

"I merely asked a hypothetical question."

Hypothetical, her foot. "You want me to help you plan the Stevases' recommitment ceremony, don't you?"

"You have to admit, you do have a knack for this sort of thing. First, the Steinbergs, then the Stevases with the moonlight cruise."

"A few suggestions does not a knack make." Although she had to give him credit. At least he didn't try and pretend he wasn't looking for input. "Isn't there a rule about making guests work?"

"A few suggestions does not work make," he replied.

Damn him, for throwing her own retort back in her face.

"Plus," he added "you've already done more work since your arrival than much of my staff."

His tone turned gentle. "I listened to you describe our cruise to the Stevases. You painted exactly the kind of picture they needed to hear. They're looking for magic, and frankly, when it comes to creating magic, I'm…" He paused to study the orchid in the center of the table. "Empty."

"Empty," Larissa repeated. An odd choice of words. It implied that once upon a time he'd had magic. The notion he lost a part of himself made her heart ache.

"All I ask is that you give me a few ideas over dinner. Perhaps things you would have done yourself."

"You want to use my defunct wedding ideas?"

"I want to hear your suggestions. Please. I would consider it a great favor."

Aw, damn, did he have to lean forward so that the

candlelight made his eyes sparkle? "What's in it for me?" she asked him.

"Pardon?"

If he was going to ask her to use her wedding to inspire someone else's happiness, she should at least get something out the arrangement. "Seems to me there should be some kind of compensation. Especially since I'm stuck paying for sixty percent of my own failed wedding." The mention of which should be causing more heartache than it was. She truly didn't seem to be missing Tom at all. Again, she slammed the worm can.

Carlos shook his head. "You are asking for me to eat more of the cost."

"Only fair, isn't it?"

He didn't answer. Probably because he had no argument. The business world survived on an unwritten *quid pro quo* of favors. Any good business man would realize that fact. Larissa sipped her sparkling water, and waited for his response.

"Very well," he said, after a moment. "I will erase the wedding charges from your bill."

"Great." Finally, something on this trip was going her way.

"But," he said, tilting his glass in her direction a warning if ever Larissa saw one, "any new expenses you wring up are completely non-negotiable."

"Fair enough." Getting a tan didn't cost much. What mattered was writing off the past.

She moved her soup to her left and learned forward. "Now, what do you say, we get to work."

"Then, we wrap up everything that evening by sending them on the moonlight dinner cruise I told them about. What do you think?"

"I will have to check on cruise availability," Carlos said, "but other than that, I'd say it sounds terrific. You're a natural at this."

The compliment warmed Larissa more than it should. "Making sure I earn my percentage is all."

"You have and then some. Are you sure you haven't planned events before?"

"Just my wedding," Larissa replied. "Told you, I did a lot of research." Not to mention that, when you spend most of your life fantasizing about something, planning became second nature.

During dinner, Carlos had shifted his chair to the side of the table so they could share the paperwork. He'd shed his jacket, as well.

You'd think the rolled-up sleeves would soften the edge she found so attractive earlier, but a relaxed Carlos was even more alluring. She couldn't blame alcohol or sleep deprivation this time, either. Beneath the table, his knee rested a hair's breadth from hers. Every shift of his body sent the seam of his slacks brushing across her skin. Good thing she had a shawl. Clutching it kept her from breakout in goose bumps.

"Well, your research has paid off for me three times this week," he said, stealing a sip of water. "I don't suppose you want to stay and replace Maria?"

"Why not? I'll chuck my life in New York and move into the Presidential Villa." Talk about the ultimate running away from your troubles. She smirked, waiting for his comeback to her pretend acceptance. What she got was a return grin that made her stomach somersault.

A soft cough broke the conversation. Their waiter hovered by Carlos's elbow, his face a combination of nerves and expectancy. "I'm sorry to interrupt, Señor

Chavez, but the rest of the staff wants to know if they could break down the rest of the room."

To her surprise, she and Carlos were the only two people left in the restaurant, the other tables long vacant. So engrossed was she in planning the Stevases' ceremony, she didn't notice the diners coming and going.

"Of course they can, Miguel," Carlos replied. "We'll be out of their way shortly."

"I didn't realize we were keeping your staff from doing their jobs," she said after the server disappeared. "Good thing I decided against having a third piece of cake or they'd still be waiting."

"Would you like—" He had his hand half up, ready to flag Miguel, when she grabbed his forearm.

"Thanks, but I've already had two pieces too many. As it is, I'll have to starve myself tomorrow to make up for the calories."

"Ah, but surely you've heard calories don't count in paradise."

"Tell that to my hips."

"Your hips have nothing to complain about." Her flush must have made him realize how his compliment sounded because she caught a tinge of pink creeping across his cheekbones. His gaze swept downward, to his forearm where her hand continued to rest. She knew she should move, but she couldn't. Like when you touch a hot stove and are unable to pull back quickly despite the sizzle.

Finally, he broke contact with her, sliding his arm free so he could straighten the paperwork. "Thank you again for all your assistance."

"Um, my pleasure." Larissa grabbed her water, hoping to hide her embarrassment. "What else was I going to do tonight? Take myself for a moonlit stroll?"

What Larissa didn't want to tell him was how much she enjoyed his company. Once you got past the stiffness, she discovered he had a very easy way about him. They worked surprisingly well together, too. Carlos was genuinely open to her suggestions, limiting his challenges to budgets and logistics. He contributed a few ideas of his own as well, which surprised her. Not that he had ideas, but the kind of ideas he put forth. For a man who claimed to be "empty" he had a knack for suggesting small, romantic gestures to complement her big picture ideas. More than once, Larissa wondered if his suggestions came from professional or personal experience. Did he, for example, leave orchids on his wife's pillow? If so she'd been a lucky woman, Larissa decided, with a pang in her stomach.

"I'm afraid you may have to take that stroll anyway," Carlos told her. He pointed to his watch. "The last launch departed ten minutes ago."

"It did?" She'd truly lost track of time. "And here I swore tonight I'd get a better night's sleep."

"Fortunately, you're on vacation. Going to bed late is part of the bargain."

"You mean like calories not counting?"

"Exactly." Slipping the papers into their file, he rose to his feet. "I'll walk you back to your villa."

"There's no need. I'm sure I'll be perfectly safe." Wasn't as though she was wandering some anonymous street in Mexico. "If not, I've got pepper spray in my bag."

"I won't ask how you got a weapon through customs," he said with a chuckle. "But I do insist on walking you. Even in the safest of resorts, unexpected accidents can occur.

"Besides," he added, the words coming out low and close to her ear. "It would be rude of me to let you travel unescorted."

Heaven forbid, Larissa thought, tugging at her shawl. With the way his voice sent shivers traveling down her spine, she'd rather the rudeness.

CHAPTER FIVE

"TELL ME ABOUT New York City," Carlos said once they'd left the restaurant. "What do you do there?"

"You mean, when I'm not planning weddings?" She gave her shawl another tug. If she pulled any tighter, she'd choke herself with the silk, but at least the action gave her something to do with her hands. She'd tried leaving them down by her sides, but felt awkward swinging her fingers near the edge of his jacket, like she was waiting for him to snatch her hand in his grip. Larissa wondered if he felt the awkwardness, too, because he had his hand stuffed deep in his pockets.

"I work for an advertising agency," she told him. "Media sales."

"Sounds interesting."

"You're being polite." Media sales definitely wasn't interesting, at least not to her. "But it pays the bills a lot better than catering."

"Ah, so you did plan events."

"Waitress. Before that, a cashier at a florist. NYU didn't pay for itself. I had to come up with the money somehow."

"You're not from New York originally, are you?"

He stated rather than asked. How they segued from her attending New York University to her hometown,

Larissa wasn't sure, although she could guess. Eight years of Big Apple living hadn't completely killed her twang. "I moved there when I was eighteen."

"Because you wanted to attend NYU."

"Because it wasn't Texas." As she expected her answer earned her a look. "In a small town, your reputation is pretty much set at birth," she told him. "I wanted to go some place where I could stretch my wings." Not to mention finding a happily ever after was a heck of a lot easier in a city where you weren't completely surrounded by taller, thinner and blonder. Wasn't as if her grandmother cared if Larissa left; she was glad to be done with her.

"How about you?" Tired of talking about herself, she decided to turn the tables. Maybe in his answers, she'd gain insight into what made him so cynical. "What made you go into the hotel industry?"

"Born into it," he replied. "The Chavez family has a long tradition in the hospitality industry. In fact, my grandfather built one of the first luxury hotels on the Baja peninsula."

"Wow. I'm impressed. Explains how you and your cousin both got sent here."

"You'd be hard-pressed to find a hotel in this country that doesn't employ a Chavez."

"So the name is like Smith."

He chuckled, the warm sound slipping under her skin. "In a way. In addition to being large, we're encouraged to learn the business from the ground up, even if that means working for our competition. My very first job was on the grounds crew for a rival property when I was fourteen years old. You'd be amazed what you can learn about the business weeding gardens. Watch your step."

They reached a section where the walkway stepped down. In spite of the area being well lit, Carlos still reached over and took her elbow. Unlike this morning, when she had a bulky terrycloth robe to protect her, this time his hand touched bare skin.

This was getting ridiculous. There was absolutely no reason for one man to cause this much physical response. Yet here she was, her entire body tingling from the slightest of contact.

"Did your wife work in the hotel business, too?"

He stiffened at the question. *You can't stop poking that nerve, can you, Larissa?* Part of her wondered if she broached the topic on purpose, to distract from the awareness stirring in her stomach.

"Mirabelle was a fashion model," he replied. "We met when I was working a property in California."

That distracted it, all right. Of course his wife had been a model. A man like Carlos, with his magnetic looks and natural virility, would attract only the best. "She must have been very beautiful." Tall, long and leggy, no doubt.

"Yes, she was."

"So you lived in California," she said, shooing away the jealousy that immediately cropped up.

"For a while. Mirabelle had…health…issues so we moved back to Mexico City. I thought being close to her family would help her feel better."

The stilted, practiced tone of his answer unnerved her. He was holding back. Larissa could sense the "but" hovering in the air, the same way she could feel the torment he fought to keep from his voice. All of a sudden, what had been awareness grew into a desire to wrap her arms around him and bring comfort.

She preferred the awareness.

They grew quiet after that. Now more aware of his proximity than ever, Larissa hugged her shawl close to her body. The flimsy material needed anchoring against the sea breeze anyway. She looked across the beach to the ocean which loomed black next to the silver land. Between the moon's brightness and the walkway lights, she could make out the white of the foam left behind each time a wave crashed. "I wonder if the tide is going in or out," she mused aloud.

"Out," Carlos replied. "See the line?" He stopped and pointed to a strip of land where the sand shifted from silver to the color of gray cement. "That is the high tide mark. The sand above the water is freshly wet, which says the water has already been there and is starting to recede."

"I'm impressed. Is knowing the high tide mark part of your job, as well?"

"More a sign that I walk this path too often."

"And how often is that?" she asked.

"Twice a day at least. It's the only way to see what's going on…"

His voice drifted off at the end, along with his attention. Following his gaze, Larissa saw that he'd focused on a shadow up beach, right at the surf line.

"Is that what I think it is?" Looked an awful lot like two people reenacting the famous beach scene from *From Here to Eternity*.

A giggle pierced the night air. Moments later, the shadows became upright and ran toward the villas. Larissa tried hard not to giggle herself. "I see what you mean about forgetting your surroundings. Love and paradise."

"Indeed." From the tension in his voice, the scene made that raw nerve flare again. Had Carlos ever rolled in the surf? *What hardened your heart? Had it been his wife? Her illness?* So many questions danced around her head.

As it turned out, the shadows were staying in the VIP section. Before Larissa realized, she and Carlos had arrived at the beachside entrance to her villa. The pathway ended only a few feet beyond, disappearing into a stretch of silver that became the lip of the lagoon. Larissa could see how the shadows had gotten carried away. With nothing but palm trees and sand, it was easy to feel like the only two people on the planet.

"Thank you for walking me home," she said.

"Thank *you* for staying so late to help me."

She went to smile up at Carlos, only to be attacked by a case of nerves dancing around her stomach. Silly, but all of a sudden she felt like a teenager saying good-night on a date. A part of her knew she should turn and head through the door, while another, stronger part, remained rooted to the spot, capable of little more than swaying back and forth on the balls of her feet. "What time are you presenting your proposal to the Stevases?" she asked.

"Nine o'clock," Carlos replied. "Why?"

"Would you mind if I joined you?"

"You have already given up part of your tri—"

"I don't mind," she interrupted. "I'm invested now. I want to see what Linda Stevas thinks of my ideas." What she didn't want to think about was how the suggestion popped into her head as soon as she realized saying good-night might be the last time she spent time with him this week. "So, do you mind?"

"Not at all. In fact, your presence would be very... welcome."

The way he said the world, rolling it off his tongue,

turned the nerves into butterflies. "Then, I'll see you *mañana?*"

"*Mañana,*" Carlos replied. "I am looking forward to it."

His gaze had dropped to her mouth, causing her breath to catch. Larissa rose on tiptoes, compelled by a need to lean closer, only to catch herself before the moment got out of hand. This wasn't a date.

Spinning around, she unlocked her hotel door and slipped inside, clapping her hand over her mouth as soon as she closed the door behind her. What just happened? Had she really been waiting for a good-night kiss?

How long he stood on the walkway after Larissa went inside, Carlos wasn't sure. Long enough for the roaring to leave his ears.

He watched as the light went on in her living room, and when her silhouette appeared in the window, he stepped closer to the building out of her line of sight. The move made him feel improper, as if he were behaving like a voyeur, instead of a man struck dumb by his reactions.

He'd almost kissed her. Staring into her eyes, feeling her body's warmth, he came a breath away from tasting her mouth. Had he lived without a woman in his bed for so long, he could no longer bury his baser instincts? And after all his warning to Jorge about leaving her be. What, he wondered, would she have done if he had kissed her? There was a voice in his head telling him she'd been expecting him to. *Wanted* him to.

Above him, Larissa stood looking outward. Looking for him or staring at the ocean? The angle and shadows combined to hide her expression, so Carlos couldn't tell.

Nothing could hide her figure, though. Every contour, every gorgeous curve was on display for the world to see. How on earth could her fiancé find another woman more attractive? And that boy in her high school. Were they both blind? She was… Awareness flared anew. Gritting his teeth, he willed the arousal away. It was the moonlight. The moonlight and all her talk about weddings making him think impractically. Larissa Boyd was recovering from a broken heart. Worse, she was an incurable romantic. He would not take advantage of either. Tomorrow he would be back in control. After all, he wasn't the same lovesick fool he was five years ago. This time he knew the difference between a moment of lust and something more.

For one thing, he couldn't feel "more" even if he wanted to.

"Señor Chavez! *Buenos dias!*" In contrast to his small size, Paul Stevas's voice boomed through the terrace lounge. Calling out was hardly necessary, as the room was nearly empty. This time of day, the guests who were interested in eating preferred the full-service restaurant or their rooms.

Paul had selected a table overlooking the ocean. Linda was there, too, her short brown hair clipped off her face. In her tank top and shorts, she looked more little girl than married woman. The woman sitting beside her, however… Thanks to her curves, Larissa's navy striped shirt and white shorts looked far more alluring than they were meant to be. Carlos's body reacted immediately, nearly stopping him in his tracks. Unwelcome, but not completely unexpected. He already decided last night that daylight would do little to dilute her appeal.

"My apologies for being late. The staff meeting ran over." Doing his best to ignore the bare leg swinging in his peripheral vision, he put on his best smile. "I trust you haven't been waiting long."

"Only a few minutes," Paul replied. "Larissa has been sharing some of her ideas with us."

"Is that so?" he asked, taking a seat across from her. Took some effort, but he managed not to drop his eyes to her lips.

Color seeped into her cheeks nonetheless. "I was telling them how we thought, since this was an anniversary celebration and not an actual wedding, they might prefer something untraditional," she told him.

He sat and listened while she described La Joya's version of the Mayan wedding ceremony. A beachside ceremony that involved offerings to the four points of the compass. He'd always considered the ritual more gimmick than following true culture, but Larissa wove the details into a magical ceremony of love and commitment even the most traditional of shamans would love. No wonder the Steinbergs couldn't wait to sign a contract. Her enthusiasm was infectious. There was no bitterness, no reluctance in her voice to give away the fact that many of her suggestions came from her own ceremony. His admiration grew.

"What do you mean purify?" Paul asked, interrupting the spell. "Do you mean with a smoke?"

"More like incense," he supplied. "The shaman will add copal to the altar fire. It emits an aroma that smells very similar to frankincense. Usually he waves the smoke around the participants before allowing them to approach. That way you are 'presentable' to the gods." He didn't go into the rest of the ceremony. It largely consisted of mystical elements best left experienced. In a true Mayan ceremony, the shaman would also make a ritual sacrifice. Thankfully, the mystic La Joya used was modern and wise enough to substitute a bloodless sacrifice instead.

"Once the shaman finishes the ceremony, he'll declare you officially committed to one another and your guests will commemorate the moment by showering you with flower petals," Larissa finished for him. "What do you think?"

The young couple exchanged a look.

"Everything sounds wonderful," Linda said. "Beautiful."

"But?"

"It's the incense," Paul said. "I get the point of the whole purification ceremony, but we don't want any smoke."

"None at all?" There was no mistaking the disappointment in Larissa's voice. Modern or not, all shaman insisted on purification rituals. Vetoing the incense meant vetoing her entire proposal. To his surprise, Carlos found himself disappointed on Larissa's behalf. Did the Stevases not realize how hard she worked on this proposal? Hours of thought and effort down the drain. He arched a brow at his surrogate coordinator. *See? Never happy.*

"It's not that we don't like the idea," Linda said, at least having the good sense to sound apologetic. "I loved everything else."

"But Linda's lungs can't handle being around smoke. She'll end up coughing through the whole ceremony, and what kind of memory is that? This is supposed to be special."

Was the kid getting choked up? His eyes had a sheen to them.

Linda reached over and squeezed her husband's wrist. "It will be special," she said in a quiet voice. "But smokeless would be better."

"No problem," Larissa said before he could. "It's possible the shaman could purify the altar beforehand. Or…" She paused. "We can always do the ceremony without the shaman. Kind of a merger of traditional and nontraditional elements." Without missing a beat, she launched into a substitute idea. Carlos was doubly impressed. Smart and sexy. A dangerous combination. Her fiancé was a fool.

Without meaning to, his attention wandered to Larissa's legs. Her thighs were pale and smooth, like her shoulders last night. Linda had pale skin, too—most of the new arrivals did—but Larissa's skin had a creaminess to it that made it stand out amid all the bronze and copper. Her skin, her style of dress, her curves…everything about her stood out.

His late wife had been so breathtakingly beautiful. Perfect-looking, some said. Certainly, he thought so first time he laid eyes on her. Larissa Boyd wasn't nearly as flawless, but she had a radiance about her that pulled you in nonetheless. There was steel in there, too. Mirabelle had been so fragile, so unable to deal with a world that wasn't forever bright and shiny. Something told Carlos that Larissa Boyd created her own bright and shiny.

Was that the reason she held such appeal? Because she was so different from Mirabelle?

"And I'm sure the resort boutique can help you find a dress."

She was looking to him for a response. *"Si,"* he replied, after clearing his throat. "Señora Pedron, our shop manager, works closely with the boutiques in town. She will help you find whatever you need."

"I don't need anything super fancy," Linda said, "but I would like to wear something a little dressier than a cotton sundress. I would have packed more appropriately if someone told me about the ceremony in advance." She gave Paul a playful nudge, which he returned.

"I told you, I wanted to surprise you. Get whatever dress you want. Far as I'm concerned, you'd look gorgeous in a flour sack."

Naturally his answer made Linda beam. Poor besotted fool. Carlos mentally added up the costs. Paul Stevas's surprise was going cost a small fortune. With every expense agreed to while wearing a smile.

It was that damn smile that tried Carlos's nerves. His insipid adoring look cut too close to home. He'd worn a similar look those first months of his marriage, too. So willing to do anything to keep a smile on his wife's face. Too lost in his romantic haze to realize the impossibility of his job.

A few feet away, Larissa watched their banter with a rapture usually reserved for romantic movies. Carlos could only imagine the smile that would grace her face if he treated her to even a tiny slice of the gestures he bestowed on Mirabelle.

But then, a woman like Larissa would also expect feelings to go along with the gestures, wouldn't she? Feelings he couldn't give even in the shortest of terms. Mirabelle, with all her need, killed that possibility.

Still…he thought, his gaze sliding back to her legs. What he wouldn't do to feel the curve of her calf beneath his palm.

His view disappeared, destroyed by the recrossing

of legs in the opposite direction. "That's every detail I can think of," he heard Larissa say. "You're going to have a gorgeous recommitment ceremony."

"I'm sure we will," Paul said, kissing Linda again. "Thank you so much for all your help."

"I still can't believe I'm actually going to have my dream wedding. I probably won't sleep between now and Friday night."

"You better. I don't want you getting sick before we've said 'I do' again." Paul's comment earned him an eye roll. Such a sugary and adoring exchange, Carlos feared he might choke from the sweetness. To think he'd once sounded that way himself. Sipping his coffee, he offered silent thanks for intense Mexican brewing habits. The bitterness made for good balance. Like reality to fantasy.

"I'll have the catering office type up the notes and make sure a copy is left for you at the front desk," he told the Stevases. "If there are any questions or changes, please don't hesitate to ask."

"Should we call your office directly?" Paul asked. He'd directed his question at Larissa.

"I—uh—don't actually work here at the resort," Larissa replied, color creeping into her cheeks.

"You don't?" Linda's eyes were wider than usual. "You're certainly familiar with the services."

"Well, that's because—"

"Señorita Boyd is a good friend," Carlos said, jumping in. "The resort is between wedding coordinators at the moment, and she, being familiar with our services, graciously agreed to step in and help with your event."

"Ahhh." The newlyweds exchanged another look, and this time the knowing glance was easily decipherable. They mistook "friend" for something else.

"Then we appreciate your help even more," Linda told her.

"My pleasure," Larissa told her, shooting him a look of her own. She, too, had read what the Stevases were thinking. "If it's one thing I love, it's weddings, or pseudo-weddings in this case. I'm absolutely positive you're going to love what we've planned."

"You're coming to the ceremony right?"

"I make a point of stopping by every ceremony to make sure arrangements are to guests' liking," he told her.

"Yes, but will you and Larissa stay?"

She was asking if they would attend as a couple.

"I hadn't..." Larissa turned to him, and he shrugged, letting her know the decision was up to her. The woman had no reason to attend. This was her vacation; the Stevases were strangers. Curiously, his pulse quickened while he waited her response.

"Please," Linda said, grabbing Larissa's hand. "We've only a few family members coming in for the ceremony, and you've done so much to create this wonderful memory. It wouldn't feel right not having you there."

"Well, if it means so much to you—"

"Oh, it does! Thank you so much." Eyes filling with emotion, the young woman leapt from her chair and wrapped her arms around Larissa's neck. "For everything."

"Yes," Paul agreed. "You have no idea." His eyes were damp, too. Clearly they were both prone to emotion as well as enamored with each other.

"Looks like I'll be attending a wedding this week after all," Larissa remarked once Paul and Linda departed. "Don't worry, I won't hold you to standing by my side."

The image of the two of them dancing on the beach flashed into his head. On their way to the elevator, Paul and Linda walked as though glued from shoulder to thigh. The thought of being glued in similar fashion while swaying to music sent his baser instincts into overdrive.

"You don't have to attend," he said, reaching for his coffee. "I could make an excuse. Tell them you aren't feeling well."

"No, I'd like to attend," she replied. "They seem like a sweet couple. They think we're dating, you know."

The remark caused him to cough into his coffee. "I assure you, that wasn't my intent when I first spoke. I was simply trying to avoid them knowing you were a guest."

"Why?"

The truth? He recognized Larissa's discomfort and felt compelled to rush in and save her embarrassment. There was no thought involved. "People expect more from a five-star resort than a guest covering a job in exchange for a discount on her bill," he replied. Perhaps not the entire answer, but truthful enough.

"I can see why you wouldn't want word to get out. Guests would crawl out of the woodwork looking for favors."

"Precisely." The shadow he thought he saw crossing her features had to be his imagination. "We are not in a position to be reducing bills left and right." No hotel was, and certainly not one who had their accounts mismanaged.

"However, I did not mean to make you feel uncomfortable," he added. "If you'd like, I will talk with them, and explain we are not together."

"You don't have to explain on my account. I mean—"

she looked down "—it's only for one evening, and it's not like I'll see them again afterward. Besides, the two of them are so wrapped up in one another, I doubt they would remember the explanation anyway."

"Probably not." He ignored the surge that overtook him when Larissa said not to bother. Whether the Stevases' thought the two of them together was moot. They weren't. "Well, as you said, it is only for one evening."

"And there is no rule that says we have to spend the event together, because of a misconception, right?"

Was that expectancy in her voice? Carlos couldn't be sure, but all of a sudden her eyes reminded him of last night. So wide and blue. Kissing her would be a mistake. A very sweet-tasting mistake.

"Si," he murmured. "There is not."

"Great." Larissa practically knocked the chair over jumping to her feet. Not her most graceful of moves, but then, she'd been stumbling mentally and physically the entire trip. "It looks like we're done here, so if you don't mind, seeing how I am a guest, I'm going to head back to my room."

"So quickly?" She couldn't blame him for being confused by her behavior. One moment, she's looking him in the eye, the next she was rushing to escape.

"There's a snorkeling trip to the ecopark leaving soon. If I hurry, I can join."

"I thought you didn't want to leave your lounge chair?"

"I wasn't, but snorkeling was on my original itinerary, and I realized last night there was no reason for me not to go through with my plans. I originally planned to go on Friday, but now that I've agreed to go to the recommitment ceremony, I need to pick a different day, so why not today?"

She smiled, hoping her smile didn't look nervous. Right before answering, Carlos's eyes had dropped to her mouth. While only a couple seconds ticked by, they'd lingered long enough to send some very disturbing thoughts into her head. First and foremost, the very clear realization that she wanted Carlos to kiss her, maybe more than she wanted him to last night.

Much as she hated to admit it, in slightly over twenty-four hours, she'd managed to develop a very serious fixation on the man. Tom, the man she should be thinking about, was barely a blip on the radar. She needed space and fresh air to clear her head.

If her departure disappointed Carlos, you couldn't tell from his expression. His eyes were as shuttered as always. "I won't keep you then. Enjoy your afternoon."

"Thanks, I will."

What did you think he'd say? Stay? The skin on the back of her neck prickled as she rushed her way to the elevator. If he was watching her departure, it was only because she acted so skittish. Anything more was kidding herself. Good thing she did decide to go snorkeling. A nice cool plunge in the tide pools was definitely what she needed to get a grip.

The launch back to her room took forever. Laid-back Mexican time did not work when you needed to stay distracted. Sitting in her seat only gave her more time to think. What did it say about her that she could be so drawn to a stranger on her honeymoon? Maybe she was as superficial as Tom said. She certainly hadn't given him a second thought while talking wedding details with Linda. If anything, she'd been excited that she would get to see her wedding ceremony take place after all. *She and Carlos.*

And with that thought the can of worms she'd fought

so hard last night to ignore, ripped open to reveal the ugly truth: She didn't miss Tom at all. And if she didn't miss him, then he wasn't really her Prince Charming. She only thought he was because he wanted her, and being wanted was such a nice feeling.

Was that the reason she felt so attracted to Carlos? Because he looked at her with desire? That was so not a good reason.

CHAPTER SIX

IT WAS, HOWEVER, yet another reason to get away from the resort for a few hours. Soon as the launch reached her dock, Larissa rushed upstairs to her bedroom, pulling off her shirt as she ran. She had only a few minutes before the launch made its turn and passed by her dock. If she missed it, she'd have to either call another or rush back to the lobby by foot. Grabbing the first bathing suit she could find, a bright red one piece she normally hated because it emphasized her paleness, she tugged the spandex up over her hips while hopping around the room looking for the rest of her beach equipment. Why was it her sunscreen and sunglasses could never stay together?

Eventually, she located both, along with the snorkel equipment she'd brought with her. She clapped the fins together, to make sure there wasn't a tarantula hiding in a toehold, stuffed the equipment and a couple oversize beach towels into a tote and headed out the door.

A look out the glass-encased staircase told her she took too long to catch the launch, giving her no choice but to take the back way. This time of day, the sun was high and hot, not the kind of weather made for rushing. Fewer than five minutes into the dash, Larissa had sweat trickling down her back. Reminding herself she would be spending the afternoon in the water, she pushed on, making it back to the lobby in time to see the bus pull away from the curb.

Fantastic. Now she'd have to come up with another field trip to keep her mind distracted. Hot and sweaty, she sank to the curb to contemplate her options.

"We do have more comfortable places to sit," she heard a voice say. The deep timbre washed over her, setting off flutters in her stomach.

Glancing upward, she spotted Carlos standing by the valet stand, his presence obliterating everything around him.

"I missed the bus," she said lamely, as if he couldn't guess by her woebegone appearance. "So I was trying to figure out what to do. I don't suppose there are taxis that go to Tulum?"

"There are always taxis. The question is how long it takes for them to arrive."

"Oh." It was beginning to sound like fate wanted her to stay on her lounge chair and think after all.

It dawned on her, that while she'd been rushing back and forth, her host had changed as well. Instead of his dark suit, he wore a pair of khaki shorts and a sport shirt, the white of which glowed against his copper-colored skin. Until this moment, Larissa had credited his black suit for his darkly sophisticated appearance. She'd been wrong. He looked sleeker than ever. "Are you going somewhere?"

"This afternoon is my afternoon off. I thought I'd take a drive off property." Looking for distraction and fresh air as well?

Just then, a battered black Jeep older than her pulled up to the curb she sat and a young man stepped out. "*Lo siento por el retraso,* Señor Chavez."

"*Gracias,* Hector."

This was Carlos's vehicle? Her amazement must have shown on her face, because he shot her an amused expression. "You look surprised."

"I am, a bit." Though she had no good reason except that based on his appearance, she'd expected something sexier. Not a mud-splattered car that looked like it fought in Normandy.

"Don't forget, we are in the jungle. When in Rome…"

Do as the Mayans do. Somehow, she didn't picture the Mayans having four-wheel drive. She could however, picture Carlos, with his jungle cat sleekness maneuvering around the jungle. Is that what he was off to do? Maneuver through the jungle? And why did the idea sound far more exotic when she included him?

She watched as he stashed a small cooler in the back before slipping a tip into the valet's hand. Right before he climbed into the driver's seat, he paused. "If you'd like, I could drive you."

Ride with him? In his car? The very man she was seeking space from? "Thank you, but that's not necessary."

"If you wait for a taxi, there's a good chance you'll waste your entire afternoon and I'd hate for a guest to miss out on an activity."

"I don't want to interfere with your plans."

"Since my plans are to take a drive, you aren't interfering with anything."

"I don't know…"

It was only a ride, right? Okay, granted the whole point of getting off site was so she could get away from his presence and think straight. On the other hand, if she continued arguing with him, she'd end up making a scene, and she didn't want that, either.

The driver behind him beeped his horn, the universe telling her to make up her mind and quick.

Carlos looked at her expectantly. "Larissa?"

"Why not?" Shouldering in her tote bag, she slipped into the passenger seat. It was only one ride.

As the Jeep bounced its way along the highway, Larissa did her best to keep her hat and sunglasses in place. Between the breeze and the Jeep's aging shock absorbers, the job was harder than she thought it would be.

Out of the corner of her eye, she saw Carlos watching her. Even with sunglasses masking his stare, his attention still caused tingles to spread across her skin. Maybe this wasn't such a good idea after all. She tugged at her shorts, wishing she could make them magically lengthen and cover more of her thigh.

For some reason, the action made Carlos grin. "What?" she asked.

"Most people come to Mexico to expose their skin to the sun. You look like you're in disguise. I'm not helping you rob a bank, am I?"

Easy for him to joke. With his gorgeous skin, he wouldn't turn into a tomato in the sun. "You caught me. I'm really planning to rob the ecopark and have corralled you into driving my getaway car."

"I knew you weren't going for the tropical fish."

He had no idea how close his joke was to the truth.

A sign by the side of the road said they still had several kilometers before their exit. "Are you sure I'm not disrupting your afternoon?" she asked again.

"I assure you, my plans are flexible. It's far more important that you be happy."

"Why?"

"Because you are a guest," he said, as though the answer were obvious.

He seemed to play the "guest" card often around her. Was it his not-so-subtle way of telling her not to read anything into his actions? Larissa wondered if her attraction was that blatantly obvious. Probably.

"Customer service is very important to you, isn't it?" she said. "I don't mean, simply because of recent events. It means a lot to you, what people think of your hotel."

"Because customers I can make happy."

"I don't understand." At first, she thought she heard wrong, he said the words so softly.

"*Lo siento.* I mean that, yes, how people view our resort is very important. The hotel's reputation is my reputation, and by extension, my family's. Discredit the hotel, discredit the Chavez name."

That wasn't what he said the first time, but she let the comment go. "My grandma used to say something similar, although it came out more like 'I won't have some high and mighty prom queen bitchin' all over town that I don't know how to sew.'"

"Your grandmother sounds like a very astute woman."

"She had her moments. I think when you're really good at your job, you can get away with being crotchety."

"And she was good?"

"Best in town. The house was always full of gowns. On the backs of closets, the china cabinet doors—basically anywhere she could hang a hook. Other kids had posters hung in their room. I had bridesmaid gowns."

"No wonder you became such an expert on weddings."

"If you can't beat 'em, join 'em, right? Do you know

how hard it was, not to play dress up when I was little? All those beautiful gowns belonging to other people. My grandmother would have had a fit if I so much as breathed on one."

Remembering how badly she'd wanted to have a dress to call her own, she felt a hollow feeling spread across her chest. *Careful. That's how you got in this mess. By wanting to belong.*

"My brother Pedro dressed up in one of our mother's gowns once. My brothers and I never let him forget how pretty he looked."

Larissa smiled, both at the image and his attempt to lighten the mood. "Sounds like Delilah and me when our friend Chloe dyed her hair. We still tease her about looking like a wire-haired circus clown."

"Your friends…the three of you sound very close."

"I don't know what I'd do without them. They're the closest thing I have to a family these—" Damn. It'd be too much to hope he didn't catch her slip, wouldn't it?

"I didn't realize your grandmother had passed. I'm sorry."

No, she was the one who was sorry, because the whole story was more pathetic. "We'd stopped talking long before, so it wasn't a huge loss."

"I'm sorry. Did you have a fight?"

"Not really. Once I turned eighteen, she um…well, she sort of retired."

"From dressmaking."

"From raising me." She cringed knowing what he must be thinking. A man like him from a large, established family. "It's not as bad as it sounds. After all, I'd left Texas behind, so why shouldn't she leave me? After all, she'd already had to raise two generations on her own." Wasn't her grandmother's fault time had wrung out the best of her.

"What about the rest of your family?"

Ah, that. She should have realized that she couldn't mention a second generation without getting a question or two. "There isn't any more. At least any that I care to talk to." If her mother, wherever she was these days, wanted to find her, she would have. Wasn't like she was hiding out.

Carlos reached over and covered her hand with his. "I am sorry if I brought up a sad topic."

"You didn't." She watched as his thumb made small circles on the back of her hand. His touch chased the hollow feeling away. If only she could entwine their fingers and hold on tight.

To her dismay, he moved his hand back to the steering wheel. "Why don't we make a pledge, to focus on pleasant topics for the rest of the ride?" he suggested. "Are you looking forward to snorkeling at the ecopark?"

"Both will be new experiences," she replied. "Have you been? To the ecopark, that is."

"I have. It's very nice. Crowded though. Most of the serious divers prefer more out-of-the-way places." He paused, and Larissa could see an idea forming in his head. "Would you be interested in trying a different location? One that wasn't so touristy?"

"Sure. Why not? I'm not all that keen on crowds myself. Where do you suggest I go?"

His profile broke in to a slow smile. Damn if the look didn't make her nerves tingle with excitement. "You willing to trust me?"

A loaded question to be sure. In spite the warnings whispering in her ear, Larissa shrugged. "Sure. Why not?"

It was only snorkling. Sitting back, Larissa watched
the road signs for clues to their destination, seeing none.
A short time later, they turned off the highway onto a
narrow unmarked road which in turn became dirt. The
narrow pathway was carved with ruts and potholes so
deep she feared one might swallow them up. Tropical
foliage formed a wall on either side of them, the broad
leaves reaching out to slap the sides of the Jeep. Forgetting about trying to save her hat, she reached up to
grab the roll bar to save herself.

"You won't fall out, if that's what you're worried
about," Carlos said.

Maybe not, but holding on made her feel more secure. "What kind of road is this, anyway?"

"I believe Americans would call it the road less traveled."

Did the road get traveled at all? They hit another
pothole and she gripped the bar tighter. Now she understood the point of driving the Jeep, as well as what
happened to the shocks. "Is it going to be this bouncy
the entire way?" She might not fall out, but another jolt
like that one, and she'd need her spine realigned.

"We're almost there," he said. Ahead, nailed to trunk
of a large tree was a wooden sign on which someone
had painted...something. The letters were too faded
to read clearly, although Larissa thought she made out
the letters *C, N* and *T.* A few feet beyond, the road narrowed even further, becoming no more than a rocky foot
path that ended with a rusty gate held shut by a chain.

The first thing that struck her when he cut the engine, was the quiet. There wasn't a sound beyond the
rustle of leaves and the occasional caw of a bird. Carlos got out and walked to the rear where he removed
her beach bag and his cooler. "We will have to go the

rest of the way by foot," he told her. "It's not a very far walk. No more than a quarter mile."

Question was, a walk to where? All of a sudden she wasn't so certain about this trip. *Serves you right,* she said to herself, as a giant mosquito buzzed her ear. A warm, earthy smell hung in the air. Without the breeze, her skin was already hot and sticky. She took a step, only to turn her ankle on a rock.

"Careful! The path is uneven." In a flash, Carlos appeared at her elbow and despite carrying their belongings, still managed to have a hand free to guide her. Larissa did her best not to shiver as his fingers brushed her bare skin.

"Is it safe to leave the Jeep parked here like this?" she asked. Every piece of literature she read cautioned about leaving belongings unattended, yet here they were parking an open car in the middle of the jungle. She was suddenly having visions of being stranded. Not because she didn't trust her companion—if anything, she trusted him too much—but with the way her luck had been running this week, who knew what could happen.

"The Jeep will be fine. Pablo will keep an eye on it."

"Pablo?"

He pointed to where the path turned into a clump of foliage. Beyond the bushes, the path split into two, one way continuing on into the trees, the other leading uphill to a small building.

She waited while Carlos rattled the chain against the gate. *"Hola!"* he greeted. *"Estamos aquí para nadir en el cenote!"*

"There's a *cenote* here?" Hearing the word, Larissa suddenly realized that's what was painted on the sign.

She craned her neck hoping to spot one of the famous Yucatán underwater sinkholes but saw nothing but dirt and scrub.

"The landowner discovered it on his property several years ago. Mostly locals use it, but the resort sends divers here when they are looking for someplace off the beaten path."

A thin gray-haired man ambled out of the building and down the path. *"Cincuenta pesos cada uno. Y no proporcionamos chalecos salvavidas."*

Carlos turned to her. "How's your swimming?"

"Pretty good," she replied. Enough so she could hold her own in deep water.

"No problema."

Larissa tried to keep up with the exchange, but her Spanish was too rusty and basic to understand most of what was being said. Based on the fact Carlos reached into his pocket and peeled off several bills, she assumed the man was the aforementioned Pablo. The old man stuffed the money in his pocket, then wordlessly opened the gate. *"Asquirese de tomar su basura,"* he said as he let them pass.

"He's really got his people skills down," she noted after the man headed back to his house.

"Now you know why only the locals visit. I think Pablo considers visitors a necessary evil. If he didn't like the money, he'd keep everyone off his property. The *cenote* is this way." He gestured toward the path on the right, leading into the jungle.

Larissa picked her way beside him, keeping an eye on the ground so she wouldn't stumble again. Stumbling meant Carlos would reach out and catch her. The way she reacted to his touch disturbed her. Tom touched her hundreds of times, and far more intimately at that, and she never broke out in shivers.

"Do you come here a lot?" Until today, she wouldn't have said he looked like the swimming hole kind of guy, although she had to admit, the shorts made him look like a different person.

"Once, when I first arrived, so I knew the kind of place the front desk clerks were recommending. I didn't want to be blindsided by a bad review."

Why wasn't she surprised? Guests seemed to be the most important part of his world.

Dear Lord, but it was hot. For something that was supposed to protect her from the sun, her hat wasn't doing a very good job. The back of her neck felt like it was on fire. "Do we have much further?"

"We're here."

Looking up, Larissa saw the vegetation had dropped away, creating a large cavern in the middle of the trees. Peering over the edge, she saw a pool a hundred or so feet below, part of the great underground river system that flowed beneath the entire Yucatán peninsula. The water was so clear, that despite the drop, she could make out rock formations in its depths.

"You're right," she said, smiling up at Carlos. "This is way better than the ecopark." Better than better; they had the entire place to themselves.

A crude wooden ladder lead into the cavern. With Carlos leading the way, they climbed to the base. There the rocks formed a natural spiral staircase leading to the water.

"I can see why the Mayans thought these places were portals to the underworld," Larissa remarked. It really was like entering another world. Tree roots twisted from above like giant gnarled fingers, their ends disappearing into the rocks beneath the water. Meanwhile, long strings of vegetation formed a curtain along one edge. Sunlight streamed through the gaps to fill the dark space with an otherworldly glow. Nature's mood lighting.

"Be careful," Carlos said. "The condensation makes the rocks slippery and unless you want to practice your cliff diving, I'd watch your step."

Larissa took the warning to heart and pressed a palm to the wall. After a few more minutes, they reached bottom. The rock formed a shelf a few inches above the water. Beneath the surface, Larissa caught sight of a school of fish darting away from one of the stalagmites and gasped with delight.

"This is amazing! I can't believe we have the whole place to ourselves."

"I did see snorkeling equipment poking out of that bag of yours, right?"

"You did." The water was so clear she could see the stalagmites rising up from the depths. She couldn't wait to jump in and explore. Ditching her hat and sunglasses, she reached for the hem of her T-shirt. No sooner did she start to lift the garment than she froze. Carlos was in the process of peeling off his shirt, and damn if he didn't make the task look effortless. The cotton slipped up and over his head in one swift movement. He'd definitely been a cat in a previous life. His body was sleek, with muscles made for action, not show. A dusting of dark hair lent an unnecessary rugged edge.

"If it's all right, I thought I'd cool off while you explored," he said, when he caught her watching. "Is that a problem?"

"Don't be silly. Of course it's not a problem." Beyond the fact he was standing shirtless while she was about to strip off her clothes. *Dear Lord, she'd pressed her hand against that chest.* She raised her own shirt, conscious of every wiggle and twist needed to pull the garment over her head. The air hit her bare shoulders in a rush, causing goose bumps. At that moment, her one-piece bathing suit felt way too skimpy. When she finally pulled her head free, she found their positions reversed, and Carlos was staring at her.

"Be careful," he said. Was it her imagination or has voice dropped a notch? "The water's very deep."

"O-okay." Her mouth suddenly dry, she swallowed, then reached for her waistband. Carlos eyes locked with hers. Without breaking their gaze, she popped the button on her shorts and slipped them over her hips. They dropped to the rock with barely a sound. They stood inches apart, the sound of their breathing magnified by the close space, making it seem as though no other noise existed.

Larissa had never felt more exposed. The whole moment was fraught with an intimacy way beyond their surroundings. As for Carlos, his eyes still hadn't released their hold on hers. In the dim light, they looked darker than ever. Predatory, even. She wished she could see past their surface to know what he was thinking, but like all the other times he'd looked at her, she found their depths shuttered.

That didn't stop her skin from igniting from the inside out. Or an ache from starting low in her stomach. She felt on the edge of a far bigger plunge than the water beside her.

"Who dives in first?" Her voice came out a whisper, the question's double meaning hanging in the air.

A strand of hair clung to her damp cheek. She shivered as Carlos brushed it away. *"Dios me ayude,"* he whispered in return. Then, turning, he dove in to the clear blue water.

Good idea, thought Larissa, ignoring the heavy disappointment in her stomach. *Take the safe plunge.*

CHAPTER SEVEN

"Surely, you are a prune by now?"

Rotating onto her back, Larissa pushed off the ledge with her feet, the water slapping the rock with a soft whoosh. "Possibly," she replied. "I didn't check."

Okay, she had checked, but she wasn't ready to dry off. So long as she stayed in the water, she could avoid dealing with what happened earlier. The tension between them seemed to grow stronger with each passing moment. At some point, the line had to snap, sending them in one direction or another. Her body knew what direction it wanted. Forty minutes in the cool water and it still tingled from his touch.

And, he'd merely brushed his fingers across her skin. Goodness knows how her body would feel if he actually kissed her. Her mind, on the other hand, wasn't entirely sure finding out was a good idea.

Which was why, pruny fingers be damned, she stayed in the water while Carlos lounged on the rock shelf like a copper-skinned god.

"You have to remember," she told him, "we don't have underground rivers and caves in New York. We have sewers."

"Mexico isn't all *cenote*s and tropical lagoons, either,

you know. We have our droughts, our poor sewage systems, our earthquakes—"

"Yeah, yeah. Stop being a buzzkill."

"I'm simply trying to inject a little reality and remind you no place is perfect."

Maybe not, but her current location certainly came close.

Using the backstroke, she glided across the surface and stared at the cloudless blue sky through the chamber opening. "I still can't believe I'm swimming in my own private underground cave," she said. Her favorite part was on the far side of the cavern. There, above two giant root systems, the water flowed from the source in a waterfall. She angled her body in that direction, prattling as she paddled.

"When I was a kid, I watched this movie about star-crossed island lovers. In it, the hero comes across the heroine bathing in a lagoon. I remember thinking how she rinsed her hair in the waterfall was the coolest thing ever."

"Should I go ask Pablo for some shampoo?"

"Would you?" She leaned back and let the stream wash off her forehead. Somehow she suspected the host in him would oblige if he thought her serious. "Anyway, the princess falls in love with the hero. Or Bob Hope. I don't remember which one."

"Sounds like you watched a lot of movies."

"Tons. My grandmother used to sew to the classic movie channel." And God forbid she should change the channel. "While other kids grew up with video games, I grew up counting satin buttons and watching Errol Flynn rescue princesses."

"I'm beginning to see where you got your romantic streak."

"What can I say? I'm a sucker for happy endings."

"Except life isn't like the movies, is it?" A soft plop echoed through the chamber. It was Carlos tossing a pebble into the water. He sat leaning forward with his body hunched over his knees, his attention focused somewhere in the depths.

"That doesn't mean happy endings don't happen."

"Don't tell me you still believe happy endings are possible after what happened with your own engagement?"

"Why shouldn't I?" She had to believe in them. Otherwise, the alternative was that she didn't get a happy ending, and that idea was untenable. Surely after sitting on the sidelines for so long, she deserved some happiness, even if she failed this time around. "Look at Paul and Linda. They're happy."

"*Si,*" he replied. His unspoken *for now* hung in the air.

The waterfall's appeal faded. Turning around, she began the slow kick back toward the ledge. "My friend Delilah has this saying," she told him. "Every puzzle has its missing piece, and I think she's right."

"I don't understand."

"It means all of us have that one special person who completes us. Our soul mate."

Carlos laughed and took a drink from the water bottle he'd retrieved from his cooler. "If that were true, La Joya wouldn't have repeat customers."

"I'm serious."

"So am I. Five years from now, at least a third of the people lounging by the hotel pool will be unhappy. What will you say about soul mates then?"

"I'll point out the two-thirds who *are* happy, that's what." Why was he so determined to rain on her pa-

rade? "I have to admit, I really don't understand why
you're so cynical. You were married."

"An experience that taught me quite definitively that
nothing lasts forever."

He tried to sound casual, but pain still leaked from
between the words. How deep his grief must run. The
thought left an ache beneath her breastbone. Was that
why he closed off his gaze? Was he trying to keep the
world from seeing how much he hurt?

"I'm sorry," she said in a soft voice.

Carlos set down the bottle. His eyes were black as
he looked down into the water. "For what?"

For the fact he'd been left alone. For his anger. "You
must have loved your wife very much."

"Why do you say that?"

"Why else would you be so angry?"

She watched as his attention moved to an invisible
spot on the rock. His finger scratched at the surface,
each stroke leaving a wet streak, black against gray. "I
fell in love with my wife the moment I laid eyes on her.
I would have done anything for her."

And she died leaving him alone. Larissa still didn't
understand the cynicism, but she did get the bitterness.

He reached down to grab her by the hand. "Your lips
are turning blue. Come out and towel off."

"My lips are not blue," Larissa protested. She
grabbed his hand anyway, marveling at how effort-
lessly he pulled her up. Once out of the water, the cold
air hit her skin and the comfortable body temperature
she'd been enjoying disappeared into a fit of shivers.
Instantly, a fluffy towel settled around her shoulders.
"See?" Carlos said. "Blue."

He tightened the terrycloth cocoon, then brushed the

damp hair from her face. The sensation of his fingers caressing her skin ignited a new set of shivers.

"You must miss her very much."

"I miss— She shouldn't have died."

"No, she shouldn't have," Larissa replied. What were the words he bit back? Did he think she wouldn't notice the sorrow in his words? The man could shutter his expression all he wanted, but clearly, he hurt and hurt deeply. With good reason. The love of his life died too young. Still, something about the way held back made her think there was more to the story.

"You stayed in too long, *querida*," he told her.

"Did I?" Based on how her insides were trembling, she wondered if she should still be swimming.

"*Si*. You need to be careful. Too long, and you'll grow weak from the cold."

"I'm not cold."

"Your shivering says otherwise."

Larissa looked him in the eye, her gaze telling him what they both already knew: that her trembling had nothing to do with the water. His hands slowed, the touch becoming sensual. "I don't…I'm not…" He struggled for words to caution her no doubt but the way his gaze dropped to her mouth even as he spoke left no doubt as to what he wanted.

"Me, neither," Larissa whispered. This was purely physical. Two people giving into an attraction and nothing more. That her heart pounded in her chest in anticipation meant nothing.

Carlos cupped her jaw. *"Tan bella,"* he murmured. *"Me vuelves loco."*

She wanted to ask the translation, but his mouth slanted over hers, erasing all thoughts of conversation. He kissed like he moved, confident and masterful, his lips coaxing a response without effort. Her eyes fluttered shut. Tom's kisses never felt like this. Carlos's kiss pulled the ground out from her feet. It made her head spin. She was dizzy, breathless, aching for more.

And then it ended, broken by a need for air. Carlos's breath was ragged as he rested his forehead against hers. A solitary Spanish oath escaped his lips. Larissa didn't need to translate the hoarsely whispered word. She felt the same way. Just what that feeling was, she couldn't say for sure, but all of a sudden, to call their attraction *purely physical,* sounded very inadequate.

"We should go," Carlos said, breaking away.

"You want to leave?"

This disappointment in her voice killed him, and it was all he could do to rein in his impulse to erase the tone from her voice. Of course he didn't want to leave. He wanted to pull her back into his arms and kiss her senseless. But with his head spinning, going back to La Joya was the better option. He turned so he wouldn't have to look her in the eye. Any kind of sad expression would be the death of him. "The evening shift starts soon. I need to go back in case there are questions."

"What's the matter, afraid the hotel won't manage without you?"

He could sense her smile. "You sound like Jorge. He tells me the same thing, although this is the longest I've stayed away since our arrival. I'm curious to see how he reacts." Originally, he planned only on taking a drive to clear his head, ironically enough, of his thoughts about her.

"I'm sorry if I screwed up your afternoon."

"Don't be silly. I'm the one who offered." He was still

trying to figure out what made him make the suggestion in the first place instead of driving her to the ecopark as planned. One moment she'd been talking about her childhood, fighting hard to keep her voice upbeat and positive while telling a story that was anything but, the next he was possessed with the urge to show her something unique gripped him.

To make her smile...

So what if he did want to do something nice? Larissa did him a great service today. Why not treat her to something out of the ordinary. His decision had nothing to do with how her story squeezed at the center of his chest. Nothing whatsoever.

As for the kiss... What could he do? She'd been stirring his blood from the moment she opened her hotel room door, and there was only so much resistance a man could muster, especially a man who'd been living as a monk for half a decade.

A soft sigh broke his thoughts. Turning, he saw Larissa folding her towel, a wistful expression on her face. She caught him looking, and blushed. His chest squeezed again.

"I know I've said it before, but thank you for an amazing afternoon," she said. "This place is unlike anything I could have imagined."

"I'm glad. Considering how helpful you were with the Stevases, showing you an underground river is the least I can do."

"Anything to make a guest happy, right?"

"Naturally." No sooner did he speak than he regretted his answer. "I didn't mean—"

"Relax. I was making a joke."

Then why did her eyes turn shadowy? Perhaps the fading light was playing tricks with his head. Too many years of weighing every sentence lest he say the wrong thing had turned him overly wary. If Larissa said she was joking, he should take her for her word.

"You're more than a regular guest," he told her.

"I should think so, unless you kiss all your guests."

"No. You're the exception."

"Good to know."

With his confession came a bout of nerves, bubbling up from place he couldn't name. He needed to explain his actions fully. So she would understand. "It wasn't planned," he rushed to explain. "The kiss, that is. I'm not..." Again the words failed him. How did you explain to a woman who talked of island princesses and soul mates that the woman you thought was the love of your life drained you dry?

She rallied a smile, saving him. "There's no need to explain. I understand."

"You do?" Because he wasn't sure he did anymore.

"Sure. Sometimes a kiss is just a kiss."

Carlos let out a silent sigh. *"Gracias, querida.* I'm glad we are on the same page."

Although he'd feel better if she hadn't quoted another movie.

Or if a tiny voice in the back of his brain didn't disagree.

It didn't take long for them to pack their belongings and climb back to the surface. When they reached the top of the ledge steps, Larissa paused to snap a photo with her cell phone. Something to help her remember paradise. On a whim, she snapped a photo of Carlos as well, catching his profile as he looked down at the water. Another memory to hold.

She lied when she told him a kiss was just a kiss.

Kissing Carlos was more like a carnival thrill ride: Exhilarating, euphoric, a dizzying freefall that left her insides trembling with adrenaline and eager to ride again. Would she, though, or was his kiss, like this afternoon's surprise trip, a one-time deal?

Above ground, the weather was as hot as the *cenote* had been cool. By the time they walked back to the entrance and waited for Pablo to unlock the gate, Larissa had gone from refreshed to sweaty again. Perspiration ran down her back and between her breasts.

"So much for blue lips," she said, pulling at the ruching on her swimsuit. "I have half a mind to turn around and head back to the cavern."

"I'm—"

Again, she rushed to reassure him. She appeared to be doing that a lot this afternoon; reassuring saved her from hearing apologies. "Evening staff meeting, I know."

They walked into the lobby to find a scowling Jorge pacing behind the front desk. "Don't you answer your phone?" he snapped.

"We were in the jungle. You know what the reception is like. What's the problem?"

"We?" His eyes switched to Larissa, and his expression softened. "Oh. I didn't realize. *Lo siento,* Señorita Boyd. I've been trying to contact my cousin regarding an issue that requires his attention."

Carlos shot her a look that said *See?* "What is the problem?"

Jorge learned close and spoke in low, rapid Spanish.

Larissa caught the words right before Carlos grimaced.

"I'm going to have to handle this right away," he said,

his eyes apologetic. "Do you mind taking the launch back on your own?"

She smiled so he wouldn't see her disappointment. Foolish, but she'd hoped…

She didn't know what she hoped. That goodbye might be more? Summoning a bright smile, she pretended the dismissal didn't sting. "Of course not. I've already taken up way too much of your time as it is. I'm sure there are many guests that need your attention now."

It took some effort, but she managed to slip her bag from his grip without brushing his fingers. "Thank you for a fantastic afternoon, Señor Chavez. I appreciate your attention."

She turned away before he could respond.

Later, as she sat on her terrace nursing another twenty-dollar cola, she wondered if she reacted too dramatically. After all, Carlos had done his best to be honest. Any unspoken words were because she cut him off. Maybe the kiss didn't have the same effect on him. It was entirely possible her reaction had more to do with his skill than any kind of connection.

What she should be pondering was how easily Tom had slipped from her mind. Six weeks ago, she'd been prepared to walk down the aisle and now here she was, kissing another man. Were her feelings for her ex so anemic they could be displaced that easily?

As far as comparisons went, the two men were like night and day. Carlos might look sleek and confident, but beneath the surface lay a sadness she'd yet to fully measure. One moment he made her pulse race; the next she wanted to hold him in her arms and tell him everything would be all right.

On the other hand Tom…Tom wanted to marry her. Oh, sure, he was a nice guy—intelligent, kind and successful—but mainly, he wanted her, and Larissa considered herself darn lucky to be wanted. Not once, though, did his kisses leave her insides trembling the way today's kiss did. At best, his kisses were like the man himself: nice.

She sighed. Much as she hated to admit, Tom did her a favor breaking the engagement. The two of them were far from soul mates. Carlos's kiss proved as much.

Listen to yourself. Sitting here acting like kissing Carlos was more than a bit of rebound entertainment. Larissa shook her head. Who knows what Carlos was to her? She didn't even know if she'd see him again the rest of the trip. His kiss, however… His kiss would stay with her a long, long time.

On the other side the lagoon, the egrets had begun bedding down for the evening. Pairs and trios swooped into the foliage, their feathers dotting the canopy white. They called out to each other, other birds joining in until the entire lagoon was alive with squawking. Her own personal nighttime serenade, Larissa thought with a sleepy smile. Swimming had taken more out of her than she thought, and she could feel her eyes growing heavy. Closing them, she let the birds' song float her away. Carlos was wrong. Flaws or not, Mexico was paradise. If she could, Larissa would never leave.

Seemed like only seconds later when she opened her eyes to dark gray and quiet. Falling asleep on the divan was becoming way too easy. Yawning, she padded her way inside to the darkening living room. From the look out her oceanside window, the sun had only recently set. Red and orange closed on the horizon line, the colors making a bright line between the black water and gray sky.

As if answering a call only it could hear, her attention moved to the walkway and the figure standing below her window. Larissa's pulse quickened. *Carlos.* He stood in the shadows, but it didn't matter; she knew what he wanted. She walked downstairs and opened the door.

"Hey," she greeted, her voice barely audible over the surf. "Crisis averted?"

"A guest thought someone stole some jewelry. Turns out she simply misplaced the items."

"So, there was a happy ending after all."

Carlos smile flashed white in the darkening sky. "For now."

He wasn't going to give an inch on the issue, was he? At the moment, Larissa wasn't in the mood to argue the point. Soon as she saw him, a twisting longing had begun spiraling through her erasing any and all of the very logical self-arguments she'd given herself earlier. "That mean your duties are done for the evening?"

"I don't know," he replied. "Are they?"

Smiling, Larissa opened the door wider and let him inside.

"Mind if I join you?"

The sight of Linda Stevas holding a plate of scrambled eggs and fruit wasn't what Larissa hoped to see when she decided to take coffee on the terrace. She'd been scanning the walkway below for a familiar black suit, hoping to catch Carlos on his morning property check. To ask him how he slept, she thought, smiling to herself.

There were times when she thought the past two

nights were dreams. Her body remembered, however. Granted, she didn't have a long list of lovers for comparison, but being with Carlos made her feel alive in a way she didn't know was possible. Like his kisses, his lovemaking left her breathless and unsteady. She couldn't get enough. Neither could he. Both nights passed in a haze of lovemaking and pillow talk that lasted until gray seeped through the cracks in the mangroves, and Larissa couldn't keep her eyes open any longer. Then morning would arrive, and she'd wake up alone, the only sign she'd had company the rumpled sheets and love bites marking the back of her shoulder. She thought of asking him to stay, but fearing his answer, decided to accept what he could give.

It was, she told herself, a vacation fling in its truest form. Hadn't both she and Carlos assured one another neither was looking for more?

Why, then, did she have this nagging feeling the rules had changed, at least where she was concerned? With each kiss, each whispered word of intimacy, she found herself hoping this would be the time she looked in Carlos's eyes and found their depths no longer shuttered.

"Larissa?" Linda looked at her expectantly. "I'm not disturbing you, am I?"

"Not at all." Swallowing her disappointment, Larissa smiled and gestured for the woman to take a seat.

"Are you sure? I thought maybe you were waiting for Señor Chavez."

Truer words… "Carlos is working. I'll see him later." She tried to contain the thrill the thought gave her, and failed. "Speaking of eating companions, however, where's your other half?" She thought the couple inseparable.

"I convinced him to take a run on the beach. We spent yesterday at the local hospital, and he's a little stressed out from the experience."

"The hospital? Is everything okay? It wasn't anything serious, was it?"

"I was having some trouble catching my breath, but everything's fine now. No big deal."

Was it really no big deal? While the young woman certainly looked fine, the way she suddenly focused on her plate made Larissa wonder. It would be a shame if, after so much effort, Linda got sick and couldn't enjoy her recommitment ceremony. It would explain why the young woman was downplaying yesterday's emergency.

"Anyway," she said, taking a bite of pineapple, "I figured he should mellow out a little before our parents arrive."

"You must be getting excited."

"You have no idea." The woman's eyes sparkled. "I found the perfect dress while in town yesterday. White with flowers hand-stitched around the neckline. It fits, too. I was so afraid I'd end up looking like I was wearing an oversize sack."

Larissa understood. Growing up, she'd heard customers uttering the same lament too many times to count, and given Linda's obscenely thin figure, she could imagine the challenge.

"I feel a little bad about how much it cost," Linda was saying, "but Paul told me not to worry."

"Listen to your husband. He clearly wants you to be happy."

"Yeah, Paul's great that way. He keeps telling me he wants me to have the wedding of my dreams this time around. I'm so lucky to have him," she said, eyes growing damp.

The Stevases' devotion to one another was enviable. Too bad Carlos wasn't here to see the love on Linda's face. Maybe it might change his cynical view to see two happy people.

"I bet if I ask, he'll say he's lucky to have you, as well."

"I hope so. I hated to think he's doing all this simply out of… Never mind." The young woman shook off whatever she was about to say. "Tomorrow is going to be absolutely perfect. You're still coming, right?"

"Absolutely. I wouldn't miss it for the world. I'm kind of excited to see what the shaman will do." After a bit of negotiation, Carlos convinced the man to compromise on his cleansing ritual, enabling the Stevas› to have the full traditional ceremony. And the man claimed he wasn't romantic.

"Me, too," Linda replied. She started to take a bite of food, only to drop the fork and rush to the other side of the table. "I'm sorry," she said, pulling Larissa into a hug. "I'm so happy, I can't help myself. You and Señor Chavez have no idea how much this ceremony means to both Paul and me."

"No, but I think I can guess," Larissa said, patting her back. Hard not to want to help the couple, what with the way they seemed so in love.

"I hope I'm not interrupting a female bonding session?"

Carlos? Larissa entangled herself from the embrace to see him striding toward their table. His black suit crisp as ever, his hair perfectly in place, he looked nothing like the lover who kept her up all night. That is, until his eyes dropped to her lips, and the flash of familiar possessive hunger she saw sent heat curling around the base of her spine.

He might as well have kissed her consider the onslaught of shyness attacking her. Tucking her hair behind her ear, she turned away with a smile. "I thought you made your morning rounds this hour."

"Actually I was on my way to call Señora Stevas's room when I spotted her on the terrace."

"You were looking for me?"

Larissa's heart started to sink, and she kicked herself. She had absolutely no reason to feel disappointed. Did she think he was the only guest at the resort Carlos thought about?

No, just the only one he was sleeping with.

"I wanted to let you know we were able to book a moonlight lagoon cruise for you and your husband Friday night."

"Really?"

"Yes. And I've directed the launch driver to take you to the outmost point of the lagoon so your anniversary can be celebrated in private. The chef will call you later today regarding the menu."

"Oh, my gosh, I'm so excited. I'm going up to the room and see if Paul's back from his run. He's going to be so excited." Jumping up from the table, the young woman drew Carlos into a hug, which, Larissa noted with a smile, he awkwardly returned.

"She's very…exuberant," he remarked after Linda had bustled off.

"Can you blame her?" Larissa asked. "You know, for a man who claims to detest romance, you went out of your way to create a very romantic evening. Directing the launch operator to sail to a remote location?"

"We direct all the operators to sail to remote locations," he replied, taking the seat Linda vacated. "Telling the guests lets them feel special. Those special touches are what lead to good reviews."

And goodness knows reviews were important to him. "Well, I'm sure Paul and Linda will sing the resort's praises to everyone under the sun."

"Let us hope so."

Judging from Linda's enthusiasm, Larissa was pretty sure she could guarantee it. She smiled over the rim of her coffee. "You look tired this morning." Dark smudges marked his bronze skin.

"I'm afraid I didn't get much sleep last night. Seems there was a rather high-maintenance guest who required my attention."

"Is that so? What a shame. Perhaps she'll be less demanding tonight so you can sleep."

A gleam appeared in his eye. "I certainly hope not. Her 'demands' have been the best part of my week."

Larissa flushed from head to toe. He'd purposely dropped his voice to a husky timbre, making her mouth run dry. "Then she'll definitely demand more."

"Good." The air stilled around them. Feeling bold, Larissa slid her leg forward until the inside of her sandal pressed against his wingtip. To anyone walking by, the position looked benign, but for them, the touch held unspoken promise. To Larissa's pleasure, Carlos actually smiled.

"Señora Stevas wasn't the only person I was heading to see," he said.

"Really?" Her stomach gave another one of those flutters. "Did you want something?"

"It appears one of our guests canceled their dinner

cruise reservation for this evening. I was wondering if you would be interested in joining me."

"You want to take me on a moonlight cruise?"

He shrugged, as though the offer was no big deal. "I remembered you mentioning to the Stevases how much you'd been looking forward to going, and how disappointed you were to have to cancel your own. I thought I'd offer you the opportunity to indulge in another one of your itinerary items. But if you don't wish to—"

"I didn't say I wasn't interested."

Next to the wedding ceremony, the moonlight lagoon cruise had been the one item she'd most looked forward to. So much so, she actually contemplated having the dinner by herself. Having dinner with Carlos, however, sounded much more inviting.

He arched his brow. "But?"

"But…" She paused, wondering how to phrase her question. Going on a dinner cruise, was very much like a public date. "Your staff will see us together."

"You have a problem with them seeing us together?"

"I don't." But a man who made a point of hightailing it from her room at dawn might. "I assumed when it came to your personal life, you preferred to maintain a low profile around your staff."

"You forget, *querida*," he said, leaning forward. "My staff knows how to be discreet. So are you interested?"

"Very."

"Good. The launch will be in front of your dock at seven o'clock."

Just in time to enjoy the sunset. If she said something, he'd probably tell her the boats always departed at sunset to increase the ambiance. She preferred not to know. "I'll be there."

"So will I." He reached over and ran a finger along the inside of her wrist, trumping her foot move by spades. "'Til tonight, *querida*."

Watching him walk away, Larissa rubbed the spot on her skin where his finger made contact, and tried not to think about how he completely dodged her comment about being public.

CHAPTER EIGHT

"Hola, chica! Que pasa?"

Chloe's voice burst over the receiver. Hearing her friend caused a ripple of homesickness. Back home, they barely went a day without chatting. "Just having breakfast overlooking the ocean," Larissa replied. After Carlos went back to his office, she remained, using the view to distract her from thinking too hard. "What about you? Aren't you supposed to be working? Or have you finally decided to quit and help your boyfriend run his coffee empire?"

"Nah, I'm saving those kinds of life-changing decisions for when you get back."

"We're on speakerphone in Simon's office," a second voice, Delilah's, chimed in. "We told him we needed to check on you. We were worried because you didn't return our phone call the other day."

She'd completely forgotten they called while she was getting sick. "I'm so sorry, you guys, I meant to."

"Relax," Chole replied. "We're only teasing. We didn't expect you to call back. International cell calls are expensive."

"Plus, you should be out enjoying your vacation," Delilah added. "How is Mexico?"

"Wonderful, now that I've recovered from your welcome present. I'm never drinking champagne again. Oh, and then there was the tarantula." Briefly, she told them about her encounter with Hairy.

True to form, Delilah expressed the proper sympathy, while Chloe giggled. "Poor La-Roo," she said. "So far paradise hasn't been very nice to you."

"It hasn't been all bad." In fact, she added silently as Carlos's midnight smile flashed before her, some of Mexico had been very, very good. "I went swimming in an underground cave the other day. And, tonight I'm taking a moonlight cruise on the lagoon."

"How lovely," Delilah said, only to pause shortly after. "Wait, I thought those lagoon cruises were a private, couples-only thing. Who are you going with? Don't tell me you're taking one by yourself."

Larissa bit her lip. Should she tell them about Carlos? Normally, the three of them shared everything, but she didn't feel like talking about her time with Carlos. Not yet anyway. She was having a hard enough time examining the circumstances in the harsh light of day; talking would only expose the flaws and bring her bubble closer to bursting.

Unfortunately, in a huge tactical error, she forgot how her friends could read between the lines, especially the lines of a prolonged silence.

"Something's up," Chloe said. "You have a date, don't you?"

"I—"

"You do!" Delilah squealed. "With who?"

"The general manager and it's not a date." This was why she didn't want to talk. Because Chloe and Delilah would force her to face reality. "Have the two of you forgotten that I'm here on my honeymoon?"

"Without your groom," Chloe shot back.

"Thank you for reminding me." Immediately, Larissa regretted snapping. Since Carlos appeared on her walkway two nights ago, she'd hadn't thought of Tom once, and she'd barely thought of him before that.

"All I meant was that you shouldn't feel bad if you want to have a little fun while you're south of the border."

"Who said I feel bad?" she asked. If anything, she'd felt way too good the past few days.

"So long as you don't let all those romantic sunsets go to your head."

"What's that supposed to mean?" She didn't like the way Delilah's comment made the hair on her neck stand up.

"It means don't get too carried away. You know what a sucker you are when it comes to romance."

"For goodness' sake, Delilah, I just broke my engagement. I'm not looking for a deep relationship." Even as she said the words, however, she could hear the distant warning bells. Suggesting she might remind herself of her resolve a little more frequently.

"Give the woman a break, wouldn't you, Del? She's going to dinner, not running away with the guy. Don't listen to her, La-Roo. The only advice you need is to not do anything we wouldn't do."

Talk about loose guidance. When it came to caution, the two women were at complete opposite ends of the spectrum. "Pretty wide berth, don't you think?"

"Plenty of wiggle room for a good time," her friend replied.

"Good Lord, there's going to be a chef and a launch operator with us. How much wiggling do you think there's going to be?"

"Depends on how creative a thinker you are. You'd be amazed what you can do when you think outside the box."

"Very amusing." She wondered if Chloe would give the same advice if she knew how much *wiggling* she and Carlos had done already.

After a few more minutes of conversation, mostly about the hotel and her room, and one last warning from Delilah to keep her head, Larissa hung up. Immediately, a server showed up to top off her coffee. Invisible, discreet service. Carlos would be pleased to see his dictate being carried out with such efficiency.

Mug cradled in her hands, she let it hover below her lips while she stared at the horizon. The sky and water met with perfect complimentary colors. Dark navy abutting cerulean. So much of Mexico's colors seemed plucked from a box of crayons. Bright, bold, beautiful.

Romantic as sin.

Delilah's remark about Mexican sunsets nagged. Everyone always teased her about being overly romantic. *Addicted to romance,* Chloe liked to say. *All those years helping your grandmother gave you tulle on the brain.*

Was it possible she was letting her surroundings color her emotions? Would Carlos's kisses be as intoxicating if they took place somewhere like the corner of Fifty-ninth and Madison? Did it even matter? In a few days, she'd be back on Madison Avenue, while Carlos stayed here. Was it really important for her to know the answer?

Wow, she thought, setting her coffee down. For a woman whose ex-fiancé accused her of not having deep thoughts, she was certainly thinking herself into a corner, wasn't she?

* * *

"I heard you booked the open moonlight cruise."

Carlos looked from his paperwork to see his cousin who stood in the doorway. "That's right, I did. For Señorita Boyd."

"And for you, as well."

"She mentioned the cruise had been a highly anticipated part of her old itinerary. I thought taking advantage of the cancellation would be a nice way to show our appreciation for her help."

"Interesting. I would have thought visiting her room the past two nights would be message enough."

Carlos washed his hands over his face. He'd been wondering how long before Jorge said something. His staff might be discreet, but they weren't blind. Nor had he been overly secretive about his rendezvous. Sighing, he got up and went to shut the door. "You could at least keep your voice down."

"Little late to be worried about discretion now, don't you think? The time to worry was before you decided to mix business with pleasure."

Carlos winced.

"Regardless, I'd prefer to at least try and protect the señorita's reputation."

"Relax, *primo,* I made sure we were alone before I said anything. I don't want to encourage gossip any more than you do."

"Gracias."

"No need to thank me. I'm happy to see you finally moving on."

"I'm not moving on." The response was reflexive.

"Then what are you doing?"

"I…" Carlos wasn't sure. He certainly didn't set out to become Larissa's lover. Quite the opposite. The other afternoon, he'd decided to take a drive precisely because he wanted to clear his head of the notion. *Until he saw her sitting on the curb.* From that moment on, kissing her had been inevitable, and after kissing…well, there was no turning back. He could no more stop himself from going to her room than he could stop breathing. His actions were no longer his own.

Jorge, if he heard such an explanation, would never let it go, so Carlos settled for a half-truth instead. "We're two people enjoying each other's company, that is all."

"Well, I have to say, you've got good taste. She is a beautiful woman. She must be very special, too, to get your attention after all these years."

You don't know by half. Leaving Larissa each morning proved increasingly difficult. She was sweet, smart and had an uncanny ability for making him feel lighter. By the end with Mirabelle, he'd had a persistent weight pressing down on him. For the first time in years, he didn't feel the pressure.

"Don't read too much into the situation," he told Jorge. Or was he telling himself? "She's only here for a few more days."

"If I remember correctly, you courted, proposed and married Mirabelle in the same amount of time."

And look where that got him. "Larissa is not Mirabelle."

"Thank goodness."

Spine stiffening, Carlos turned away. On other side of the glass the ocean looked particularly blue today. Perhaps he'd take a perimeter walk. Clear his head. *Because doing so worked so well the last time….*

Behind him, the leather guest chair crinkled as Jorge shifted his weight. His cousin gearing up for another comment. How foolish for him to think the conversation over. He held his breath, waiting for what he knew was coming.

"What happened to Mirabelle wasn't your fault. No one could have loved her more than you if they tried."

And yet he still failed her. Did his cousin ever stop to think that Carlos might not want to fail again? Some mistakes were too awful to repeat. The most he and Larissa could ever be were two people incredibly and insatiably attracted to one another.

Not that more could happen anyway. Even if he were capable of having a deeper relationship, come the end of the week, Larissa would leave for New York, and their affair would be in the past. Which, he thought rubbing a sudden pang in his sternum, was exactly what he wanted.

"Why is it women always keep us waiting?"

Carlos shot the chef a look. "I would hardly call five minutes a wait," he replied.

"*Lo siento, señor.* It seemed longer."

Yes, thought Carlos, it did. Fortunately, his employees knew better than to call him on the fact the launch arrived at Larissa's villa ten minutes early and coasted around the lagoon to kill time.

Turning so his back was to the boat, he wiped his hands on his slacks. "I'm sure the señorita will be outside any moment."

"She's outside now," Larissa said.

She hustled toward him, wearing a curve-hugging red dress and platform sandals. As he watched her hips swing back and forth, Carlos's mouth began to water.

"Sorry I made you wait," she said, her voice breathy. "I ran into Paul and Linda by the pool. We ended up talking about tomorrow's ceremony and the time slipped away."

He couldn't care less about Linda Stevas. The only thing he could think about was how much Larissa's body resembled an hourglass, and how he couldn't wait to run his hands over every blessed inch of time. *Two people incredibly and insatiably attracted to one another.*

Suddenly the launch was over capacity by two. "Disembark," he barked at the crew. "I'll handle the boat from here."

Both staff members' mouths opened. "But this is the VIP section. How are we supposed to get back to the main hotel?"

"Call for another launch." There were plenty of boats still available. "Or walk." So long as they didn't set sail with them. The men grumbled but did as he requested. Tomorrow there would be gossip, but at the moment, Carlos couldn't be bothered to care. The gleam in Larissa's eyes told him that neither could she.

He held out his hand. "Ready to board?"

It didn't surprise Larissa that Carlos could maneuver the launch on his own or that he looked completely in command standing at the wheel in his suit. Everything the man did oozed confidence; why shouldn't steering a boat?

Lifting a hand from the wheel, he slipped an arm around her waist. "You're standing too far away," he said. The hum of the engine required that he bring his mouth close to her ear so when he spoke, his lips tickled the outer shell. Larissa shivered.

"How about I open the bottle I saw chilling?" she whispered back, slipping from his grip. Ever since the boat pulled to the dock, her insides had been a jittery mess, more in keeping with a first date than two people who'd been sharing a bed for days. After the things Carlos and she had done the past two nights, that she should feel any shyness was absurd. For goodness' sake, didn't she pour herself in to this dress knowing full well what kind of message it telegraphed? A message Carlos received loud and clear, she might add.

The nerves were Delilah's fault. Her comment about not getting carried away kept replaying itself. The warning was completely unnecessary; both Larissa and Carlos understood the parameters of their *relationship*. She wasn't about to build their affair into anything more. Didn't matter how gorgeous and romantic the setting.

Unlike the regular launches, which featured rows of benches to accommodate multiple passengers, the dinner boats had counter space and cooking equipment. A gauzy curtain divided the stern from the rest of the space, so guests could maintain the illusion of being alone of the water. Since she and Carlos really were alone, the curtain remained open. She made her way to where the ice bucket sat on the floor next to the cushioned bench seat. The bottle had already been opened and left to breathe.

"I see, you're going to make me break my no-alcohol rule," she teased over her shoulder.

"What?"

No sense talking over the engine. Clearly, conversation would have to wait. She lifted the bottle only to stare at the label in surprise. *Spring water.* Carlos must have directed the chef to replace the usual wine for her sake.

How silly, getting a lump in her throat over a bottle

of water, but there it was, thick and large, and causing her chest to grow tight.

"Everything all right?" Carlos called back.

Everything was great. Pouring two glasses, she made her way back to his side.

Carlos steered the boat west to where an inlet divided the jungle into two before cutting the ending. From there, they floated in silence toward the trees, where the last rays of sunlight broke through toward the water. "I'm afraid this is the best sunset I can do given how they built the resort," he told her. "You would get a far better view from the oceanside."

"It's perfect," Larissa told him. Handing off one of the glasses, she used her free hand to pull him close for a deep kiss. "Thank you," she whispered against his lips.

"If this is how you thank me for an obstructed sunset, perhaps I should arrange for a glass-bottomed boat cruise so you can see the real deal." He swiped his thumb over her lower lip, a tease in comparison to the mouth hovering near hers. "Of course, on an ocean cruise, we wouldn't have as much privacy. My boating skills are limited to small launches."

"I can't believe you told your employees to leave."

"Would you rather I'd asked them to stay?"

"They're going to talk."

"They are already."

"And you don't mind?" He never did address her comment from earlier.

"Naturally, I'd prefer they didn't. For your sake, as much as mine."

"You're trying to protect my reputation."

"Shouldn't I?" he asked, thumbing her lip again.

"Is that why you leave before dawn?"

A look flashed in his eyes, but he shuttered them before she could decipher what it meant. "Ah, *querida,* I'm not keeping you a secret if that's what you're asking."

"Then…"

"Because if I waited until you woke up, we'd stay in bed all day."

That wasn't the reason; the fearful flash she saw said as much, but before she could challenge him, Carlos bent his head and nipped, vampire-like, at the curve of her neck. "Have I mentioned how incredibly beautiful you look in that dress?" It was a distraction of the finest order, because Larissa's knees immediately buckled. She'd let him skate by for now, but promised herself that at some point, she'd find out the truth.

"There is one problem," he whispered, after a moment.

"A problem?" She found it hard to think clearly when his lips were exploring. "What's that?"

"I may have dismissed the chef prematurely."

"In other words, we don't have anything to eat on our dinner cruise." Larissa started to giggle. She couldn't help herself. The unplanned nature of his confession, implying he'd been too overwhelmed by her to think clearly, only made the evening more romantic. Pulling back the curtain, she saw for the first time, the containers of food neatly stacked on the counters. "It shouldn't be too difficult to whip something up."

"You know how to cook Yucatán cuisine?"

"No, but I can turn on a stove."

Laughing at Carlos' expression, she began peeking in containers. "We've got marinating meat, chopped vegetables, beans, spices. Might not be authentic, but we can throw something together. Sort of a Yucatán stir-fry?"

"Carnita," he said, over her shoulder.

"That's a much better word. How is it everything sounds so much more exotic in Spanish?"

"You only think that because it's a foreign language."

"A foreign language where people roll their *R*s. *Car-r-r-rnita*." She imitated his pronunciation. "I love how the words drip off the tongue."

"Just words, *querida?*"

Heat flooded her from head to toe. He'd added the Spanish endearment on purpose for that exact reason, she bet. "Cook," she said, directing him to the stove.

While the meal wasn't authentic or even close to gourmet, they managed to mix the ingredients into an edible concoction. Carlos also found a fruit platter and prepared appetizers in the refrigerator. More than enough to make a satisfying meal.

They ate from a shared plate, forgoing the dining table in favor of sitting side by side on the bench, forks and hips invading each other's space. While cooking slowed the physical part of the night, it lent an added layer of intimacy. There was a teamwork required of cooking that made Larissa feel as connected to him as she had during their nights together.

With the sun gone, the jungle had turned black, leaving only the light from the boat reflecting off the watter. Her interest in food long gone, Larissa leaned against Carlos' shoulder and listened to the waves as they lapped against the launch. Somewhere in the darkness, an animal screeched.

"Monkey," Carlos said, teasing her lips with a piece of papaya. "They live in the canopy. If you watch long enough, you'll catch one swinging across the branches."

"Sure don't see that in New York. In fact, you don't see any of this in New York. Just buildings. Lots and lots of buildings." Her sigh sounded overly loud thanks to the silence. "You don't get this kind of quiet in the city, either."

"Sounds like Mexico has cast a spell on someone."

"Maybe Mexico has." *Or someone in Mexico.* Delilah's warning whispered in her ear.

"Well, there's always the wedding coordinator position here at the resort if you want to stay."

"Tonight, your offer is very tempting." Only it wouldn't be the job luring her to stay.

"I know something else that is very tempting." Carlos's breath tickled her cheek as he leaned close to press kisses along her jaw. Fingers cupped her chin, turning her face to his. His tongue flickered over her lips, tasting, teasing. "Why is it I can't get enough of you?" he asked her.

Larissa had been asking herself the same question. Everything about Carlos—the way he moved, the way he spoke, his very existence—was like an aphrodisiac. He'd spoiled her for other men. And now, to top it off, looking into his eyes she saw a tenderness that took her breath away.

She combed her fingers through his thick curls. Maybe she was falling for a fantasy, but right now, she didn't care. Reality was overrated. "Do you need an answer?" she asked him?

"No," he replied. "Not tonight." He lowered his mouth to hers.

"Tell me about her."

Nestled against his chest, Larissa felt him stiffen. He didn't like the question, but she needed to ask. From the moment the two of them began this attraction, there'd been a third presence in the room. Mirabelle's ghost clung to Carlos. She was the distance Larissa felt when they made love, and the reason for his shuttered expression. After giving herself so freely, Larissa felt she deserved to know more about the woman who kept her from getting closer.

"I don't know what tell you," he replied.

"You said she was beautiful. Start there."

His laugh was soft, sad. "Women. Always comparing. Yes, she was very beautiful. First time I saw her, I swore my heart stopped beating. I decided then and there I wanted to spend the rest of my life with her. We married three days later."

Three days. The same length of time they'd been together. The coincidence stung. "Love at first sight."

"*Si.*" What was it he said in the *cenote?* Mirabelle had been the center of his universe? Larissa shoved the tightness in her chest aside. If she didn't want the answer, she shouldn't have asked the question.

"How long were you married before she got sick?"

Again, he stiffened. "I think she was sick all along. I didn't see the signs, is all. We seemed so happy in the beginning. Everything was such a whirlwind. The rush of falling in love had us high for weeks. But eventually, it wore off. I tried to keep her happy, but…" His voice drifted off, despair hanging heavy in the words he didn't say, and it was then Larissa realized Mirabelle's sickness hadn't been physical. She wrapped her arms tighter about his waist. If she held him close enough, perhaps she could soften the hurt. "What happened?" she asked. The hair on the back of her neck stood on edge. Maybe she didn't want to know.

"She drowned," Carlos replied. "In the pool."

Dear Lord. She expected something about fighting

or their struggle with mental illness, not such a blunt, flat answer. "I'm so sorry," she whispered.

"Jorge and I found her. We tried to revive her, but it was too late." His body trembled along with his voice. "She'd been drinking heavily those last few days. The authorities said she probably tripped and her legs became tangled in the gown she was wearing."

In her list of imagined horrors, drowning was one of the worst. Your body screaming for air. Nothing but water filling your lungs. How the poor woman must have suffered. No wonder he'd been so frightened when housekeeping called him to her room.

There was more to the story; she could tell because Carlos's body had grown tenser than ever. With her heart in her throat, Larissa held on tight and waited for him to go on.

When he did, his voice was barely above a whisper. "She was a strong swimmer."

Larissa sat up. "I don't..." Understand? But she did; she simply didn't want to contemplate. "Are you saying she deliberately...?" She couldn't even say the words.

Carlos shook his head. "She was so unhappy. I tried—we all tried so hard—but nothing every worked. The darkness, the insecurities, they always won."

"Oh, Carlos." Larissa couldn't imagine living with such uncertainty. Carrying all that grief and guilt. No wonder he emanated such pain. She'd only heard his story, and her own heart ached on his behalf.

"You can't know for certain," she said. Cradling his jaw, she forced him to meet her eyes so he could see the reassurance she so badly wanted him to feel. "It still could have been an accident. The authorities— they have ways of knowing what happened. They'd know if..."

"If she got tired of trying?" He brushed the hair from her face, his hand coming to rest in a mirror image of her own. "You're right, *querida*. We will never know for sure. It doesn't matter. I hate her all the same."

"What?" The harshness caught her off guard. How could he hate the woman who owned his heart?

Giving her forehead a kiss, Carlos eased himself away from her. The absence of his body made the bench a cold and lonely place, and she drew her knees close to stay warm. She watched as he poured himself a glass of water, graceful even in distress. "I suppose you think I'm heartless for saying so."

"I— No."

"You don't?"

"No, I don't."

In fact, she understood better than he realized the questions those left behind were stuck dealing with. Why did she leave? Weren't you enough to make her happy? Hadn't she asked all those questions herself as a child? When a person walked away, the betrayal lingered.

"You're angry with her."

"*Angry* is not a strong enough word for what I feel." He jammed the bottle into the melted ice. "I loved her. I *worshiped* her. But my love wasn't enough. She always needed more. Excitement, fireworks. She wanted the honeymoon to never end, and I obliged. I gave and I gave until I was drained dry. And it still wasn't enough. I wasn't enough." The sentence came out close to a sob.

Her poor, poor Carlos. His cynicism made sense now. How else could he feel when he gave his heart, only to come up short.

"I was such a fool," he said. "I believed love would solve everything. But no. Love does nothing. And now…" He looked away with a sigh. "And now, I can't love anyone anymore. I'm empty."

"No," Larissa whispered. "That's not true."

"Yes, *querida*. I am. Best I can do is a night like this."

A wonderful, magical night. He wasn't empty. Far from it. The ache in her heart shifted, deepened. If only she could make him see. Knew the right words to say. She opened her mouth, but inspiration didn't come.

Without words, she'd have to use the next best thing. She closed the space between them. He looked so beautiful standing in the dim light, his skin streaked by shadows. Unable not to, she traced the patterns with her finger. Across his collarbone, down his breastbone. The beat of his heart rose up through his skin to greet her. Strong, full. Not empty at all.

For three days, she'd been standing on the edge of an emotional crevasse, and now the gap wrenched open, propelling her over the edge. She pressed her lips against the sound, and gifted his heart with her own.

A groan broke the silence. Carlos's hands tangled in her hair. "Larissa…"

She held him tight, and prayed for Mirabelle to disappear.

Morning was streaming through the mango branches when Carlos pulled the launch to Larissa's villa. Long— long—past when the other cruises had returned.

Standing in the cabin doorway, Larissa hugged her coffee mug, and watched as he neatly abutted the dock. "You were right," she told him. "Café D'orzo is way better than regular coffee. I'm going to have to tell Chloe's boyfriend to add it to the coffee shop menu. He can call it Carlos's Special."

The specter of a smile graced Carlos's mouth. Since they woke up, awkwardness had hung between them, heavy and uncomfortable, more in keeping with a one-night stand than two people who shared an intimate encounter. Their lovemaking had been open and honest, but immediately afterwards, Carlos closed down. Regretting he'd shared too much or afraid of the way he let Larissa in? Most likely both.

There was a soft bump as boat met wood. "Guess this means the moonlight cruise has come to an end," she said.

"Seeing as how the moonlight ended a few hours ago, I'd say so." He took the coffee cup from her hands, then pulled her in for a cinnamon-flavored kiss. The ardor was the same as always, along with his guarded expression. She'd so hoped things might have changed.

Since they only had a couple days left, she decided it was better to go with what they had than push a fight. "Sleep well?"

"When you finally let me sleep."

"Let you sleep? I wasn't the one demanding thirds." She smacked his shoulder. This, they could do. Banter and light conversation.

"I was simply going the extra mile to keep my guest happy."

His teasing stung more than it should, largely because, after his confession, Larissa wasn't sure he didn't partially mean what he was saying. The line delineating commitment and casual still existed, and she remained planted firmly on the temporary side.

A voice in her head reminded her she should be fine with the position. *You're not looking for more, remember?*

She turned to topics more practical to keep from listening. "Thank you for the jacket. It made for a very comfortable blanket."

"You mean I wasn't enough?"

Pink crept into her cheeks. "Would you like to come in?" she asked. "You know, to shower before work?"

"Oh, *querida,* if only I could." He brushed her cheek with the back of his hand, igniting the now familiar shivers. "But I need to return the boat to the boathouse before people on the staff start to wonder what happened."

Of course, he did. Thank goodness for convenient excuses. Larissa kept her disappointment to herself. At least now she understood his reasons. Maybe after she got some sleep, she wouldn't take the rejection so personally.

"It's just as well," she replied. "I wanted to head over to the resort to check on preparations for Paul's and Linda's ceremony later this morning anyway."

"You don't have to do that. I'm sure catering will have everything well in hand."

"I want to." She was invested in the couple having the perfect ceremony. "Will I see you there? At the ceremony?"

"I'll be by."

"Good. Maybe we could steal a dance." As much as it killed her, she managed a smile as she rose on tiptoes and kissed his cheek. "Thank you for last night. I couldn't ask for a better memory."

"Larissa, I—" She gasped as he gripped her shoulders. His dark eyes searched her face. He was on the edge, she could feel him struggling to open up. Instead, he kissed her long and hard. When she tasted his desperation, Larissa knew he'd backed away. "I'll see you at the ceremony," he told her.

She waited in her doorway as he steered the launch back toward the center of the lagoon. After tomorrow, she'd never see Carlos again. She'd leave him and paradise behind. Her heart began to splinter.

Delilah's warning sounded. *Don't let the atmosphere go to your head.* Larissa had a very bad feeling she'd failed to listen.

It wasn't technically a lie. Carlos did have to return the launch to the boathouse. It simply wasn't the real reason he rushed off. Staring at the sky half the night didn't clear his head. If anything, he seemed to be losing his grip.

Once Larissa was safely in her villa, he pulled away from the dock. He intended to drive straight to the boathouse, but when he reached the center of the lagoon, he suddenly cut the engine, letting the early morning silence envelop him. Perhaps the quiet would settle his thoughts.

Last night was... He didn't know what to call it. A rawness assaulted his body as if he'd been cut open and his insides exposed to the world. Certainly, he didn't expect their lovemaking to feel so intimate. Or for him to share so much of himself. The latter he blamed on the former. Larissa's arms gave him courage and before he could stop, his history with Mirabelle poured out. The exchange left him torn in two, with one half wanting nothing more than to lose himself in Larissa forever while the other screamed to push her away.

Closing his eyes, he saw Larissa's blue gaze. So full of comfort and reassurance. An indefinable longing gripped his soul. The desperate sensation reminded him of the days when he first met Mirabelle. Those heady, infatuated days of new love he swore would never happen again.

Fear squeezed at his chest. They *wouldn't* happen again. They *couldn't*. He'd only fail, and Larissa was far too special for him to hurt.

CHAPTER NINE

"WAIT! ISN'T IT supposed to be the red flowers at the top of the altar and purple on the bottom?" The shaman had been very specific about the flowers position. Last thing she wanted to do was give Paul and Linda bad energy because they stuck the tulipanes in the wrong location.

Larissa took out her phone and double-checked the compass app she downloaded earlier. She was right. North was indeed the top of the altar. *Phew.* She smiled at the workers, who she was pretty sure didn't understand a word she said, and switched the flower positions herself. Catering was setting up early to allow the shaman to purify the altar in advance of the ceremony. That way, Paul and Linda wouldn't have any lingering smoke.

She arranged the flowers around the candle, stepped back, then arranged the flowers again. You'd think she was the one getting married, she was being so obsessive with details. Delilah and Chloe would be making Bridezilla comments left and right.

Thing was, she liked wedding details. She liked planning weddings. A lifetime of listening to brides-to-be left their mark because she took pleasure in the nitty-gritty details. Stressing about seating numbers was way more fun than typing media contracts and coordinating sales department meetings. The only fun she had with those was trying to top the previous meeting's snack menu.

Besides, obsessing over these details kept her from fixating on Carlos.

I hate her. All morning, she replayed the painful declaration. She was pretty sure he didn't truly hate his late wife, even if there was a thin line dividing the emotion from love. The anguish lacing his voice had been too strong. She couldn't begin to imagine what life must have been like for him during those years. Loving a woman so deeply only to see her slip away to depression.

Her eyes began to water. They'd been doing that a lot this morning. Blinking rapidly, she turned away from the workers so they wouldn't notice. If they did, she'd blame the sand. On the other side of the beach, near the pool, she spied a familiar figure talking to one of the assistant managers. If they were in a movie, he'd sense her presence, and their eyes would meet. Being real life, however, Larissa found herself watching while he spoke. Did Carlos have any idea how captivating a figure he made? How much strength he exuded merely by standing still? Larissa smiled. She bet Mirabelle fell in love with him at first sight, as well.

Carlos said something and the other manager smiled. Beamed actually, like he'd paid her the biggest compliment in the world. Who wouldn't? Carlos's attention would make anyone feel special. Damn Mirabelle's demons for letting Carlos think his devotion wasn't enough.

"Did the flower do something to upset you?" Paul Stevas suddenly appeared at her shoulder.

Looking down, Larissa saw she was crushing a tulipane in her fist. "Keeping a firm hand, is all. If you don't show flowers who's boss, they'll run amok," she told him. Hopefully her cheeks weren't too flushed.

Speaking of flushed, Paul was red and sweaty himself. Back from running the beach, no doubt. "Let me guess, Linda threw you out."

"She, her mom and my mom were doing some sort of spa thing up in the room," he replied. "Minute I saw the nail polish, I was out of there."

"Wise choice. While I'm pretty sure the bad luck before the wedding rule only applies to couples who aren't already married, you're still smart to stay clear of her until she's ready."

"Believe me, I know. I didn't survive a year of marriage without learning something."

Larissa laughed. "By the way, Linda showed me a picture of her dress. She's going to look gorgeous."

"Hope so. I know she won't be happy unless she looks perfect in the pictures. I wish I could get her to realize I don't care what she wears. To me, she'll always look beautiful." Using the hem of his shirt as a towel, he wiped the sheen in his voice, although with the way his voice cracked at the end of his sentence, he might have well been wiping his eyes. If the day's emotions were getting to him this early, heaven help him when they reached the actual ceremony.

"If Linda's having a spa day, I guess that means she didn't get sick after all. I heard you two took a trip to the emergency room," she added when Paul looked at her.

"Did she tell you why?"

"Only that she had a little trouble breathing."

"I was afraid she was having a pleural effusion."

"A what?"

"Sorry, I forget not everyone lives with medical

speak. It's a kind of breathing complication people can get when they have lung cancer."

"Linda has cancer?" Larissa's stomach dropped. No wonder the poor girl looked so frail.

"Stage four," Paul said in a soft voice. "Untreatable. We decided to stop treatment and go for quality of life for however long she has left."

But she was so young. Larissa felt sick. "I'm sorry." Unable to say anything else, she stared at the crumpled flower.

"Thanks," Paul replied. "It's been a long couple years. We actually thought we might lose her last year, so she and I got married while she was in the hospital. Linda says she didn't care, but I know she did. She'd always wanted a big fancy wedding, ever since we first talked about getting married."

Which was why he wanted to pull out all the stops this year. This trip was their last hurrah. Here Carlos thought Paul was a lovesick fool spending himself into debt, when in actuality, he and Linda were creating one last, amazing memory. Larissa's eyes began to water again.

Immediately, Paul was in front of her, fussing and patting imaginary pockets for a tissue. "I'm sorry. I didn't mean to upset you. Sometimes the story pops out before I've had a chance to think."

"Please, don't apologize," Larissa told him. *Don't ever apologize for being that much in love.* "I think it's wonderful that the two of you are making up for the missed opportunity."

"Are you kidding? Linda's my world. I'd do anything for her."

"I'm sure you would," Larissa murmured. Paul reminded her of someone else she knew. A man who'd been willing to give his wife the moon if it made her happy. How ironic that the man whose wife had a whole life in front of her didn't appreciate the effort while the woman who didn't…

For the first time in days, Tom popped into her head and all of a sudden, Larissa felt very unworthy.

"My father and father-in-law are waiting on me in the restaurant. I should go meet them," she heard Paul say. "Is there anything I need to do here?"

She shook her head. "Señor Chavez and his staff have everything under control."

"It's important everything to be perfect."

"It will be. Let the resort worry about the details. The only thing you need to worry about is enjoying yourself."

Funny that she would tell Paul not to stress about details. She who changed wedding venues three times and gave new meaning to the term *wedding obsessed.* Her sense of unworthiness swelled larger. All that time and effort planning the perfect ceremony. Would she have chucked all her plans if Tom—or she—had gotten sick? For that matter, would she have moved heaven and earth to make her partner happy the way Paul did? The way Carlos did?

The answers came back a resounding no on all counts. Tom, it appeared, had been right again. The man was still a jerk for cheating on her, but he also had a point. How many times had he tried to get her to dial back her plans, to talk about something other than the wedding. But as far as she was concerned, it had been all wedding, all the time. She was so happy someone wanted to marry her—that she was going to finally get to be a bride—she didn't stop to think about what was really important.

She really did love the wedding details more than she'd loved him.

Paul and Linda, Delilah and her husband, Simon, even Chloe and her boyfriend Ian—they had real love. You need only look at their faces to see how much they cared for one another. Oh, sure, she'd loved Tom, but never with the bone-deep intensity the others did.

Or the way she felt when she was with Carlos.

Flower petals dropped to the floor. She could not be in love with Carlos. Being drawn to the man did not make her in love, no matter how deeply his story touched her, or how badly she wanted his heart to heal.

No, that was attraction, concern, infatuation. Like Delilah said, it was the atmosphere playing tricks with her emotions. For crying out loud, she'd known the man for a few days. The only people she'd ever heard of falling in love that quickly were Simon and Delilah. And Chloe and Ian.

Carlos and his first wife.

Oh, damn, was she in trouble. She needed to have a good long think and figure out where her mind was truly at.

First, though, she needed to make an international phone call. She owed Tom a very big apology. Then, she would figure out the rest of her feelings.

The ceremony went off flawlessly. Husband and wife were beaming as they held hands before the floral altar. Their parents offered sacrifices of fruits and vegetables and lit candles to represent each point of the compass. Then the shaman had them proclaim their commitment to one another "…for as long as the commitment lasts."

As she listened to Linda repeat the shaman's translated vows, Larissa felt a tear slip down her cheek. Weddings always made her cry. At Simon and Delilah's she'd bawled like a baby. This ceremony of two virtual strangers hit her far harder.

Paul and Linda were so brave. The depth of their courage and love amazed her. They didn't need all the bells and whistles to prove they belonged to one another. They simply did.

That, thought Larissa, was what she wanted next time around. Not a big fancy wedding, but a marriage. For richer or poorer, in sickness and in health. She sniffed back another tear.

There was only one problem: She wasn't sure a second time around would ever happen. A real relationship required two fully committed hearts, and she had the sinking feeling her heart had gone and found a mate that refused to open his.

She stole a look to her right. Carlos's face was as handsome and unreadable as ever as he watched Paul and Linda seal their vows with a kiss. Just once before she left for home, Larissa wished he would look at her with clear, unguarded eyes. A pipe dream, she knew. She'd come close last night, and yet even then, when sharing his darkest secret, Carlos still refused to fully let her in. If he couldn't open his heart at his most vulnerable, what made her think he ever could?

Leave it to her to come on her honeymoon nursing a bruised ego and return home with a worse broken heart than before.

Their vows complete, Paul and Linda turned to the altar where the shaman lit the center candle, the merging of male and female. Maybe it was because she knew Paul and Linda's story, but the moment held a profound solemnity. Looking around, she saw that she wasn't the only one affected. Both sets of parents were openly weeping, as well. The true meaning of what they were all witnessing hung heavy in the air.

When the ceremony ended, she was the one hugging Linda for a change. "I don't know why you were worried about looking bad in the photographs. You look so beautiful," she told her. It was true. The peasant dress camouflaged her skinniness while someone, her mother, maybe, had taken extra care with her makeup so that she looked radiant and healthy. Her visible happiness helped with the glow, too. "Are you happy with how the ceremony turned out?"

"Are you kidding? Everything turned out better than I could have ever imagined."

"I'm glad," Larissa told her. "You deserve a memorable afternoon." She was trying not to get weepy, but it was difficult.

Apparently she failed, for the young woman met her eyes with a long look that said, "You know, don't you?" The only answer Larissa could give was to squeeze her hands.

Paul slipped up behind his wife to kiss her on the cheek. "Hey, babe, your mom wants to take some group shots in front of the altar."

"Again? Good Lord, how many shots of the same scenery does she need?" Linda asked. She was smiling, however, as she rolled her eyes. "Will you excuse us?"

"Congratulations, *querida*. Your ceremony was a success."

She watched Carlos approach, wondering if there'd ever come a time when she didn't marvel at the way he moved. "Not my ceremony," she told him. "Your catering staff did all the work."

"Yes, but you provided the inspiration." He handed her a goblet of golden liquid. Xtabentún. In an oddly prescient moment, she suggested the Mayan liquor yesterday to toast to Paul and Linda's health and happiness. Lord knew the two of them could use all the good vibes they could get.

"Plus," he continued, "you were down here first thing supervising the arrangements when you could have been home catching up on your sleep."

"I wasn't that tired."

"No? Then I must be losing my touch." His smile was full of wicked promise as he tapped the rim of his glass to hers. "Regardless, I am very impressed. This is exactly the kind of ceremony that made La Joya's reputation. It's traditional, it's memorable—"

"Magical?"

"Exactly," he replied. "You've definitely raised the bar when it comes to hiring a new wedding coordinator."

"Too bad I'm only temporary, right?"

The sour tone slipped out before she could stop herself. Too bad. She didn't feel much in the mood for compliments right now. Especially when they both knew how meaningless his comments were.

She raised her glass only to wrinkle her nose at the sweet scent. Between the flowers and the fruit, the air was cloying enough. A tight ball found its way behind her left eye where it throbbed every time she inhaled. She needed fresh air.

Actually, she thought, as Carlos's warm presence abutted her, she needed space. Having him close only made her head worse.

The shoreline stood only a few feet away, but it was downwind enough to feel like miles. Setting her drink on a nearby table, she made her way past the tide line to the water's edge. Damp sand slid between her toes reminding her of the other night, and Carlos's lesson about the tides. How different this trip might have been if she hadn't agreed to help him that night. If, instead of insisting on enjoying her wedding dinner, she'd hid in her room.

She heard Carlos making his way through the sand. No surprise there. Her departure had been abrupt. "Is something wrong, *querida?*"

"A little headache, is all."

"See? You are tired. Would you like me to take you back to your room?"

So he could make her feel like the only woman in the world for another few hours? Tempting, but after witnessing Paul and Linda's courage, she wasn't in the mood for indulging in fantasy. "I'll be fine in a few minutes," she told him.

His hands settled on her shoulders, his fingers gently kneading. "If you change your mind," he whispered as his thumbs pressed the muscles on either side of her spine, "I know a way to help you relax."

Temptation won for a moment, and her eyes fluttered shut. She would miss this, his touch. Unless...

"What would you do if I told you I wanted to stay?" she asked.

"You just did, *querida.*"

"No, I mean stay at La Joya. Take you up on your offer to be the wedding coordinator."

The hands stopped moving. "I—"

That's what she thought. "Don't worry," she said, pulling away, "I wasn't serious. We both know my staying would completely mess up your plans."

"Plans?"

"Sure. I mean, you can't keep having a fling with your wedding coordinator, can you? Your predecessor already took care of that. Far better I leave and never come back. This way you don't have to worry about any messy loose ends, right?"

Carlos looked utterly confused. "What are you talking about? I never had any plans. You were always leaving at the end of the week."

"Exactly." Her head started to pound. Maybe she was overtired after all. She was being childish and surly when he'd done nothing but be honest from the start. Wasn't his fault she fell for him. "Forget I said anything. I'm being overly emotional. Paul and Linda…"

"Did something happen?"

Something, all right. She looked him in the eye. "She's dying."

"Who?"

"Linda. She has lung cancer. Paul told me this morning. That's why he went to all this trouble. For one last memory."

The color drained from his face. He muttered something in Spanish. Soft, but from the sharpness, Larissa knew it was some kind of obscenity.

She turned her attention to the horizon. "Doesn't seem fair, does it? Both so young and in love."

"Poor bastard would be better off if he never fell in love in the first place."

Larissa's insides died a little. He really believed that, didn't he? It broke her heart.

Spying a half-buried seashell, she dug it free with her big toe. Immediately the tide sent the shell tumbling end over end. She scooped it up, letting the sharp edges dig into her palm.

"Growing up, I used to watch the women getting their fittings," she said. "No matter who they were or what they looked like, the minute they put on the dress, they transformed. They were beautiful. Everyone would gather around and fuss over them."

In a flash she was back in her grandmother's living room. A poor, chubby, motherless girl surrounded by white satin and sequins. "It was like they'd become princesses. I always figured that someday I'd put on a white dress and become a princess, too. Then I'd live happily ever after. Like in the movies.

"Except it's not about the dress, is it?" she asked, turning to him. "It's about what the dress represents. What the whole wedding represents. Loving the person with all your heart."

"Love isn't the answer, either."

"I hate that you think that way." Then again, that was the whole crux of their problem, wasn't it? She'd chuck all the romance in the world to have him think differently.

"Why shouldn't I?" he asked her. "I loved Mirabelle. I loved her with all my heart and what did it mean? Nothing. Same with Paul and Linda. So he moved heaven and earth to give her this recommitment ceremony. She's still going to leave him. This whole celebration means nothing. Their love means nothing."

As he spoke, the words flew faster and faster, like angry spittle hurling into the air, his tone growing so sharp it frightened her. He kicked at the sand, sending the grains flying, and that seemed to take some of the anger out of him.

"Like I said I told you, it's better to not love at all."

Maybe he was right. God knew anything would be better than the way Larissa's heart felt right now.

She looked up, hoping he could read the emotion in her eyes and understand what she was trying to tell him.

"Unfortunately, you're too late."

No... Carlos froze. She couldn't love him. He clamped down the thrill rising in his chest. "But in the *cenote,* you told me... You said that you weren't looking for a relationship."

"Apparently my heart had other ideas."

Maldita. What did he do now? Back at the top of the beach, a mariachi band had started playing. The partygoers would be dancing. Dancing to chase away the darkness. How many times had he done the same during his marriage? Too many and to what end? Larissa might see Paul's gestures as noble and romantic, but they weren't. They were foolish and painful. They could dance all they wanted, but Linda was still going to die. Paul will have failed. Like he failed Mirabelle.

Like he would eventually fail Larissa.

Icy fingers clawed at his insides, warning him to back away. He scrambled for purchase. "I told you from the start, Larissa. I don't have anything left to give. I can't love you. I can't."

Her eyes, her gorgeous, soulful eyes searched his face. "You say that, but the man I've been with the past few days... There's life inside you, Carlos. I've seen it. In the *cenote,* on the cruise."

Did she have to look so hopeful? Carlos couldn't stand to see the light in her eyes. "Those were field trips." He'd been using the same excuse all week, only the words sounded hollow this time around. "I wanted to make sure you enjoyed your visit."

"And sleeping with me? Was that another guest service?"

"No." That was him being selfish. "We agreed—"

"Stop telling me what we agreed!" Something sharp smacked his cheek. She'd thrown a seashell at his head. The ragged edge nicked the skin; he could feel the salt-water sting. "I don't want what we agreed. Not any-more."

"I can't give you anything more!" he shouted at her. Didn't she realize, what she wanted would only end up in heartache? "I was honest with you from the very start. I told you the truth."

"Did you?" she asked, calling him on his excuse. It scared him how she was starting to see through his fa-cade. He hated the anger in her eyes, and the sadness. Seeing her in pain ripped a hole in his chest. If only they could go back to last night. When her eyes shim-mered with happiness. Perhaps, if he tried, he could make her forget.

He reached for her. *"Querida..."*

"Don't!" She pushed him away before he could touch her. "I'd rather deal with reality."

She stomped away, leaving him standing alone.

CHAPTER TEN

"ACCORDING TO OUR RECORDS, Señorita Boyd, you're not scheduled to check out until tomorrow. Was there a problem?"

Larissa rested her sunglasses on top of her head. "No problem," she replied. "Just decided it was time to go home."

The clerk's expression said her excuse wasn't fooling anyone. By this point, the entire hotel had to know about her and Carlos. If not the affair, then yesterday's argument. They hadn't exactly been discreet.

Oh, well, she thought, handing over her credit card. She attracted looks checking in. She could deal with a few heading out.

The clerk typed a few keystrokes, then frowned.

"Is there a problem?" she asked.

"Uno momento, señorita. Por favor."

It was Larissa's turn to frown while he disappeared behind the rear door. Hearing him switch to Spanish made her uncomfortable. "Guess they don't like when you try to leave early," she said to the couple checking in beside her.

Clearly newlyweds, they were too wrapped up in each other to hear. Watching them whisper and exchange secret caresses made her stomach hurt. Twenty-four hours ago that had been her and Carlos. Maybe she was being stupid, taking off like this. Theirs was never supposed to be more than a few-day fling to begin with. Why let stubbornness stand in the way of their last twenty-four hours?

Because a few-days fling wasn't good enough anymore, that's why.

The rear door opened. Spying the cuff of a black suit jacket, Larissa's heart stopped. She thought for sure she wouldn't see Carlos again. After their argument on the beach, she took refuge in her room and while she hoped and hoped he'd knock on her door, he didn't.

Another reason not to extend her stay. Even if her heart could stand being around him one last day, Carlos clearly agreed the fling had ended.

What hurt the most, though, wasn't the fact that she'd developed feelings for the man, or the fact he'd walked away. It was the certainty in her heart that if Carlos had let her in, if he'd allowed himself to be close to her, that they could have had something truly spectacular. The kind of relationship she'd been searching for.

The door opened wider. The cuff became an arm, followed by a torso. Jorge.

Her heart sank. Did she really think Carlos would want to deal with her?

The assistant manager said a few quick words in Spanish to the clerk and stepped to the desk. "You're leaving us a day early, Señorita Boyd."

"Afraid so, Jorge. Manhattan calls."

Sober eyes met hers. "I'm sorry."

"Me, too," she replied. "But sometimes these things can't be helped."

After a couple silent beats, she nodded toward the computer. "Is there a problem?"

"Since we weren't expecting you to check out until tomorrow, we haven't had a chance to go over your bill. With the credits and changes Carlos made during the week, we want to make sure the charges are accurate. It will only take a moment or two." He rattled off a series of keystrokes, moved to hit Enter, and paused. "Are you sure we can't convince you to stay through tomorrow?"

Larissa shook her head. "I think I've stayed long enough. Don't worry, I promise when I give you all an online review, I won't mention our eight-legged friend. I know how Carlos likes his five-star reviews."

"He likes to know people were happy."

That he did. "Maybe too much."

"Look, I don't know what happened on the beach yesterday, but whatever happened, I'm sure Carlos didn't mean—"

"Actually," Larissa interrupted. "I'm pretty sure he did." Last night's silence confirmed the message.

"You know, he was a different person this week. More like his old self than I've seen in a long time. Not since…"

"Mirabelle? It's okay," she told the man. "Carlos told me about her."

"He did?"

Flashing back to the night on the launch, she felt her cheeks grow warm. "I might have pushed a little."

"Ah, that makes sense." He dropped his voice. "I was with him when he found her. He was inconsolable."

Apparently she was going to get an explanation anyway. "He must have loved her very much." The words stung to say.

"*Si*, maybe too much," Jorge replied. "It scarred him when she left."

And so he drew the curtains around his heart to

keep from loving too much again. That's what Larissa was afraid of.

"Hopefully someday his scars will heal," she said.

"I had hoped that's what I was seeing this week."

It was exactly what her stubborn heart didn't need to hear. Hope was hard enough to shake. Thank goodness she had sunglasses with her to hide their moisture. "Is the bill settled?" she asked, slipping them in place.

"*Si.* I'm printing you a copy now."

"Great. Could I ask one more favor? Could you make sure Paul and Linda Stevas get this when they check out?"

Reaching into her bag, she pulled out the note she wrote last night apologizing for leaving their ceremony so abruptly and wishing them as many happy days as possible.

"I'll make a note on their file," Jorge said.

"Thank you."

Time to leave. A few more hours, and paradise would be a distant memory. Kind of already was, she thought as she started toward the door.

"You're going to leave without saying goodbye."

This time she didn't need to see a dark suit. Carlos's voice washed over her like a deep dark wave. He stood midway between the reception desk and the lobby, breathing heavy, as though he'd rushed. Was he the reason for the delay? Out of the corner of her eye, she saw Jorge disappearing back into his office.

"I'm pretty sure we said everything we had to say yesterday afternoon," she replied. Or in his case, didn't say. "I didn't think you'd care if I cut my trip short."

"Of course I—" He stopped short. Saying the word might imply feelings. "I'm sorry if my behavior led you to believe there was more to our relationship than there was. It wasn't my intention to hurt you."

"I know," Larissa replied. "But you did." See? She could be honest, too. "Don't worry, though. I bounce back. I'm nothing if not resilient."

"Querida..."

"Don't." Larissa stiffened. As far as she was concerned, he lost his right to use any endearment yesterday. *"Querida* is for a man who's brave enough to admit his feelings."

"This isn't about whether I'm brave enough."

"Oh, I know what you say it's about. You made your point very clear."

Over at the concierge desk, a pair of heads turned to look at them. She lowered her voice. "I do have to wonder, though. When exactly was it you decided your heart was too dead to have feelings for me. Was it when you spontaneously kissed me in the *cenote* or after you took me sailing in the moonlight? I'm curious because both of those are pretty sentimental activities for a guy who's dead inside.

"Goodbye, Carlos." That's what he wanted, right? A proper goodbye? Now he had one.

She got about three feet when one final thought occurred. "For the record, I didn't fall in love with you because of the moonlight. I fell for the lonely man I saw living inside you."

"Doesn't matter," Carlos whispered as he watched her march out the door. The end result was the same. "You still left."

"There's still time to get her, *primo*." Jorge appeared at his shoulder. "I could stop the taxi."

To what end? A twenty-four-hour postponement? She'd still leave. "It wouldn't make a difference."

"But you could—"

Carlos held up his hand. "Señorita Boyd is gone. Better to focus on the guests we still have."

"Next time I decide to go on a luxury vacation by myself, shoot me. Better yet, shoot me anyway." She was already miserable.

"Here." Delilah nudged Larissa's upper arm with a bowl. "This will make you feel better."

"What is it?"

"Brownie sundae. Don't tell Simon, though. It's the last brownie."

"I'll buy Simon a new batch." Larissa offered the brunette a watery smile. God bless good friends. Unable to bear going home to an empty studio, she'd been curled up on Delilah's sofa since her plane landed. "I'm sorry to intrude on you two. I figured since I crashed at Chloe's when Tom dumped me..."

"You'd give me a turn?" Delilah smiled and handed her the bowl. "No worries. You know you can crash here anytime. If I had a dollar for every time Chloe knocked on my door in the middle of the night, Simon and I could buy every ad agency in town."

"Honestly, I don't know how she survived all those back-to-back breakups."

"By stuffing her face and having a good pout. Since she was never very emotionally invested, she usually bounced back pretty quickly. God forbid she and Ian break up. She'll be inconsolable."

"Like that'll ever happen," Larissa muttered. "To either of you." It was clear both her friends had found lasting love.

"True, but if it did, I imagine she'd be as messed up as you are. Forgive me for saying this, but you're more upset over this Carlos than you were when you and Tom broke it off. Granted, you're not crying the way you did then."

"I think I'm too sad to cry. I feel more numb than anything. Like someone stomped on my heart." Was this how Carlos felt after losing Mirabelle? Probably worse. No wonder he was so afraid to put himself out there again.

Understanding the man's position did not make her feel better. "What am I going to do?"

"I'm afraid there's not much you can do. You can't make a man interested in you."

"That's just it," Larissa said. "He is interested. I know he feels the same way I do, but he's too scared to let himself feel anything. Oh, Lord, I sound like one of those letters in an advice column, don't I? Desperate in Manhattan."

"Dramatics aside, are you sure this isn't a rebound thing or the atmosphere getting to you?"

"Of course I'm sure," she said, stabbing the brownie with her spoon. Best friend or not, Delilah's question annoyed her. "Look, I know you and Chloe think I'm some kind of romantic ninny, but what I felt when I was with Carlos.... I can't explain. It's like something inside me clicked into place."

And there'd been a hole inside her since the moment she walked away on the beach. "It wouldn't matter if he was in Mexico, Manhattan or Mars. I don't feel whole without him."

She looked up at her friend. "Is it possible to find your soul mate only to have him not want you?"

"That's not really how soul mates work."

"That's what I was afraid you'd say." Appetite gone, she set the sundae aside. It was going to take a lot more than brownies and ice cream to make her feel full again. "So what am I going to do? And please don't say, give myself time, because I'll scream."

"Okay, I won't. I will, however, tell you to give *him* time."

"Excuse me."

Delilah reached across her to take the sundae off the end table. "Do you remember when I first fell in love with Simon? How he insisted he and I couldn't be together?"

Larissa remembered. A terrible trauma in Simon's past had him believing he wasn't good enough to be with Delilah.

"Well, my mother passed along some advice. She told me that if Simon was really my soul mate, he'd find his way to me. And he did. Took a while, but he did. If you remember, same thing happened with Chloe and Ian."

"But you and Simon worked together. You might not have been in a relationship, but you still saw him every day. And even Chloe and Ian were in the same city. Carlos is in Mexico, for crying out loud. What am I supposed to do, take the wedding coordinator job?" The idea crossed her mind more than once. That's how crazy she was about the man; she would relocate to the other end of the continent to be with him.

"Why don't we wait a couple weeks before trying something so extreme?" Delilah suggested.

"You think I'm being dramatic again."

"No, I think you're truly in love, and it stinks. Those weeks Simon and I were apart were some of the worst weeks of my life. You have to have faith that he'll miss you as much as you miss him, and that the loneliness will motivate him to do something."

Terrific. Her happiness rested on Carlos's ability to cope with loneliness. Larissa had a feeling she'd be waiting forever.

Wasn't heartburn supposed to clear up after a few days? It'd been almost three weeks, and the horrendous burning ache behind his breastbone hadn't eased up one bit. He shook out a handful of antacid tablets. Surely there was a limit to how many of these a person should take, as well.

"Those won't help, *primo*." Jorge walked into his office without knocking, an annoying habit that seemed to have increased over the past two weeks. "Antacid doesn't cure stupidity."

"I need it to survive your bad jokes," Carlos groused.

"No offense, but are you sure you're surviving?"

Carlos tossed back the tablets with a wince. Other than the heartburn, and a few bouts of insomnia, he was surviving perfectly fine. Business was doing well, the last of Maria's mistakes had been rectified, and every time he closed his eyes he saw Larissa walking out the door. What could be wrong? He pinched his brow. "Did you want something?"

"A letter arrived today that you should read. And before you ask, no, it is not from New York."

"What makes you think I was going to ask?" He knew better. When Larissa walked out the door, she walked out for good. He knew from the very start he wouldn't hear from her again.

The return address indicated the letter was from somewhere in Colorado. Carlos didn't recognize where. Upon opening, he found a gold-and-white note card.

Nothing fancy. The hotel received dozens of similar cards every year. For some reason, however, this particular card made his stomach tighten. Slowly, he opened it and read:

Dear Señor Chavez:
I wanted to take this time to thank you for the incredible recommitment ceremony you and Señorita Boyd arranged for us. Linda didn't stop smiling the entire day and must have said a hundred times that it was better than she imagined. It truly was the trip of a lifetime.

Unfortunately, Linda suffered complications shortly after we returned. She passed away last week. Whenever I start to miss her, I pull out the photographs from that day. Seeing her smile, and remembering how happy she was helps ease the pain. Thank you for helping us make one last memory.
Sincerely,
Paul Stevas
PS: Could you please tell Señorita Boyd again how much Linda and I appreciated all her help? I don't have her address. Thank you.

The card slipped from Carlos's fingers. Poor Paul. Life kicked the poor lovesick bastard in the teeth exactly as Carlos knew it would. All that love and what happened? The kid was stuck at home with nothing more than memories.

Proof what he'd told Larissa was right.

Jorge picked up the card. "I remember this couple. They seemed like nice people."

"They were." Too nice for something like this to happen. "Have Louisa send flowers with our condolences."

"Are you going to let Larissa know?"

He nearly missed the question. It was the sound of Larissa's name that pulled him from his thoughts.

"The card says they don't have her address," Jorge said. "She'd probably want to know what happened."

She would be heartbroken, as well. Paul and Linda had become special to her. "Will you call her?" he asked his cousin.

"Don't you think she'd rather hear the news from you?"

He couldn't. Memories of her visit plagued him enough without hearing her voice.

Funny how Paul's memories brought him comfort, while thinking of a weeklong affair brought him nothing but insomnia and heartburn.

The ache in his chest started to spread. So much for antacid. "Given how we said goodbye, I'm sure hearing from me would be awkward."

"Since when has 'awkward' ever bothered you? I've heard you talk to guests over some pretty sensitive subjects."

"I never slept with any of those guests." *Slept with.* Sounded way too crude a term for what he and Larissa shared. When he was with her, he felt…

He felt.

Heaving a sigh, he shoved the thought from his brain, where it joined the countless other thoughts waging war in the center of his chest.

"She doesn't want to hear from me, Jorge," he said. Looking to the papers on his desk, he made a production of fishing through them. Perhaps his cousin would get the hint that he didn't want to have this conversation any longer.

No such luck. "I think she does, *primo*. I think she wants to hear from you quite badly."

"She also wants more than I can give her," Carlos snapped. "My calling would only open the wound. I'm asking you to do it. Now, if there's nothing else, I have work to do." He went back to shuffling through his paperwork.

Jorge stood, but rather than leave, he crossed around to the other side of the desk. Carlos tried to ignore him, but his hulking presence cast too big a shadow.

"What are you afraid of, *primo*?"

"Other than not signing off on these contracts in time?"

"You know what I mean. Larissa. I watched you when she was here. She was special."

More than special. "I'm not afraid of anything. Larissa and I had a weeklong affair that ended badly. I wish it hadn't, but it did. Life goes on." Eventually his guilt and regret would fade away. That's what this ache in his chest was, right? Guilt over leading her on?

"Rich talk, coming from you."

"What does that mean?"

"It means, dear cousin, that Mirabelle is dead."

"I know that," Carlos snapped. Dear God, but he knew that. Why were they talking about Mirabelle all of a sudden anyway?

"Because Larissa isn't," Jorge said when he asked. "She's alive and waiting for your phone call."

"No, she's alive and in New York City," Carlos replied. Even if he did call her, what good would talking do? Eventually she'd hang up, and he'd be faced with her absence again. "Calling her won't bring her back."

"Are you sure?"

"She has a life there. A family. A career."

"So?"

"So, she's not coming back," he said, slamming his hand on the top of his desk. Jorge's questions served nothing other than to churn up the acid in his stomach. Needing space, he shoved himself to his feet.

Outside his office window, the beach reached out to meet the crystal-blue water. It was a view he'd tried to avoid all month long. Too many associations.

"How do you know? Have you asked her?"

Of course he didn't ask her. "You saw how we ended things." Her asking him questions he didn't have answers to.

Not true. You know the answers.

Carlos closed his eyes. The voice had been taunting him more and more over the past three weeks, as well. Pushing him to have unwanted thoughts, asking him to open doors he'd be better off keeping closed.

"You know, I don't think I've ever hated her as much as I do right now," he heard his cousin say.

"Hate who?" Although he already knew the answer. Certainly couldn't be Larissa. She'd done nothing wrong. Nothing at all.

"I know it's wrong for me to say because she had so many demons. She needed so much. Too much. I saw how much you loved her."

"She was my world. Not that it did any good."

"I know, and that's why I hate her. Because she was too sick to see that and because when she died, she passed on her demons to you. I hate that she turned you into a coward."

Carlos shook his head. "I don't know what you're talking about." He didn't want to talk about Mirabelle.

Lately, when he thought of his late wife, the thoughts morphed into memories of Larissa. Her laugh, her innocent sense of wonder. He pictured her eyes when she saw the *cenote* for the first time, and her face every time their bodies joined together. Each and every memory twisted in his gut, begging for him not to push them away.

Perhaps Jorge was right. He was a coward. But couldn't his cousin see, cowardice was the only thing keeping his heart from ripping into pieces a second time?

Hasn't it torn already? The truth finally won the battle. All his lying to himself, all the walls he so desperately tried to keep erected, and in the end, Larissa still claimed his heart. Somewhere between the moment she opened her hotel door and their fight on the beach, despite all his best defenses, he'd fallen in love with her.

Whoever said the truth would set you free, lied. His pain was worse than ever.

"Call her, *primo,*" Jorge urged.

"I can't."

Can't or won't? Larissa's final question came floating back, mocking him. So desperate to hear him admit his feelings. "She isn't coming back."

"How do you know unless you ask her?"

Before Carlos could argue otherwise, the two-way radio on Jorge's waist went off. A problem in the ballroom. "You better go," Carlos told him.

"Sending me off on an errand won't change my opinion, you know."

"Go."

"Fine, I'm going, but we will revisit this conversation. Along with the fact that we need a new wedding coordinator so I don't have to deal with catering crises every five minutes."

His cousin faced failure on both points. Carlos was done talking about Larissa. And as for a wedding coordinator, he doubted any future candidates would ever be as good as the woman who checked out a few weeks ago.

No one in general would be as good as her.

How long he stayed staring out the window, he didn't know. As he watched the sun drift from one corner of his window to another, hundreds of thoughts raced through his mind, all coming back to one central question. *What are you afraid of?*

Turned out his fear had been a self-fulfilling one, didn't it? With all his effort to hold Larissa at arm's length, to keep from feeling pain, he created even more.

Slowly, he walked back to his desk, where Paul Stevas's letter lay. What was it Larissa said that day on the beach? About Paul and Linda facing the bad together? He wished he could remember her exact words, but he'd been too busy scrambling to protect himself and they didn't permeate his brain until now.

Before he realized what he was doing, he'd taken out a piece of hotel stationery and started writing.

Dear Paul,
I am so sorry to hear about Linda. She seemed like a very wonderful person. It was obvious the two of you loved each other very much. I'm glad we could help you enjoy your final days together.
Cherish the memories. Love is too precious a gift to forget.

He folded the note and set it aside to accompany the condolence flowers. Love was a precious gift, he thought. Mirabelle's demons hadn't let her see that. And as a result, his demons hadn't let him see the same thing when Larissa came into his life. If only he'd been brave enough to realize how lucky he was to be given a second chance at happiness.

How do you know until you ask her?

He reached for the phone.

CHAPTER ELEVEN

Two weeks, five days and twenty-seven hours. That's how long it had been since she said goodbye to Carlos and flown back to New York, and the hole in Larissa's heart loomed larger than ever.

"If you love him set him free," she muttered. What a joke. She heaved her pen across her desk where it hit the postcard pinned to her wall before landing on a stack of media contracts. A nice red dot now marred the sky over the La Joya swimming pool. She should take the darn pictures down anyway. Looking at them only made the longing worse.

God, but she missed Carlos. Why did she have to be so stubborn about insisting he admit his feelings? She should have stayed the extra day and had one last wonderful memory. Granted, she'd still be sitting here in New York without him, but at least she wouldn't keep picturing the way his forlorn expression reflected in the glass as she walked out of the lobby.

No, you could torture yourself with some other memory.

"We brought you back a sandwich." Chloe rattled a white paper sack as she and Delilah invaded her cubicle doorway. "Roast beef with slaw."

"Thanks, I'll eat it later." Ignoring the look between

exchanged between her friends, she set the back on the corner of her desk.

"You should have joined us," Chloe said. "Feels like summer has finally kicked in out there. It's even warm enough for you."

"Sorry I missed it, but I had too much work."

"Interesting how that's been happening a lot lately," Delilah remarked. "Work keeping you from lunch, that is."

"I don't see what's so interesting about it. No different from the way you work late all the time." Actually, it was a lot different and all three of them knew it. Her work might be piling up, but it was because she'd been unable to focus. While her body sat in New York, her mind and heart were back in Mexico. The other day she went so far as to see if La Joya hired a wedding coordinator yet. At least if she were physically in Mexico, she'd feel like she was putting up a fight.

A hand settled on her shoulder. She looked up into Chloe's brown eyes. "It's going to be all right," her friend told her.

"Would you say that if this was Ian?"

Her friend's eyes widened a second, and she shook her head. "No."

"Exactly. It's not going to be all right as long as he's not part of my life." That's what she got for wanting real. Her life wasn't a life at all without him. She was no better than Carlos right now, existing in a void.

"You know what? I'm going back." Time she took a piece of her own advice. How could she expect Carlos to reach out and take a chance, if she wasn't willing to do the same?

She reached for the phone, only to have Delilah's

hand curl around her wrist. "What will you do when you get there? Pick up where you left off?"

"Maybe."

"And then what?" Delilah asked. "Six months from now when he still won't open up to you, are you going to feel any better?"

"I don't know." She certainly couldn't feel any worse.

In the end, her phone rang, ending the argument. "Hi, Larissa, it's Jenny from first-floor reception. Can you come down for a moment?"

"Sure. I'll be right there." She hung up with a frown. "That's odd. First-floor reception wants me."

"Maybe someone sent you a present," Chloe teased.

A present indeed. She and Delilah had been doing everything under the sun to cheer her up. They'd probably ordered a balloon bouquet or something equally silly. Forget what she said about not being able to feel worse. As horrible as she felt right now, she'd be completely lost without these two.

"I'd better go find out."

After four years of working at CMT, Larissa had come to expect all sorts of sights in their corporate lobby. None of them prepared her for the man standing at the reception desk.

Her heart leaped to her throat. "C-Carlos?" She whispered the name in case she was dreaming.

Carlos turned around and smiled. The shyness nearly broke her. *"Buenos dias."*

"Buenas tardes," she corrected. "It's afternoon."

"I guess I've got my time zones mixed up."

As he started toward the elevator, everything else in the lobby faded away. The only thing worth looking at was his face. Habit already ingrained, Larissa looked to his eyes. They shone like two dark jewels, bright and open. So incredibly, wonderfully open that she wanted to cry.

"*Querida,* no…" He cradled her cheeks in his palm, smoothed her trembling lip with his thumb.

"I can't believe you're really here," she whispered.

"I can't believe it myself, but I needed to tell you something, and face-to-face was the only way."

"Tell me something?" She felt her heart skip with a hope she dared not acknowledge.

Carlos nodded. "I wanted to tell you that you were special. That's the reason I did everything I did. Because you were…are…special."

He pressed a kiss to her forehead. To feel his lips after all this time…Larissa had to squeeze her eyes tight to steel herself against the thrill building inside. "I spent so many years thinking I was dead inside," he whispered. "Then this beautiful drunk blonde opened a door and I found out I wasn't dead after all. I was waiting for her. Only I was too scared to take a chance. Too afraid of how badly it would hurt when she walked away. So I tried to lock her out.

"Except," he said, smiling down with shining eyes, "she got in anyway. I've tried to deny the feelings for three weeks, but I miss you, Larissa. There's been a hole in my chest since you left."

Oh Lord, how she'd longed to hear those words. "There's been a hole in my chest, too. I've missed you so much."

"Same here, *querida.*"

It felt like an eternity, but at last, Carlos swept her into his arms. His kiss was honest and real, the connection instant. Gone was the distance she used to sense. Larissa wrapped her arms around his neck and kissed him back with an intensity that left them both breathless. When they finally broke, and she remembered where they were, she started to giggle.

"What's so funny?" he asked.

"Nothing." Looked like his kisses did have the same impact while standing on Madison Avenue.

Still, kisses weren't everything, and while she would far rather spend the next twenty four hours wrapped in Carlos's arms, they needed to talk. "So where do we go from here?" she asked, putting some distance between them.

"What do you mean?"

It meant dealing with nitty-gritty reality. Carlos coming to New York was a start, but if they were to make a real go of things, they needed to negotiate life beyond La Joya's romantic facade.

"For starters, we live three thousand miles apart. I have a job here. Delilah and Chloe are here." That she had been about to fly back to Mexico was beside the point. That was when she was depressed and thinking illogically.

"I'm well aware of the distance, and I've got a solution."

"Already? You've only been here five minutes."

"I've had a long time to think before I got here, and I realize I've been a selfish bastard."

"No—"

He held up his hand. "No, *querida,* I have been for a long time. By shutting myself off from the world. And, just because I've woken up, doesn't mean I have the right to ask you to give up your life. Not yet."

Larissa's heart started pounding. "Carlos, what are you trying to say?" She knew what it sounded like, but...would he really make that kind of commitment?

"I've put a call in to Kent Hotels regarding a position here in New York."

Oh my God, he was making that kind of commitment. "You're leaving La Joya?"

"The hospitality industry has always been a little nomadic. I've moved from hotel to hotel before. What's another move?"

"But it's your family's business."

"It's a business. Businesses can be replaced. Hearts can't."

"Wow." She didn't know what do say. He was willing to leave his family's business and move to New York City for her when neither of them knew what the future had in store. An incredibly gigantic chance for a man who feared getting hurt. That Carlos would take such a leap of faith *for her...* "I'm so humbled," she murmured.

"You're so worth it," Carlos replied.

If Larissa's heart ever had any doubt whether she belonged with him, those four words erased it. There was still one more question to ask, though. "And when things get rough?" She needed to know.

"We'll deal with them together."

"Are you sure? Because I want it all. The good, the bad and the ugly."

"So do I, *querida.*"

They were both tired of keeping space between them. When Carlos stepped close again, Larissa melted into him. "I love you," she said, resting her head against his chest. "I don't care if it's too soon to say the words, but I—"

"Shh..." He pressed a finger to her lips. "Say them all you want, *querida.* I love you, too."

His kiss showed her just how much.

"Now," he said, planting one last kiss on the tip of

her nose. "Why don't you take me upstairs to meet these best friends of yours? Then tonight, after you finish work, you can show me around my new adopted home."

"Okay, but I've got a better idea. How about I introduce you to Chloe and Delilah, and then, I show you how much I missed you."

He smiled. "I like your idea better."

"What can I say? I'm a terrific event planner." As she led him to meet the two most important women in her life, Larissa thought of how lucky she was. She'd gone to paradise to lick her wounds over lost love and discovered a love that was even better. What's more, with Carlos in her life, it wouldn't matter if she ever travelled to paradise again. Because paradise was wherever the two of them were together.

One year later...

"Tell me again why we came on this trip?" Simon Cartwright lifted himself from the infinity pool. Water dripped from his Olympic-fit body as he walked to the nearby lounge chair to grab a towel.

"Near as I can tell," Ian Black replied, "it's so we have someone to talk to while our wives ignore us."

He smirked at the nearby table, only to have one of the women stick her tongue out in return. "Watch it, Mister. I'm not your wife yet," Chloe Abrams said, waggling her index finger at him. "I still have twenty-four hours to change my mind."

"Idle threats, Curlilocks. You and I both know you're stuck with me for life."

Rolling her eyes, the brunette turned back to the other women at her table. "I hate when he's right."

"You think he's bad now, wait until the two of you

decide to have children," Delilah told her. "Simon's been strutting around like a peacock ever since the ultrasound. You'd think I was giving birth to the king of England." She squealed as Simon splashed water in her direction.

From her seat at the far end of the table, Larissa watched the whole exchange with misty eyes. She missed this—spending time with her friends. It'd been nine months since she returned to Mexico. True to his word, Carlos did stay in New York, although he took a year's leave of absence rather than find a new position. While Larissa knew beyond a shadow of a doubt the two of them belonged together, she told him they should take things slow, and he agreed.

New York lasted exactly six weeks. Surprisingly, it was Larissa who initiated the move back to Mexico. The decision came while she and Carlos were sitting in Bryant Park one brutally hot Sunday afternoon. If she was going to endure oppressive heat, she told him, she wanted egrets to sing her good-night. They returned to La Joya two weeks later. She didn't regret the decision for a moment.

Fishing the pen from behind her ear, she flipped open the file folder on the table in front of her. "Before Simon tosses Delilah into the pool, I want to make sure you're absolutely okay with the plans for tomorrow's ceremony. Are you sure you don't have any changes?"

"Other than the size of my bridesmaid dress?" Delilah quipped. "It appears the future king has decided to take up residence in my rear end."

"No worries," Larissa told her. "The dresses I picked out are very figure-forgiving. You're not the only one whose rear end has decided to expand."

"Perhaps because someone feels the need to sample every wedding cake that comes through the hotel."

Carlos came strolling out from the restaurant, resplendent as always in his manager's suit. Twelve months together, and the way he moved still sent shivers down her spine. He smiled at her, his eyes warm and bright. "I guarantee tomorrow's ceremony will be flawless. After all, you're using the finest wedding planner in all of Mexico."

"She's also the only wedding planner who didn't have a wedding of her own," Delilah noted. "Noontime at City Hall? Seriously, what kind of wedding is that?"

Her cheeks growing warm, Larissa reached up and entwined her fingers with the hand resting on her shoulder. She and Carlos got married right before their return. "I had everything that mattered."

"And so do I," Chloe said. "I've got the man of my dreams and my best friends. Tomorrow will be the icing on the cake as far as I'm concerned." She giggled. "Sorry, La-Roo, did saying the word *cake* made your butt get bigger?"

"It did Delilah's," Simon said with a laugh. Before the brunette could retort, he gathered her in his arms and gave her a kiss. "And I love every inch."

"You better," she grumbled, kissing his nose.

"Ah, the sparkling cider is here."

At Carlos's announcement, a waitperson appeared bearing a tray with six glasses. "I thought we should have a toast to start the weekend," he said.

"To the bride and groom," Simon said, once the glasses were in hand.

"And good friends," Ian added.

Chloe leaned over and gave him a kiss. "To family," she corrected.

"No, to soul mates," Delilah said.

Larissa looked at the people around the table. The six of them had endured a lot to find one another and now had nothing but lifetimes of happiness ahead of them. Who knew, when she walked into CMT Advertising four years ago, that a corporate orientation would bring her such enduring happiness? As far as she was concerned, the six of them shared one thing worth toasting above everything.

"To love," she said raising her glass. "To love."

* * * * *

MILLS & BOON®
By Request

RELIVE THE ROMANCE WITH THE BEST OF THE BEST

A sneak peek at next month's titles...

In stores from 9th March 2017:

- **A Secret Seduction** – Kim Lawrence, Elizabeth Lane & Wendy S. Marcus

- **The Beaumont Children** – Sarah M. Anderson

In stores from 23rd March 2017:

- **Mothers in a Million** – Susan Meier, Michelle Douglas & Dianne Drake

- **Winning his Heart** – Cara Colter, Alison Roberts & Melissa McClone

Just can't wait?
Buy our books online before they hit the shops!
www.millsandboon.co.uk

Also available as eBooks.

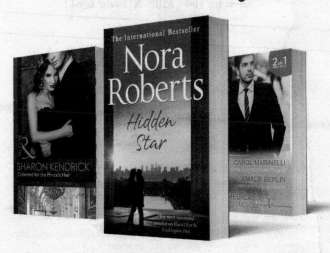

MILLS & BOON®

Congratulations
Carol Marinelli
on your 100th Mills & Boon book!

Read on for an exclusive extract

How did she walk away? Lydia wondered.

How did she go over and kiss that sulky mouth and say goodbye when really she wanted to climb back into bed?

But rather than reveal her thoughts she flicked that internal default switch which had been permanently set to 'polite'.

'Thank you so much for last night.'

'I haven't finished being your tour guide yet.'

He stretched out his arm and held out his hand but Lydia didn't go over. She did not want to let in hope, so she just stood there as Raul spoke.

'It would be remiss of me to let you go home without seeing Venice as it should be seen.'

'Venice?'

'I'm heading there today. Why don't you come with me? Fly home tomorrow instead.'

There was another night between now and then, and Lydia knew that even while he offered her an extension he made it clear there was a cut-off.

Time added on for good behaviour.

And Raul's version of 'good behaviour' was that there would

be no tears or drama as she walked away. Lydia knew that. If she were to accept his offer then she had to remember that.

'I'd like that.' The calm of her voice belied the trembling she felt inside. 'It sounds wonderful.'

'Only if you're sure?' Raul added.

'Of course.'

But how could she be sure of anything now she had set foot in Raul's world?

He made her dizzy.

Disorientated.

Not just her head, but every cell in her body seemed to be spinning as he hauled himself from the bed and unlike Lydia, with her sheet-covered dash to the bathroom, his body was hers to view.

And that blasted default switch was stuck, because Lydia did the right thing and averted her eyes.

Yet he didn't walk past. Instead Raul walked right over to her and stood in front of her.

She could feel the heat—not just from his naked body but her own—and it felt as if her dress might disintegrate.

He put his fingers on her chin, tilted her head so that she met his eyes, and it killed that he did not kiss her, nor drag her back to his bed. Instead he checked again. 'Are you sure?'

'Of course,' Lydia said, and tried to make light of it. 'I never say no to a free trip.'

It was a joke but it put her in an unflattering light. She was about to correct herself, to say that it hadn't come out as she had meant, but then she saw his slight smile and it spelt approval.

A gold-digger he could handle, Lydia realised.

Her emerging feelings for him—perhaps not.

At every turn her world changed, and she fought for a semblance of control. Fought to convince not just Raul but herself that she could handle this.

Don't miss
THE INNOCENT'S SECRET BABY
by Carol Marinelli
OUT NOW

BUY YOUR COPY TODAY
www.millsandboon.co.uk